SACRAMENTO PUBLIC LIBRARY

D0375114

CENTRAL LIBRARY
828 "I" STREET
SACRAMENTO, CA 95814

SEP - 1998

WHITE
CHOCOLATE

WHITE CHOCOLATE

ELIZABETH ATKINS BOWMAN

A TOM DOHERTY ASSOCIATES BOOK
NEW YORK

This is a work of fiction. All of the characters and events portrayed in this novel are either fictitious or are used fictitiously.

WHITE CHOCOLATE

Copyright © 1998 by Elizabeth Atkins Bowman

All rights reserved, including the right to reproduce this book, or portions thereof, in any form.

This book is printed on acid-free paper.

A Forge Book
Published by Tom Doherty Associates, Inc.
175 Fifth Avenue
New York, NY 10010

Forge® is a registered trademark of Tom Doherty Associates, Inc.

Library of Congress Cataloging-in-Publication Data

Bowman, Elizabeth Atkins.
 White Chocolate / Elizabeth Atkins Bowman.
  p. cm.
 "A Tom Doherty Associates book."
 ISBN 0-312-86306-3
 I. Title.
 PS3552.O8757114W48   1998
 813'.54—dc21   98-5522
                                              CIP

First Edition: May 1998

Printed in the United States of America

0 9 8 7 6 5 4 3 2 1

I'm dedicating this book to my parents, Thomas Lee Atkins and Judge Marylin Atkins. I feel incredibly blessed to have been born to such a genuine, loving couple, and I try to emulate your hard work and good nature every day. Thank you for teaching me that love is colorblind . . . and that it's the most important thing in life. Daddy, I know you're smiling down on me during this proud moment. Thank you for inspiring in me a passion for reading, writing, and exploring my imagination. And Cap, I'm grateful to you for being such a strong, awe-inspiring role model. I'm so proud to be your daughter and your friend.

And to my husband, Victor Bowman: Your support while I toiled day and night on this book only reinforced what I already know—you're the most wonderful man on the planet. With you as my soul mate, every day is Nirvana . . . especially now that Lavender is real.

A special thank-you to my sister, Catherine Atkins, for being my best friend.

I'd also like to thank my editor, Natalia Aponte, for sharing your literary expertise and thus bringing to life my wish of being a published novelist.

And to my agent, Susan Crawford—I love your enthusiasm! Thank you for all those great adjectives.

One more: Thank you, Bill Proctor, of WXYZ-TV, for letting me tag along to study the details of TV reporting. I learned from the best.

Lastly and very importantly, let me express heartfelt appreciation to Jeff Wardford, for stroking my literary dream with your Midas touch.

WHITE CHOCOLATE

PROLOGUE

After two days and nights, the fatigue and visceral revulsion of masquerading as a white supremacist had become excruciating. Now, as bursts of flame bristled the fine hairs on her body, Taylor James prayed for the stamina to endure the climax of her mission.

She watched yellow and crimson flames slithering up huge crosses, hissing and licking into the black sky, charming the hundreds of white supremacists encircling her. As their blood-hungry shouts assailed her ears and their frenzied applause jostled her body, the orange haze of hatred over their contorted faces flogged her heart.

It astounded her that this venomous nest could thrive in mid-Michigan woodland, breeding paramilitary racists, spawning bloody revolution.

Yet Taylor sculpted phony admiration on her face as she watched the dictator of this madness, Rocky Pulaski, who stood in full military camouflage and jackboots on an elevated platform between the flaming crosses.

"I am the superman, and I will lead my Aryan brethren as I execute the final solution to America's race problem," he shouted, his auburn mustache and crew cut glowing orange under the fire, casting shadows on his ordinary, oval face. His large black eyes lingered on individuals in the sea of faces before him, as if entrancing each one with his spell.

"You must join the racial revolution," Pulaski bellowed, pointing an admonitory forefinger at the crowd, "because it will return to us white Americans the power and privilege that we once had, before our government condemned us to second-class status behind blacks and Jews and homosexuals and illegal aliens and the mongrel race formed by their degenerate cross-breeding. Comrades, we will take back our land by blood!"

Below him, the crowd roared. Taylor—and the video camera concealed in her denim baseball cap—monitored him. When Pulaski suddenly locked intrigued eyes on her, she smiled at him, a wide, face-cracking smile, because her mouth was watering with the triumphant taste of annihilating him and everything he symbolized.

I have to stop him. And I will. God, please get me and Andy out of here safely without anyone blowing our cover. Just twelve more hours . . .

Pulaski's voice, echoing from rooftop speakers on the four-story, U-shaped brick building surrounding the courtyard, crescendoed as he continued.

"The government sends noble white men to fight pathetic wars in the jungles and deserts of despicable lands," he roared. "All the while it endows millions of dollars to the inferior races of Israel and Africa. It enacts NAFTA, thieving jobs from productive white men, handing them on a silver platter to the subhuman Mexicans. While illegal aliens crawl across our borders like insects, leeching off our welfare system, making us foreigners in our own land. Comrades, I say enough is enough!"

The frenzied throng thundered.

"You've all read William Pierce's brilliant fantasy in *The Turner Diaries,*" Pulaski bellowed. "Well, for us, comrades, the fantasy is real. We will overthrow the government. We will conquer it! An Aryan utopia will be ours!"

Taylor clenched her teeth to stifle a shudder of disgust. One man had no right to execute his own demented vision of the perfect society. If Pulaski's doctrine were allowed to flourish, he could spawn another of the world's racial horrors: apartheid in South Africa; the Black Codes that enslaved African-Americans; the Nuremberg Laws that preceded Hitler's slaughter of six million Jews; Hutus killing Tutsis in Rwanda; Serbs murdering Muslims in Bosnia; the United States laws that once would have prohibited her own parents' marriage.

She stared at him, drawing strength from her anger. *If you only know that I'm the little biracial girl your son used to torment. I'm the daughter of the interracial couple you used to shout at in all those meetings with the principal. And I'm the friend of the little brown-skinned boy who'd wallop your son Billy Joe when he hurt me. Now I'm going to bring you down.*

Taylor glanced to Pulaski's right, where his camouflage-clad son, Billy Joe, stood at attention. The sight of Billy Joe, even after fifteen years, clawed the wounds he had inflicted on her childhood psyche. It was still vivid in her mind, that day in fifth grade, when her lungs had ached as she fled across the playground.

Billy Joe was getting closer; teachers and classmates faded in the distance.

"Leave me alone! Julian! Mrs. Stein! Help me!"

Taylor's stomach ached at the sight of Billy Joe's rabid blue eyes and wet, open mouth. She was sick of his meanness. Just last week he had said that the police would arrest her family because interracial marriage was illegal.

"Leave me alone!"

Billy Joe, smelling like a wet dog, knocked her to the grass. "I hate you, Taylor James. My dad says niggers like your dad aren't supposed to do it with white women and have baby freaks."

Taylor glared through a curtain of yellow curls. "My parents said you're a demon child. People aren't s'posed to hate each other because of race. God said."

"You're wrong," Billy Joe said, pulling a black bottle from his pocket. "My dad said it's nature's way for whites to stick with whites, not dirty up the race with mutts like you. You got clean white skin on the outside, dirty black inside."

Taylor threw a rock against his thick stomach. "You're the meanest boy in fifth grade and the whole world!"

"You little brat!" Billy Joe squeezed the bottle. Black ink splattered on Taylor's head and arms.

"Stop it!" she shouted.

Laughing, Billy Joe danced around her. "Now you look like the little black freak that you—"

There was a deep thud. An agonized moan. Silence.

Relief flooded Taylor's aching stomach; Julian was calling her name, holding her, pulling stained hair off her face. Tenderness radiated from his tawny face and brown eyes. "Shhh, Taylor. I'm here now. You're safe."

Taylor clung to him. She glimpsed Billy Joe, sprawled on his back on the grass. He was still. She closed her stinging eyes, hoping that Julian would always be there to protect her.

"Whites unite, fight for our rights!"

The deafening chant wrenched Taylor from the memory. She focused on Billy Joe's still stormy blue eyes. The red tinge and chubbiness had faded from his cheeks; his mop of brown curls was now a crew cut. As if sensing her contempt, he glanced her way. Taylor's stomach cramped, her pulse raced.

"I know you," he had slurred the night before, glassy-eyed and reeking of whiskey. An icy chill had snaked down Taylor's spine; her leg muscles had tremored like so many rubber bands.

Rocky Pulaski, who at the time had been urging Taylor's undercover partner, Andy Doss, to use his keen marksmanship in the revolution, had told Billy Joe to take his "drunk ass" to bed. But Billy Joe's retreat did not calm Taylor's nerves, even after Andy assured her that the playground bully could not possibly recognize her as an adult in a wig and glasses.

Still, the suspicion now roiling in Billy Joe's eyes alarmed Taylor so much that she contemplated feigning illness to escape from the heavily guarded compound. Tonight. Before he figured out their true identities and staged a pogrom, offering the half-breed and the white traitor to Odin, pagan ruler of the universe in Norse mythology.

Taylor inhaled deeply to calm her nerves. *Don't be paranoid. We can make it until the morning. But I wish Julian were here to hold me.*

Or at home, waiting for my safe return. Six years without him, and I'm still craving the sanctuary that was his embrace. Let go.

She yelled Andy's alias in his ear. "Look at Billy Joe. Think he recognizes me?"

"No," he said. "Be cool. You've been brave enough to go where no reporter has gone before, so don't freak out now. We're almost done. Besides, you should be more worried about Rocky's biker-chick girlfriend."

Taylor fixed on the platform where, next to Billy Joe, Jess Stevens was scowling at her with the same malice as the previous night in the bunker.

"Guess it really pissed her off," Andy said, "when Rocky looked like he wanted to sop you up in some gravy and slurp you down whole. She was just ticked that Rocky showed us the arsenal. Shot some great video, though."

Jess's violent eyes intensified Taylor's trepidation. Taylor now retained mere slivers of the confidence she had possessed Friday when this so-called open house had begun in celebration of Adolph Hitler's birthday. Its purpose was to recruit members to the White Power Alliance, and Jess had the responsibility of promoting the organization to the female visitors.

"Women are the lifeblood of the revolution," Jess had said, wearing brown cowboy boots, jeans, a flannel shirt, and a holster, "because it's up to us to reproduce the superior race."

Before her sat about a hundred women in that recreation room, reeking of beer, displaying such vulgarities as an SS helmet and a black doll in a noose. Jess sharpened her eyes on individuals as she spoke. "But that's not all. Take me, for example. I'm in charge of all telecommunications here. The White Power Alliance has Web sites, E-mail with chapters as far as Australia, the whole bit. And I'm doing this to make society better for white women."

The room was silent as several women nodded at Jess.

"After the revolution," Jess continued, "once we get all the minorities out of the way, life will be different. No more fear of rape and robbery. No more walking down the street, having some lusty-eyed nigger leer at you."

Jess, tall with a prominent chest and round hips, squinted, deepening tiny furrows around her eyes. "No more gettin' passed up for a promotion, having some unqualified minority get the job instead."

"Hallelujah! It happened to me," snickered Sue Mathews, the fiftyish wife of a Ku Klux Klansman.

Jess scowled. "And what about the day your kid comes home and says, 'Mommy, today African dancers came to our class and taught us Swahili.' You like it when the schools shove multicultural hogwash down the throats of your beautiful Aryan children?" Jess asked. "Making them ashamed to be white!"

"No!" shouted Lula Wallace, stroking her little girl's chestnut mane.

"And here's the kicker," Jess said. "A Negro doctor's kid wins a Harvard scholarship for blacks only, while your white child doesn't get a dime! That's reverse racism. And we're not puttin' up with it anymore!"

After rousing applause, Jess led the women through a paramilitary training ground, then a library stocked with white supremacist scripture: *Mein Kampf,* by Adolf Hitler; *The Clansman,* by Thomas B. Dixon; *Race and Reason,* by Carleton Putnam; and *The Hoax of the Twentieth Century,* by Arthur Butz. Jess's tour also included the set of Pulaski's cable TV show and the offices of the group's newspaper. All the while, Taylor and her camera captured every detail.

Now, on the final night in the compound, Taylor pried her eyes from Jess's glare. *Yes, I can get through the last stretch.* She noticed that Pulaski's preaching was becoming increasingly fervent.

"We've seen the results of race mixing," Rocky shouted. "In Detroit. Los Angeles. Newark. We've seen time and again the flames, the gunfire, the murder. I say these race riots prophesy the dawning of the white revolution."

Around Pulaski's neck, an Iron Cross glimmered under the flames. Taylor wondered what dead Nazi war criminal had once worn that same World War I medal awarded to the young Adolf Hitler.

"You see, comrades," Pulaski continued, "nature did not intend for Aryans to breed with blacks and Jews and Arabs. Wolves don't mix with storks, and horses don't breed with sharks. Every species sticks with its own kind. But the defiling of Aryan blood has inspired this fiery violence. In response, we try to protect ourselves, practicing our right to bear arms according to the Second Amendment of the Constitution. But what does the vile government do? It passes the Brady gun-control bill. They want to disarm us! They want to seize our weapons while they slaughter innocent women and children at Ruby Ridge and Waco! This is blasphemy!"

The crowd roared as Pulaski shoved fists in the air, his face glistening with perspiration beneath the flames.

"Nietzsche spoke of a natural aristocracy, of social Darwinism that ranks some humans above others," Rocky yelled. "And I, comrades, I am the superman! Brave enough to confront danger in the name of progress! Leader of the master race! I am commanding us—a Nordic, superior people—into the twenty-first century!"

Inwardly reeling with disgust, Taylor calmly faced the crush of people, videotaping their evil exhilaration. Countless distorted faces—darkened mouths, empty eyes, shadowy complexions—reminded her of the Siqueiros painting *Echo of a Scream*.

To her left, Taylor glimpsed a cluster of skinheads, bald heads glowing yellow, swastika-tattooed arms saluting Hitler style. Fearless and young, these storm troopers of the white revolution were hungry to terrorize and kill.

Among them was twenty-year-old Melvin "Spike" Thompson, who had boasted to Taylor, on camera, that he had murdered a black man at a highway rest area to earn a spiderweb tattoo. And when she had foolishly followed him to the compound's underground "jail" alone, to videotape it, she had fended off his attempt to grope her—and discover her hidden camera—by duping him with an absurd lie that the plastic he felt in her sweatshirt was a colostomy bag, and that if he pawed further, it would spew waste. Taylor chilled at the memory of the terror she had felt with him and his rottweiler.

Near Spike was Lula Wallace, Lula's daughter, and her platinum-haired husband, Nick, who had welcomed Taylor and Andy under a Nazi flag in the rustic dining room. Now the veins in Nick's neck bulged as he joined the crowd in an earthshaking chant of "Whites unite, fight for our rights!"

Taylor closed her eyes. Everything and everyone around her, except Andy, were the antithesis of what her parents had ingrained in her since childhood. For the sake of her sanity, she recoiled into the cozy recesses of her mind, envisioning her father's warm brown eyes, his nutmeg complexion, and his salt-and-pepper beard as he took her in his lap. "You're a beautiful symbol of America's melting pot," he often said. "But sometimes the pot seems to hold an impossible stew—big chunks of stuff that won't mix with the other ingredients. That's why God made people like you, a catalyst to blend all the elements, no matter their color or creed."

And her mother, a schoolteacher whose Scandinavian ancestry was apparent in her cloud of gold hair and aquamarine eyes, would add, "Taylor, honey, people have been unkind because you're biracial, but always hope for a better day. Your grandparents disowned me when I married your father, but I still pray that one day we'll all be together again. Always remember that love can overcome anything."

Taylor adored her parents, but their tendency to be overprotective sometimes angered her. She hoped that this undercover investigation would show them that she could take care of herself, anywhere.

"By blood, comrades!" Rocky thundered. "We will take back our land by blood!"

After a quarter hour, the tumult finally subsided into a highly charged din as Rocky, Jess, and Billy Joe descended into a swell of reverence. The rest of the group disbanded for country line dancing to a live band, a skinhead heavy metal group and slam dance in the barn, and plenty of racist fellowship, footloose and fancy-free under steady streams of cheap Tennessee whiskey.

Taylor and Andy headed for the compound, a former boarding school that towered ominously with rooftop riflemen against the midnight sky.

Out of the crowd emerged Nick, calling their fake names.

"Hi, buddy," Andy said.

His wife, Lula, and her little girl, clutching her black-haired Dolf Bear, approached Taylor. "Kate, doesn't this make you feel proud?"

Taylor nodded. "It's overwhelming."

"Gives me gooseflesh," Lula said, shaking short, dark curls. "Everything Führer Pulaski says is right on the money."

Her daughter saluted, shouting, "Whites unite, fight for our rights!"

Lula kissed her forehead. "That's right, sweetie. You remember that."

The little girl smiled up at Taylor, who masked disgust under a smile. *God help that poor child.*

Nick grinned. "My daughter is growin' up proud to be a white American."

Andy, in jeans, a denim jacket, and a Detroit Tigers baseball cap over his light brown ponytail, put his arm around Taylor. "We're going to the rest room. We'll meet you right back here for the dance."

Nick smiled. "You two—such a cute couple. Bet I hear wedding bells."

Andy's eyes sparkled. "Oh, I don't know, man. That's a long way off."

Taylor was pleased that their boyfriend-girlfriend act was duping everyone, but as they walked hand in hand toward the compound, a pang of longing shot through her. Her yearning for Julian—his soothing touch, his calming voice—was now exacerbated by shell shock in this horrific place.

Julian doesn't want me anymore. I can deal with this alone. Get over it.

Taylor squeezed Andy's hand as they headed inside. However, there was no substitute for Julian. It was not Julian's handsomeness that Taylor still loved; it was his innate ability to understand her. Half French and half African-American, he knew how she felt, balancing on that shaky bridge between black and white, aching and wincing from the stones and verbal assaults slung from both sides. So being, Julian had provided a sanctuary where Taylor could be not black, not white, but simply Taylor—the little girl and teenager who loved watching movies and swimming and using a camcorder to report fires and accidents around the neighborhood. Nowhere did she feel the security, serenity, and passion that his presence proffered.

But their childhood dreams of marrying and working together as journalists had vaporized in a sudden, mysterious cloud of irascibility and sex years ago. And Julian never called, never wrote, never apologized. However, she still saw him every day—on television, anchoring the Los Angeles–based show *Entertainment Exclusive.* But seeing his happy, handsome image, and hearing his smooth baritone, stabbed at her heart. She wanted him live and in color, in her life, not on television. If he were to call on Monday and say, "Let's get back together," she would demand an apology, then welcome her soul mate back into her arms.

Be for real. That's not going to happen. Let go already.

Taylor released Andy's hand and stepped into the rest room, where Sue Mathews, the Klansman's wife, was pinning back her hair to display diamond stud earrings. As Taylor waited in line, Sue clasped her hands.

"Honey, you feel all right? You look pale. All this excitement—"

"Oh, I'm fine," Taylor said. "Just overwhelmed, I guess."

"I know the feeling," Sue said. "Well, you be sure and get some rest. And I hope we'll be seein' you again real soon."

Taylor smiled. *And you'll be sure to hear from the IRS real soon, after they see you admitting on the news that you and your KKK hubby haven't paid taxes in ten years because you hate the government.*

As the line inched ahead, Taylor unbuttoned her denim jacket, then stooped to scrape mud off her hiking boots. She stopped when two cowboy boots appeared, facing her.

"You think you're real cute, don't you?"

Taylor's heart galloped.

"Uh, no," Taylor said, meeting Jess's glare. Around them, a half dozen women gawked. Everyone knew that Jess was Rocky's woman; the tattoo atop her left breast—a red heart inscribed with ROCKY—left no doubt.

Eyes wide with rage, thin lips pursed, Jess shoved Taylor's shoulders. "I saw the way you were lookin' at Rocky last night. Askin' all those questions about our weapons. And that little innocent voice. I can see right through you. What're you gonna do, meet Rocky in the woods for a quick fuck?"

Only in my worst nightmare . . .

Taylor's hands trembled, but her face was stiff. "No, of course not. I'm here with my boyfriend."

Jess combed her fingers over dark roots, letting loose blond hair fall on her shoulders. One strand caught on the silver crucifix at her neck. "Chicks like you are always tryin' to elbow in on Rocky. It pisses me off!"

Taylor shook her head. "No, really, I would never—"

Jess pointed a forefinger, its nail bitten to half its normal size and topped by a raw, red strip, in Taylor's face. "You go near him again, I'll kick your ass." Then she left.

The other women whispered while Taylor breathed deeply to calm frantic nerves. She cringed at the thought of Rocky touching her, with his thick, oarlike hands, his odor that reminded her of beef jerky, and those lecherous eyes.

Finally Taylor entered a stall, where she inserted a fresh videotape in the recording deck sewn inside her sweatshirt. She checked the wire running from the lipstick-sized camera in her hat through her wig and into her shirt. Another wire laced down her sleeve to her cuff, which held a microphone and the camera's remote-control record switch.

Ten and a half more hours . . .

The sour taste of danger seeped up from her aching gut as Billy Joe's suspicious expression suddenly flashed in her mind. Glancing in the mirror, she was nearly a stranger to herself in the wig and blue-framed glasses. She recognized only the anxious green eyes, her father's full mouth and roundish nose, and her mother's arched brows and dainty jawline.

If these people only knew I'm half black. It baffled Taylor that the genetic fusion of her father's brownness plus her mother's whiteness equaled more white, instead of café au lait like Julian. But now her appearance was a tool. Without it, the investigation would have been impossible.

Moments later, Taylor met Andy outside the rest room.

"Thought maybe you fell in," he said, chuckling. "You all right?"

Taylor nodded. "Just ready to go home."

"Hang in there," he said. "Let's have a drink with Nick and Lula, maybe dance a little. In the morning we're home free."

Taylor clung to those words as they penetrated the noisy crowd. To her left was a man in black leather chaps, passing out swastika armbands. Among the takers was state senator Ned McCleary.

Taylor stepped toward him with an extended arm. "Excuse me, Senator McCleary. I'm Kate Lawson. It's a delight to meet you."

"Hello, young lady," he said, smiling and shaking her hand.

"That was so generous of you to donate a half million dollars to the White Power Alliance," Taylor said.

McCleary grinned and removed black-rimmed eyeglasses. He was short with a wild band of gray waves around a freckled dome. "Yep, I know a good cause when I see one."

"You must see a lot," Taylor said with a girlish tone. "I mean, since you're chairman of the Senate Appropriations Committee and everything."

"Well, aren't you a sharp little cookie. Yeah, I'm fed up with money going to the minority this and the minority that. So I say, let's give some money to a valid effort. Couldn't find a better cause than this here."

Taylor feigned confusion. "But, Senator, you won't get in trouble, will you? Since this is kind of, well, an underground movement and all."

McCleary chuckled. "It's called coverin' your tracks. See, I can account for the money with doctored-up paperwork. Say it's for some cultural project. Which it is—preserving white culture. Nobody'll ask questions."

"That's clever," Taylor said.

McCleary nodded as a tall man, probably six six, with a broad face, gray-brown hair, and a protruding Adam's apple, approached. "Kate, meet Fred Lutz. Private developer by trade. White Power benefactor by belief."

"Hello," Lutz said. "You sure ask a lotta questions."

Taylor smiled. "Yeah, me and my boyfriend are just trying to learn all we can before we join up."

Lutz nodded. "There's no better way to spend your free time and money. We got, what? Five hundred people here tonight. Here's the man himself."

Taylor's heart pounded as Rocky Pulaski approached. He was about six feet tall, barrel-chested, and radiant. All weekend he had appeared fresh-scrubbed clean; his ears and the slight hump on his nose shined like polished wax. And up close, his black eyes emitted hair-raising potency.

"We were just schooling your young admirer here," Lutz told Rocky with a macho chuckle.

Rocky put his arm around Taylor. She concealed her repulsion under an anxious smile. As he spoke, his deep voice resonated through her chest, intensifying the nervous ache in her gut.

"Yeah, Kate here's a real hoot," Rocky said. "Full of questions."

That's because I'm a journalist. Smile for the camera . . .

A short time later, with Andy, Nick, and Lula, Taylor headed for the grassy dance area. *Ten more hours and we're out of this wicked—*

She froze.

Billy Joe was storming toward her. Shoulders hunched forward, furious eyes. A half dozen skinheads, including Spike, flanking him.

"I know who you are, bitch."

Icy fingers of fear slithered around Taylor's neck, clutching her chest.

Andy stepped in front of her. "Don't talk to her like that."

"Your bitch set me up," Billy Joe said. The skinheads, in steel-toed combat boots and black leather jackets, glared at her and Andy.

This is it. We're busted. They're gonna strip us . . . torture us . . . kill us. Sweat prickled under her arms and across her groin. Her quick breath formed little white clouds in the crisp April air.

Then, with a sudden burst of adrenaline and courage, Taylor stepped from behind Andy and faced Billy Joe. "I never met you before yesterday," she said. "You must have me confused with someone else."

Andy scowled. "Yeah, Kate just met you last night."

Billy Joe balled his fists. "Oh no she didn't."

"Hey, man, cool down," Nick said. Lula, confused, held her daughter close.

Billy Joe squinted at Taylor. "I said if I ever saw you again, I'd beat the shit outta you."

God, please help us . . .

Dizzy with terror, Taylor met his glare. "Please leave us alone. We're trying to enjoy the party."

"Leave her alone," Andy said.

Billy Joe shoved Andy's chest, then glared at Taylor. "You're gonna be sorry you ever set foot in here."

He raised his fist.

Oh God, no . . .

White-hot pain cracked across her cheek. She teetered. Blackness, lights, and faces swam before her.

Julian can't save me this time . . .

CHAPTER 1

A sudden pang of apprehension froze Taylor midstep in the center of the bustling newsroom.

Why are cops at my desk?

She did not want any interference today. In just a few hours she would face Rocky Pulaski again. And she was primed to gloat that her work had dismantled his Reich to little more than the swastika tattoos on his arms and the vile thoughts in his head.

Taylor glanced at Shari Gordon, the executive producer, who was briefing a reporter at producers' row, a central bank of desks around which several producers fixated on computers.

"Go," Shari told Tony Martin. "We got three kids dead in a house fire. Ask the mother why the hell she left her kids alone. Find out if police are pressing neglect charges."

Tony blew past Taylor.

The assignment editor, a freckled, bespectacled man named Jerry Spinx, yelled after him: "The dad is on the scene, ready to dish dirt on the crackhead mom."

Jerry disappeared behind a gray tweed divider into the newsroom's high-voltage nerve center, where he monitored computers, crackling police, fire, and ambulance scanners, and several ringing phones. Behind him were wall maps and the huge white, erasable storyboard. In red letters, the top slot said: TAYLOR JAMES, WHITE POWER RALLY, 4 PM, DOWNTOWN DETROIT, VIDEOGRAPHER PATRICK MCIN-TYRE.

"Shari, what's going on?" Taylor asked, drawing her boss's attention from a television monitor. Shari, somber in a high-necked gray pantsuit, darted toward her, chic muss of brown hair bouncing.

"Taylor, I'm glad you're here early. We need to talk."

"I hope you're going to tell me why the cops are here," Taylor said.

Shari's thick, arched brows drew together over piercing hazel eyes while she fingered her diamond tennis bracelet, an action that always signaled that Shari was more high-strung than usual.

"You got death threats," Shari said.

"From who?" Taylor set her leather shoulder bag on the black circular Newsflash desk, where journalists conducted live newsroom reports.

"From Pulaski, about the rally," Shari said.

Taylor crossed her arms over her red linen suit, causing the two-carat diamond ring on her left hand to sparkle. "So what else is new? Pulaski's been sending me nasty letters for three years now. I'm not scared of him anymore."

"This is different," Shari said. "Those letters came from prison. But now he's out, in Detroit, and you're going to shove a microphone in his face. Could be dangerous."

Taylor shrugged. "There'll be enough cops at the rally."

Shari shook her head. "Come up to my office."

"Don't tell me you're taking me off the story," Taylor said.

"No, not that," Shari said as they climbed the open, black marble staircase that ascended one side of the newsroom's arched entryway and descended the other side. Silver railings lined the steps and the balcony.

"Then what?" Taylor asked, annoyed, as they hurried into Shari's spacious office.

Shari rushed to the phone and punched buttons. With anxious eyes, she twisted her bracelet as Pulaski's message played: "If that half-nigger, white traitorous bitch Taylor James shows up at our rally today in Detroit, she's dead. I'll kill her with my own hands and come all over the bloody pulp that's left of her."

Beep.

Taylor shrugged. "That's no worse than anything else he's—"

"Wait," Shari said. "There's more. I think this is his son."

The message played: "Secret reports and exposés, taken in sneaky, mongrel ways, will bring the death of Taylor James, a freak I shoulda killed in our childhood days."

Beep.

Taylor caressed the tiny white scar on her left cheek. "Yeah, that's definitely Billy Joe. They teach poetry in prison?"

Shari snickered. "Listen, here's the third one."

"Hi, Kate. It's Spike, still in the slammer, thanks to you, but I'll be watchin' the news tonight when they show Rocky and Billy Joe beatin' the shit outta you. I'll see you in hell."

A chill snaked down Taylor's spine as she remembered that skinhead's mouth smashed against hers, the terror of being alone with him in that underground jail.

"Who was that?" Shari asked.

"The skinhead convicted of killing the black man at the rest area," Taylor said.

"Right, I remember."

"Shari, this is nothing new. What's the big deal?"

"The big deal is they threatened to kill you and I'm worried about it," Shari said. She leaned against her black marble desktop and lit a cigarette. Behind her, track lights illuminated silver-plated media awards.

"If they wanted to hurt me," Taylor said, "they would have done it when the Feds seized the compound and threw those morons in jail."

Shari squinted and blew out smoke. "Unless they wanted to wait and hurt you themselves. They know you'll be out there today."

Against clear, white skin, Shari's eyes were grim with gray liner and shadow the shade of her pantsuit. Balancing an elbow on an arm across her waist, she held the cigarette between short, raisin-colored fingernails. The dark lipstick smudges on the tip of the cigarette matched her tense, narrow mouth.

"You look like you're going to a funeral," Taylor said.

"Yeah? Well, I don't want it to be yours," Shari said.

"So what are you saying?" Taylor set her bag on the gray leather couch and sat down. Staring at Shari for an answer, she resolved not to let her boss's gloom and paranoia spoil the enthusiasm that had awakened her early.

Over the past three and a half years, their friendship had culminated in Taylor asking Shari to stand in her upcoming wedding. Seven years her senior, Shari was a mentor and a role model as a woman who had excelled in this arduous, male-dominated business. Early on, if Taylor had blundered on-air or misunderstood an assignment, Shari had been patient and supportive.

She and Taylor, who both thrived on the hectic, unpredictable chaos of breaking news, were a productive pair. One night, when Taylor was upset after reporting the murder of a woman whose assailant used a knife to steal her unborn baby from her uterus, Shari had prepared a cup of chamomile tea for Taylor and consoled her in the employee lounge. Another day, when a commuter plane crashed into a suburban home, killing fifteen people, Shari directed Taylor and much of the reporting staff in tracking down victims' families, survivors, and FAA officials. After soaring on adrenaline all day and evening, Taylor and Shari descended together over Coneys at the nearby Lafayette Coney Island. Indigestion the following day prompted them to move nighttime chitchats about men, office politics, and current events to a downtown piano bar. When Shari fought with her husband, or argued with the news director, Taylor provided tequila shots and emotional support. But their friendship never eroded the professional respect Taylor showed Shari at the office.

"Oh, there's William," Shari said, opening the glass door. Taylor stood, perplexed at the surprise meeting with Channel 3's news director.

"Good afternoon, Taylor. Please, sit down," said William Monroe. She studied his and Shari's somber faces as she sat down.

"We need to talk about your story," said William, who wore round, pewter-rimmed glasses, which magnified his eyes, the same shade of gray as his Caesaresque coif. As he sat on the couch, his navy blue suit jacket opened to reveal the gold chain of a pocket watch that dangled from his vest. In an electronic business that moved daily at breakneck speed, William's frequent caressing of the antique time-piece in his palm, and flipping it open to check the time, seemed as unlikely as replacing the anchor studio's Klieg lights with candle-sticks.

Taylor's cheeks burned with uneasiness as she faced William. She sat erect, hands clasped in her lap.

"We want you to have a police escort today," William said from a leather chair facing her. His deep, gentle voice reminded Taylor of when her grandpa Duke warned her as a child not to bicycle in the street or ride without a life jacket on his forty-foot Sea Ray on Lake St. Clair.

"I beg your pardon?" Taylor shot a questioning look at Shari.

"I agree," Shari said, raising her eyebrows. She stabbed her cig-arette into an ashtray on the glass coffee table. "We discussed this when your series ran three years ago. But the federal raid, the trials, everything happened so fast, I don't think Rocky Pulaski had time to plot your demise."

William nodded. "But today, well, this guy is out for your blood."

"So what am I supposed to do?" Taylor asked. She was relieved that the anger surging through her did not crack her voice. She did not want to appear disrespectful to her superiors.

"We told the FBI and the Detroit police about the threats," William said. "And the two cops downstairs will be your bodyguards at the White Power Alliance rally today."

"Bodyguards?" Taylor asked incredulously.

"Yes," William said.

"I don't think that's necessary," Taylor said. "The time for body-guards was when Andy Doss and I were watching crosses burn with howling racists and secretly filming Pulaski's arsenal. Back then I was scared, but now I'm not. My exposé castrated Rocky Pulaski. I won."

"You won round one," Shari said. "But this guy is back with a vengeance to rebuild what he had, what *you* destroyed. That's what the rally is for, to recruit members and get attention for their cause."

Taylor shook her head. "You're overreacting. Do you really think that with all the cops and TV cameras out there today, Pulaski would be stupid enough to hurt me?"

Shari fingered her bracelet.

"Don't know," William said. "And it's not worth the risk to find out."

Taylor sighed, then struggled to summon a calm voice. "This happened when I worked in Miami," she said. "The Francisco drug lord sent his goons after me during his double-murder trial. Said if I didn't back off, they'd send me scuba diving in a cement wet suit. But I did my reports anyway, and lived to tell about it."

William sighed. Shari lit another cigarette.

"I didn't back off then, and I won't now," Taylor said, crossing her arms.

"Nobody said back off," William snapped. "Go out there and make us proud. But don't get killed in the process."

"Right," Shari said.

Taylor knitted her brows. "But I—"

"End of story," William said as he stood up, pulled his watch out of his pocket, and flipped it open. As he left the office, he added, "We'll decide tonight if the cops need to stick around."

"Stick around?" Taylor bolted to her feet, annoyance ringing in her voice.

Shari touched Taylor's arm and cast a concerned expression. "If it gets rough out there, you're getting round-the-clock protection."

Taylor closed her eyes and shook her head. After a few moments, she looked at Shari. "I can't believe this."

"Believe it," Shari said, blowing out smoke. She hurried behind her desk and grabbed a leather-bound day planner. "As your boss and your friend, I think this is a smart move."

Taylor's limbs hummed with irritation. She did not need bodyguards to help her do her job. She had survived the dangerous undercover investigation, so surely she could handle a rally crawling with police.

She retrieved her bag and strode toward the windows facing the newsroom below. Through ficus trees and silver blinds, she saw Andy Doss and the back of a tall, dark-haired man as they walked toward the large purple neon "3 Sports" at the sports desk. Then she glanced at the police officers.

"This is so paranoid," Taylor said.

Shari hurried toward the door. "Think of it this way. How'd you like Philip going to your funeral instead of your wedding?"

Taylor shook her head. "That's not gonna hap—"

"I have a meeting," Shari said as she walked toward the large conference room adjacent to her office. "Talk to me before you leave."

As Taylor walked along the balcony toward the elevators, she watched Andy laugh with Buck Norton, the lead sportscaster, and the other man she did not recognize. She could not see his face, just black curls trimmed in a perfect line above a brown neck. Maybe he was an athlete in for a studio interview with Buck. Craning to see him, Taylor almost bumped into the anchor of the six- and eleven-o'clock shows.

"Hi, Taylor."

"David, I didn't see you."

"No problem," he said. "You look great in red."

"Thanks. Excited about your new job?"

Dimples formed on David Dwyer's made-up face as he smiled. He was about the same height as Taylor, five eight, with wavy brown hair.

"Yeah," he said. "My first assignment in D.C. is to interview the president."

Taylor smiled. "You've hit the big time now."

"Huh," he said. "I just hope I'm not so nervous that I'm tongue-tied. But you guys won't miss me. They're already interviewing some guy from California to fill my anchor chair."

"We will miss you," Taylor said, "especially your band at the Christmas party."

"Thanks. I won't be around for your wedding, but good luck with Philip. I have him to thank for this dream gig in D.C."

"Hey, if he likes you, the sky's the limit."

"Yeah, but if he doesn't, look out," David chuckled. "You hear about Rick Hilton?"

"I've heard of him," Taylor said. "A Wolf reporter in Chicago, right?"

"Used to be," David said. "He and Philip had a major blowup. We're talkin' nuclear bomb here. There's probably still a mushroom cloud over the Windy City."

"What happened?" Taylor asked.

"Well, Rick's had an ego since the second grade," David said. "And believe me, being on TV hasn't humbled him any. So put him in a room with Philip and—"

"I get the point," Taylor said, smiling.

"Then you can imagine how Rick's contract negotiations went last month," David said. "Those two fought like inbred pit bulls. Course, Philip ripped Rick's throat out and left him in the gutter to bleed to death."

"Bad news." Taylor crossed her arms. "Philip never mentioned—"

"Of course, there are two sides to it," David said. "Rick says Philip has some vendetta against him. But my sources in Chicago say Rick built his own house of horrors. Demanding a monster salary, a BMW, a huge wardrobe allowance, stuff like that. Then he bad-mouthed Philip to any and everyone."

"What an idiot," Taylor said.

"Yeah, an unemployed idiot," David said. "Philip ripped the contract to shreds and said Rick would never work in broadcast news again."

Taylor shook her head. "You reap what you sow. Rick should've known better than to cross Philip Carter."

"True," David said, then smiled. "Well, you have nothing to worry about. As Mrs. Philip Carter, your future is paved with gold."

Taylor frowned. "Hey, don't start. I've heard enough comments from people around here. Why can't anyone understand that Philip swept me off my feet and we're in love? And no, I'm not trying to wed my way up the company ladder."

David frowned playfully and tapped her shoulder. "Course not. I've seen the softie under Philip's barracuda facade. It was at one of those inner-city journalism programs he supports. There was this little black kid having a hard time. Philip sits down with him and voilà, the kid writes a great story."

Taylor smiled. "There's a lot more to Philip than meets the eye. Like with his own kids, he spends at least one weekend a month doing something fun with them, I guess to make up for all the time he spends on the road."

"Good luck, Taylor. And be careful with your new police friends."

Taylor glanced down at the two police officers at her desk, then rolled her eyes. *How embarrassing and insulting to have cops baby-sit me on my job. This is ludicrous. Maybe I can sweet-talk Philip into nixing the idea.*

Taylor stepped toward the elevators, a tide of anger rising within her.

CHAPTER 2

Taylor rode the elevator to the twenty-eighth-floor atrium, where beams of yellow sunshine filtered through palm trees and leafy plants, making fernlike patterns on the marble floor. Across a dark cherry-paneled wall in silver letters was WOLF MEDIA CORP. MIDWEST HEAD-QUARTERS.

"Hello, Ms. James," the snow-haired receptionist said. "Mr. Carter is expecting you. Go right in."

"Thanks."

When she glimpsed Philip across the cavernous, paneled office, Taylor's stomach fluttered. *I love being in love.*

Philip stood with his back to the door, looking out a large window facing tall office buildings. He was talking loudly into a cordless phone.

"Put me in the kill zone, Greg," he said. "I don't care if you have to skewer Franklin like a roasted pig in the process. The K.C. station is mine. Simple as that."

Taylor padded across the vast forest green carpet. She slipped her arms around his firm waist, pressing her breasts into his back. His deep voice vibrated through her as she inhaled an intoxicating blend of Lagerfeld, his natural scent, and herbal shampoo.

"I don't care about the risk, Greg," Philip said. "If that sleaze-master Wilbur Franklin so much as thinks he can block me this time, I'll make pâté of him and serve it to his mother for lunch. Later."

Philip spun around, then kissed Taylor gently on the mouth.

She flushed.

"Darling," he said softly, his cornflower blue eyes aglow. "I knew you'd come storming up here when you saw the men in blue downstairs."

Taylor bristled; she pulled out of his embrace and studied the usual omnipotent expression on his tanned, clean-shaven face.

"You know about the police?" she asked.

"It was my idea," he said.

"Well, I think it's ludicrous," Taylor said, a geyser of anger deepening her voice.

"I knew you would," he said. "But I'm not gambling with your safety. Not when it comes to that barbarian Pulaski."

Taylor crossed her arms. "You, everyone, you're overreacting."

"Better safe than sorry, darling. I've been in this business since before you were born; I know what I'm doing." Concern radiated from

Philip's eyes. He put his hands in the pockets of his beige, pleated trousers and jingled change.

Taylor cast her eyes down to his monogrammed shirt pocket. *I'm sick of everyone treating me like a child. My parents, my bosses, now Philip. Why can't they see that I can take care of myself?*

"Pout all you want," Philip said. "The bottom line is, you're not going out there alone. Pulaski's only redeeming value is what he's done for you and me. I discovered a rising star and a gorgeous new wife, and your exposé dazzled the network powers that be. It's only a matter of time before you're giving the news in every living room in America."

Philip tickled a manicured finger under her chin. "Come on, flash that million-dollar smile."

Taylor drew back the corners of her mouth.

"That's better," he said, fine lines fanning the corners of his eyes and around his smiling mouth. "You'll be a superstar out there today. A safe superstar."

The intercom buzzed: "Mr. Carter, Horace is on the line."

"Christ," Philip said. "Put him through."

Taylor sat in one of the burgundy wing-back leather chairs near Philip's six-foot television screen, which divided into dozens of boxes that allowed Philip to watch simultaneously from his desk Wolf's stations, those he wanted to buy, and competing stations.

"Philip," his brother said over the speaker phone.

"What is it, Horace?"

As Horace rambled about plans for Channel 3's future morning program, Taylor watched Philip tense behind his wide cherry desk. A finger width of his combed-back blond hair fell to his temple. He sighed, then fidgeted with the remote control, causing dizzying images to rotate on the screen.

Philip grimaced. "Goddammit, Horace, I told you—"

"Wait, Philip, just listen a minute."

Taylor hated to admit to herself that she pitied Philip when she thought about him in the context of his family. The one time she had met his family—his parents, two older brothers, and a younger sister—at a formal dinner at their Beverly Hills mansion, his father had viciously berated him for divorcing his first wife, leaving her with two teenagers. A puritanical lecture about God and morality followed, casting a humiliated silence over the family.

"You bring me shame in the eyes of God," Gerald Carter had bellowed, his swarthy features radiating fury.

Later, at Philip's oceanfront mansion, a hot wave of empathy had consumed Taylor as Philip described a lifetime of alienation and pain in a family whose paternal blood he did not share. It was then that Philip confessed to Taylor the Carter family's most scandalous secret: that Gerald Carter had chosen to raise his wife's love child as his own rather than suffer the shame of cuckoldry and divorce in 1948.

Hearing that, Taylor had then understood why Philip, with his slim build, chiseled features, and blond hair, did not resemble his father and brothers, who had bulky physiques, fleshy faces, and dark, wavy hair. She had also comprehended why his mother had stared at him with that odd glazed expression throughout dinner. Also that evening, early in their courtship, Taylor had realized that both she and Philip were outsiders: he in his family; she in a black-or-white world.

And so, for the past three years, Taylor had soothed Philip's ache while he helped her forget her own. She never expected to marry a white man; she had always dreamt of marrying Julian, a métis like herself. But while she tired of waiting and wishing for Julian, Philip was making her feel like a princess—all the trips to New York, the tropics, Europe; the gifts; the promises of media superstardom under his guidance. It was a passion-swept haze that bloomed into engagement.

His proposal had been a reverie of luxury and romance. He had taken her to London for a long weekend of Christmas shopping at Brompton Cross, when, in their room at the Savoy overlooking the Thames, Philip kissed her passionately, declared his love, and presented a diamond ring. Taylor remembered being dizzy with ebullience, barely able to sleep in the handmade bed in that elegant late Victorian room.

Now, when it sounded like Philip and Horace were concluding their contentious chat, Taylor stepped toward his desk and looked at the large brass-framed picture of herself and Philip on his father's yacht, *Lady Virtue,* near Acapulco. They were radiant—both tanned, their sun-bleached hair blowing over the azure sea as she, in a white bikini, perched on his lap in the teak captain's chair. That photograph always evoked happy warmth within Taylor, and she hoped that it forecast a lifetime of love and elation.

Thank you, God, for letting me find love again.

It had been nearly ten years since her breakup with Julian, but seeing his face on newsroom TV monitors every night when he anchored *Entertainment Exclusive* in Los Angeles still provoked a dull ache deep within her. If she allowed herself to think about him long enough, sorrow stabbed through the tough scars that had formed over the place he once occupied in her heart. But now her love for Philip, coupled with twelve- and fourteen-hour workdays, left little time or energy to lament the loss of her first love.

Tension gripped Taylor as she approached the police officers at her desk.

"Ms. James, I'm Officer Edwards," said a thirtyish, clean-cut man with brown hair and a warm smile. His partner, a broad-shouldered woman, smiled and extended her hand. "I'm Officer Young, nice to meet you."

Taylor shook their hands. "So how does this work?"

"We'll follow your news van to the rally and we'll escort you through the crowd," Edwards said. "If we're needed beyond this afternoon—"

"You won't be," Taylor said. "I have to do some work at my desk, so have a seat at producers' row."

They looked at Shari, who was scolding a reporter for not getting sound bites from the mayor about the city's efforts to open a gambling casino.

"What the hell kind of story do we have without the mayor? Get a quote from him if you have to ride a scaffold to his office and climb through the window. Don't come back without it." As the reporter slunk away, Shari smiled at the police officers.

"Welcome," she said. "There's a cafeteria upstairs, if you'd like some coffee or chips."

"We're fine, thanks," Officer Young said. Taylor suppressed a chuckle as the officers looked at Shari as if she breathed fire.

On a gray tweed chair that matched the walls of her cubicle, Taylor spun to face her desk, a computer, a phone, and phone books. On the wall hung her Journalist of the Year award and a certificate from Columbia University thanking her for using her prize money to start a scholarship for biracial students. Next to that hung awards from Channel 3, community organizations, and the Girls Center, founded by her close friend Carla Jackson, where Taylor mentored girls interested in journalism.

On the desk sat the Emmy Award she had won for investigative reporting following the White Power Alliance exposé, along with a clay statue of two cherubs, one white and one brown, holding hands with outstretched wings. In small frames sat pictures of Taylor and Philip, her parents, and her with Shari, Carla, and Danielle Mancini, her best childhood friend since fifth grade at the Detroit Country Day School.

Even after ten years, Danielle still reminded Taylor of Julian. They had all been so close once, her and Julian, Danielle and Peter, always going to movies, concerts, and sporting events. They even took their senior high school trip together, a week of hedonism in Fort Lauderdale. Skinny-dipping in the ocean at two in the morning. Spending a drunken day and night on the yacht of a rich man they met at a trendy restaurant on the Intracoastal.

But graduation ended the foursome's fun times. Danielle and Peter went to Michigan State, married, and opened Mancini & Anderson, a public relations firm in Detroit. They bought a house in the suburbs and had two children.

Now, glancing at Danielle's picture, Taylor felt a twinge of envy that her close friend had married her first love. The foursome had always talked about being in each other's weddings, letting their children play together, and enjoying friendship as they grew old. Taylor sighed. *Not everything is meant to be. I'll be just as happy with Philip.*

Taylor punched a pass code into the phone to access her messages. "Message one," the electronic voice said.

"Taylor, it's Carla. Listen, since you're covering the rally downtown today, could you do me a favor and keep an eye out for Officer Gus Lemer? His beat is downtown, but it would be pretty suspect if he just happens to be strolling through a white supremacist rally. Call me later."

Taylor made a mental note to watch for Officer Lemer. The one time she had seen him on a downtown street corner, she had felt a pang of contempt because beneath his friendly smile lurked a murderer, perhaps even a racist murderer. Here was a man, a police officer, who had killed Carla's father during Detroit's 1967 riots, yet he was free to enjoy his family, his career, his life. It was only after Lemer had pumped two bullets into Gregory Jackson's chest that he learned that Mr. Jackson was not looting the very grocery store that bore his name and was his livelihood. Regardless, an all-white jury acquitted Lemer of manslaughter.

Carla, devastated that her father was never coming home, had made it her life's mission to bring Lemer down. As a prosecuting attorney, she knew the law backward and forward, and spent much of her free time searching for new evidence, or an eyewitness, anything that could reopen her father's case and put Lemer behind bars forever. Taylor had promised to help Carla gather information whenever possible, and today might just provide a new lead.

The phone rang. Taylor glanced at the police officers, who nodded.

"Channel Three, this is Taylor James."

"Hello, honey."

"Hi, Mom." The officers turned away.

"Honey, I'm worried about you going out to that hate-fest today."

"You can rest easy this time, Mom. I have a police escort."

"Wonderful. Tell Shari that's very smart," Monica James said. "Now, about the bridal shower, Janice and I need to know which cheesecake flavor you prefer. We love the white chocolate because it reminds us of that cute nickname Julian used to call you, but since you're not marrying him as we'd all hoped, we wanted to check with you first."

Taylor rolled her eyes. *When will Mom ever let go?*

"I'm not having this conversation again," Taylor snapped.

"I know, I know. It's just that, well, we liked Philip when he was just a company executive, not our future son-in-law. It's no secret that we all wanted you to marry Julian."

Taylor turned to the wall and spoke softly. "Guess what, Mom. Julian didn't want me anymore."

"I know, I just think in time—"

"Mom, what's your question?"

"The cheesecake. Which flavor do you want, white chocolate or regular with strawberries?"

"The latter," Taylor said impatiently.

A few minutes later, she pulled a file from her drawer and flipped through newspaper clippings chronicling the demise of the White Power Alliance. Under the headline FBI SEIZES WHITE SUPREMACIST COMPOUND, HUGE ARSENAL AFTER TV REPORTER EXPOSES ALL was a picture of wild-eyed Rocky Pulaski being led away from the compound in handcuffs. Under him were pictures of Billy Joe and Jess, handcuffed in a blue flannel nightgown.

The exposé had earned Taylor and Andy exclusive access to the predawn raid by Michigan State Police and the Federal Bureau of Investigation, who, in an assault of gunfire, German shepherds, and tear gas, seized the property, weapons, and computers. In the muddy courtyard, Taylor, in a bulletproof vest, had stood tall with victory, dizzy with euphoria. She had conquered Pulaski's bloodthirsty Reich, in effect stitching up a pus-oozing ulcer on the belly of America's racial beast. And she hoped that this was just the first victory in a lifetime of similar work.

Another article, with a picture of Rocky, Billy Joe, and Jess in front of the federal courthouse, said: NEO-NAZI LEADER SENTENCED TO PRISON FOR CONSPIRACY, WEAPONS OFFENSES. Rocky had been

WHITE CHOCOLATE / 39

fortunate that his lawyer was able to manipulate legal technicalities and loopholes to have several charges reduced and dropped, enabling Rocky to qualify for parole after just two years in prison. Jess and Billy Joe both served eighteen months.

Other fallout from the exposé included a political scandal: SEN-ATOR MCCLEARY IMPEACHED, IMPRISONED FOR FUNNELING STATE FUNDS TO RACIST MILITIA. He went to prison, as did Spike. The family of the man he killed thanked Taylor for helping to solve a senseless crime and incarcerating the perpetrator for life. But she received no such accolades from Sue and Larry Mathews, who were pictured handcuffed in front of their sprawling lakeside home: KKK LEADER AND WIFE JAILED FOR TAX EVASION.

Taylor's mouth curled up in a half smile. *If I had to do it all over again, I would. It was worth every goose bump.*

It was almost time to leave for the rally, so Taylor went to the rest room. In the mirror she noticed that some of the fire had dimmed in her green eyes; she blamed the humiliating police tagalong. And now, suddenly, her red suit seemed too flashy, its padded shoulders and tapered waist accentuating her shape too dramatically for this gritty assignment. She pushed her long, blond curls off her shoulders to her back, then wiped a lipstick smudge from the corner of her mouth. Hurrying back into the newsroom, she bumped into Andy Doss.

"Hey," he said somberly. "Can I borrow your bodyguards if the skinheads come after me out there today?"

"Why are you going?" Taylor asked. "Patrick McIntyre is my cameraman today."

"I'm taking this guy out to do a package for his tryout. He wants Dwyer's job." A hard glint flashed in Andy's eyes. "I'm surprised Philip is even letting you go out today."

"What's that supposed to mean?"

"Seems like Mister Big Shot wouldn't want his precious bride around danger anymore."

Taylor sneered. "Marriage will not hinder my reporting. And you need to stop it with your childish grudge."

Andy raised his hands the same way he had when that soldier had pointed a gun at him as they entered Pulaski's compound. "Hey, hey, relax. It was just mighty strange how you told me you don't date co-workers, then you go and get engaged to the head honcho. But let's be real. I'm just a cameraman. I can't offer you a private jet and a vacation pad in Maui."

Taylor blinked. "You're being so juvenile, Andy."

"You weren't complaining about me up north when you were shaking like a leaf. I gotta go." With a bitter glare, Andy walked away.

What a jerk. As Taylor headed toward her desk, her annoyance intensified when she saw reporter Kendra Vaughn hurrying toward her.

"Taylor, girl, I *know* you're pissed, having those cops follow you around all day," said Kendra, whose tone of voice barely masked her amusement over Taylor's predicament. Wearing sunglasses, a designer suit, and her usual not-a-hair-out-of-place bob, Kendra was carrying a take-out lunch and a diet soda.

Taylor could not even glance at her without remembering the day that Kendra had called her "a high-yellow bitch" who had no business attending National Association of Black Journalists conventions. And when Taylor was hired at Channel 3, Kendra, a two-year veteran of the station, loudly contested the station counting Taylor as a black employee in their annual report. It also seemed that important press kits and videotapes mysteriously disappeared from Taylor's desk when Kendra was around.

Meanwhile, Kendra was always trying to hijack Taylor's stories. Just last week, Kendra had convinced Shari to send her to a triple shooting at a suburban high school while Taylor was in the rest room. The story—about a teen girl who killed her algebra teacher/lover and his cheerleader class pet—ran at the top of the newscast for days. All the while, a devious gleam in Kendra's eyes broadcast her desire to usurp Taylor's status as newsroom star.

Not in this lifetime.

"Hi, Kendra. No, actually, if covering the big story means having a police escort, then so be it."

Kendra raised her eyebrows. "Well, I sure don't envy you, having to face that racist maniac this afternoon. I bet he'd love to pump some lead into you."

Taylor tensed. "As a matter of fact, he would. But that's not stopping me from doing my job. Excuse me." She brushed past Kendra and walked toward the purple neon "3" that stretched from the newsroom floor to the top rail of the balcony near producers' row.

Taylor approached Shari. "You wanted to talk to me?"

Shari rested a gentle hand on Taylor's shoulder, a cloud of Shari's expensive perfume engulfing them both.

"Right," Shari said. "Ask Rocky Pulaski if he's trying to rebuild what he had. The weapons, the computer network, the soldiers, all that. And I want a lot of color, natural sound—let the viewers experience the rally themselves. And, Taylor, be careful."

CHAPTER 3

Philip Carter smiled as he watched Taylor, a larger-than-life vision of red curves and flowing yellow hair, execute the four-o'clock Newsflash on his enormous television.

"A neo-Nazi rally draws hundreds to downtown Detroit this afternoon," she said in a strong, smooth voice over the din of the demonstration behind her. "I'm Taylor James and I'll have a full report at six o'clock."

42 / Elizabeth Atkins Bowman

Philip's groin stirred. "Do your thing, darling."

A menacing feeling had been gnawing Philip for the past two days, but its source still eluded him. Perhaps it was the threats against Taylor, or jitters about taking the plunge a second time, desperately wanting—needing—it to work. His marriage was far too momentous for anyone, especially that uneducated savage Pulaski, to interfere by hurting her. No, Taylor James was his ticket to the plush leather CEO chair of Wolf Media Corporation. He had never told her that, but then again, there were a lot of things he never planned to tell his young fiancée.

A few minutes later, Philip entered Shari Gordon's office, where she and news director William Monroe were discussing the neo-Nazi rally.

"Listen," Philip said. "I want Taylor to have that police escort all weekend."

Shari twisted her bracelet. "I don't know if that's necessary. And Taylor will have a fit. She already thinks we're being over—"

"I don't care," Philip said. "Who knows, if we play this right, we can get some pub from the competition. Could be great for ratings."

Philip noticed William's aggravated smirk. "You got a problem with that, pal?"

"As a matter of fact, I do," William said with a harsh tone. "Let's just for once think about safety. Not ratings."

Philip glared at him. *What a wuss in a cheap, off-the-rack suit.*

He had disliked William for years, ever since that incident involving a chemical fire at a downriver factory. Philip had ordered a cameraman to go up in the Channel 3 News Chopper to shoot video of the captivating green-blue flames bursting into the black sky. But then, unbeknownst to Philip, William had reversed the order, citing the fire marshal's warning about hazardous fumes. As a result, competitor Channel 5 was the only station in town to capture the deadly blaze from the air. That sent Philip into a rage; he threatened to fire William if he ever disrespected Philip's authority again.

"So tell me, William, what's the word on talent for the morning show?"

"You'll see a stack of résumé tapes in the morning," William said.

"They better be so good my eyes pop," Philip said. "Or it's your job on the line, pal. Shari, tell Taylor about the police when she gets back."

"Will do," Shari said.

"What's your take on Julian DuPont?" Philip asked. "You can't be anything less than impressed; I taught him everything he knows. He'll do one helluva job here at Channel 3."

"He's very sharp," Shari said. "Articulate, down-to-earth. Comes across on-camera as real. Very sincere, at least according to what I saw of him in the studio this morning."

Philip nodded at Shari. For the past several years that he had known her, he had always respected her direct, rapid-fire style. Shari had real news savvy—she initially approved Taylor's proposal to investigate the White Power Alliance. She had strong instincts for making intelligent, split-second decisions. And her long hours and talent had helped make Channel 3 the top-ranked local news station in Detroit.

"I disagree," William said. He adjusted his glasses, which magnified the bellicose expression in his eyes. "We'll see if DuPont can think on his feet once he gets to the rally. But my first hunch is that he's a long shot. After all these years of reporting about movie stars and Hollywood gossip, I'd bet money he's too lightweight for hard news."

Philip smacked William's shoulder blade. "Loosen up, pal. DuPont is a ratings magnet for *Entertainment Exclusive*. He gets mountains of fan mail. Everybody loves him. You'll see."

Philip returned to his office in time for the weekly Carter family conference call. He chewed several Tums and rolled his neck before punching the phone line. "Hello Dad, Jonathan, Horace, Emily."

Horace and Emily said hello, but Jonathan was silent.

"Jon, greet your brother," said their father, Gerald Carter. "Last week's bickering will not repeat itself today. You ought to be ashamed. Vice presidents of this corporation acting like children fighting over a cupcake."

Philip tensed. *We are. Four years until Dad retires and we're already at each other's throats, trying to outshout and outshine each other. I deserve the CEO chair more than my punk-ass, lazy brothers do.*

"Hello, Philip," Jonathan said with the same annoyed tone as when he was a kid, forced by their parents to apologize for calling Philip "Goldilocks" or banning him from the playroom with a NO BLONDES ALLOWED sign.

"Hey, sport," Jonathan said. "How's the weather in that abyss of blight otherwise known as Detroit? It's a gorgeous day here in the City of Angels."

Philip stiffened. "Good for you, pal. I think the smog is corroding your brain cells. Emily told me how you mucked up the Mega-Com deal last week. Christ, they oughta put your picture in the dictionary under incompetent—"

"Philip, stop it!" their father shouted. "Your grandfather did not found this company eighty-some years ago for you to quarrel like this. Now, let's act like civilized professionals here, or I'll fire all of you."

Philip ground his teeth. All the conflicting emotions of his love-and-loathe relationship with his father and siblings turned his insides to boiling water. He munched a few more Tums, trying to ignore the fact that he had always been the Carter family outcast, always trying to compensate for his ill-fated birth to earn his father's approval. Earning straight As in school wasn't enough. Nor was rowing his college crew team to first place. And now, though his incessant work was earning the company high ratings and tremendous profits, Philip still got the feeling that his stellar accomplishments were deficient in his father's eyes.

"Dad, I sign on the dotted line for the Kansas City deal tomorrow," Philip said. "I won't let that lowlife Wilbur Franklin toss a bomb into the deal. He called today, bluffing. Said GNN wants the K.C. station, so I'd better back off."

Philip let out a chuckle. "that only whetted my appetite for battle. And believe me, I'll make Wilbur Franklin bleed on this one. Can't stand that unscrupulous bastard."

Philip ground his teeth harder at the thought of Wilbur Franklin, whom he had hated for nearly two decades. Franklin, a Global News Network executive, had once planted informants in Wolf newsrooms to steal ideas for stories and projects. As a result, GNN had scooped Wolf on several important reports. And Wilbur Franklin had become Philip's mortal enemy.

"I don't care what you do," Gerald said, "just buy the station. We need to break into that market. I want Wolf to own twenty-eight television stations by the end of the year."

Philip tensed. "Twenty-eight? What happened to twenty-five?"

"I tried to tell you this morning," Horace said. "We need to get into fifth gear now if we want to reach next year's profit and expansion goals."

"That's right, sport," Jonathan said. "It's only June. You're so big and bad, Philip, you can do it. But who knows? If this marriage is as catastrophic as your first—"

"Cut the crap!" Philip shouted. He could feel the vein at the center of his forehead throbbing.

"Philip, your brothers and I reached this decision earlier in the week," Gerald said.

Philip shook his head. "It really pisses me off, Dad, when you leave me out in the dark. How am I supposed to make important decisions when you got me walkin' around blind without a cane?"

Jonathan chuckled. "Pretty naïve for you to think we're all equals here, sport. You know better than that."

Philip grimaced. Little had changed since that day when he, right out of the University of Southern California business school, had realized the full extent of his estrangement from power in the family business. Philip had thought that he and his two older brothers had been given equal jobs as advertising and sales managers at Wolf, until he crept up on them with Dad in the family dining room.

That day a quarter century ago was still distinct in Philip's mind: his father at the head of the table with his tall, bulky frame balanced on his elbows, his wide, fleshy face and dark waves close to Jonathan and Horace at his sides, leaning close and speaking low. The scene resembled his mother's mirrored vanity, a triple reflection of one image, except the center face was older than the ones flanking it.

And they were talking about the family business, its future, its progress and growth, and how Gerald would pass it to his sons, just as he had inherited it from his father, who founded Wolf's newspaper chain in 1915. It was only after Philip announced his presence by clearing the lump in his throat that his father invited him to sit down. From then on, Philip had always felt as if he were interrupting a meeting where he did not belong. And his brothers had eagerly perpetuated that feeling. The only person who treated him with warmth had been his mother.

I can't believe it'll be a year in September. Way too young to die. Doctors said heart attack, I still say heartache. Boy, do I miss her.

Today Philip longed to call his mother, hear her soothing voice, because his constant sense of alienation and anger was more acute than usual.

"Jonathan, enough," Gerald said. "Can you acquire eight more stations this year? You say K.C. is practically in the bag, so that leaves seven. Can you do it?"

"Yes," Philip said.

"Horace, son, what was it you said the other day at the club?"

"A source tells me the top station in Atlanta is ripe for picking," Horace said.

"That's yesterday's news—old and stale," Philip snapped. "Stick to your own work, Horace. I'll do mine."

Philip closed his eyes. Sometimes he truly loathed his brothers. They would never outgrow their childhood sport of insulting Philip.

"You're not our brother," they would taunt. "Aunt Bea says you didn't come out of Daddy and Mommy like we did. She says you came from a bad place where sins come from." Comments like that, and an argument he had overheard between his parents, helped Philip deduce why he did not resemble his parents and siblings.

He could still hear his father yelling at his mother, forty years ago, behind the closed double doors of their immense gold bedroom: "Bella, I fired that son of a gun because he's supposed to work on the pool, not my wife. I'm raising his bastard child, for God's sake, just to protect my own reputation. But you disrespect me by asking me to hire him back? I ought to throw you and that little blond bastard out on the street. See if the bum will put a tramp like you up in a palace like this!"

Philip heard his mother weeping. "He wants to see his son once in a while," she said. "Gerald, I'm tired of this life with you. You pretend you're the most devout Christian on the planet, but your affairs . . . your so-called business trips. You think I'm stupid, but I know what's going on. So I just pretended everything was perfect, until I got a chance to get you back."

A loud slap and a scream followed, sending Philip to his room in tears.

"Philip?" his father said sternly. "Are you listening?"

"Of course, Dad."

"How are things going with the morning program there in Detroit?" he asked. "That'll be the prototype for the other stations."

"Fine," Philip said. "My staff is recruiting talent; we have a meeting in the morning. The set is under construction and the cameras should be here any day."

"A lot is riding on that," his father said. "It's got to be exceptional."

"It will be," Philip said.

"Emily, how do things look in the newspaper division?" their father asked.

"Better," Emily said. "It looks like we'll be able to reach a contract agreement with the unions in Cincinnati. For a while it looked like a strike was only a matter of time."

"Keep me posted on that," the elder Carter said. "Horace, how are network operations?"

"Running like clockwork," Horace said. "I have nothing new to add since we spoke earlier in the week."

"Good, son. Jonathan, programming?"

"Ditto," he said. "I've got that conference this weekend in Washington to discuss the V chip and the television industry's rating system."

"Good, son. What do we want?"

The four siblings recited the Carter mantra in unison: "We must always strive for stability and productivity, to bring success, revenue, and respect to our family."

"That's right," Gerald Carter said. "I'll talk to you all next week. Philip, stay on the line. I want to talk about your marriage."

"Yes, Dad." Philip stared at the picture of himself and Taylor on his desk. She was the key to him fulfilling the first goal of the Carter mantra: stability. Though he had achieved the other four, his divorce was a wart on his character in Dad's eyes. Once it was removed, Philip believed he would be a flawless candidate to succeed his father at Wolf's helm.

"You know how disappointed I was when you divorced Andrea," his father said. "Leaving her with two teenagers after fifteen years. It was an outrage, a violation of Carter family ethics."

Philip sunk deep in his chair, hanging his head. He abhorred how his father's stern voice still made him nervous. "I'm sorry, Dad."

"Well, I had about enough embarrassment and gossip when you divorced three years ago," his father said. "Don't make the same mistake twice. I want this union with Taylor James to work. Marriage legitimizes you, lets people know you're not having sex outside the sanctity of wedlock."

Philip closed his eyes. *Dad, you're such a hypocrite.* He was certain that his father had had many affairs because he once caught Dad humping a copy editor from one of Wolf's newspapers. Philip had been working at the paper during a summer vacation from college when he entered his father's office and found the woman spreadeagle on the desk, newspapers crumpling noisily beneath her as Dad banged away.

But Gerald Carter's own philandering must not have registered when he constantly preached to his children about the sins of the flesh. Once, when Philip was about twelve, an erection inflated his blue Speedos as he climbed out of the swimming pool. That prompted his father to rant about the wickedness of masturbation and sexual daydreams. Philip often chuckled to himself that his father's puritanical ways had implanted in him the seed that spawned his insatiable sexual appetite. Now, with Taylor, he could have both superb sex and legitimacy in his father's eyes because she was, somehow, both wholesome and knee-buckling sexy.

Philip had also learned from his father the art of projecting the image to the world—and Taylor—of a hardworking, highly moral man, while secretly enjoying certain indiscretions forever unknown to his family, colleagues, and future bride.

"Taylor and I will be good together," Philip said. "She's perfect for me."

"Well, I still think it's shameful that you chose a woman twenty years younger than yourself, but let's hope it works," he said. "Your siblings have stable families. Put family first and business will flourish."

After they hung up, Philip gripped the back of his tense neck. Nothing would arrest his quest for the CEO chair. He deserved the chief executive office more than his brothers, who spent more time at the golf club than at their desks. Emily worked hard, but Dad would never forfeit the company reins to a woman.

It's mine. A new wife, eight more stations this year, I can do it.

As Philip psyched himself to toil even more rigorously, a sudden pang of paranoia made him feel as if he were sprinting breathlessly on a treadmill, chasing an illusion.

CHAPTER 4

The sunbaked haze of hostility, exhaust fumes, and body odor shrouding the cement square bristled the fine hairs on Taylor's body. *I can feel the violence in the air. It could happen any moment.*

She half listened to Jerome Wilkins, an antiracist protester in a red, black, and green knit cap and a Million Man March T-shirt.

"This reminds me of the 'sixty-seven riots," he said into her microphone as Patrick McIntyre, a fiftyish man with a gentle manner and award-winning video skills, filmed him. "I was just a kid, but I remember the flames and the gunshots. Forty-three people dead. I can still see the tanks rolling past my house after President Johnson called in the National Guard."

As he spoke, Taylor discerned a nearly inaudible pitch in the air, like a dog whistle, that forewarned danger. Her police escort and cameraman surrounded her, but the hundreds of people cramming Kennedy Square were a mere spark away from exploding.

"Whites unite and fight for our rights!" shouted camouflage-clad Rocky Pulaski from the cement perch, where he stood with Billy Joe, Jess, and about fifty neo-Nazis. A red, white, and black swastika flag and a White Power Alliance banner fluttered on poles held by skinheads.

In response, a white man with dreadlocks screamed, "Die, Nazi pigs!" A black woman waved a placard on a stick that said PULASKI = SATAN. Others sang "We Shall Overcome" and shouted, "Hey, hey! Ho, ho! White supremacists have got to go!"

Taylor found some comfort in the sight of dozens of police officers with shields and helmets, their walkie-talkies crackling as sirens wailed and red and blue lights flashed from squad cars ringing the park. That and the half dozen media vehicles with microwave masts raised caused traffic snarls, stranding cars and buses full of gawkers around Kennedy Square. Above, office workers stared down from the windows of high-rise buildings.

"We won't let the White Power Alliance spread their hatred here," Jerome Wilkins said. "Here's my partner, Lloyd Pryor. We founded People United."

Taylor switched her microphone, adorned with silver disks and a purple "3," to Lloyd Pryor, the white man with brown, shoulder-length dreadlocks.

"Ms. James, my favorite reporter," he said, hoarse from yelling.

"Thank you," she said. "What do you think about this?"

He grimaced. "You remember after 'sixty-seven when the Kerner Commission reported that 'Our nation is moving toward two societies, one black, one white—separate and unequal'? Well, here we are. But I'll tell you one thing. Pulaski won't have his race war here. Our kids play together and hold hands just like Dr. King said in his 'I Have a Dream' speech. We're not in the promised land yet, but we'll sure die trying to get there."

Taylor's pulse quickened. It was time to face Pulaski. She led Patrick and the police officers through the crowd toward the elevated area.

There a mob of TV crews, radio correspondents, newspaper reporters, and photographers surrounded Rocky Pulaski. At his sides were Billy Joe and Jess—now brunette with deeper wrinkles, angrier eyes—handing pamphlets to reporters. Behind them, skinheads chanted over the crowd.

Taylor's heart pounded. Sweat rolled between her breasts and plastered her panty hose to her legs.

She stood just feet from Pulaski, who was glaring at a reporter from under his camouflage hat. He did not notice Taylor as she studied his black marble eyes, his taut mouth, his red-brown mustache and crew cut. His death threat echoed in her mind; repulsion clawed her gut.

I'm back and I won't let you poison more minds. I abhor you and everything you represent.

"You'll read here," Rocky said, glowering at cameras, "that when the country is engulfed in the flame and battle of revolution, the White Power Alliance will conquer its enemies and establish all-white states. We'll outlaw interracial marriage. The Jew-controlled media and the scheming government will cease to exist. We'll bear arms at all times. And we'll live without the interference of minorities and homosexuals and immigrants who're dirtying the wholesome white fabric of America."

Sheila Dane, Channel 5's star reporter, held her microphone near his mouth. "Is it true that you're planning a race war?"

Rocky answered, "America's on the verge of self-destruction. When reality as we know it explodes in chaos, the White Power Alliance will triumph. And we'll get revenge."

Billy Joe grabbed Sheila's mike. "We want to tell all the white people in the world that we're here, we're strong, and we're ready to fight until—"

Sheila snatched it back.

Pumped with adrenaline, Taylor pushed through the circle of reporters with Officers Young and Edwards at her sides. She shoved her microphone toward Pulaski's face.

"Rocky, have you resumed the stockpiling of bomb-making materials and biological warfare on your farm?" Taylor asked, her voice strong over the roaring crowd and sirens.

Rocky stiffened when he saw her. His left eye began twitching.

Taylor stared back without blinking. *That's right, look at me. Remember that naïve girl three years ago. Your destroyer. And I'll do it again if I can.*

She noticed that the red record button glowed atop Patrick's camera and several others. In her peripheral vision was Andy Doss, and the dark man she had seen with him earlier.

Cameras clicked and reporters—having witnessed Rocky's obscene outbursts at Taylor during his federal trial—watched hungrily, as did a half dozen police officers.

Pulaski was still, his eyes locked on Taylor like metal clamps. Next to him, Billy Joe glowered. Jess glared, chest heaving, pursed lips white.

"Please answer my question," Taylor said.

Rocky lunged.

Thick fingers, like daggers, stabbed at her neck.

"You die!" he shouted.

Her microphone hit his mouth. Officers Young and Edwards shielded her. At the same time, two more police officers grabbed Pulaski's shoulders. As he twisted in their grasp, his camouflage hat fell off.

"The pariah of the white race!" Pulaski shouted, his eye twitching. "I'll rip you apart with my hands."

Taylor held his glare. *Anything you say can and will be used against you in a court of law. Again.*

Suddenly Billy Joe dove toward her.

"I shoulda snuffed you out when I had the chance," he said, nostrils flaring.

Two police officers grabbed him.

Taylor watched him calmly. *How was prison, Billy Joe?*

Rocky, writhing in the policemen's grip, cursed Andy Doss.

"There's only one name for you: traitor! Conspiring with that mongrel, selling out your white brothers and sisters. When the revolution comes, you'll beg for mercy."

Andy, with one eye closed, the other on the camera viewfinder, continued filming. Next to him, Taylor saw the tall, dark man.

Oh my God. Cold, dizzying shock rippled through her.

Everything blurred except that angular, bronze face that she used to kiss, the cinnamon brown eyes that were once her emotional sanctuary, the silky jet curls she once stroked, the full lips that knew every inch of her body.

Good God, yes. It's Julian.

He met her stare with gentle eyes, and the corners of his mouth curled up slightly.

A jolt of rage stiffened her. *Why is he holding a Channel 3 mike? He can't be here for Dwyer's anchor spot. No . . . not now . . . it's too late . . . I love Philip now . . . I'm getting married in three weeks . . .*

Taylor realized her lips had parted in bewilderment. Her ears filled with the staticky sound of rushing blood. Her heart thundered.

Billy Joe's hostile shouts penetrated her trance. "We're not through with you, freak."

Then Jess charged through the media pack.

Alarmed, Taylor stepped back.

"You and your mother are a disgrace!" Jess screamed.

Officers Young and Edwards grabbed Jess, leaving Taylor suddenly exposed.

"Your day of damnation is dawning," Rocky hissed.

Taylor stared into the malicious depths of his eyes.

God help me, he really does want to kill me. Goose bumps prickled across her body. But when she remembered the good deed she had done for society by destroying Rocky's blood-hungry, racist empire, her confidence surged. *I'll do whatever I can to stop him.*

"C'mon, folks, let's break this up," a police officer said. Other officers led Rocky, Billy Joe, and Jess back to the perch, where Rocky shouted about "reclaiming America."

Officer Young asked Taylor, "You want to leave now?"

Taylor—her mind a spinning kaleidoscope of Julian and Philip, Pulaski and Jess, police and protesters—shook her head. "No, no. I have a lot of work to do. But thanks for being so quick."

"We're just doing our job," Young said.

Suddenly cameras and reporters, including Julian and camera-toting Andy Doss, engulfed Taylor, thrusting microphones.

"Taylor, how do you feel about Pulaski's threats?" asked Sheila Dane. "Afraid? Is that why you have a police escort today?"

A male radio reporter pushed closer: "Ms. James, do you think

Pulaski hates you because you're biracial and he condemns race mixing?"

Startled, Taylor said, "I'm here to report the news, not become it." Then she hurried toward Patrick, who had set his camera on a cement planter. She was trembling from Pulaski's glare, and the shock of seeing Julian, who was approaching.

Not now, after ten years . . .

Patrick grimaced. "Taylor, just a minute. I need to check my camera."

"Okay," she said, pacing. Her gold watch with free-floating diamonds, a gift from Philip, said quarter to five.

I can't talk to Julian now. I have work, and Philip, and—

"White Chocolate," Julian said. The words sliced across her heart. She looked up, stunned.

Oh my God. No, don't let me feel the serenity of his presence. I can't succumb to those eyes.

"Don't call me that," Taylor snapped. "What are you doing here?"

"Trying to get a job," he said, smiling.

"At Channel Three?"

"That's right. I want to come home."

A heavy, ominous feeling sucked at her composure like a riptide.

Oh no, what if he wants me back? It's too late—

With her left hand she wiped perspiration from her upper lip, causing her diamond to sparkle. She watched Julian's face droop.

"Your engagement brought me home," he said.

Taylor scowled. "Why? You figure you haven't hurt me enough, so you want to crash my wedding with that actress you married?"

"No, I—"

"Taylor, I'm ready," Patrick said as he and Andy approached.

Andy, dangling his camera by his knee without looking at Taylor, said, "So you two have met. Patrick McIntyre, this is Julian DuPont. He's applying for Dwyer's job."

Patrick smiled, pumping Julian's arm. "Nice to meet you."

"Thanks," Julian said. "This rally is some welcome to town."

"It's a shame," Patrick said. "Taylor, you okay?"

"I'm fine. I expected that from Pulaski. Or worse."

Andy smiled without looking at her. "She sure has changed. She was like a scared cat three years ago, but now she looks like she'd sucker-punch Pulaski. Sweet little Taylor turns out to be just as ruthless as—"

Taylor glared at him. "I'm sick of your attitude, Andy."

She glanced at Julian. Bitterness and anger rumbled through her.

"Patrick, we better go," she said.

Patrick waved to Julian. "Good luck with your interview, buddy."

"Thanks," Julian said. "It was a pleasure meeting you, Taylor."

She did not look at him. *Please go back to California now and leave me alone.*

CHAPTER 5

On the sidewalk near the Channel 3 truck, an eerie pitch rang in Taylor's ears. She scanned the raucous crowd. *What's hap—*

A man, blood spurting from his forehead, tumbled at her feet.

"Somebody help him!" a woman screamed.

Taylor froze.

This is a race riot.

Before her was a writhing, shrieking mass of bodies. Skinheads punching, kicking everyone in sight. Protesters whacking neo-Nazis with wood sticks holding placards. Sirens blaring. Police with shields and billy clubs closing in.

Suddenly a man with a blond crew cut charged at Taylor.

"You're gonna pay, bitch!" yelled Nick Wallace, the man who had caught her when Billy Joe punched her at the compound.

A cold fist of fear squeezed Taylor's chest.

Nick was just feet away. He ran right into the grasp of Officers Edwards and Young. As Officer Young led Nick away, Edwards told Taylor to stand near the van.

From there, Taylor watched the crowd. Rocky and Billy Joe, shouting, "White traitor!" knocked Lloyd Pryor, the protester with dreadlocks, to the ground. Skinheads covered him like piranhas on a carcass. Nearby, others attacked Jerome Wilkins, kicking, punching.

A gray gloom blanketed the sky and the odor of blood hung in the muggy air. More helmeted police with Plexiglas shields and billy clubs penetrated the throng, breaking up fistfights.

Nausea burned in Taylor's gut. *This is so horrible . . . exactly what I want my work to prevent. Yet it's happening here and now, twenty-eight years after the riot ripped the city apart, welcoming me into the world.*

Taylor noticed, just yards away, Detroit Police Chief Bernard Goodson, giving orders to officers. Nearer was a policeman watching the melee with folded arms.

"Why are you letting this get so out of control?" Taylor asked him. "People could get killed."

A malicious glint in the officer's silver-blue eyes startled her as he stepped closer. He nodded at Young and Edwards. His silver nameplate said J. Scarlin.

"The White Power Alliance has the constitutional right to assemble and express their beliefs," he said. "The protesters started the trouble."

Taylor, searching for Patrick and his camera so that he could film this man, said, "Are you defending the White Power group?"

"I'm stating the facts, ma'am," Scarlin said over sirens. He turned toward the crowd, jaw muscles flexing on his thin face.

Taylor stifled a shiver. *This guy sympathizes with Pulaski.*

Chilled, she watched ambulances double-park beside news

trucks and police cars. Paramedics ran toward people moaning on the sidewalk. A black woman shrieked and held a grotesquely twisted leg. Then Taylor noticed Officer Gus Lemer—the policeman who killed her friend Carla's father—approach Scarlin, speak in his ear, and quickly walk away. If Scarlin sympathized with Pulaski, Taylor wondered, did Lemer endorse White Power Alliance doctrine as well?

Suddenly tin rattled on cement. Tear gas. Yellow-beige smoke plumed.

Another column of masked, shielded officers marched toward the crowd, holding cans high, misting people with pepper spray.

Coughing, shouting men and women scrambled everywhere, even into the clogged street. Horns blared. Tires screeched. Drivers shouted.

"Get inside the van," Officer Edwards told Taylor. Through the glass she watched Patrick film at the edge of the crowd, a bandana around his nose and mouth, his left eye closed, his right eye pressed to the viewfinder.

And he was focusing on Rocky and Billy Joe, kicking Lloyd Pryor's unconscious body on the ground. Nearby, Jerome Wilkins coughed and tried to crawl away from a burly, bearded man wearing a swastika armband.

Finally police officers in gas masks cuffed the Pulaskis and led them to a squad car. Paramedics rolled Lloyd Pryor past on a gurney, giving Taylor a closeup look at his blood-caked dreadlocks, his motionless body. After him was Jerome Wilkins, unconscious with a swollen-shut eye.

A skinhead with gushing arm wounds thrashed on a gurney. The burly, bearded White Power supporter ran past, coughing and holding his face. Paramedics wheeled another bald white youth in black combat boots and jeans, unconscious and bloody-faced.

Taylor cringed. *This is a nightmare. And if Rocky has his way with the race war, this would happen everywhere. But not if I can help it.*

"I need to interview people," Taylor said, opening the door. Her eyes and nose stung from the tear gas and pepper spray. She coughed.

"You should stay in the van," Edwards said.

"No, I have to work," Taylor said.

She and Patrick headed toward the police chief, who was surrounded by reporters. He was standing near a bronze and stone monument to the Civil War's Iron Brigade, which included Detroit soldiers. Two American flags fluttered above.

Reporters shouted questions simultaneously.

"Chief Goodson, why did the police respond so slowly when those men were being beaten?" Taylor asked.

Goodson appeared surprised. "Our officers kept this rally peaceful until that moment. As an African-American who watched this city go up in flames in the 'sixty-seven riots, it pains my heart to see this racial animosity and violence in the city of Detroit."

"But you didn't answer my question," Taylor said loudly. "Why did it take so long to respond to the violence right in front of you?"

Goodson sighed. "We've arrested dozens of people. We have the situation under control."

"But it clearly was not earlier," said GNN reporter Amy Chang. "How can the police not recognize the danger of this type of demonstration, given Detroit's history?"

"Like I stated before, we have the situation under control," Goodson said. "Mr. Pulaski had a permit for this demonstration, and we provided adequate protection."

Taylor and Patrick returned to the Channel 3 van, where Patrick climbed into the back, pushing buttons and turning knobs on a wall of electronic equipment.

"Eh, Channel Three, this is truck fifty-six ready to get established," Patrick said into a two-way radio. Morse code–like beeps filled the truck as Patrick prepared to send via microwave all the video and audio he had recorded at the rally. Once it was received at the station, a videotape editor would use it to create a "package," or story, with a voice-over that Taylor would send from the van. Then the package would air during Taylor's live report.

"Ready, Patrick," a man said over the radio. "Got your signal. Let 'er rip."

In the passenger seat, Taylor retrieved a cellular phone from her purse and called her producer.

"Shari Gordon, Channel-Three."

"Shari, it's Taylor. We're sending pictures now, and I'm about to send audio over the live mike."

"Fabulous," Shari said. "Give it all you got, Taylor. You're the star of the show. Philip is drooling over this story since Channel 5 ran a promo with video of Pulaski shouting at you."

"Oh, great," Taylor said sarcastically.

"Great for ratings. Good luck," Shari said.

Taylor quickly composed her script and recited it into the microphone, which, hooked up to the microwave mast, beamed her voice back to the station. Then she stepped onto the sidewalk, where Patrick was setting up for her live report.

"You look upset," he said.

I am, from seeing the two things that hurt me most: Julian DuPont and racial conflict.

"This violence upsets me," Taylor said. "I mean, my parents marched right here in 1963 behind Dr. King. It's more than thirty years later, and this happens. I can't believe it."

Patrick untangled red, black, and yellow cables. "I can't believe the Irish and the English are still at each other's throats. And look at my grandfather in Dublin—cursed the English till his dying breath. What I'm saying is, madness and despair get you nowhere. So don't get discouraged, Taylor. God put you here to do just what you're doing."

Taylor followed his warm eyes as he positioned the tripod and camera facing Kennedy Square.

"In all my thirty years in the business, you're the most caring reporter I've seen," he said. "It's not the money and glamour you're after. You really care. And you're making a difference, believe me."

A smile lifted Taylor's cheeks. "Thanks, Patrick. I needed that.

Now, let's get this live shot set up and tell the world what happened here today."

"That's my girl," he said, smiling.

In front of him, Taylor inserted her IFB, which blared static into her ear.* Then she heard the show director, Mike Covey, who was in the studio control room.

"You have five minutes to go on-air. Are you guys all set?" Mike asked.

"Yes," Taylor said.

"We have the pictures edited and we're ready to go," he said. "Taylor James, you have two minutes at the top of the show. We'll go to your wrap, then answer David Dwyer's questions. Stand by."

Taylor focused on what she would tell millions of people across southeast Michigan. As if turning a knob on her brain, she tuned out a barrage of questions about Julian and Pulaski.

Then the jazzy Channel 3 theme song played in her IFB: "Quick! Current! Caring! Channel Three News you can use. News you can trust."

"Taylor James, ten-oh-eight," Mike said.

"Good evening everybody. Welcome to Channel Three News at Six. I'm David Dwyer. A neo-Nazi rally erupts in a violent race riot this afternoon in downtown Detroit. Reporter Taylor James is standing by live to give us the very latest. Taylor, what happened out there?"

Taylor sucked air deep in her abdomen and stared into the black camera, letting her adrenaline-fueled autopilot take control.

"Well, David, what started as a peaceful demonstration by a white supremacist group became a bloody race riot here in the heart of downtown Detroit. I'm standing in front of Kennedy Square, where just a short while ago, Detroit police used pepper spray and tear gas to stop a violent clash between white supremacists and an-

---

*IFB is short for "interruption feed broadcasting," and is the name given to the earpiece a reporter or anchor wears on-air. The IFB enables the show director to give directions.

tiracist demonstrators. You can see that the air is still smoky from the tear gas." Taylor raised her left arm to point to the square.

"At least six people are hospitalized, including two antiracist protesters who were beaten unconscious," she said. "A spokeswoman at Detroit Receiving Hospital told me the men were in critical condition, but she would not disclose their injuries. More than two dozen people were arrested and they are expected to be formally charged with various offenses tomorrow in Thirty-sixth District Court."

Taylor continued looking into the camera as if it were a friend and she were describing her day.

The show director said into Taylor's earpiece: "Roll tape, Taylor. One forty-five. Kendra Vaughn, you're up after Taylor James. Stand by."

Patrick signaled a thumbs-up at Taylor as she listened to her recorded voice narrate the video package, prepared by editors at the station. After nearly two minutes, Mike said she had ten and a half seconds before the package finished.

"Go," he said.

"David, as you can imagine, many people here expressed dismay that this could happen in the 1990s," Taylor said. "However, I did speak with one police officer who blamed the antiracist demonstrators for instigating the violence. But most eyewitnesses say just the opposite is true, that the neo-Nazi protesters started this bloody conflict."

"Taylor," Dwyer said, "it looked like Rocky Pulaski was pretty angry at you and the media in general."

Pulaski's hateful eyes flashed in her mind. "You're right, David. He threatened to kill me as revenge for my exposé that destroyed his organization, but he would not answer my questions about whether he was stockpiling the kinds of bomb-making materials and illegal weapons that authorities seized from his military compound in northern Michigan," Taylor said. "But he did give me this pamphlet."

"What does it say?" David asked.

It says they'll destroy all the people like me, the half-breeds, the mud people who blur the lines of white purity— Suddenly Julian's face flashed in her mind. And for a second she yearned for him to hold her, just as she had on that horrific night three years ago in the heat of the burning crosses.

Stop. You're still on-camera. Focus on the story.

"It explains," she said, pausing, "the group's prophecy of a revolution in which white people would overthrow the government and create all-white states."

Damn, I can't believe I blanked out on-air.

"Pretty scary stuff, Taylor," Dwyer said. "Thank you for that live report."

The director said, "Clear Taylor James. Kendra Vaughn, stand by."

Taylor removed her IFB. "Patrick, could you tell I spaced out?"

"When?" Patrick asked, breaking down the camera and tripod. "You did fine, especially since this kind of story gets to you."

A few minutes later, as they pulled away from the curb, Taylor glimpsed Julian and Andy on the sidewalk.

"That Julian DuPont had eyes for you," Patrick said. He slammed on the brakes behind a bus on Woodward Avenue. "Boy, oh, boy, where do they get these drivers? Anyway, that Julian DuPont sure took a shine to you."

Taylor, still astounded by his sudden appearance, watched Julian in the rearview mirror. "Sorry, I'm already taken."

CHAPTER 6

The camera lens symbolized a black hole into the future as Julian DuPont braved the deadline of his life. He could afford no mistakes.

"Let's try that stand-up once more," Julian said.

"No problem," Andy answered.

Sharp arrows of remorse stabbed Julian's chest as Taylor's champagne-bottle green eyes flashed incessantly in his mind. *This is Julian DuPont reporting live in Detroit, where I plan to seduce my mentor's fiancée, Taylor James, because I still love her.*

Julian focused on the story that would help him accomplish that goal.

"A violent race riot here today is what the White Power Alliance declared as its first effort to rebuild after a Channel Three investigation led federal authorities to dismantle the organization three years ago," Julian said, his voice coached as smooth as the low notes of a double bass. "But protesters vow to stop the racist militia by any means necessary."

Julian remembered Rocky, Billy Joe, and that woman threatening Taylor.

I should be at her side protecting her, always. I should have been there all along.

"That was good, man," Andy said. He began breaking down equipment.

"Thanks," Julian said. "So I take it you and Taylor James don't get along."

Andy scowled. "I liked her back when she was a street slave, doing fires, murders, and press conferences like everybody else. Then comes this White Power stuff and boom! Awards, high ratings, and now she's marrying Philip Carter."

No, she's not. She's going to marry me.

"Man, he's like the Wizard of Oz behind the curtain, pulling the strings of everybody in the newsroom," Andy said. "Makes me sick how everybody would give their left nut for Philip. I don't see what Taylor sees in him, man."

Andy loaded his camera and equipment into the van. "Don't get me wrong. I'm not jealous that Taylor snubbed me."

A twinge of envy quickened Julian's pulse.

"Up north we kissed," Andy said, "part of our boyfriend-girlfriend cover, you know. But soon as we got to Detroit—business as usual." Inside the van, he blasted the air conditioner and played a Top 40 radio station.

"I saw you checkin' her out, man," Andy said. "Don't even try it. She's only got eyes for Philip."

Just watch me. Julian realized that everyone at Channel 3, including Philip, was unaware of his past with Taylor. And he intended to keep it that way. For now.

"So what kind of slant does Channel Three have—conservative, sensational?" Julian asked.

Andy chuckled, pulling into the snarl of traffic. "If Philip is around, it's flash over substance. Like this story Taylor and I were doing about a black guy who shot and killed an Arab party-store owner. Philip wants to hype the racial-tension angle—interview the screaming Arab widow and the most hostile black people around. All he cares about is ratings and ad dollars."

"So what happened?" Julian asked.

"Huh, Taylor's clever," Andy said. "She gave the report some depth while hyping the racial angle, too. Now, Shari and William, they're more responsible and compassionate. But man, what does Taylor see in Philip? She's too wholesome for him. I bet he's got a whacked-out dark side, like dominatrix whippings on his lunch break."

Julian laughed with Andy as he remembered that night a few months ago, in Philip's limousine in Los Angeles, when those girls— teenagers made up to look twenty-two in spike heels and skimpy dresses—were massaging Philip, sharing his cocaine, licking their lips for the video camera that Julian held at Philip's request. Julian had been overwhelmed with repulsion at that scene, and the countless ones before it. Now those wild times with Philip blurred in his mind like a bad hangover.

Why was I ever attracted to that lifestyle? And why did I become Philip Carter's road dog?

"Philip has a noble side, too," Julian said. "You could say he made me."

Andy shot him a confused look. "Made you?"

"Yeah, after I graduated from UCLA, I was busting my ass reporting for *Entertainment Exclusive*. One hellacious day I got a scoop about assault charges filed by this chick against an actor. I was all over L.A. interviewing the mistress, the wife, the lawyers, even the actor. It was *EE*'s lead story, and all the competition picked it up the next day. My work caught Philip's attention, and the rest is history."

"Man," Andy sighed.

"It shocked the hell outta me," Julian said. "There I was, a kid from Detroit, being groomed for greatness by Philip Carter, heir to the Wolf Media empire."

Andy nodded. "Yeah, Philip gives tons of cash to inner-city charities."

Julian raised his eyebrows and looked coolly at Andy. "Are you suggesting that I'm one of those?"

Andy quickly fanned his fingers on the steering wheel. "Oh, no, man, that's not it."

"Then what did you mean?"

"I mean, uh, that Philip . . . has a compassionate side," Andy said.

The disappointing chill of a racial slight stung Julian's cheeks. He closed the vent blasting cold air in his face, then watched people at bus stops along Woodward Avenue.

"Hey, man, I didn't mean to—"

"Don't worry about it," Julian said.

Philip's attention, however, did occasionally smack of charity. Like the day Julian signed his anchor contract. Philip had put his arm around him and said, "DuPont, your success just goes to show that with the right grooming, black men can be saved from drugs, gangs, and prison." Other times, Philip refused to acknowledge that Julian was half white: "A chocolate shake has vanilla ice cream, pal, but the syrup makes it brown, so we call it chocolate." Another day, Philip asked Julian to demonstrate his fluent French for Parisian television executives at the Wolf offices. He did so, very elegantly, but the incident made Julian feel like a dog ordered to bark for his master. Shortly thereafter, Philip introduced Julian at a reception as his "dark shadow" because they attended so many parties and professional functions together.

So despite all that Philip had done for Julian, uneasiness always chafed their friendship—and expedited Julian's strategy to heist Philip's fiancée. Employment at Channel 3 was phase one of his ambush.

CHAPTER 7

As Taylor entered the newsroom, she longed for relief from the ghastly images of the riot that were still vivid in her mind. Just as bothersome was the mental vision of Julian. The emotional shock of seeing him, and the violence, made her physically ache.

She headed toward her desk, eager to sit down and regroup.

Instead, red-hot rage exploded inside her.

At her desk she saw Kendra Vaughn, rifling through drawers.

Taylor stormed toward her. "What the hell are you doing?" She demanded, slamming shut the drawers.

Kendra looked up, obviously surprised by Taylor's presence. "Oh, I thought you were still out on your story."

Taylor sneered. "What are you doing in my desk?"

Kendra stood up straight, running her perfect manicure over the front of her designer suit, as if to iron out a wrinkle. "I was just . . . Shari wanted me to do a piece for eleven to help you out. You know, recapping your investigation. So I—"

"Do that in the library," Taylor snapped. "You have no business in my things."

"But I know you keep all the newspaper clippings of your stories," Kendra said. "I just wanted to look them over."

Taylor stared into Kendra's dark eyes. *You devious liar.*

"Don't ever do this again," Taylor said. "I don't care if I'm out on a story, out of town, whatever. My desk is off-limits to you."

Kendra scowled, hostility radiating from her eyes. "High-yellow bitch," she said under her breath. "Can't even share. Think your shit's better than everybody."

Kendra spun on a heel and walked toward her own desk.

Taylor clenched her teeth, closed her eyes. Her limbs hummed with rage and distrust. She took a few deep breaths, trying to quell the indignation trembling in her fingers.

"Hey, Taylor, smile," said the eleven-o'clock producer, Alan Blum. "You were phenomenal out there today." Alan was a lanky man who always made Taylor think of the Age of Aquarius with his ponytail, Birkenstocks, brown-bag lunches of bulgur and alfalfa sprouts, and passionate debates about nuclear weapons and toxic waste.

Taylor attempted a smile.

"I was just thanking Detroit's finest for shielding you from that lunatic," Alan said. "Smart move to have them go with you."

"Thanks, Alan."

"I don't know how you do it," Alan said, leaning on producers' row. "When I covered the Nazi march in Skokie, they called me kike and every slur in the book. I was so mad I couldn't see straight."

Officer Young nodded. "I have to commend you, Ms. James. You seemed fearless out there today. A lot of women couldn't do what you do."

"I just concentrate on the story," Taylor said, a flat tone masking her fury at Kendra. "I'm not letting Pulaski or anybody else ruin my work."

Taylor sat at her desk and retrieved her phone mail. "Message one."

"Hey, girl, it's Carla. I won my trial today, sent another wife-beating murderer to prison for life. Just wanted to make sure we're still on for tomorrow. Call me later. I might be out late. Marcus claims he's cooking for me tonight. We'll see."

Taylor noticed Alan to her right, diving over another producer's desk to answer the phone.

"Oh, man!" Alan said, lifting his sleeve. Chalky liquid dripped down his arm and spread across the desks. A bottle of Mylanta teetered on its side, then tumbled to the floor. Almost every desk on producers' row had a jumbo bottle of Tums, Pepto-Bismol, or Di-Gel. Such were the hazards of the news business.

Alan, though, had his own remedy for stress. Taylor had once found him in an editing booth, sitting Indian style, chanting.

"Message two."

"Taylor, honey, we're very worried. Your father and I saw your report this evening. Did you see Julian today? Call me when you can, honey. We love you."

"That was your last message," the electronic voice said.

Taylor paced her cubicle, infuriated that her parents were conspiring with Julian. First her mother's comment about white chocolate and everyone's desire for her to marry Julian. Now this. They knew of his scheme but had not warned her. Sweat prickled under her arms as she dialed her parents.

"Hello?"

"Hi, Daddy."

"Taylor, are you all right?"

"Of course I am."

"Every station is running video of Pulaski lunging at you."

"I'm fine. I had police with me."

"Thank goodness. I ought to take my rifle down to the Wayne County Jail and put those bastards out of their misery."

"Now, how would that look in tomorrow's paper, Daddy? I can just see the headline: BLACK, MIDDLE-AGED ARCHITECT TURNS RAMBO: BUSTS INTO COUNTY JAIL, GUNS BLASTING."

Her father chuckled. "You're right. But your mother and I have been worried sick about you. At least Julian was there. He could have protected you."

Taylor rolled her eyes. "I don't need him. Why didn't you tell me he was trying to bogart into Channel Three and act like he needs some urgent conversation with me? After all this time, what's he thinking?"

"I don't know," her father said. "All I know is what his folks told us—Julian is ready to come home and settle down, and you're the one he wants."

Taylor tensed. "What nerve! Why does he think he can just traipse into town and sweep me off my feet?"

"Cut the melodrama, Taylor."

She shook her head. "I don't know—"

"Just hear him out," her father said. "You and Julian were made for each other. Everything was perfect until—"

"Until he ripped out my heart," Taylor said. "Now all of a sudden, this. Julian is crazy if he thinks I want him now. And if he crosses Philip, he might as well take a nosedive off the Renaissance Center. No way am I gonna jump with him."

"Taylor, you know your mother and I have only lukewarm feelings for Philip. He's too old, too slick for our little girl. Maybe you don't see it, but we do. And we love Julian like a son. Maybe this is a sign that . . ."

"That what?"

"That you should hold off on the wedding."

Taylor closed her eyes, bullets of anger shooting through her. "Wrong. I'll see you tomorrow when I bring my gown and veil to Mom."

Taylor walked past the glowing purple "3" sign toward the staircase. Jerry Spinx, the assignment editor, was shouting toward Alan.

"We got a drive-by shooting with three wounded teens on the west side!" he said.

"Art Jones is already there for a drug bust," Alan answered. "Call him in truck fifty and give him cross streets."

"Gotcha." Jerry disappeared behind his counter and tapped a keyboard.

As Taylor ascended toward Shari's office, she scanned the newsroom, but Julian was nowhere around.

"Taylor," Shari said, putting out a cigarette in an ashtray on her desk. "Come in. I want to talk."

"What now?" Taylor asked. "You want me to get a CCW permit and pack a pistol while I work?"

Shari laughed. "No, this is personal."

"What?" Taylor sat in a chair before Shari's desk. Her hazel eyes were melancholy. Her eyeliner and shadow had smudged slightly, making her look tired.

"My husband is such a fuck."

Taylor leaned on the desk. "Shari. Charles is a nice man. What are you saying?"

Shari held a cigarette and flicked a gold lighter up to her mouth. She squinted and inhaled.

"I think he only married me for my frickin' uterus," she said, smoke pouring from her mouth. "After ten years, two miscarriages, and news that I can't get pregnant, he stopped loving me."

"I thought you decided to adopt," Taylor said.

"We did, then Charles changed his mind," Shari said. "He comes from a huge Catholic family, and he started getting all uptight. Some excuse about not fulfilling his role in God's eyes about procreation."

"What?" Taylor picked up the crystal-framed wedding picture of Shari and Charles on the desk. "You two always look so happy. And at my engagement party you seemed okay."

Shari shrugged her shoulders. "I don't know what happened. The love is gone. He's at the bank from dawn to dusk; I work twelve-hour days here. I dread seeing him tonight; we're having dinner with friends. I don't know, I'm at a turning point or something."

"Divorce?" Taylor asked.

Shari took a long drag on her cigarette. "Maybe. We'll see. Things sure can't go on the way they are. I can't even remember the last time we had sex. And believe me, I need it bad."

"What about counseling?"

"Charles would never do that."

"So he won't adopt even though he still wants kids?" Taylor asked.

"Right," Shari said. "Stupid, huh? I could love any child. God knows our house could hold a whole brood of kids. That's why we bought it."

"I think you should do what makes you the happiest, Shari."

"Thanks for listening, Taylor. You're the only girlfriend I can confide in about this, because my other friends are either married to Charles's friends or gabbers who'd blab my business all over Oakland County. You know those women on *Saturday Night Live* who do 'Coffee Tawk'?"

Taylor smiled. "Yeah."

"My friends are sort of like them," Shari said. "But, Taylor, I'm happy for you and Philip. I'm a little jealous, too. I mean, you're perfect for each other."

Taylor beamed. "Remember, tomorrow. You, me, Carla, and Danielle. The woman at the bridal shop said she'd make last-minute adjustments if any of us gain or lose weight."

Shari laughed. "That might be me. Can you tell I've put on five pounds since Easter?"

"No."

Shari stood up and pressed her raisin-colored fingertips to her rounded hips, camouflaged under her gray suit. "It's all right here. All thanks to my new late-night lover, Mr. Häagen-Dazs. That's about all the excitement I'm getting in the bedroom these days."

Taylor laughed. "Well, with all those cigarettes you smoke and the way you run around this place, your metabolism should be faster than the speed of light."

Shari smashed her cigarette in the ashtray. "I think when I turned thirty-five my metabolism all went into my libido. It's torture, honey, let me tell you. Especially when Charles neglects his duty. But don't worry. I'm sure you and Philip will have a great marriage."

"I hope so," Taylor said softly.

CHAPTER 8

Julian scanned the wig shops and boarded-up buildings lining Woodward Avenue. Up ahead was the Fox Theater, home of the Christmas Day Motown Revue that his parents frequented in the sixties. But the scores of empty, decaying buildings, short and tall, modest and grand, were what had earned Detroit its label as a dead city. The corridor on which they now drove was a mere ghost of the bustling commercial strip that their parents had known when the Hudson's department store thrived decades ago.

Julian studied the building's renovated facade, the coffeehouse, sidewalk café, and restaurant on the first level.

"Wolf has really done a job on the old Hudson's building," he said.

"Yeah, it's a good sign," Andy said. "Used to be an eyesore, just like the old Motown Records building up the street. But soon as Wolf bought it, they gutted it and built our studios. Could be a rebirth for Detroit. And the empowerment zone, that'll bring a bunch of jobs, too."

"Yeah," Julian said. "But I still think I'll get culture shock. This ain't Melrose Avenue, if you know what I mean. And judging by an article I just read in a magazine, you'd think Detroit was Sarajevo."

Andy chuckled. "Man, go to spots on the east side, it is. Burned-out cars, condemned buildings, lots full of garbage. You wouldn't believe how many shootings I've covered over there. One kid I met said he sleeps in the bathtub. It's bulletproof."

Elizabeth Atkins Bowman

"Sounds like South Central L.A.," Julian said. "Man, this downtown is sad. It went from industrial Emerald City to the set of a Mad Max flick."

Andy shook his head. "My parents are always talkin' about how Detroit used to be white and middle-class. But after the riots, boom! White flight. The city turns black and poor almost overnight. Hey, you wanted hard news, Detroit is the place. We got car-jackings, Kevorkian the suicide doctor, the Jimmy Hoffa mystery, you name it."

"Yeah," Julian said, "it's time for change."

"Maybe that's what I need," Andy said. "I been here all my life. Are they hirin' at *EE*?"

"Don't know, but I can put in a good word to Philip," Julian said. "You'd love it out there. I know I did. Like a kid in a candy store. Gorgeous chicks, fast cars, hot clubs, slammin' houses."

"That's it," Andy said, smiling. "I'm quittin' my job tonight and movin' to Cali."

Both men laughed as Andy pulled into the Channel 3 garage, but Julian's lust for the L.A. scene had deflated long ago. Now he wanted to start his life all over with his first love, right here at Channel 3.

In a small, windowless room, Julian and a video editor produced what Julian believed was an engaging report.

Then, as Julian walked along the balcony past the conference room, he saw Taylor, talking heatedly with Shari and two police officers. Julian's heart swelled; he was at least close to her, inching toward his dream.

"Hello, Julian," William Monroe said as he emerged from his office. "How'd it go out there?"

"It got pretty tense for a while," Julian said, shaking William's hand.

"Come in, sit down," William said.

Inside the large office with recessed lights and ficus trees, Julian sat in a gray chair in front of the black marble desk as William played the tape.

"Good start, grabs my attention," William said. "Great stand-up. You project authority and concern." He watched the rest in silence, then ejected the tape. "Good kicker. A lot of reporters would have started with the violence. Why did you start with skinhead chants and protesters, then show violence?"

Julian met William's eyes. "I wanted to show how quickly a peaceful protest can escalate into violence. And to me, the rally was a microcosm of society. We live side by side with simmering prejudices that can explode into riots like this. Today wasn't just about a White Power Alliance rally in Detroit. It was about the race problem that lies just below the surface of everyday life in America."

"Good point," William said.

"I think that television news should do a better job of looking at these issues," Julian said.

William shook his head, then appeared somber. "I'll be honest, Julian. I'm worried about your transition from entertainment to hard news."

Julian's pulse quickened with the hard glint in William's eyes. "I think my piece speaks for itself," Julian said. "I'm confident that I can do well here."

William knitted his brows. "Your résumé said you interned at the Global News Network bureau in Los Angeles. You were in that minority program they have, the one that lasts four summers. Why'd you leave after one?"

Julian did not flinch while images of the incident flashed in his mind. "I decided to go into entertainment news. But the one summer I was at GNN, I learned a lot. I went out with news crews all over, helped out in the studio, got a taste of what TV reporting is all about."

"Do you know Wilbur Franklin?" William asked.

Sweat prickled under Julian's arms. "The vice president of news, of course."

William eyed Julian suspiciously. "Wilbur said he never heard of you. He and I go way back, to college. So of course, I called him when I saw your résumé."

"I was only an intern, and that was ten years ago," Julian said coolly. But inside he stewed with the memory of that life-altering day with Brad Hastings, the rich-boy intern who had criticized the way Julian angled the studio's klieg lights.

"I'm doing it exactly like the technical director said," Julian had answered.

"You're a cocky son of a bitch," Brad said.

Julian, then nineteen, continued working. Nearby, Wilbur Franklin and an anchor were chatting.

"You're nothing but a stupid, half-breed Mandingo stud," Brad said. "You're wasting your time here. Nobody wants to hear the news from a nigger."

Julian glared at him. Then the wheezy laugh of Wilbur Franklin, a rotund, gray-haired man with fat earlobes, made him spin around.

"Face it," Franklin said. "You can forget about being a reporter. I've seen the dimwits in that minority program you're in. Half of 'em can't make a full sentence. Christ, last year we sent one to cover a mud-slide. Couldn't make heads or tails of what he was mumbling into the mike. But we get rid of this program, the NAACP will sure as hell make a big brouhaha."

Stunned, Julian stared at Mr. Franklin. Here was a man who could wave his hand to get him a job, yet he was predicting Julian's failure based on his complexion. And next to him was a guy Julian's age, who was Mr. Franklin's darling and nothing more than a rich, educated Billy Joe Pulaski.

Julian's parents had always taught him to believe in himself regardless of outside influences because his talent and intellect could get him through anything. But at that point he realized that racists were not just the playground bully. They were people who could influence and sabotage his long-dreamed-of broadcast career. And that realization hurt him to the bone.

When Wilbur Franklin left the studio, Brad pushed a shoulder into Julian and said, "Don't look at me like that, nigger."

Like a reflex, Julian punched him in the face. Brad fell into a camera, breaking it, and threatened to press criminal charges.

But when Julian vowed to hire a lawyer and sue for racial harassment, and call the NAACP, management paid him for the last two weeks of his internship, dismissed him, and purged his file. Then everyone acted as if nothing had happened.

It wasn't so simple for Julian. The blinding rage he had felt that day, like red-hot flames licking at his every thought, profoundly altered his personality. He plunged into a vacuum of indifference toward everything, even Taylor. He never told her, or his parents, what happened, and he rarely returned to Detroit to visit. Nothing had mattered but his career, proving Wilbur Franklin wrong.

Julian now realized that all this time, he had been cruelest to the people who loved him most. It was time to make amends for the horrible mistakes he had made, but the mere mention of Wilbur Franklin's name sent his heart racing, his anger surging.

"I'm sure Wilbur Franklin has seen hundreds of interns since I left," Julian said.

William stood up. "You're right. I like your style, Julian. Good job today, and we'll let you know our verdict in the morning."

CHAPTER 9

Hope welled inside Julian as he greeted Philip, who was watching the six-o'clock news on Wolf stations in the central time zone on his huge television.

"You dazzling them downstairs with all the tricks I taught you?" Philip asked, smiling in a wing-back leather chair.

"Hope so," Julian said. "William Monroe seemed pretty positive."

"I know raw talent when I see it," Philip said, holding up his palms. "It was like molding Adam out of clay. I created a media masterpiece. Now you want to hide yourself in Detroit, but hey, it's your choice."

Julian took a seat. "Philip, man, you know I appreciate everything you've done for me. But like I said, it's time for change."

"I hear you, pal. But I'll sure miss you in L.A. Running buddies like you don't exactly grow on trees."

"You won't need a road dog anymore, after the wedding," Julian said.

Philip chuckled. "You're crazy if you think a wedding ring is going to deliver me from temptation. Thought you knew me better than that, pal."

Julian met his laughing eyes. *You bastard, you're not even gonna get the chance to cheat on Taylor because you're not gonna marry her in the first place. I am.*

"I don't know, man," Julian said. "I met Taylor James at the rally, and she's a knockout. And tough. You should've seen how she handled those white supremacists."

"That's my Taylor," Philip said, smiling. "Three weeks from tomorrow, she's all mine."

Wrong. Julian smiled. "She'll make a gorgeous bride. Just make sure you clear out all the hula dancers at your Maui place before the honeymoon. Man, that was one wild time."

"Sure was," Philip said, shaking his remote control. "This damn thing is out again." He buzzed his secretary on the intercom: "Thelma, get me some new batteries."

Julian studied the picture of Philip and Taylor on the desk. "Where was this?"

"Acapulco," Philip said as he took batteries from his secretary. "On my dad's boat, before we told anybody about us. She was so worried people would think she was humping her way to the top; she wouldn't fuck me again until the divorce was final."

Again? So Taylor slept with him while he was married? A dull ache gripped Julian's gut at the thought of Philip having sex with Taylor. He wondered if Philip played video charades and naked newscast with Taylor like he did with *EE* correspondent Shanna George, whom Philip had bedded many times before promoting her to anchor.

"Philip, I was wondering, why'd you keep Taylor such a big secret?" Julian asked. "I'm surprised you never brought her to the studio or introduced us when she came to L.A. Close as we live to each other, you could have brought her by one day."

Philip returned to his TV. "I wanted to keep it under wraps. Besides, you're my link to the dark side. She doesn't need to meet the guy who knows all my dirty secrets."

"The key word here is 'secrets,' man," Julian said. "I got a Ziploc mouth when it comes to that stuff. Relax." Philip had that same I-own-the-world expression as when he announced his engagement. Julian's blood still boiled at the memory.

It had been a February night when Philip had invited a dozen friends to an upscale strip club in Los Angeles for what he said was a surprise. In a private room with a half dozen topless women slow-dancing on the table, Philip stood up. From Julian's seat, the women framed Philip in his gray, wide-chalk-stripe gangsteresque suit, the smoking Cohiba cigar in his hand, the arrogant expression on his always-tanned face.

"I brought you all here so you'd be the first to know," Philip had said over a sultry singer and bass beat, "that I'm about to walk down the aisle with a blond-haired, green-eyed, half-black nymphette who's the hottest thing to hit a newscast since color TV."

The words slammed Julian's chest like a sledgehammer. He couldn't breathe.

Not my Taylor. Not the woman Philip is talking about like some porn star. Philip can't have my White Chocolate. His face felt cold, as if the blood had suddenly drained from his head.

". . . a TV reporter in Detroit," Philip said. "On her way to the network. Her name is Taylor James, and we met when—"

Julian went numb. Fragments of Philip's description of their budding romance filtered through the shock that gripped Julian like a giant fist, but he heard nothing after Philip called Taylor a "mulatto tigress in bed." Julian felt as if a tight metal coil inside him would spring, releasing fury at Philip and at himself for letting this happen. He could never forgive himself for treating her so badly, ignoring her calls and letters, and getting engaged to Brooke. He'd thrown away Taylor's love like an old pair of shoes, well worn to hug and caress every inch of his feet, and replaced them with a closet full of cheap, flashy pairs that left him nothing but chafing and blisters.

Julian bolted to the men's room, where his mirror image sneered. *You fucked up the most precious thing in your life, and this is fate's way of punishing you.*

But no, she's mine. I can't let it happen.

He devised a plan, then congratulated Philip.

"What's on your mind, DuPont?" Philip squinted behind a veil of cigar smoke. With his legs crossed, a dancer massaged his shoulders.

As Julian sat down, a cool expression concealed his newfound disdain for Philip. Julian felt oddly like he was meeting with the Godfather, asking him for a life-altering favor that, when the truth came out, would turn this powerful man into a mortal enemy.

"I'm ready to make some serious changes, too," Julian said.

"What's that, pal?"

"Hard news," Julian said. "And being closer to my dad. His heart attack, the fiasco with Brooke, I don't know. I think something's telling me to go home. My contract is up June first. What I want is to be a news anchor for Wolf in Detroit."

Philip's eyes were sharp as blue steel hooks as they probed Julian. Smoke plumed from his nostrils.

"You're different, DuPont, but that's why I like you. You're real. You got substance. Yeah, it's a little crazy to give up your gig out here, but your heart's in the right place."

Julian did not blink under Philip's penetrating stare. If Philip said no, Julian could always apply for a job at one of Detroit's other three stations, but he wanted to stay with top-ranked Wolf. And if he did this right, Philip could hook him up with the best salary and perks.

The tip of Philip's cigar glowed red as he sucked it. "Sure thing, pal. I'll see what I can do."

"Philip, you don't know what this means to me. Thanks, man."

"For you, pal," Philip said, "anything is possible."

Julian had smiled. *You're gonna regret you said that.*

Now Philip pointed at the enormous television in his office. "Look at that bimbo meteorologist in Omaha," he said. "I bet she doesn't know a weather balloon from a rubber." He dialed Omaha's news director as the woman giggled, pointing to a storm center over the Rockies.

"Frank, who the hell is doing the weather? She looks like a fuckin' showgirl with that big hair and her tits pushed up. Get her a makeover or replace her now. This isn't the frickin' Playboy Channel."

The office doors blew open with a blur of red and yellow. It was Taylor, scowling. Julian's palms dampened; he ached from head to toe to feel her approval and affection again.

And he devoured every inch of her, from her flowing hair to her red lips, her hourglass curves, her muscular calves. With her arms crossed, her red fingernails and diamond ring sparkled under the recessed lights. She hurried past Julian, the soft scent of her perfume and her vibrant eyes turning his insides to mush.

How could I have let this exotic creature go? And how can I ever explain and make up for my horrible mistakes? Julian wanted to fall to his knees and beg for her forgiveness. But her stern expression told him that his exoneration was the last thing on her mind.

"Darling," Philip said, rising from his seat with outstretched arms. "What's the matter?"

Julian stood, smiling. "Hello, Ms. James."

"Darling, you met my friend Julian DuPont?"

"Your friend?" Her words pierced the air like bullets.

"Yes, I've been his mentor over the years."

Taylor raised her eyebrows. "Mentor? You never told me that. What does someone as famous as him need a mentor for?"

Philip chuckled. "He wasn't always famous."

"Is he invited to the wedding?" she asked.

"Of course he is, darling."

"He's not on the invitation list."

"I hand-delivered his invitation at the *EE* studio in L.A.," Philip said.

Julian grinned when Taylor stared at him. He was so physically close to her, he wanted to kiss her, wash away the years of pain and betrayal with sweat-soaked passion. But first he'd need to pour on the charm like a blowtorch to penetrate the Plexiglas tent of hostility around her.

"Darling, why do you look so angry?" Philip asked.

Taylor sighed. "The cops. Shari just told me I'll have them all weekend. I told you I don't need a baby-sitter. This is ridiculous."

Philip stroked her shoulder. "It's for your own good. Pulaski's in jail tonight, but his commandos are still out there. And if he gets released tomorrow, I don't want that barbarian anywhere near you. You know it would crush me if anything happened to you."

The intimacy of their exchange—the touching, the affectionate gazes—agitated Julian to the point where he wanted to flee the office. But he maintained a cool mask, underneath which his rage at himself and at Philip fueled his resolve to earn Taylor back. *She can't possibly love him as much as she loved me.*

"So this was all your idea?" Taylor asked.

"Yes," Philip said. "Besides, your face is on every station in Detroit. We couldn't pay for pub like this."

Taylor rolled her eyes. "Oh, so now I'm part of a ratings gimmick."

"Wrong," Philip said. "Think of it like this. You're a rare porcelain statue. There's a bulldog that wants to smash you into a thousand pieces. We put a shield around the statue; the dog can't smash it."

Taylor shook her head as she walked to the window.

At the same time, Philip smiled at Julian as if to say, in an exasperated tone, "Women."

"Taylor, relax," Philip said. "High-profile people have bodyguards all the time. Look at Madonna, Michael Jackson, the president. Come here."

She turned around. "What?"

"Come here."

Philip pulled her close—two white faces, two blond heads of hair—and whispered in her ear. She smiled and glanced up at Julian.

There was sadism in her eyes, as if she wanted Julian to wallow and writhe in the defeat that he had brought upon himself.

Julian excused himself from the room. With every step, his heart ached with immense regret, because he realized that losing Taylor was the worst mistake he had ever made.

CHAPTER 10

Taylor tossed her head back as Philip's lips tickled her neck.

"Philip, stop. I'm still working."

"I can't help it," he whispered. "You were so sexy tonight on the news, it made my dick throb."

Taylor stiffened. "Yeah, tear gas and men being beaten unconscious really got me in the mood. How could you think of sex and watch a race riot at the same time?"

Philip nuzzled her ear. "Lust is my opiate. Numbs me to the wicked ways of the world. Taylor, baby, a quick erotic diversion might relax you, make you forget about all that for a while."

Taylor pushed him away. "Philip, you just don't understand, do you? What I saw today really upset me." She retreated to a wing-back chair.

Philip leaned down and licked her ear. "Oh, come on, darling. You know it stokes my fire when you get sassy."

Taylor scowled. "Stop it, Philip. I'm too stressed to think about sex. Can't you wait a few hours until I get off work?"

The corners of Philip's mouth turned down as he caressed her shoulders. "All right, but then my tongue is going to ravage every crevice of your body. How 'bout a little nude newscast, huh?"

Taylor stood up and hooked her forefingers in his braces. "The only newscast I'm thinking about is the one at eleven o'clock when I'll be standing in front of the Wayne County Jail, happily reporting that Pulaski is inside."

Philip tried to kiss her, but she pulled away.

He'll never understand how I feel. His lust annoyed her; he should instead have been talking to her, letting her explain how it pained her to see that racial clash, hear Pulaski's threat, look in his eyes. And there was more to her mood.

Julian.

She could not shake his face from her mind. *What does he want to talk to me about?* Since she saw him, her imagination had spun a thousand scenarios of working with him at Channel 3, wondering what could have been. Clashing anger and curiosity swirled inside her like a noxious chemical reaction, adding to the queasy feeling she'd had since the riot. If Julian was hired, they would be living their childhood dream. But she would be married to someone else.

Taylor twisted out of Philip's arms. "Philip, what's up with the secret friendship with Julian DuPont? I mean, he's from Detroit. Why didn't you ever introduce us, or even mention his name?"

Philip shrugged. "What's there to tell?"

"A lot, since you secretly invited him to our wedding," Taylor said. She hoped that Julian had not told Philip about their past. It was irrelevant now and would only raise Philip's suspicions. "Any more surprise guests?"

"Roger Gold, executive producer of *EE*. That's all."

"Are either of them bringing spouses? The caterer needs an exact—"

"Taylor, relax. Roger's getting a divorce, but he might bring a date. DuPont, he'll be solo. Seems like he's got tunnel vision all of a sudden."

"That's what he told you?"

"Yes, Taylor. Why the inquisition?"

"I'm a reporter. I ask questions for a living. And I just wondered why, when I saw him at the rally today, he'd leave such a glitzy job to come here."

"DuPont is different," Philip said. "I don't know, something about his dad having a heart attack, returning to his roots. Hey, cheer up. He's cool people. He'll be good for Channel Three."

"We're already number one," Taylor said, crossing her arms. "So he's hired?"

"Is my Taylor jealous?" Philip grinned.

"No, I'm not jealous. I hear he's an arrogant playboy."

"Arrogant, no. Playboy, used to be. He's calmed down a lot over the past six months, since he dumped Brooke. Christ, Taylor, you look like somebody drowned your cat."

Pangs of anxiety and anger gripped Taylor's insides when she saw, in the center of the newsroom, Kendra Vaughn smiling and talking with Julian.

Hoping to avoid them both, Taylor darted past the neon "3" toward producers' row, where she needed to discuss her eleven-o'clock report with Alan. But she could not walk fast enough. Julian strode toward her.

"Taylor."

Her heart thundered.

"Hi," she said coolly. She looked up at his face—he was a head taller than she, even in heels—and felt annoyed by his absorbing stare. She hated looking at the face whose every detail she had memorized, from the shiny beige scar at the edge of his black curls to the smooth arch of his ears to the perfect points of his upper lip and the luscious curve that was his bottom lip. Her eyes lingered on that mouth that had once spoken so many comforting words, calming her fears, expressing love. Mostly she loathed staring into his eyes, the place where she had once sought solace from the world's cruelty— only to discover that his eyes were the most brutal place of all.

"Amazing job out there today," he said. "I watched it on the monitor in the news van."

"Thanks."

"Listen, Taylor, is there an employee lounge around here where I can get some soda or juice?"

"Yeah, have one of the PAs show you up to the cafeteria."

"Can't you show me?"

"No, I'm too busy."

"Please?"

"Okay, go through that archway, take the elevator to the eighth floor, get off the elevators and turn left, then right at the library, then go down the long hallway, cut through the renovation area, and stop near the room full of colored wires and blinking equipment. You'll see the employee lounge and cafeteria on your right."

Julian laughed. "I'm supposed to remember all that?"

"Yes."

"Come on, Taylor, show me. It'll only take a minute."

"I have to meet with the producer. He might want to send me out."

Taylor felt odd, talking to Julian in the newsroom. It had served as the backdrop for her finally pushing him out of her mind and heart, yet it was also the place where they had dreamed of being to-gether. She ran her left thumb over the back of her engagement ring.

"C'mon," Julian said.

"Fine," Taylor said. She waved to the police officers at her desk and held up five fingers, as if to say, "Five minutes."

In the elevator, Julian turned to her. "I have to talk to you."

"So talk." She crossed her arms and stared at the panel of num-bered elevator buttons.

"Don't act like you hate me," he said.

She glared at him, fury rising inside her. "I should hate you for what you did to me. If you want to know the truth, I think you're a heartless, selfish, womanizing bastard."

As she lifted her eyebrows to show indifference to Julian's bruised expression, the elevator doors opened.

"Hello, Taylor," said Mia Lee, a production assistant.

"Hi, Mia. Busy night, huh?"

"Yeah. I'm going up to the Wolf offices to give this to Mr. Carter." Mia held up the latest copy of the glossy *Broadcaster's Weekly* magazine. On the cover was Philip, standing in front of the Wolf World Report anchor desk in New York. The headline said, MEDIA HEIR PHILIP CARTER BRINGS PIZZAZZ, PROFITS TO BOOMING WOLF NETWORK.

"That looks great," Taylor said. Philip, wearing his usual I-own-the-world expression on his tanned face and a three-button, navy blue suit, stood with crossed arms and feet wide apart, in front of the glass backdrop etched with a world map.

"Here, take a look." Mia handed the magazine to Taylor. "Hi, Julian. They've kept you pretty busy since you got here yesterday."

Taylor glanced up from the magazine and hardened her eyes at Julian. "You were here yesterday?"

"Yes," Julian said. "From William's office, I saw you rush out of the newsroom with Andy."

"Oh," she said. How odd that he had been watching her and she had never suspected, or sensed, his presence.

"Julian knows my cousin who's a writer at *EE*," Mia said, her straight black pixie hairstyle bouncing.

"That's nice," Taylor said, flipping through the six-page spread of pictures and text about Philip and Wolf. A pang of annoyance shot through her when she saw a large picture of Julian and Philip, both smiling, on the *EE* set. The caption said, "Carter discovered Julian DuPont and molded him into a superstar of entertainment news. The Wolf executive points to DuPont's success as an example of the network's commitment to diversity in hiring and coverage."

Julian glanced over her shoulder. "I hope that reporter quoted me right," he said. "He hung around the set for three days."

"Your job sounds so exciting, Julian," Mia said. "Maybe we can have coffee sometime, if you get hired, and you can tell me all about it."

Julian smiled. "Sure."

The elevator beeped and the doors opened. "The cafeteria is on eight," Taylor told Julian in a businesslike tone as they stepped out. "See you later, Mia."

In the deserted hallway, Taylor looked around, then turned to Julian. "Don't you dare tell Philip about our past. Have you?"

"No," he said softly. "I've never mentioned it."

"Well, don't do it now," Taylor said, walking quickly, her pumps echoing on the tile floor. "I never want Philip to know about us."

"It's funny," Julian said. "Philip never mentioned you until a few months ago. That's when I decided that Philip Carter couldn't have you. Because Julian DuPont wants you so bad it hurts."

Taylor froze. Shock snaked through her like fire and ice in her veins.

"What?" she shouted in a whisper. "What did you say?"

Julian took her hands in his. The expression in his eyes was soft as brown velvet. "Taylor, you're the reason I'm here. You and I belong together."

Taylor snatched her hands back. "You're delusional."

"Just listen to me, please."

"I don't want to hear this."

"Please."

"What kind of sick trick is this?" she asked. "Don't you think you've screwed with my mind enough?"

"Please listen to me."

Taylor glanced around the empty hallway, then stepped over a barricade to a suite of offices that was being renovated. She walked through two dark rooms smelling of paint and cluttered with giant cans, ladders, and brushes. Plastic crinkled under their feet as Taylor stopped by a window, crossed her arms, and looked out at the pink-orange sunset.

"Talk. Hurry up. I have to get back to work."

Julian stepped close.

God help me, he still wears Arrazo.

"Taylor," he said softly. "I have a lot of explaining to do. Words can't express my regret over losing you."

"Losing me? That's not quite what happened. You lose a pen or a wallet. Our breakup would have been more humane if you had taken a Ginsu knife and sliced my heart out."

Julian sighed and stepped closer. "Taylor, I'm sorry. I still love you. I want you back. I want my White Chocolate back."

Dizziness swept through her like a tornado. Julian's voice, distorted in slow motion and a bass pitch, echoed like a gong in her mind. *Give me strength . . .*

"You heard me right," he said. His lips were inches away. Heat radiated from his broad chest. "Don't marry Philip. Give me a second chance."

The impulse to slap Julian and the desire to hear him out clashed in Taylor's trembling body. She could smell her perfume, rising in humid wafts, as her chest rose and fell. She hated that he was so handsome, that his voice was so enchanting, that his presence penetrated her to the bone, like a blazing hearth during a blizzard.

But she knew that her Julian would understand the hatred and the heartache she had experienced at the rally. And he would appreciate the triumph she had felt over the Pulaskis and the White Power Alliance. He would applaud her drive to make the world a better place without calling it a gimmick, as Philip did. But was this the same Julian she had known as a child? Or was he that monster she had encountered ten years ago in Los Angeles?

Taylor looked up at him with questioning eyes. An instinct from deep within urged her to explore his mind and motivations. At the same time, another urge sent a bolt of fire through her body, straining her nipples against the lace of her bra.

Julian slowly bent down and kissed her mouth.

She whimpered and tried to pull away.

No, you can't do this. You can't just kiss me and—

Julian's lips were startlingly hot and soft. He smelled delicious.

Taylor shook her head, but he stilled her by cupping the back of her head with his hand. His other hand circled her waist and pulled her close.

She tried to twist away. *I'm trapped. He can't trap me in his arms in a dark, half-finished room between the newsroom and Philip's office. But his lips feel so good . . . so soft and hot . . .*

Taylor closed her eyes, just for a second, to remember the passion and the hungry teenaged curiosity that first united their bodies.

Her head, light as a cloud, whirled. Julian, with lips pressing gently on her mouth, pulled her closer. Her breasts crushed against his chest.

Oh my God . . . I'm kissing Julian again and I don't want to stop . . . ever.

Fiery sparks sprayed through her abdomen, down her thighs, igniting a hot swell between her legs. She was melting. Just for an instant, she longed to run her hands through his hair.

No. Philip. No, I can't do this. Can't do this.

She whimpered and pressed her hands against his chest. He pulled. She twisted her lips away from his, then gasped. He buried his face in her neck and hair. Her fingernails dug into the padded shoulders of his suit.

"Stop it! Julian, stop it!" Her pulse raced.

He held her close, his hot breath tickling her neck. "I still love you, Taylor. I want you. I need you. Nothing matters but getting you back." His voice was raspy with desperation.

"Stop it! Get off me!"

Julian clung to her waist.

Taylor kneed him in the kneecaps.

"Ow!" Julian reeled back and massaged his knees. "That hurts!"

"Good."

Taylor stepped back, panting. Hot tremors and cold goose bumps wracked her body. Her stomach cramped. With her sleeve, she wiped the taste of Julian off her lips. Unable to speak, she closed her eyes.

This can't happen.

When she opened her eyes, Julian's stare seemed to penetrate to her soul. "Taylor, I decided to come to Channel Three so I could be close to you. I'm risking everything for you. You can't marry Philip. He's a snake. He doesn't deserve you. I know a side of him that would make you cringe."

"*You* make me cringe!" Taylor shouted. "You took the most beautiful, precious love that two people could ever share, and you stomped on it. You meant everything to me. But you took away my comfort zone, where race didn't matter. You left me out in the cold, and for years I was so stupid to beg you to take me back. But you didn't, and now I hate you, Julian. I hate you."

Blood pounded through her veins, throbbing in her ears. "You're crazy. This is so outrageous. And don't talk about Philip like that."

"Taylor, you have a right to be upset, but give me a chance," Julian said.

"You don't deserve a chance," Taylor said. "You deserve nothing less than me pushing you out this window. Maybe all the women in the newsroom are drooling over you, but you make me want to heave."

Taylor held up her left hand. The diamond sparkled in the dim light.

"I'm about to become Mrs. Philip Carter. You, Julian DuPont, are ancient history. Nothing more. Even if, God forbid, you get hired here, I will have nothing but indifference for you. Besides, I'll be at the network by my thirtieth birthday."

Julian put his hand over hers, covering the diamond. "I don't care about your wedding or Philip or your future plans. All I want is you. Here. Now. Forever."

Taylor snatched her hand from his grasp. "Don't touch me! You have a bad case of memory loss. Don't you remember how it ended between us?"

"Yes, I was there."

Taylor's insides jittered. "No, if you remembered what happened, you wouldn't have the gall to just pop into my life, at my job, three weeks before my wedding, to say you want me back."

Julian leaned against the brick wall, crossed his arms, and tilted his head back.

"Think back, Julian, to our first college summer, when I visited you in L.A. before school started back up. Usually you were ecstatic to see me. But all of a sudden, this time, you were mean and cold.

"Starting when you picked me up from the airport. No hugs, no dinner, no expression. You were another person. At your apartment, we didn't make love. You fucked me in a disgusting way. All rough, slapping my butt, pinching my skin. Am I ringing any bells here?"

"Yeah," Julian said softly.

"And the next day, I was crying, and you just left. Gone for hours! All those girls, coming to the door asking for you, calling nonstop. And the bra under your bed. The panties, not mine, in the bathroom."

"Taylor, you don't have to do this," Julian said. "I know I was a dog, but I've changed. Please."

"No, just so you know where I'm coming from," Taylor said. "That night you made me wear that slutty dress to that cokehead actor's party. You flirted with every tramp in the place, like I wasn't even there. And then, horror of all horrors, back at your apartment— those bimbos in bikinis come in from the pool, blasting music, dancing all nasty. You loved it, probably screwed them all after I left. I still can't believe—"

"Taylor, please."

She cut her eyes at him and shuddered. She felt sweaty and nauseated. Vivid images of those women and Julian's cold smirk made her stomach feel like a gurgling vat of acid. The eleven-o'clock producer, the police officers, and Philip lingered in the back of her mind, but the horrific images of Julian, ten years ago, and the anger over his outrageous scheme today, overwhelmed her.

A hot lump burned in her throat. *No, I will not cry in front of him. I've shed too many tears for him already. He doesn't deserve any more.* She twirled her engagement ring on her clammy finger.

"The worst thing, Julian, was after that night, after I took a cab to the airport and flew back to New York, I never heard from you again. Until today. Imagine how I feel. No calls, no letters, no explanations. My parents and your parents always asking me what happened, and I didn't even know. Then I saw you on TV. And in *People* with your girl of the week. Imagine how I felt!"

Taylor scowled. "I moved on with my life long ago, and you're not part of it. No sudden kissing or begging or bad-mouthing my fiancé can change that."

Julian stepped toward her. "Taylor, I am so sorry. Please believe me. Please. I want to spend the rest of my life making you the happiest woman in the world. We can start over. I want my White Chocolate back."

Goose bumps danced across her skin. "Don't! Don't call me that."

"Taylor James, I still love you."

Fat tears welled in her eyes and rolled down her cheeks. She bit her lip and looked out the window. After long moments, she faced him.

"Julian, you know this wild scheme of yours to woo me back, break off my marriage, and work at Channel 3?"

"Yes," he said eagerly.

"Take it all back to L.A. and shove it!"

Trembling, Taylor fled. Her shoes echoed in the hallway and stairwell as she bounded back to the newsroom. With every step, she summoned all her will to keep from crumpling to her knees and bawling.

CHAPTER 11

Rocky Pulaski squared his shoulders and raised his chin to a haughty angle as he and his son stepped into the jail cell. He ignored the racial heckling of a dozen black men as he mentally cordoned himself and Billy Joe in a corner near the iron bars.

This brief imprisonment, like the two years he had spent at Milan, would further galvanize his cause, just as Hitler's nine-month incarceration at Landsberg in 1924 had incubated his magnificent rise to führer of the Third Reich.

My master's Munich putsch failed, but in the end he was victorious for his reign; our rally today was defeated by the Jew-dominated media and the malicious government, but ultimately we'll triumph.

As he had since childhood, Rocky sensed Hitler's spirit with him, guiding him on a journey past racial injustices and oppression toward a totalitarian Fourth Reich. And like Hitler, who had composed *Mein Kampf* during his incarceration, Rocky had nurtured his mind and will by reading, writing, and strategizing the white revolution while confined to that cramped, cold cell. Similarly, he would meditate tonight until his release.

And, as he had done in prison, he would sharpen and shine his obsessive lust to avenge the mongrel whore who had dared to impede his ascension to power. She had destroyed everything, and for that she would suffer unfathomable brutality.

I am Nietzsche's strong man, a warrior carrying on the brave Pulaski tradition of racial activism.

Rocky derived courage and strength to execute his mission from his forefathers, who had forged a long, proud history of racial activism in Detroit.

A jolt of inspirational fury always surged through Rocky when he thought of Stanislaw Pulaski, his great-great-grandfather who had fled Russian oppression in Poland in 1855 and sought a better life in Detroit. Here, with a wife, three sons, and work at a meat-processing plant, the American Dream had glittered on the horizon.

But the dream vaporized in 1863. Civil War inscription forced him to forfeit his work to the growing influx of blacks, as he was enlisted to fight for issues irrelevant to his life. To vent his rage, he joined like-minded Irish, Polish, and German immigrants—armed with guns, clubs, axes, and a rope—in rampaging Detroit's black neighborhood on Beaubien Street, beating people, looting stores, and torching buildings. But the protest was in vain; Stanislaw went to war and died at Gettysburg.

How ironic that we rallied today beneath the Iron Brigade Civil War memorial in Kennedy Square. Grandpa Joseph would be proud of my perseverance.

Joseph Pulaski had participated in the upsurge of Ku Klux Klan activity in Detroit in 1925 as Henry Ford's five-dollar-a-day factory wage beckoned thousands of blacks, southern whites, and immigrants to Detroit. As the overcrowded city became a virtual cauldron of racial and ethnic tension, Joseph joined ten thousand whites in cheering KKK speakers who preached for segregated housing laws and against the growing numbers of Jewish merchants. The hostility exploded when a black man, Dr. Ossian Sweet, bought a house in an all-white, Polish neighborhood near Grandpa Joseph's house on Charlevoix near Garland on the east side. A white mob stormed Sweet's house, a shot was fired, and a white man died. Despite two trials, Sweet was acquitted of murder.

But the racial tension left in the wake of that world-watched drama festered for two decades, inspiring Rocky's father to partake in racial activism as well. Like his father, Karl Pulaski earned a good living at Chrysler's Packard plant. During World War II, when car production halted and Chrysler began producing tanks, the United Auto Workers successfully lobbied for an integrated work force. Naturally, Karl Pulaski and 250 of his Polish and white colleagues protested working alongside Negroes by staging a forty-minute sit-down strike at the Packard Motor Company in September 1941.

Then, furious that the federal government had built black housing near his home in the Polish enclave off Ryan Road and Nevada in northeast Detroit, Karl Pulaski joined the Klan and a huge white mob in burning a cross and picketing before the Sojourner Truth housing projects in 1942. At the same time, Karl was a supporter of Father Coughlin, whose magazine, *Social Justice,* openly defended Hitlerism, and Rev. Gerald L. K. Smith, a southern Democrat who preached white separatism in his publication, *Cross and Flag.*

Racial fury continued to simmer until July 1943, when a race riot ignited on the island park in the Detroit River known as Belle Isle. It soon consumed the city—thousands of whites viciously attacking blacks—claiming thirty-four lives. Blacks burned and looted Jewish businesses in the ghetto, and the cops, many of whom sided with whites, killed a fair share of blacks.

And it happened all over again in '67.

Can't they see that the races are not meant to live together?

Throughout Rocky's fifty years, each character-molding experience had confirmed the beliefs instilled in him as a child by his father. First came the civil rights laws, starting with *Brown v. the Board of Education of Topeka, Kansas* in 1954, the Civil Rights Act of 1964, and the 1967 U.S. Supreme Court decision *Loving v. Virginia,* which struck down laws banning interracial marriage. Rocky and his family believed that these further forewarned of the racial chaos that would grip the once glorious United States.

But Pulaski's most gut-wrenching, life-altering experience had been his service in the marines in Vietnam. What had sucked Rocky into a haze of black despair for years was witnessing his brother Joseph's horrifying, gruesome death in that godforsaken jungle.

There wasn't even enough left of Joey to bring home to Mom and Dad in a body bag. And it was all Nixon's fault.

Pulaski loathed the politicians in Washington, playing war games with the precious lives of white men, sending them by the planeload to get slaughtered in a foreign land not worth the rice in its paddies. In the war he lost countless friends, and despised the Negroes in his platoon—their speech, their smell, and mostly their collective sense of entitlement, as if the United States owed them compensation for slavery. Hell, the Pulaskis sailed here with nothing, yet settled in Detroit and found employment, made a life, without asking the government for one dime.

Another reason Vietnam infuriated Pulaski was his apprehension over leaving Loretta alone with Billy Joe in a city already ravaged by race riots. Even worse was the day, just months after Joey's death, when he received the letter from Loretta saying his parents had died in a car wreck, and he could not even return for the funeral.

Months later when he did come home, however, Rocky was overcome by the torturous hypochondria of wondering if and when the carcinogenic Agent Orange to which the government had knowingly exposed him in the jungle would trigger cancer. At the same time, he returned to his assembly-line job at the Ford plant, where it infuriated him to hear and feel antiwar spite and scorn. It made him wish he had never gone to Vietnam. And it further enraged him that the government had forced that nightmare upon him.

But always, as now, he had persevered, and one day his adversity would culminate in victory for hardworking white Americans like himself. He owed it to his deceased parents, his ancestors, and his butchered brother to become someone great, a man who would make the Pulaski name proud.

Rocky pressed his fingers to his spastic eyelid. It always twitched when he was incensed, ever since that Negro inmate in prison bashed his forehead into the shower wall when he saw the White Power Alliance tattoo across his back.

"Dad, when are we gettin' outta here?" Billy Joe asked. "I don't like the way those guys are lookin' at us."

Profound anger surging through Rocky's body made his head feel like a red balloon, full of hot water, stretched to the point of bursting. He wanted to slap that effeminate pout off Billy Joe's round face.

"What?" Rocky snapped. "You love to whack girls and those goons this afternoon, but you shudder like a coward when you face jailhouse degenerates? Is that the kind of pansy I raised?"

Billy Joe's eyes widened. "No, Dad, I just don't like jail."

"Maybe you need something to toughen you up," Rocky said. "I have just the solution."

"What is it, Dad?"

"It's time for you to earn your spiderweb," Rocky said.

CHAPTER 12

Shari Gordon pounded her cigarette in the ashtray of her gray Dodge Stealth as she pulled into the driveway. The garage was empty.

"That fuck."

Shari drove inside, closed the garage door, and leaned back in the bucket seat as the stereo played a melancholy love song. She flicked her gold lighter and stared at the flame, lit a cigarette and watched the fire disappear. Blazing one instant, extinguished the next, just like her and Charles.

He could've called to say he'd be late. He better get home in time for dinner. We don't need that embarrassment, again.

Shari dreaded entering their half-million-dollar dream home in Bloomfield Hills. Every step would remind her of how, a decade ago, with visions of babies in their heads, she and Charles had christened each room by making love on the floor before the furniture arrived.

They had even made love one night on the back deck overlooking the wooded ravine.

Back then, their lives had been flawless. Shari, at twenty-five, was climbing the ranks at Channel 3, and Charles, five years older, had been recently promoted to his executive position at National Bank of Michigan. His impressive stock portfolio, and his inheritance from his late father, assured that their children would have private schooling, college, and the best of everything.

Shari closed her eyes, envisioning Charles. The man who used to cook shrimp stir-fry in the wok and feed her with chopsticks, massage her feet after hours of dancing, and sponge her all over during bubble baths now made her feel as if she were married to a cadaver. His love and vitality had expired somewhere between the second miscarriage and that heart-wrenching appointment with her gynecologist.

Lost in her thoughts, Shari headed inside. Minutes later, she stood zombielike under the shower.

Maybe Charles forgot about dinner. Maybe he has a mistress. A fertile one. I don't care anymore. I'm going out, with or without him. No more lamenting.

In the spacious bedroom, with its cathedral ceiling, floor-to-roof windows, and beige decor, Shari flipped on the last segment of *Entertainment Exclusive.* As she passed the dresser in stockings and underwear, she laid a brass-framed picture of herself and Charles on its face.

A grief-stricken heaviness consumed her, as if she were mourning the death of a close friend. *I am. My husband.*

The forty-year-old stiff who now shared her bed was not the lusty man with the satin tongue she had encountered at Club Taboo in Detroit's warehouse district back in the wild eighties. Shari, in a snug blue dress that hoisted her breasts into two creamy mounds, had flaunted her most sultry smile and sway when clean-cut Charles, wearing a gray three-piece suit and Italian loafers, invited her to dance. They danced until the club closed, then spent phase two of that fateful night at the after-hours City Club. Their mutual attraction sizzled amidst a relentless bass beat and a dance floor undulating with trendy youths in black leather. Phase three, lustful French kissing in the parking lot, led them to the downtown Westin Hotel, where wild sex—the best Shari had ever had—kept them in a sweaty, panting tangle until checkout the next morning. Shari's body was raw for days, but she and Charles had ignited insatiable eroticism within each other that she mistakenly believed would last forever.

Now a barrage of questions rattled in her mind, amplified by rage to a maddening pitch. She longed to escape again into the oblivion of passion, the serenity of a man's embrace.

Shari vacantly slipped on a short, black Donna Karan dress and Kenneth Cole pumps. The ensemble that had once made her feel elegant and sexy while dining by candlelight and dancing with Charles now scratched under her arms and pinched her hips. In the lighted mirror of her built-in vanity, Shari's hazel eyes appeared sorrowful. Tiny crow's-feet spread like fans around her eyes, and her skin seemed doughy. And she noticed for the first time a circle of fat around her neck, like a choker of pudge.

"I'm getting fat and old," Shari said to herself in the mirror. Her life was spinning by like a movie on fast forward, and she was careening into an abyss of lovelessness and desperation.

I have to act now, before it's too late. I don't want to end up like Mom.

Shari spritzed her hair with hair spray, then rifled through shelves holding enough expensive lipsticks, foundations, powders, and eye pencils to rival a department store cosmetics counter. Her fondness for primping for parties with Charles and friends now felt like a chore; she was languidly going through the motions, painting a mask over her discontent.

The phone rang.

Maybe it's Charles, calling to say he ran off with his fertile secretary.

"How's my Shari?" Her mother's high-pitched voice startled her.

"Ehh, I've been better." Shari lit a cigarette.

"What, you don't feel good?"

"I feel fine. It's Charles again. I'm very unhappy. He's turned into a cardboard robot who gets up, goes to work, comes home late. And when he is home, he schleps around with this obnoxious smirk, like the sight of me gives him diarrhea."

"Shut your mouth, Shari. I'm sick of your complaints. When I was your age——"

Shari watched smoke billow out of her mouth in the mirror. She knew exactly what Mom would say.

"——I had four kids. We were barely getting by on the money your father, rest his soul, brought in at the butcher shop. It never crossed my mind to leave. Forget divorce, that wasn't an option for me. I had no education, no job skills. You think I sat around worrying about passion when the mortgage was due? I never dreamed of taking off to the Bahamas like you and Charles do."

Shari did not speak when her mother paused. There was more.

"At least your brothers are happy with their wives and kids. You get divorced, you'll end up like your sister Wilona. Always complaining there are no men out there."

Shari blew out smoke. "Mom, if Wilona stopped inhaling so much pizza and doughnuts and cheeseburgers, maybe she wouldn't weigh three hundred pounds. Maybe then she'd find a man."

"Don't be so shallow, Shari, and I don't want to hear about it with Charles. Marriage is marriage. Passion fades. Get over it and re-decorate the house. Take a vacation. Adopt if you still want children. But enough of your complaints."

Shari dotted foundation on her face, then rubbed it around with a cosmetic sponge. "Thanks for your understanding, Mom."

Unconsciously she fingered her diamond tennis bracelet—a self-congratulatory gift when she was promoted to executive producer. She poked the nail of her forefinger into the spaces between the gold links and diamonds, thinking about how she disagreed with her mother. Passion did not have to dissolve in a marriage. Shari re-membered Taylor's parents as they had kissed and smiled at each other over the barbecue grill in their backyard at Taylor's birthday

party last July. Married thirty-two years, and they still beamed when
the other entered the room. Shari longed for such eternal love.

"I just want you happy," Mom said. "Cheer up. You're better off
than most. Call me tomorrow."

"Okay, Mom."

Shari was quite different from her mother and sister. She was far
more motivated and ambitious than Wilona, who drifted from receptionist jobs and store-clerk positions in a fog of fatness and self-
pity. Nor was she bound to her husband by children or a lack of
education and job skills as Mom was.

No, Shari made a point each day to appreciate her exciting,
award-winning career in which she made major decisions that in-
fluenced public opinion in southeast Michigan. She adored being
around creative, interesting, and industrious people, and she relished
watching young, hungry reporters like Taylor blossom. She thrived
on the rush of deadline pressure, of choreographing scores of performers every day to create perfect dramas at noon, six, and eleven.
And the new morning program that Philip was designing promised
to bring even more exciting challenges.

Through her career, Shari was realizing a dream that had
sparked within her at age fifteen. When her class at Berkley High
toured the Channel 3 studio at its former home near the General
Motors headquarters, she experienced an instant adrenaline rush in
the high-voltage newsroom. She saw reporters and producers hurrying around with the fire of deadline pressure in their eyes, and she
wished that she could have joined the excitement right then. It was
as if she felt an innate sense of belonging that was not surprising to
her; she had always loved watching television news and reading
newspapers. So inspired, she earned a communications degree from
the University of Michigan, then was hired as a production assistant
at Channel 3. After that, she climbed from writer to field producer to
assistant producer for the six-o'clock show, then six-o'clock producer.
And here she was, at thirty-five, executive producer of Detroit's top-
ranked news station.

And I haven't had sex in six months. I deserve more than this. I deserve love and passion. A divorce. And a lover. Someone to fill this awful ache and emptiness inside me.

As she puckered and spread on lipstick, a shade called Burgundy Passion, she heard the deep rumble of the garage door. Charles. The clock said 8:55.

Shari lit a cigarette, then noticed gray smoke already spiraling from the ashtray on the vanity. She snubbed out the old one.

A few minutes later she heard Charles deposit his briefcase in the den down the hall. As he entered the bedroom, Shari watched him in the vanity mirror, her nerves jingling. Golf. He was wearing a pink polo shirt with yellow and brown plaid shorts, a red sweater over his shoulders, and a brown and gold striped visor.

What a dork. Did he get dressed in the dark? No, not the pink socks, too.

Shari bit her lip to stifle laughter. How could a man who wore thousand-dollar suits and ordered shoes from Italy walk into the exclusive Oakland Hills Country Club looking like a melted banana split?

He did not even glance at her as he stormed to the television and turned it off. "There's nothing I hate more than a blaring TV," he snapped. "You aren't even watching it. Don't you get enough of that crap at work?"

Shari's neck muscles tensed.

"Hello to you, too," she said without facing him. She wiped a lipstick smudge at the corner of her mouth. "You do remember our dinner plans with Jenn and John, don't you?"

Charles sat on the bed and leaned down to remove his shoes. "Damn. No, I forgot. Our golf outing was today. That heat and humidity really zapped me. I'm beat."

Shari applied another coat of lipstick. "Our reservations are at nine-thirty. As in a half hour from now. I'm going. And John is your friend, so if you don't want me to embarrass you by telling him and Jenn that you forgot and don't feel like coming, then the shower is right through there."

Without turning around, she pointed to the bathroom door near her vanity. "By the way, you could have called me at work today to tell me you had your golf outing. Why wasn't I invited to the wives' luncheon this year?"

Charles snatched off his visor, raising damp clumps of thin, wheat-colored hair. He spun around and glared. His down-turned, widish nose was sunburned, his lips twisted with annoyance.

"Because," he said, "every other year you're always too busy working to come to the luncheon or the outing and too many other things. Why waste my breath telling you when I know you won't show up?"

Shari charged at him. "You've been neglecting a lot of things around here lately, Charles," she shouted down at him. "You don't talk to me unless it's to complain. You don't call me at work. You don't even fuck me anymore."

Charles stood and leaned toward her. "Maybe if you didn't taste like an ashtray, I'd want to. And if you weren't such a smokestack, maybe you wouldn't have fumigated your ovaries and charbroiled your uterus."

What a shit-head.

Shari huffed. "Now I know you only married me for my womb. But you know what? I'm glad I can't have kids with you, Charles. I wouldn't want to wake up one day and realize how much I despise you, only to be stuck with you for the kids' sake. We know too many people like that."

Charles scowled.

"What happened to us?" Shari asked softly. "One minute we're madly in love, then I wake up one day and realize you're never in the same room with me. And when you do come around, you look constipated. Why did you stop loving me?"

Charles sighed, running a hand through his hair. "I don't know, Shari. I've been wondering the same thing myself. And frankly, I'm too tired to care right now." He plodded toward the bathroom.

Shari wanted to kick him. "That's it? That's your answer?"

He stopped at the bathroom door, his hooded eyes blank and

dull. "Yes, Shari. That's my answer. I'm too tired to care about our marriage right now. Maybe we can talk about it tomorrow."

Shari grabbed the open lipstick tube from the vanity and threw it. A burgundy line stained his shirt. Then, fueled by rage, she pelted him with a bottle of foundation, a comb, and her gold lighter.

"You're such a prick!" she shouted.

Charles watched her calmly. He ignored the broken glass and beige foundation pooling at his feet.

"You've lost it, Shari," he said flatly. "You've got problems."

"No, you're my problem. You're my only problem in life."

"You need help," Charles said. He closed the door and turned on the shower.

Shari's body quaked. Plunking into the vanity chair, she studied herself in the mirror. Tears brimmed in her bloodshot eyes. When Charles's emotionless face flashed in her mind, she sobbed.

After a few moments, she dabbed her face with tissues and reapplied her makeup. Her body ached to feel a man, a perpetual erection ravishing her hungry flesh. Her nipples stiffened, two points under her black dress.

I'm going to get a divorce and find a lover. And probably not in that order.

CHAPTER 13

Billy Joe Pulaski's eyes glowed with malice as his father described how they would kill Taylor James.

"That's right, with your hands," Rocky said. "You're going to rip her limbs apart, one by one. Make her suffer a bloody, painful death."

Billy Joe nodded. "Yeah. I shoulda done that a long time ago. I hate that bitch. Always have."

Rocky held his son's hands. "It'll avenge you and me and Jess and all of our white comrades, and it'll galvanize the movement. It'll send a message to the Jew-controlled media, the government, and every law-enforcement bully out there that they shouldn't mess with us."

"Yeah," Billy Joe said. "But, Dad, what if we get caught? I ain't spendin' the rest of my life in prison with gorillas like those guys over there. I ain't doin' it, Dad. Eighteen months almost did me in. I don't know how you lasted two years."

Rocky's eye began twitching again. "Frickin' sissy. Sometimes I think your sister Suzette came back to life and took over your mind."

Billy Joe stuck out his jaw and looked away, staring through the bars toward an adjacent cell holding a dozen skinheads.

Rocky sighed, exasperated. Billy Joe had never recovered from Loretta's death. But if she had not been so mouthy, maybe she would still be alive. Every detail of that night twenty-three years ago was clear as a glass of vodka in Rocky's mind.

Like Hitler, he made a habit of staying up until three or four in the morning, reading and talking with comrades about the revolution. But on that particular night, he had been drinking and playing cards at the local bar before he climbed into bed with Loretta in the small, wood-frame house on Ryan Road in Detroit. He needed sexual satisfaction, but Loretta, asleep in a flannel nightgown, was not in the mood. She never had been, since Suzette was born.

"Don't come in here drunk tryin' to screw me after you been out gamblin' and whorin' around," Loretta shouted as she scrambled out of bed.

"Get back here and give me what I need."

"No!" Loretta darted into the hallway where five-year-old Billy Joe, in Spiderman pajamas, stood outside his bedroom, his blue eyes enormous with terror. She ran into Billy Joe's bedroom, grabbed the baby, then clutched Billy Joe's hand.

"C'mon, Billy Joe, we're goin' to Grandma's," she said, heading toward the wooden staircase in her nightgown.

"You're not going anywhere but back to bed, Loretta." Rocky grabbed her thin arm. "Billy Joe, go back to bed."

Billy Joe stared up at his mother, whose stringy brown hair flew as she screamed and slapped his father. The red-faced baby wailed at a deafening pitch.

"Get the fuck back in the bed and give me what I want," Rocky shouted.

"No! I ain't your whore!" Loretta screamed, pulling back. "Don't hit me when I got the baby! I'm leavin' you. C'mon, Billy Joe. Come with Mama."

Red-hot anger surging through him, Rocky lunged at Loretta. He spun her around and shook her. Then, as if in slow motion, he watched in horror as the baby flew from her arms and bounced down the staircase like a basketball. In a split second, Loretta thudded down the steps. She landed in a grotesque heap atop Suzette.

"Mama! Mama!" Billy Joe shrieked, running down the stairs. He looked up at Rocky with wild eyes. "You killed my mama!"

No, she brought it on herself, being so careless at the top of the stair-case.

Rocky called an ambulance, which arrived with a young police officer named John Scarlin, whom Rocky had met at one of the white separatist meetings he frequented with his late father's colleagues. At the most recent meeting, Scarlin had seemed to sympathize with Rocky and some of his co-workers at the auto plant who were angry that they had suddenly gotten a Negro foreman.

Lucky for him, because Scarlin made sure the death report said that Loretta Pulaski and six-month-old Suzette Pulaski had died accidentally when Loretta slipped during a feeding.

But after that, Billy Joe became a terror. He kicked cats and blew up frogs with firecrackers. He threw bricks through garage windows. He cussed at Rocky's steady stream of girlfriends. One day he set fire to his schoolbooks. And he was always getting in trouble at school for fighting and disobeying teachers.

In tenth grade, after they had lived in the country for five years, he quit school. He was arrested for petty crimes and developed a fondness for marijuana and whiskey. At eighteen Billy Joe finally calmed down. When Rocky founded the White Power Alliance, Billy Joe sunk all of his energy and fury into its mission, funneling his anger toward minorities and women. Soon afterward, Billy Joe traveled to Germany to study Nazi doctrine, living in a compound with neo-Nazis in Berlin.

Still, Billy Joe displayed despicable cowardice. Perhaps the murder of Taylor James would bolster his valor. Rocky fingered the Iron Cross—the medal Hitler received after his bravery in the Bavarian Sixteenth Regiment during World War I—that he always wore around his neck, as he scrutinized his only living child.

"It smells like a fuckin' zoo in here," Billy Joe said. "Shit, I don't know why they arrested us. We were just actin' in self-defense."

"You're right, son, but our day of Aryan dominance will come," Rocky said. "Just wait until the revolution when we—"

"Hey, who the fuck are you," a Negro yelled from the back of the cell, "commander of the honky army with all that camouflage?"

Those degenerates don't deserve the breath it would take for my response.

Rocky faced him. "And if I am?"

"You mothafuckas got a lotta nerve comin' up in here with them swastika tattoos on your arms an' shit," said the man, who was short but muscular in blue jeans and a mesh T-shirt.

"Yeah, they sho do," another man said. "Look at the young one's shirt. What kinda bullshit is the White Power Alliance?"

"Sick-ass white boys!" a man said as they formed a semicircle behind the muscular man and glared at Rocky and Billy Joe.

"Shut up!" Rocky shouted, waving his hand to discharge the men from his sight.

But the man in mesh punched Rocky's stomach. He clenched his teeth as pain radiated through his gut.

Billy Joe spun to face the bars. "Guards! Guards! They hit my dad! Get over here! Help!"

The next few moments were a painful blur as the man pummeled Rocky nonstop. Compact fists hammered his abdomen, his chest, his arms. Rocky tried to raise his arms to protect his face, but the man punched him in the jaw. The back of his head slammed against the metal bars.

Yes, give me more pain. It only prepares me for revolution. Raises my threshold. I don't feel a thing.

Then Rocky pummeled the Negro until he retreated.

"Guards!" Billy Joe sounded like a whining girl.

Rocky heard thuds and grunts coming from his right, where Billy Joe stood.

The room spun. The man in front of Rocky was a glistening black blur. Rocky laughed, ignoring the throbbing pain.

"All you men are soldiers in our revolution, but you're too ignorant to know it," Rocky said.

"What did you say, mothafucka?"

"I said all you men in here for black-on-black crime are working for our Aryan cause. You shoot each other, get addicted to drugs, have babies that don't amount to shit in life. Then you end up in prison. I know, I've been there."

The man who had punched him said, "I know I ain't hearin' you right."

"You don't want to hear me," Rocky said. "You're destroying your own race, leaving less work for the White Power Alliance and our revolution. So I say, good riddance. White power!" Rocky saluted Hitler style.

"Sick-ass honky!" a man shouted.

"Mothafucka, I know you got a death wish now!" The man buried his fist in Rocky's thick gut.

"Uuugghh!" Rocky doubled over.

"Guards! Help us!" Billy Joe shouted.

A sheriff's deputy sprinted to the cell. "What's going on here?"

"These baboons are beatin' us up, me and my dad," Billy Joe said.

"Excuse me?" the officer asked. "We got no place else to put you guys. So get along." The guard walked away.

"No, you gotta get us out of here!" Billy Joe shouted after them. He looked back at the black men, then toward the guards. He shook the bars. "Get us outta here!"

Rocky grabbed the back of his son's shirt. "Billy Joe, shut the fuck up. You sound like a bitch in a hissy fit."

The black men clustered in the corner while Rocky and Billy Joe stood near the bars. Rocky pursed his lips. "Billy Joe, this is a revolution. I'll be führer one day, and you'll succeed me. But not if you act like a faggot."

"I'm sorry, Dad. I get scared sometimes, ya know? Guys like them scare the shit outta me."

Rocky glared at Billy Joe. "Don't give those subhuman animals the satisfaction of knowing you're scared. You're a white man, superior to them in every way."

Billy Joe stared back with frightened eyes. "Okay, Dad."

"Führer Pulaski."

Scarlin and Jess appeared outside the cell.

"You come to let us out?" Billy Joe asked loudly.

Alarm filled Jess's eyes. "Rocky, what happened to your face?" She turned to Scarlin. "How can they let this happen?"

"Jess, relax." He held her hand through the bars.

"Führer Pulaski, I'm doing what I can to get the prosecutor to lower the charges from assault with intent to do great bodily harm to a lesser assault-and-battery charge," Scarlin said.

Scarlin's thin face was taut with concern. "I'm sorry you men got arrested. I think the nigger police chief was tryin' to get good PR with all them damn reporters. So he tries to make himself look good by lockin' you guys up. I can't stand that cocksucker."

"And the other comrades in jail?" Rocky asked.

"I'll do what I can before court tomorrow," Scarlin said, his eyes sharp and serious.

"Thank you, comrade," Rocky said. "We'll remember how you helped white brothers in need."

"White power," Scarlin answered. He stepped away.

Rocky held Jess's hand through the bars, feeling warm inside as she gazed at him. "Thanks for coming, Jess."

"This is wrong," she said. "You men were acting in self-defense."

"I know," Rocky said. "This is just part of the revolution. We'll be out tomorrow with a plan. I've made Billy Joe the mongrel's assassin."

"Rocky, you know I've been itchin' to hurt that bitch," Jess said.

"You can help out, but Billy Joe gets center stage."

"When I saw her today I coulda spit bullets," Jess said.

Rocky stroked her cheek. "Relax, Jess. Her day of damnation is near."

CHAPTER 14

Julian DuPont shoveled the last morsels of collard greens and smothered pork chops into his mouth, scraping a silver fork across china for the remaining drops of gravy.

"I'm about to burst," he said, blowing out his cheeks. Limbs heavy and loose, he stretched bare feet under the lace-topped table and yawned.

A CD of Chopin's Piano Concerto no. 2 played softly, lulling Julian. Also mellowing him were the scents of home cooking and the warmth inside the DuPonts' white-shuttered Georgian Colonial in Detroit's exclusive Palmer Woods neighborhood. At the head of the long table in the gold-draped, paneled dining room, François DuPont rested a hand on his slightly rounded stomach.

"I am stuffed too," he said, his French accent still thick after thirty years in America. "Pork chops and gravy are a treat these days. Your *maman* feeds me salad, fowl, and fish when I'm craving *du foie gras, du brie, et du quiche.*"

"Doctor's orders," his mother said.

Julian watched the brightness fade from her dark eyes. The silver streaks in her black hair, swept into an elegant roll, and her cream silk ensemble, complemented her skin, which was as unblemished and smooth as polished mahogany. Julian admired his mother's ageless beauty in the chandelier's glow.

"François, I love you too much to let you have your way with cholesterol and cigarettes," she said. "That's what got you sick in the first place."

François's eyes averted to his plate.

A pang of sorrow struck Julian. His father's once sturdy shoulders appeared thin, and a sickly pallor dulled his once robust complexion. Papa was sixty now, and though he had recovered quickly from the heart attack, doctors said he would never recapture his previous vitality. They said another heart attack could come at any time, thus forcing Papa to retire after decades with Ford Motor Company as an engineer. Sudden death seemed too real a possibility.

Julian closed his eyes to obliterate the image of Papa in a casket. *I've been selfish and cruel to stay away.*

"Papa, I'm sorry I was gone so long," Julian said. "From here on out, I plan to spend a lot of time with both of you."

Papa's eyes lit up. "Julian, your *maman* and I are proud of you. I want nothing more than having my son home."

Julian shuddered with emotion.

Papa smiled, then winked at Mom.

"We're thrilled about your decision, baby," she said.

"Me too," Julian said. "Today went well. And Philip said—"

Mom rolled her eyes. "I'm sorry, Julian, but I don't like him. I'm catering Taylor's shower, but only because her mother is my best friend. Philip gave me the same bad feeling as this hustling numbers man named Slim who knew my father."

Papa threw his napkin on the table. *"Philip, il est serpent. Taylor, elle est angélique. Ce mariage est horrible."*

"I agree, Papa," Julian said. His father always spoke French when angry. "Philip will marry Taylor over my dead body."

His mother folded the linen over a basket of petites baguettes. "Julian, you're not a boy beating up the playground bullies anymore," she said. "Don't let that machismo of yours make you do anything foolish. Did you see her today?"

Taylor's face, dazed from his sudden kiss, appeared in his mind. There was torment in her eyes, fury in her heaving chest. And Philip's diamond on her hand. Julian dug his toes into the Oriental rug.

"Yes. I talked to her. She told me to shove it."

His mother coughed on her Chardonnay, laughing. "Lord, that child sure has changed."

"I know," Julian said.

Papa shook his head. *"La guillotine pour Rocky et Billy Joe Pulaski."*

"That boy was a monster," Janice said. "And for the principal to suspend you all those times, when you were protecting Taylor. Thank goodness Country Day didn't allow that kind of nonsense."

Julian closed his eyes. Taylor's puffy, red face and black-splattered hair flashed in his mind. That awful day in fifth grade, all he could do was embrace her and soothe her cries, especially when her mother cut off most of her hair because the black stains would not wash out.

"I want to protect her now at all costs," Julian said. "You don't know how I wanted to shove my fist down Pulaski's throat today."

"Her mother was frantic when we talked earlier," Janice said. "So what else did Taylor say?"

"That she's marrying Philip and, basically, she hates me," Julian said. "But I can't let her. I know she still has feelings for me. I saw it in her eyes."

Mom sipped her wine. "I'm cheering for you, baby, but as a woman, I have to say you're a day late and a dollar short. You can't break the girl's heart, then show up before her wedding for a re-union."

Julian spread clammy hands over his jeans.

"*Oui,* yes he can," Papa said. "If it's true love."

François gazed tenderly at Janice. "Her family did not like me, but I didn't care. They were thinking I was a wild Frenchman who wanted to bring their daughter to the red-light district in Paris."

Mom blushed. "Oh, Daddy only said that because he was scared, François. He didn't really think you were a pimp."

Julian chuckled.

"I can still see the look on Daddy's face," Janice said. "I come home after my year in Paris and announce I'm in love with a French-man. He and Mama about fell out. Especially when François trans-ferred to the University of Michigan to be with me.

"I can hear Daddy now," she said, lowering her voice. " 'Girl, I didn't work all these years in the plant to pay for college, to have you turn around and be some Frenchman's washerwoman.' "

François laughed. "Then comes your brother to threaten me."

Julian chuckled. "But even though Granddad said he'd stop pay-ing your tuition—"

"And banned François from the house," Janice added.

"—you still got married," Julian said. "Love won."

His mother sighed. "But, baby, it's different. You broke up with Taylor."

Julian's cheeks burned. Decade-old images—the nearly nude girls in his apartment, Taylor's horrified face—flashed through his mind. He'd been so mean, so coldhearted. "You're right, Mom, it's all my fault. No wonder Taylor hates me."

"But you were so in love, *mon fils,* laughing all the time," Papa said softly. "I'll never forget that one night," he chuckled. "During your senior year. I came downstairs for a glass of milk, and there you were. You and Taylor, asleep by the fireplace. Such a precious sight, all cuddled up together."

Mom smiled.

Julian looked down, embarrassed. That was the night he and

Taylor had seen Prince's Purple Rain concert at Joe Louis Arena. They came home, drank wine, and made love by firelight while his parents slept.

At the time, sex in his parents' house did not seem disrespectful. Taylor and Julian had been spending the night at each other's houses for as long as they could remember. When they reached puberty, their parents allowed weekly sleep-overs to continue. At sixteen when they first made love, they realized how fortunate they were to have such liberal parents. And with hormones electrifying his growing body, Julian could never get enough of Taylor's long legs, caressing hands, and hot, eager mouth.

"My baby boy," Mom teased. "What in the world is on your mind? If you could see your face!"

Julian frowned. "We had the perfect relationship until I ruined it."

"But why?" Papa asked.

"I guess when I got to L.A., I saw all the women. They liked me, I was curious about them, and I lost sight of how special Taylor was. Is."

"So you dated other women, big deal," Mom said. "You don't think, pretty as Taylor is, men didn't notice her in New York?"

Julian bristled at the thought of other men kissing Taylor. Especially Philip. But Julian could not reveal to his parents the real reason that he had exiled Taylor from his heart.

"It's sure stumped us all these years," Mom said, frowning. "But Lord knows, I'm glad you didn't marry that girl in California."

François sighed and said, "Oh no. Big mistake. I want our grand-children to have triple-digit IQs. Impossible with that girl."

Julian shook his head, wondering why he ever wanted to marry Brooke Jacob. They had met on Philip's yacht two years ago, and her thong bikini and request that he rub coconut oil on her curves had pushed Julian's lust into overdrive. Then she ensnared him with temptress wiles: fixing breakfast wearing only a tiny apron, picking him up from the studio in a limousine wearing only a mink coat. A San Diego native, Brooke had honey hair, long legs, and sun-kissed skin, making her the quintessential California blonde.

At first Julian had been impressed by Brooke's hard work—daily acting classes and countless auditions. But then she demanded that he use his position at *Entertainment Exclusive* to introduce her to producers and casting directors, and even do a feature story about their engagement to jump-start her acting career. Julian's refusal provoked in Brooke screaming tantrums. Then, on several occasions, he caught her vomiting in his bathroom after dinner. She said it kept her thin, but he, disgusted, suggested bulimia counseling. Later she asked for a clothing allowance. Then he discovered that her silicone breasts were a gift from a married boyfriend, who was still financing her acting lessons in exchange for sex.

And the few flippant comments Brooke made about race revealed her cluelessness about his identity as a half-black, half-French man in a polarized city. Brooke was in love with Julian DuPont the TV star, not the man who had started a basketball camp and literacy program in South Central.

"Why do you spend your Saturdays slumming with those ghetto thugs when we could be shopping or sailing?" she snapped one morning. "People don't even think of you as black. You're above that because you're famous."

"Well, I am black and I don't care what people think," Julian said.

That night over lobster at Gladstone's, he said, "Brooke, I don't want to marry you."

She dropped her engagement ring in his drawn butter and stormed away, but she was at his doorstep the next day, begging him to take her back. He refused, but she'd been calling and coming over unannounced ever since.

Now, at his parents' dining room table, Julian shook his head. "Are you disappointed in me?"

"No," his mother said. "Everyone makes mistakes. Fortunately for you, yours aren't permanent. It's not too late for a second chance with Taylor. But we sure have been confused all these years about what happened between you two."

Julian loved his mother's dark eyes, the way they demanded an answer but sensed his uneasiness and pain.

"It's a grand mystery to me, too," Papa said.

"And don't tell me," Mom said, "that when you got to California, race was no longer an issue for you, baby. I've been a black woman in America long enough to know that no matter how good you are at what you do, there are folks out there who'll try to hold you back. If I can say anything good about Philip Carter, it's that he's taken care of my child."

"*Oui,*" Papa said.

Julian ran damp palms over his legs. The story, the Wilbur Franklin incident, perched on the tip of his tongue.

"I'm sorry, Mom, Papa, I'm too ashamed to explain why we broke up."

"Ashamed?" Mom walked around the table. A cloud of the sweet perfume she'd worn all his life enveloped him as she caressed his tense shoulders. "Baby, we love you more than you know. Don't think you can't talk to us."

Julian bit his lower lip as a torrent of emotions crashed through him. Closing his eyes, he savored his mother's voice and touch. He swallowed the aching lump in his throat.

"I'm sorry. Maybe someday I'll tell you. Let's just say that I hurt Taylor for my own selfish reasons, and now I can't think about anything but winning her back."

Julian stared blankly at the silver candlesticks on the table. "I have to. If Channel Three doesn't hire me, I'll go to Channel Five. After all my years on national TV, somebody in Detroit has got to give me a job."

His mother massaged his neck. "Julian, baby, you know we're always here for you."

"I know, Mom."

"And don't give up on Taylor," Papa said. "Three weeks till the wedding. That's long enough for a DuPont man to capture a woman's heart."

Julian stood and kissed his mother's cheek. He put his hand on his father's shoulder. "Thanks Mom, Papa. I need to be alone. Excuse me."

Mom smiled. "Can I tempt you with my cherry cobbler? I baked it just for you. A nice big piece, with ice cream and milk. You'll sleep like a baby."

"Maybe later," he said. Restless with the sense that he was flailing in an emotional abyss, Julian walked through the spacious foyer to the back hallway and into the family room.

Get a fuckin' grip on yourself, man.

Julian passed the double fieldstone fireplace where he and Taylor had made love countless times. He glanced at the plush carpeting, then the blue afghan and the sectional's big pillows that they would use to construct a fireside love nest. He dashed into the game room on the other side of the fireplace.

Hanging his head, he pressed his palms on the jukebox, whose flashing red, yellow, and orange lights glowed eerily. A blue glow seeped through the windows from the underwater lights in the in-ground swimming pool.

The names of the Motown hits in the jukebox's lighted selection box mirrored his thoughts. He set it on auto-mix, then flipped on the lights.

Across the room at the bar, he remembered himself as a child, standing on a box of records, preparing root beer floats for himself and Taylor, who sat on a red vinyl and chrome stool. Then he saw them competing on the two pinball machines, or playing hours of Scrabble at the game table near the shelves of board games. Through the windows, he saw himself chasing her, giggling, across the patio and into the kidney-shaped pool.

As the music played, Julian racked the balls on the pool table and chalked his cue. That reminded him of Taylor's Diana Ross imitation. In his mother's minidress, which hung to her ankles, platforms, and a huge black wig, Taylor used the shortest cue as a microphone. She danced around the room belting out, "Someday we'll be together . . ."

Julian's Michael Jackson imitations, with a specialty of "Rockin' Robin," were just as hilarious.

He positioned the cue ball, struck it, and watched the colorful balls scatter across green felt. The orange ball fell into the corner pocket, drawing his attention to the nearby glass case. It held a sequined dress once worn by one of the Supremes, a harmonica played by Little Stevie Wonder, and a scarf that Marvin Gaye autographed for Mom at a concert back in the sixties.

His parents were always going to auctions for Motown memorabilia. One of Julian's favorites was the framed black-and-white photograph of his parents in front of the Fox Theater marquee that said MOTOWN REVUE. Julian stepped closer, smiling at his parents' giddy-in-love expressions. Papa, in his black beret, goatee, and shoulder-length brown hair, had his arm around Mom, wearing fake eyelashes, a jet black bouffant, and white patent leather boots.

The next picture frame held six tickets and—

Julian's heart skipped a beat. He fixed on an enlarged picture of the DuPont and James families at the Jackson 5 concert at Cobo Hall. The corner of the picture said 1971. In it, he and Taylor, then four, balanced on their fathers' shoulders. Flanking them were their smiling mothers in sunflower minidresses and platforms.

What a bunch. A black man, a white man, a white woman, a black woman, a brown little boy, and a white little girl. No wonder they drew stares and whispers in restaurants, stores, and everywhere else. But that did not matter. The happy aura glowing around the families in the picture was a sort of emotional armor against the disapproving world.

Julian smiled at his own round, happy face and the way his father was looking up and holding his little hands out at his sides. Taylor's wild halo of blond curls and those laughing eyes were adorable. Her chubby little legs draped Uncle Ramsey's chest as he gently gripped them with large brown hands.

He chuckled at the next picture. He and Taylor, maybe eight years old, sat in a Corvette at Detroit's annual auto show. Nearby was his senior prom picture. In it he wore a black tuxedo and an ear-to-ear grin. His arm stretched around Taylor—hair flowing over bare shoulders, gazing up at him, looking like a bride in that white gown. A beaming bride.

At the same time, the love-lorn lyrics booming from the jukebox caught his attention.

Julian hurled the pool cue onto the table. He burst through the patio door, paced near the shimmering turquoise water.

She's mine.

CHAPTER 15

Taylor rested her head on Philip's bare chest, listening to his heart-beat.

"It feels so good to just lie here and relax," she said as he stroked her hair. "I can't wait until our honeymoon. I'm going to bring new meaning to the term 'beach bum.' "

"You mean beach bunny," Philip said. "I talked to the keeper at the Maui house today. They finished the pool. You'll love it. Two weeks of just you, me, and servants waiting on us hand and foot."

Taylor tapped him playfully on the chest. "I'm holding you to that, Philip. I want hours and hours of you and me in the sun. No phones, no pagers, no laptop. The whole time on Grand Cayman, you were always on the phone. It was like I only had half of you."

Philip chuckled lustfully. "No chance of that this time. It'll be our private slice of Keawakapu Beach. Paradise for two. I'm going to squeeze kiwis and papayas, let the nectar and pulp drip all over your naked body. Then I'm going to slurp it up and rub against your sweet, sticky flesh."

"You're so naughty," Taylor said.

"I know." Philip laid her on a pillow. Resting on an elbow, he traced her eyebrows, nose, and lips with his index finger. "I love you, Taylor James."

She smiled as warmth spread through her. "I love you, Philip Carter."

Yes, I love Philip. Not Julian. Taylor sighed, looking up at his tender expression. "Finally, relaxation. I feel a million miles away from that horrible race riot this afternoon. It made me feel so bad—"

"I don't know why," Philip said, frowning, "you let it bother you so much. Look at you. You're as white and blond as I am. Nobody would even know you were half black if you didn't talk about it so much. You shouldn't be so obsessed with all that racial shit."

His words scraped across Taylor's raw feelings like steel wool. She sat up.

"Race has been the single most traumatic issue in my life, Philip," she said, tension gripping her muscles. "I've told you about all my problems, like my mean cousins Yvonne and LaTonya, always calling me 'whitey,' locking me in the closet at their birthday party so their friends wouldn't see their white-looking cousin." Taylor remembered the spiteful expressions on her then eight- and nine-year-old cousins' brown faces as they slammed the creaky closet door shut, abandoning her in the musty darkness where they said mice lived.

Taylor closed her eyes to rid herself of the still-disturbing memory. Then she glared at Philip. "Not to mention the Billy Joe Pulaskis of the world. You think that stuff doesn't hurt?"

Philip exhaled loudly.

"And my friend Danielle, she said if she'd gone through all the stuff I did, she'd be in a mental hospital by now," Taylor said. She could still see clearly in her mind the horrified expression on Danielle's face when black classmate Tawanda Johnson screamed racist obscenities at Taylor in a fast-food restaurant after school. Tawanda had been angry that their tenth-grade teacher had chosen Taylor to head the science project that Tawanda had wanted to lead. "And you know I—"

"Enough!" Philip said. "Calm down. I admire that you want to make a difference, Taylor, but you take it too far. Your reports, your exposé, the rally—that's work. Don't bring it home with you."

Taylor scowled. "Oh, so I can bring my police escort home, let them stand outside the door all night, but I can't think about why they're here? Makes a lot of sense, Philip. Thanks for the advice."

"Lie back down," Philip said. "Let me hold you."

Taylor remained sitting up. "No. You just don't understand that I filter everything through black and white, twenty-four seven, and what I see and feel hurts. I've told you that fifty thousand times, but you don't get it. So if you can't appreciate such a fundamental part of me, then maybe marriage is a bad idea."

Philip sat up. "Darling, let's rewind here. Don't get so upset—"

"I am upset."

"I think your racial background is beautiful, darling. You're a golden treasure right out of the good old American melting pot."

Taylor looked at him. *He's just saying that to calm me down.*

Philip growled playfully. "And that black blood makes you a savage tiger in the bedroom."

Nice stereotype, Philip. The mulatto sex kitten. Taylor's cheeks burned with insult as she stared into his smiling eyes. *He'll never understand. He didn't when we met . . . he doesn't now . . . he never will.*

A hot wave of sadness surged through her, filling her eyes with tears.

Taylor darted into the bathroom and slammed the door. In the mirror, her hair was a yellow cloud around bloodshot eyes. She splashed cold water on her face, easing the same sting from Philip's words and manner that she had endured during their first lunch date three years ago.

He had taken her to the exclusive Whitney restaurant to congratulate her on the White Power Alliance exposé, which had recently aired locally and nationally. When she told him it was her life mission to bring racial unity and understanding to Americans through her television reporting, he replied, "It's good to have a gimmick. It helps you stand out from the pack. And believe me, I meet journalists all over the country, but none have gimmicks as catchy as yours."

He deepened his voice to imitate a TV anchor: " 'Taylor James, the blond bombshell whose black heritage drives her to weed out racists for the good of society.' That's ingenious self-promotion." Chuckling, he quickly cut and chewed his salmon and julienne vegetables.

Stunned, Taylor felt her cheeks sting with insult. "Mr. Carter—"

"Call my father Mr. Carter. Call me Philip."

"Philip, it's not a gimmick. It comes from my heart."

He smiled. "Of course it does. My commitment to work nonstop, flying all over the country making deals and shaping what Americans watch on TV, comes from my heart, too. So does my lust for gargantuan bonuses at the end of the year when I've made Wolf's stock value skyrocket."

Taylor lost her appetite.

"And it doesn't hurt," he continued, "that you're talented and smart. If you don't mind me saying so, you're the most spellbinding woman I've ever met. Wholesome yet ballsy. I like that."

Taylor regretted that she had accepted his lunch invitation. Prior to that day, she had known of him only through the company newsletter and references to him by Shari. After lunch, in the limousine en route to Channel 3, Philip said, "Let me be the first to say you're a superstar in the making."

Taylor refrained from answering, "You're a real jerk." She declined subsequent invitations, but his persistence, coupled with Shari's advice that Taylor should not snub the man who could promote her to the network, made her accept several lunch and dinner invitations. Then Taylor began seeing his softer side—spending time with inner-city kids in the journalism programs he sponsored, and talking lovingly about his own children and mother. At the same time, Philip charmed Taylor, complimenting her work and dazzling her with promises of a phenomenal career at Wolf.

Several months later, she and her parents flew in his jet to New York to Wolf headquarters, where Taylor, at twenty-five, was named the network's youngest ever Journalist of the Year. That night inspired an epiphany for her. First, standing onstage before applauding network executives, a few Columbia professors, and her proud parents, with a five-thousand-dollar check and plaque, Taylor realized that she was pioneering new journalistic territory, and that a vast horizon, in Detroit and at the network, awaited her exploration. Second, as she stood under the lights, beaming with pride and appreciation for the award, she longed for Julian to share her exhilaration. But a soft voice inside her whispered, *Let him go. Enjoy your success, even if you're alone.*

As if he had heard that voice, Philip seized Taylor's newly liberated heart. After the banquet, he took her and her parents in his limousine to a private nighttime visit to the top of the Empire State Building, which made Taylor feel as if she were literally floating above a sparkling world. Then Philip invited Taylor to his spectacular apartment, where, on the terrace overlooking Central Park and Manhattan's lighted skyscrapers, he toasted her with champagne. Tipsy and exuberant, Taylor welcomed his hungry kisses and the ensuing hours of exquisite lovemaking. After so many lonely nights, yearning for a man who never came, Taylor loved being in Philip's arms, melting under his kisses, trembling with mind-numbing ecstasy.

But the fantasy ended in the morning, when dirtiness and guilt consumed her. *I sinned. I slept with a married man. And I think I'm falling in love with him.*

Later, over fruit and bagels on the terrace, she said, "I can't do this, Philip. You're married, and even if you weren't, a relationship with you would look like I'm prostituting myself for my career."

Philip, in a monogrammed robe, tousled hair, and with a rosy, passion-swept glow on his cheeks, gazed at her tenderly. "Then I'll divorce my wife. We're not in love anymore. My lawyers say now is as good a time as any."

Taylor was dumbstruck. "Really?"

"Yes, Taylor. I've been happier with you over the past months than I've been in years. You make me feel young again. I knew the minute I saw you that I had to have you."

Taylor stiffened. "I'm not a car or your latest TV station. I'm a woman with important work to do."

Philip smiled. "I know. You're one in a million." He caressed her hand on the table. "I'm in love with you, Taylor, and you light up when we're together, so don't tell me you don't have feelings for me."

She stared into his eyes, feeling light-headed with infatuation.

"Until my divorce is final," he said, "we'll be discreet. You can visit my apartment in Detroit. I'll move out of the Bel Air house. And listen to me. I don't think you slept with me to get ahead. I pursued you, and you found me irresistible."

Taylor smiled. "And so humble."

"Besides," he said, "with my schedule, I'm in Detroit seven days a month, tops. But I want to be with you and only you. I can make your dreams come true."

And he did just that—trips to Paris, London, and Monte Carlo, shopping, eating at the best restaurants, taking in countless Broadway shows. But when it came to one of the most important, sensitive issues in Taylor's life, Philip repeatedly mangled her emotions. Tonight was just one of too many similar conversations.

"No, Andrea, I don't give a rat's ass about your credit-card bills," Philip said into the phone.

Taylor rolled her eyes. *His ex-wife. One more thing to irritate me tonight. What a witch.* She remembered her single encounter with Andrea at a party at the Hollywood Hills mansion.

"You're nothing but the latest prize in Philip's stable of whores," Andrea had spat. Framed by the blue glow of the swimming pool in the background, her flame red hair had formed an eerie silhouette from which blazed spiteful eyes.

Taylor had glanced at the gorgeous view of the sparkling city below, then smiled at Andrea. "Nice meeting you, too," Taylor had said, then laced her arm through Philip's as he talked business with colleagues.

Now Andrea was merely an annoying nag who telephoned at all hours to complain and harass Philip about everything from the Akita's diet to their children's grades.

"Your alimony is more than sufficient already," Philip said. He glanced up at Taylor, who was setting the alarm clock. "Taylor, darling, are you all right?"

Then, through the phone, Taylor heard Andrea scream.

Taylor shook her head. *That woman is so disturbed.*

Philip hung up, then embraced Taylor from behind. He wrapped his arms around her waist and rested his chin on her shoulder.

Taylor ignored him, staring through the huge windows at the luxury boats bobbing in the marina twenty-nine stories below. A U.S. Coast Guard boat cut through the Detroit River, forming a wake that glowed lavender in the moonlight. Across the river in Windsor, Canada, the red neon CASINO sign flashed as a large luxury cruiser with several couples on deck floated toward the lighted arches of the Ambassador Bridge.

"I'm sorry, darling," Philip said. "But you need to let go of this fantasy of being America's race martyr. And another thing—you're not doing any more dangerous work. I'm talking about investigations, stories that require police protection. It's too risky."

No, God, please tell me he didn't just say that.

Taylor spun around, anger hissing through her like steam.

"Let go? Philip, dammit, I do what I do so that other little girls and boys don't have to face all the horror that I did. From now on, we're not talking about this subject. And I'll cover any stories I please."

Aggravation glinted in Philip's eyes in the dim light. "Let's go to bed. Tomorrow I'm going to Kansas City, then to L.A., and I won't be back until Friday. So I want you in my arms now. All night."

Taylor climbed into bed and lay next to Philip. As he stroked her hair, she hoped that he could not hear her hammering heart.

I can't believe what he said. If marrying him means he'll tell me what stories I can and cannot cover, then I'd rather be alone. But no, I wouldn't have to be alone—Julian wants me. No, I have too much anger and distrust to ever get back with him.

Taylor craved sleep, but when she closed her eyes, she saw images of the rally—bloody Lloyd Pryor, skinheads kicking and punching people, Rocky's glare, Julian's pleading eyes. And she repeatedly heard his voice, in her mind, saying, "White Chocolate," the nickname he had given her one Easter when they were very young, eating white chocolate bunnies. "This is like you," he had said. "Chocolate, but it's white. And sweet."

For the past six hours, Taylor had replayed his stolen kiss in her thoughts countless times, which only provoked wicked pangs of guilt and curiosity.

"So what'd you think of DuPont?" Philip asked.

Taylor's eyes flew open. *Do I look that guilty? It's probably written all over my face—I kissed another man tonight and enjoyed it. This is so bad.*

"What?" she asked.

"Julian DuPont," Philip said. "I went to the newsroom to see you, and that cute Asian chick said you went to the cafeteria with DuPont. So what'd you think of him?"

Oh my God, what if Julian told Philip about our past? "Uh . . . I didn't get to talk to him much, and I haven't seen his work. All I know is he's famous for entertainment news. I don't know how that would translate if he were talking about the murder du jour on the six-o'clock news."

"So you weren't impressed?"

"I have no opinion," Taylor said. "All I can say is, it would be good to have a person of color at the anchor desk."

"And?"

"Shari said he's sharp," she said.

"DuPont is my buddy," Philip said. "With his looks and talent, he's a shoo-in at Channel Three."

Taylor's chest constricted. Clammy sweat glued her nightgown to her skin. *No . . . I'll have to see Julian every day—as Philip's wife.*

CHAPTER 16

Philip hurled his fountain pen onto the black marble table.

"Eject! She looks like a goddamn horse. This is a morning news show, not *Tales from the Crypt*. What are you trying to do, William, scare the shit out of our viewers?"

He glared at William, standing red-faced next to a tape deck and the five-foot television screen in the Channel 3 conference room. *Dammit, if I wasn't around to tell him what to do, Channel 3 would go to hell in a handbasket. Even Shari has more balls than this joker.*

"Give her a chance," William said. "She's very talented. Mindy Shane, an anchor in Fayetteville, Arkansas."

Philip shook his head. "Even if she's the next Barbara Walters, she needs time in a bigger market before she's ready for Detroit. And no broad that ugly will ever disgrace a Wolf newscast. Show me the next tape."

Philip retrieved his gold monogrammed pen, then leaned back in the silver and black leather chair.

William studied the label on the beige, palm-sized videotape case as the tape began to play. "This is Julie Shrinkermeyer."

A geyser of anger shot through Philip.

"Tell her to change her name and visit Jenny Craig," he said. "Then maybe we'll consider her. William, what the fuck are you thinking about? This morning show has to set the standard for the network. Only the best and brightest need apply. Show me another dud and you're out on your ass."

Tense-faced, William slammed another tape into the VCR. "Joyce Roark, a reporter in Seattle. She's been doing a morning show for two years."

Philip watched for a moment. "She makes the cut. Next."

William played another résumé tape of an African-American woman with shoulder-length hair and a bright smile.

"Hailey Washburn, a Detroiter. She's worked in Dallas for five years."

"Great voice," Philip said. "Sounds intelligent. Put Hailey Washburn and Joyce Roark in the 'maybe' pile. And do some more recruiting. This business is in sorry shape if this is the best you can find. Now show me the male candidates."

"Bobby Yoon," William said. "Grew up in Southfield. He's an anchor in Pittsburgh."

"Personable," Philip said. "A face viewers might like to see when they sip coffee in the morning. Keep him in the maybe pile, too. What's with the ugly smirk, William?"

William removed his silver-framed glasses. "Philip," he said angrily, "I don't like your tone. I'm not a PA. I'm the news director and I deserve some respect." He turned away and inserted another tape.

Philip crossed his arms. "I'm senior vice president of this network and I'll use whatever goddamn tone I want. Push play already."

William's complexion turned a shade closer to his gray Caesaresque haircut. He faced the screen, his jaw muscle flexing as if he were clenching his teeth.

On the screen, a young blond male appeared, doing a stand-up in front of a city hall.

"And who's this?" Philip asked.

"Randy Mitchner, a reporter in St. Louis."

"He makes the cut," Philip said. "Put him and Yoon on the maybe list. I've seen enough. I don't care if you have to crawl into every newsroom in America. Find me some good talent for this show, pal, or you'll be wishin' you'd never seen a TV set before."

"Last week at our board of directors meeting," Philip said, glancing across the table at William, "we heard the results of a poll that showed what Americans want from television news. I suggest you take notes."

William poised a pen over a notepad.

"First, the poll showed that we need more news-you-can-use," Philip said. "Health stories, safety tips, ways to save money and time while traveling. And promotional efforts, like helping viewers buy smoke detectors at a discount."

Philip leaned back in his chair. "And, according to the poll, we need a more sensational spin on news stories. Reporting with balls. Stories that reach out and grab viewers.

"Tough, fearless reports that go where no other news channel has dared go before," Philip said. "If it bleeds, it leads. Tears, tragedy, terror. Get the idea?"

William slammed his hand on the table. "We're sensational enough. If you push a story too far, it turns people off. Joe Schmoe relaxing after work in his La-Z-Boy and his wife Susie Q in the kitchen fixing dinner, they don't want to see bad news all the time. They want to see hope. Triumph. Positive stuff once in a while. Get too gory and they turn to reruns of *Wheel of Fortune* and *Gilligan's Island*. I think Shari and I are doing just fine when it comes to sensational news."

Philip stared at William with a bored expression. "Next," Philip said, "Wolf wants more in-depth, documentary-style reports and discussions with live audiences about important issues. Think about quarterly, two-hour-long programs for reports about local issues. Take crime, for example. We could look at how it affects the lives of metro Detroiters, what people are doing about it, so on and so forth."

William nodded. "Now, that idea, I can work with."

"And Wolf wants more viewer involvement," Philip said. "In our jazzy new talk-show studio, we can invite the public in for an evening of debate about important issues. One example might be the White Power Alliance and what the violent rally means for Detroit and the country."

William met Philip's eyes with a glare. "The last two ideas, I like a lot. The sensational it-bleeds, it-leads mentality, it really rubs me the wrong way."

Philip rocked his chair. "This is the gospel according to Wolf Media CEO Gerald Carter. Our opinions are irrelevant."

Philip scanned a list in his leather-bound day planner. "Next item—DuPont. Does he have Emmy written all over him or what?"

William played Julian's news package. When his deep voice boomed over angry skinhead chants and rowdy protesters, Philip smiled. "My boy DuPont. Do your thing."

"He's very bright," William said. "Talented, down-to-earth. I'm impressed."

Philip grinned. "I knew the second I saw him that he'd make it big. We'll start taping promos ASAP."

Someone knocked on the door. Through ficus trees and silver blinds, Philip saw DuPont in a navy blue suit with his agent, Thaddeus Wilson.

"Come in." Philip patted Julian on the back. "DuPont, how you feel today, pal? Have a seat."

"I'm good," Julian said as he sat down.

"Thad, it's always a pleasure," Philip said, shaking his hand.

Seated, Philip pulled a document from his folder. He pushed it across the table to Thad. "Here it is in black and white. I had our lawyers draw up something I thought would suit DuPont's needs."

William appeared bewildered.

"Philip, I'm hired?" DuPont asked.

"You're sharp, DuPont. Real sharp."

DuPont grinned. "Oh, man, I can't thank you enough."

"Just make me proud," Philip said. He ignored the questioning stare from William.

Philip watched Thad, gold half glasses perched on his nose, read the contract. Thad was the epitome of style in his herringbone double-breasted suit. Every detail was impeccable: the onyx cuff links, the stiff, rounded collar and monogrammed French cuffs. The manicure, polished loafers, gold watch, and silk tie with matching pocket square.

Philip smiled. Thaddeus Wilson was the black Philip Carter, in clothes and business style. During Julian's first contract negotiations with *EE,* Philip had marveled at Thad's fearless demands for DuPont's salary and perks. One of *EE's* lawyers had visibly shuddered under Thad's verbal lashing. As a result, DuPont had received exactly what he wanted.

"I couldn't have done it better myself," Thad said. "Julian, read it over. If you like it, you know where to put your John Hancock."

Philip smiled at DuPont, who was grinning like a virgin in a whorehouse. He felt warm inside that he'd helped DuPont excel, and in return DuPont had shown the world that Philip cared about diversity. *And I made Wilbur Franklin choke on his own words.*

William cleared his throat. "Philip, can I see you outside for a moment?"

"Sure thing, pal."

On the balcony, with the conference room door closed, William glowered. "What the hell is going on? You completely disregarded me. Yeah, I want to hire DuPont, but for you to draw up a contract before I gave final approval, that was underhanded and inconsiderate. You have no scruples."

Philip cast a bored stare at William. "Better no scruples than no balls."

William barely concealed a sneer.

"Call it efficient," Philip said. "I'm trying to cram as much as I can into the next three weeks. After that, I'll be one lazy bum on the beach with my new bride. Excuse me."

Philip led William into the conference room.

DuPont beamed. "Philip, let me use your lucky pen, man."

"Sure thing."

Julian gripped the pen and signed the contract. Thad did the same.

"Let's get you a copy and you're all set," Philip said as he signed the contract. "Smile any wider and your face'll crack, pal."

DuPont shook Philip's hand. "Philip, I can't tell you what this means to me, man. You have no idea."

CHAPTER 17

In the locker room of the Downtown Gym, Taylor hugged her friend Carla Jackson.

"Congratulations on your trial," Taylor said. "You've won every trial this year."

Dimples formed around Carla's bright smile. She pulled her relaxed black hair into a ponytail, off her heart-shaped face, the same smooth hue as coffee beans.

"Yeah, they love me." Carla's speech pattern was rapid, her voice naturally raspy. She lifted a foot to the wooden bench to tie her Reeboks. "Yesterday the Wayne County prosecutor told me I'm the best thing since handcuffs," Carla said, her round, dark eyes sparkling. "Five years out of law school, and I really feel like I'm making a difference."

Taylor pulled off her sweatshirt. "I'm proud of you, Carla."

"Thanks." Carla smiled.

They had met four years ago, on one of Taylor's first assignments at Channel 3. Taylor remembered how, after interviewing her during a double murder trial, Carla had stared curiously. Then, a few weeks later during a rape trial, Taylor again saw Carla in the courthouse.

"You're a sister, aren't you?" Carla had asked.

Taylor smiled. "My mom is white and my father is black."

"I knew it the second I saw you," Carla said. "I have a Creole cousin in New Orleans who could be your twin."

Later, while meeting for coffee, movies, and occasional happy hours at Detroit's popular black professional watering hole, Flood's Bar & Grille, Taylor learned of Carla's pursuit of justice for her father's death.

"It was Lemer's gun and Lemer's bullets," Carla had said, the rim of her button nose and her shapely lips quivering. "But the jury, it was all white, and they believed Lemer's lie about self-defense against the guys looting my dad's store. As if my dad was looting his own store. Please. Lemer's partner, a brother, backed up his story, but I still don't believe it."

"I don't understand," Taylor said. "As a prosecutor, you have to rely on police testimony. How can you do that knowing a racist cop killed your father?"

"First," Carla said, "I think most cops are good. And someday I'll get Lemer. A friend in police Internal Affairs is keeping tabs on him for me. One slipup, and I got Lemer's badge."

Carla's quest for justice had endeared her to Taylor, who was reminded of her own vendetta against Rocky Pulaski.

Now, as Taylor put her gym bag in the locker, she said, "Carla, I saw Lemer at the rally yesterday. It looked like he was just patrolling his beat, but something wasn't right."

"What?" Carla asked eagerly.

"The whole scene was crazy," Taylor said, "and when the violence broke out, it was mayhem. That's when I spoke with this cop who defended the neo-Nazis. Then I saw Lemer talking with this same guy! Then again, my police escorts spoke to the guy, too, so maybe I'm reading too much into it. He just gave me a bad feeling. A real bad feeling."

Carla looked pensive. "Wouldn't surprise me one bit if Lemer was secretly a White Power Alliance member."

"I don't know if I've helped any," Taylor said, "but this story isn't going away overnight. I'll keep an eye out for more clues. Have you seen Shari or Danielle yet?"

"No, there's still ten minutes until class," Carla said. "Girl, I need to work off my anger."

"Uh-oh," Taylor said. "Marcus?"

"You don't even want to know."

"What?"

Carla shook her head. "He says come over, I'm making you dinner at eight. Now, here I am thinkin' this brotha is so fine. He's a concept designer at Chrysler, goes to church, and drives a sweet Jeep Cherokee."

"So what's the problem?"

Carla drew the corners of her mouth back. "I get to his apartment a few minutes early, and he comes to the door in a bathrobe." Carla paused. "Then a *naked man* walks out of his bedroom and calls his name in this girlie voice: 'Marcus, who is it, sweetums?' I fell out."

Taylor's eyes widened. "What?"

"Yes! The man swings both ways. AC/DC. Bi."

"Yeah, good-bye," Taylor said.

"You're lucky you found a husband," Carla said. "The man market has taken a plunge so low, I'm surprised it doesn't just crash."

Taylor let herself fall against the metal lockers with a thud.

"Why are you rolling your eyes, girl? Philip is the finest white man out there. Don't tell me there's trouble in paradise."

Taylor shook her head. "I don't know. He doesn't understand me, never will."

"But he's in another generation," Carla said, "and it's hard for people, black or white, to understand the racial nuances that you're so sensitive to."

"I know," Taylor said. "But Philip has been privileged all his life and he's never had to stop and think about race. He drives me crazy sometimes. He can be so insensitive."

"You're still lucky," Carla said. "You're in the same field, and you said yourself that since Julian DuPont dissed you so bad, you thought you'd never fall in love again. So why do you look so depressed?"

Taylor fingered her diamond ring. "Carla, guess who's trying to get hired at Channel Three because, all of a sudden, he wants me back."

Carla knitted her brows. After a moment, her mouth dropped open. "No!"

"Yes."

"What!"

"Yes, Carla. Julian DuPont is in Detroit as we speak, trying to bogart into my workplace and into my love life. Then I got this ridiculous police escort, Pulaski threatened to kill me, and—"

"Say what?" Carla sat down. "I prayed for you all day, girl."

Taylor sat down, her face drooping.

Carla put her arm around her. "It'll be okay. You scared?"

"No, I'm furious that there are two Detroit police officers waiting for me outside the locker room. Pulaski and his son aren't so stupid that they'd try to hurt me or they'd be right back in jail."

Carla's eyes filled with worry. "No, Taylor. I see the workings of the criminal mind every day in court. Logic and reason ain't part of the equation."

Taylor closed her eyes and sighed. "Whatever. I'm hoping this will blow over, I'll get married and get on with my career. I'm not letting either one of them interfere with my life."

Carla shook her head. "Poor thing. My mother always says everything happens for a reason, so maybe the death threat and Julian coming into your life together mean something deeper."

"Yeah, a deep pain in the butt," Taylor said.

Shari and Danielle, laughing and talking loudly, entered the alcove of lockers and looked down at Taylor and Carla.

"Who died?" Shari asked.

Taylor smiled. "Nobody, I was just telling Carla about Pulaski."

Danielle hugged Taylor. "I'm so worried about you."

"I'm fine, really," Taylor said.

"Well, I hope you perk up before we go to the bridal boutique," Shari said. "With a frown like that, you'll jinx the place."

Danielle hugged Carla. "You still putting criminals in jail?"

"Yeah, I won my murder trial yesterday," Carla said.

"So what else is new?" Danielle asked.

"Congratulations," Shari said.

"Thanks," Carla said. She looked at her watch. "It's nine o'clock. We better get out there."

"Sorry we're late," Shari said. "I got in another fight with Charles and there was an accident on the freeway."

Taylor, feeling heavy and lazy, said, "Let's take a sauna and skip aerobics."

The three other women smiled.

A few minutes later, naked in the steam, Taylor could feel tension ooze from her muscles as sweat bubbled from her pores.

Taylor's mind wandered as she noticed the contrast between her friends' skin tones. Shari was small and milky next to caramel-colored, curvaceous Danielle. Side by side in the nude, Taylor and Carla were like a Tootsie Roll and a marshmallow. Carla wore a shower cap, while Danielle's wet hair was like a black cape.

Later, as they dressed, Taylor pulled on a white lace thong and matching strapless bra.

Carla stared. "Damn, girl, you're gonna wear that scandalous stuff when you try on your wedding gown? It's white, but it ain't virginal."

Taylor's cheeks burned with embarrassment. "I'm not trying to look like a centerfold, I just don't want a panty line. And I want my boobs pushed up."

"You can have some of mine," Danielle said, looking down at her D cups.

Taylor smiled as she put on jeans, red leather sandals and belt, and a sleeveless, V-neck red sweater cropped to flash belly button.

As the women primped in the mirror, Taylor applied makeup

and let her curls fall down her back and shoulders. Danielle pulled her hair back with a pink bow. While Shari blow-dried her hair into a stylish mess, Carla curled up the ends of her shoulder-length black hair.

"I love this bouncy swoop," Shari said as she cupped her hands under Carla's curls. "It's very chic."

At New Parthenon, a restaurant on a bustling Detroit street known as Greektown, Shari started coughing.

"All those cigarettes," Carla said. "That's why you hack like that."

"I quit," Shari said.

"As of when?" Taylor asked.

"As of last night when my shit-head husband said I taste like an ashtray," Shari said. "And he called me a smokestack. That fuck."

Carla raised her eyebrows at Taylor, who shrugged.

"That's good that you stopped," Danielle said. She glanced at the police officers at the next table. "Taylor, these bodyguards, I can't believe it."

Taylor rolled her eyes. "I don't see the need for it now."

"We don't want anything to happen to our star reporter," Shari said. "As hardheaded as she is."

A Greek waiter came to the table with an iron platter. He poured a shot glass of liquor over it, then flicked a lighter. A hot yellow-red flame whooshed above the plate.

"*Opa!*" the waiter shouted.

Taylor recoiled.

"I always think my hair will combust," Shari said.

"Me too," Carla said as she spread a piece of the bubbling cheese on a thick piece of bread. "Mmmmm."

"I love the greasy, salty taste," Danielle said. "Want some, Taylor?"

"No. I don't want my hips to bust out of my gown."

Carla took another piece of cheese. "Considering my luck with men lately, I won't have to worry about fitting into a wedding dress for a while."

"Consider yourself lucky," Shari said. "I hate my marriage."

Danielle put her bread down. "What?"

Shari stabbed the greasy blob and sliced off a piece. "I hate my husband. We have no passion, no love, not even common courtesy anymore."

Danielle's dark eyes projected concern. "My brother had huge problems until they saw a marriage counselor. It saved them. They just had another baby."

"We're past that," Shari said. "I decided to make some changes."

The waiter put a plate in front of Taylor. "Greek salad with vegetarian stuffed grape leaves."

He set a plate before Carla. "Spinach pie and gyro for you."

To Danielle and Shari, he said, "Gyros and fries."

Danielle lifted the round, flat bread rolled around lamb and spicy sauce.

"I decided to have an affair," Shari said.

Danielle froze with her mouth open.

Taylor widened her eyes. "Isn't divorce the first logical step?"

"I'll do that, too, but my immediate goal is to find a lover," Shari said in the same tone she used to direct news meetings. "I haven't had sex since New Year's Eve."

"And I thought I was having a long dry spell," Carla said. "That's six months, Shari."

"Thanks for the calculation, Carla."

Danielle's jaw closed. She set her sandwich down. "Shari, I think you should either get counseling or get a divorce. Then find a lover."

"I already made my decision about an affair. I want revenge. Charles doesn't want me, but I want to prove to him that I'm still a red-blooded woman who needs her pussy pumped."

Taylor gasped. "Shari."

"Well, don't you?" Shari asked.

"Yes, but—"

"But nothing. You have Philip, and the way he looks at you, I know you two get it on all the time."

Taylor stabbed her fork into a stuffed grape leaf. "I guess if you're getting a divorce, you have no kids and your own money, then it's not such a bad idea. Men have affairs all the time. Women should play their game once in a while."

Shari smiled. "Thank you."

Danielle chewed her sandwich and shook her head.

"It still boggles my mind," Shari said. "How Charles and I could go from love-struck sex fiends to mortal enemies. I guess my mom is right. Passion fades. All that true-love, prince-charming bullshit in the movies is a crock."

That's true. It didn't last with me and Julian. Taylor's stomach cramped as Julian's pleading eyes appeared in her mind. Then she saw Philip's tanned, chiseled face. And the two of them, smiling, together in *Broadcaster's Weekly.* She set her fork down and placed a hand on her stomach.

"No, Shari, true love is not a myth," Danielle said. "I married my first love, and we're still crazy about each other. Taylor's parents are still together, and they've been married . . . how long, Taylor?"

"Thirty-two years."

"Yeah," Danielle said. "And my parents, after seven kids, are still going strong."

"That's something," Carla said. "Before my father got killed, my mother says they had passion. But believe me, I've prosecuted too many men who just kill their wives when the urge strikes."

"I'm finding a lover," Shari said. "I'm thirty-five years old and as much as I love it, my career doesn't keep me warm in bed at night."

"I hear you," Carla said. "But it's hard out there. Last night I found my latest love interest with a naked man."

"Get outta here," Shari said.

"It's true," Carla said. "And the guy I dated before that was married, unbeknownst to me for three months. His wife lived in D.C. for her job and he had an apartment here. When she walked in on us having a candlelight dinner, I ran for my life."

Taylor shook her head. "Carla, you could write a book on dating nightmares."

"I know," Carla said. "In law school at Wayne State, I dated this guy from negligence class until I found him in my apartment in the middle of the night, when he thought I was asleep, making a long-distance phone call to some heifer in Atlanta. When I got the phone bill I enlarged it real big on a copy machine and taped it to his back during class. He was so embarrassed he wrote me a check right there."

"That's a shame," Taylor said.

Carla touched Shari's arm. "Shari, here we are complaining about men when Taylor has two handsome studs clamoring for her hand in marriage."

Taylor went numb. *No, she didn't. Shari can't know about Julian. She's too close to Philip.*

Shari and Danielle froze, then spoke at once: "Two men?"

Hot blood rose to Taylor's face as she turned to Carla.

"Ooops," Carla said. "I guess I wasn't supposed to say anything."

Taylor closed her eyes.

Carla bowed her head while Shari and Danielle stared, wide-eyed.

"Who?" Danielle demanded.

Taylor took a deep breath and blew it out hard. "Shari, you have to promise me you'll never tell Philip."

Her eyes grew bigger. "I promise. I confided in you yesterday, so tell me. It won't leave this table."

"And, Danielle, don't go scheming with Peter."

"I won't. What are you talking about?"

"Julian DuPont."

Danielle gasped.

Shari knitted her brows. "Yeah, so, what about him? You wanna have a fling before you tie the knot? He's drop-dead gorgeous. I can't say the thought hasn't crossed my mind, but if he gets hired, he could accuse me of—"

Danielle raised her eyebrows. "Hired?"

"Yeah," Shari said. "It would be sexual harassment if I came on to him. So, Taylor, go for it, if you want a last-minute fling. Just be careful."

Taylor pursed her lips. "No, that's not it, Shari. Julian DuPont's parents are my parents' best friends. We grew up together. He was my first love and we planned to marry after college."

Shari's mouth fell open.

"But yesterday was the first I saw him in ten years," Taylor said.

"Then what does Carla mean that he's clamoring for your hand in marriage?" Shari asked.

"He wants to steal me away from Philip," Taylor said.

Shari stared, stunned.

"So that's why he's in town," Danielle said. "He called last night to talk to Peter. I thought he was just visiting his parents."

Shari, with a glazed look, said, "So you're the reason he wants to work at Channel Three. Now it makes sense. But exactly three weeks from now, we'll be standing at the altar with you. And Philip, Julian's mentor. This is too scandalous."

Paranoia suddenly gnawed Taylor's gut. "Shari, you can't tell anyone. Please. If Philip finds out, I'll just die. I'm not going for Julian's crazy scheme, anyway. I wish he'd go back to California and get swallowed up in an earthquake."

Danielle scowled. "Taylor."

"Listen, I'm marrying Philip. Julian is ancient history. I told him to take his wild idea and shove it."

Carla drew back the corners of her mouth. "Yeah, right."

"I did!"

"That man is too fine for any woman to have the guts to say that," Carla said. "I've seen him on TV. I can't even imagine how good he looks in the flesh."

"Very," Shari said.

Danielle smiled. "Unbelievably gorgeous. And smart and funny."

Shari nodded.

"Taylor, I think you should reconsider," Danielle said.

"Reconsider what?"

"Julian," Danielle said. "You two were the perfect couple. You shouldn't let something that happened when you were nineteen deprive you of each other forever."

Taylor sneered.

"Why'd you break up?" Shari asked.

Taylor's stomach ached. "Julian had fifty thousand girlfriends in L.A., he ignored me at a cokehead actor's party while he flirted with every girl in the room, then girls in bikinis came in his apartment dancing seductively with him, so I left."

Shari scowled. "That is bad."

"What a dog," Carla said. "D-o-g. It's one thing to date other women while you two were apart, but there's no reason to put it in your face. I don't blame you for being pissed, but maybe he realized what a low-down dirty dog he was. People can change."

"I agree," Danielle said. "Him leaving a great job like that shows he's serious about you. You should at least talk to him."

Taylor rubbed her stomach.

"What about Philip?" Shari asked. "Taylor, don't even consider crossing him. All that mumbo jumbo from Julian is just a ploy to get in your pants. Philip can help your career. It's your face and your name and your work in front of millions of people. Don't jeopardize that. Take it from me."

Taylor leaned into the table. She looked each friend in the eyes.

"I'm marrying Philip. Now, let's go try on our wedding dresses."

CHAPTER 18

With her police escort in the hallway, Taylor stormed into her apartment. She had just left her parents' house, where Julian had been drinking champagne from their best crystal—bought on their trip to Sweden and only used for very special occasions.

My engagement to Philip didn't even merit the Orrefors, but Julian's homecoming and new job does? Shaking her head, she hurried past the cream leather sectional in the living room toward the window wall that faced the sparkling blue Detroit River and the green expanse of Windsor, Canada.

She picked up her orange Angora cat, Puff, and stepped onto the balcony, her limbs humming with rage that her parents were so insistent that she give Julian a second chance. It seemed that they had no respect for her decisions and opinions as an adult.

Taylor watched a few boats pass along the river, twenty-five stories below, then walked to the answering machine in her bedroom. She pushed the message button, then dove into soft, peach linens and pillows on her wrought-iron canopy bed. Puff nuzzled her cheek as the message played.

"Nigger bitch, you're dead."

Taylor bolted up.

Oh my God. How did Rocky get my unlisted number? Could he also know where I live?

Taylor's blood froze. Terror numbed her limbs, raced her heart, quickened her breath.

She ran to the hallway and told Officers Young and Edwards. After listening to the threat, they reported it to police headquarters. A few minutes later, there was a knock on the door.

"Sergeant Scarlin, that was quick," Officer Young said.

Taylor was stunned. It was the man with the creepy silver-blue eyes and birdlike face who'd made sympathetic comments about the White Power fanatics at the rally. Icy fear squeezed her chest when she met his contemptuous glare across the room.

"What's the problem?" he asked, gripping his holster. His voice was low and hard.

Puff meowed loudly, then fled to the bedroom.

"Pulaski threatened her," Edwards said, handing the answering machine tape to Scarlin.

"What makes you think it was Pulaski?" Scarlin asked.

"Ms. James recognized his voice," Young said.

Scarlin put the tape in a plastic bag and wrote on a white pad. "The Pulaskis were released from jail this afternoon," he said, casting malicious eyes at Taylor. "You'd better be careful."

Goose bumps prickled across her body.

"Thanks, Sergeant," Edwards said.

"I'll always be minutes away," Scarlin said, a corner of his thin lips rising as he opened the door to leave.

Taylor studied the unsuspecting expressions on the faces of Officers Edwards and Young.

"There's something bad about that man," Taylor said. "I think he's a White Power sympathizer."

Edwards scowled, then shook his head. "Scarlin? Naw, he used to have a black partner. He's cool. If he were a neo-Nazi, I'd know it."

"How?" Taylor asked.

"Well," Edwards said, "he would tell racist jokes and treat minorities rudely. He doesn't. And our chief is black. Goodson wouldn't tolerate that crap on the force."

Young shook her head. "No way. Don't worry about that, Ms. James."

Skeptical, Taylor returned to the bedroom and called Philip's Skypager.

"Hi, Philip. I miss you. I tried on my wedding dress today. Just three weeks, we'll be at the altar saying 'I do.' I can't wait. I'm home. Call me."

Then she stared at the phone. *Please call me, even if you're in a meeting. I'd feel so much better if I heard your voice.*

Minutes later, the phone rang. She answered eagerly.

"Taylor," Julian said.

She exhaled loudly. "If I wanted to talk to you," she snapped, recalling the tense moments a half hour ago at her parents' house when she saw Julian and his parents, "I wouldn't have run out of my parents' house like that."

"Just give me an hour," Julian said.

"No. So what if our parents are conspiring with you," Taylor said. "You and I are history, Julian."

"Then why does your voice sound so shaky?" he asked.

"Because I—"

"Because you only half believe that," Julian said.

"No, because Rocky Pulaski just left a death threat on my answering machine. Satisfied?"

"That bastard," Julian said. "The cops still with you?"

"Yes."

"Please, Taylor. I need to talk with you."

Taylor lay back on the bed. The soft pads of Puff's feet kneaded her stomach, tickling her, easing the nervousness and annoyance stiffening her muscles.

"I want to look into your eyes, see your smile," Julian said.

Taylor rolled her eyes. "If I see you, I won't smile."

"Then I'll kiss you," he said.

"Forget it." Taylor hung up and threw the phone against the pillows.

It rang. She wanted the answering machine to click on, but the police had removed the tape. And maybe it was Philip.

"Hello?"

"Taylor, please," Julian said. "How 'bout ice cream, cappuccino? Feeding ducks on Belle Isle? Just give me an hour."

Taylor's stomach fluttered in the mahogany and marble lobby of her apartment building. *It should be illegal for a man to exude so much sex appeal. Especially when he smiles.*

"Hi," Julian said. He wore all black: jeans, a crew-neck cotton shirt, and Gucci loafers. His upper body was a flat, upside-down triangle resting on a slim waist and long legs.

God, give me strength.

In Taylor's banana yellow Mustang convertible, with the police in tow, an awkward silence hung between them as she sped across the white arcs of the Belle Isle Bridge. There—the site of a deadly race riot in July 1943—the James and DuPont families had spent countless summer days visiting the zoo and canoeing on the island's canals.

"Damn, Taylor, you drive like a bat outta hell," Julian said, gripping the seat. "I know they're setting up for the Grand Prix here, but you won't be driving any of the race cars."

Taylor worked the black stick shift as they sped around the edge of the island, offering a view across the blue water of downtown Detroit's Renaissance Center—five cylindrical, mirrored towers that held a hotel, offices, restaurants, and boutiques—tall office buildings, and the Ambassador Bridge stretching across the river to Canada.

"I forgot how pretty this view is," Julian said. "And how beautiful you are."

Taylor rolled her eyes, hidden behind black sunglasses. "You're wrong if you think I'm vulnerable to your charm while Philip is in Kansas City."

"Hmm, Kansas City," Julian said. "That would be the brunette, Caroline, a reporter at the station Wolf wants to buy there."

"What?"

"Come on, Taylor, you can't be that naïve about Philip," Julian said. "You name a city where Wolf has a station and I'll name his girlfriends there."

Taylor slammed on the brakes. "I'm taking you back. Don't sit in my car and accuse Philip of cheating on me."

"Sorry," Julian said. "I want to talk about us."

"That's even more infuriating," she said.

"It's all I care about right now," Julian said, staring with pleading eyes.

Taylor remembered Carla and Danielle, and her parents, saying she should listen to Julian's plea.

"Fine," she said, accelerating. A few minutes later, she parked in front of the white marble Scott Fountain, and they bounded up the stairs. The police officers sat on the balustrade several yards from Taylor and Julian at the edge of the fountain.

"Remember our game?" Julian asked over the roaring water.

"Yeah," Taylor said, picking a quarter from his outstretched palm. She closed her eyes. *I wish Julian DuPont and Rocky Pulaski would go away, leaving me with a successful career and happy marriage to Philip.*

She tossed the coin and heard it plunk with Julian's into the water, joining a carpet of shimmering silver and copper wishes.

"That reminds me," Julian said, "of when we used to picnic here with our parents and—"

"Ride the giant slide until we were dizzy," Taylor said. She fought a sudden twittery feeling in her stomach.

"Taylor, I'll cut to the chase," Julian said, squinting in the bright sunshine. "I owe you the apology of the century."

"You can say that again," Taylor said somberly.

"I'm ashamed for what I'm about to tell you," Julian said.

"You should be," Taylor said, sitting on the cold lip of the fountain.

He sat next to her with a humble expression. "Taylor, the reason I was such a monster ten years ago, well, it had to do with race."

Taylor removed her sunglasses and studied his morose expression. "What?"

"I mean," Julian said, "I had a racial incident that summer, just before you visited. It changed my whole outlook on life."

"A racial incident," Taylor repeated. "What else is new? If you and I counted how many racial incidents we had as kids, the number would be—" She shook her head. "Julian, what's the point here? What's this got to do with you being so mean back then?"

"A couple things," Julian said. "First, women were coming on to me left and right."

Taylor's blood turned to scalding water. "Thanks for that detail. I really needed to hear that. What the hell is your point?"

"Please listen," he said. "I had never been with any girl except you, and I was curious. First semester, I fended girls off. When I saw you at home for Christmas, I knew I was doing the right thing. But the next semester, I caved in. I kind of went wild. The whole L.A. scene, the clubs, the women, it all went to my head."

Taylor stared at him, dumbfounded. *What a sadistic bastard.*

"Taylor, I've never told my parents or Philip about this."

"What?" she snapped.

"Remember how I was supposed to spend four summers in that minority journalism program at GNN?"

"Yeah," Taylor said. "Your parents said you only did one summer because you wanted to go into entertainment news."

Julian looked down at his hands. "That's what I told them. The truth is, I loved hard news. I worked my butt off at GNN, going with reporters to stories, editing video, working in the control room. It was a great experience."

Taylor concentrated on making sense of his story. So far, it was only confusing her more. "And? Why'd you leave?"

Julian sighed. A pained expression dulled his eyes as he explained the incident with Brad Hastings and Wilbur Franklin.

As she listened, a heavy wave of empathy flooded Taylor's senses, making her physically ache for the pain Julian must have felt. The anguish in his eyes stabbed at her heart.

"Julian," she said softly, "of all the people in the world, why didn't you tell me?"

Julian stared at the ground. "I was devastated. I felt so much rage, Taylor, it was like I couldn't see straight. I hated that people were judging my ability on my brown skin. I *hated* it. Our parents taught us to be our best, and not cave in under prejudice, but with the Klan running the network—"

"But," Taylor said, placing a hand on his back, "didn't you want me near to comfort you?"

Julian ran large hands over his thighs, then gazed at Taylor with a strange expression, one she had never seen. One that frightened her.

"I'm ashamed to say this," Julian whispered.

Taylor leaned closer, every inch of her being pining for an explanation.

"You were at your internship in New York," he said, "having a wonderful experience, but when this happened to me, I started to wonder, what if you became a superstar journalist, while I was stuck in some racist choke-hold, my complexion holding me back."

Grief welled inside Taylor. *I can't believe I'm hearing this.*

"But, Julian, I was your comfort zone. And there was never competition between us."

"No," Julian said, "but this was my first racist experience in the so-called real world. I didn't know if every other network was the same."

Taylor shook her head. "I'm sorry, Julian, but I still don't see the connection to me. This makes no sense."

He sighed, glanced nervously at the river, then met her eyes.

"I resented you," Julian said, "because you look white."

CHAPTER 19

Carla Jackson sneered at Shari Gordon over a rack of satin nightgowns in Victoria's Secret in the upscale Somerset Collection mall.

"You're trippin'," Carla said over Ravel's *Bolero* piped through the store. "You should be happy for Taylor, not jealous."

Shari shrugged as she examined a purple satin bustier. "Oh, quit with your high-and-mighty virtue. I can't help how I feel. It's not fair that she's got everything—talent, beauty, and two men after her when I'm stuck with the dud of the year at home."

"Don't forget the white supremacist who wants to kill her," Carla snapped. "That's something to covet."

A yellow silk gown suddenly fluttered between them.

"Flag on the play, catfighting, fifteen yards," Danielle said play-fully, waving the gown. "C'mon, girls, we're here for a happy occasion. We'll get Taylor's bridal shower gifts and go our separate ways, okay?"

Shari, in a leather bomber jacket and black jeans, ignored them both, her messy hair blocking her face.

Carla was antsy with anger and suspicion as she stepped toward a wall of demi-cups. *If Shari were a real friend, she wouldn't be jealous of Taylor. Hell, my love life is a joke, but I'm thrilled for her.*

"I'm getting this," Shari announced, holding up the purple ensemble, "for Taylor and myself. And for my lover."

Danielle, in a black frock, clogs, and one of the crystal pendants she always wore, this one amethyst, shook her head. "Shari, you're serious about this affair, aren't you?"

"As serious as the six-o'clock news," Shari said.

Carla was sick of hearing about Shari's wicked thoughts. "Are you both ready?" she asked impatiently. "Let's pay. I have to go." Carla headed toward the cashier.

"Carla, wait," Shari said, joining the line. "I know it sounds bad, but when you reach my age and realize that life isn't fair, I don't know, it makes me hold a grudge against people who have it so easy, I guess."

Danielle snickered. "Easy? Not the Taylor James I know. She's had to go through more torment than anybody I know. You wouldn't believe how mean people can be, like in sixth grade once, these black girls circled her, walking around and around, saying they wouldn't let her go till she said she wasn't black."

Shari cast her eyes down to a table of lace panties.

"She never told me that," Carla said.

"But Julian defended her all the time," Danielle said. "I always thought they were made for each other, but when Julian dumped her, it was bad. Very bad. I mean, Taylor was dazed and glassy-eyed for a year. Then she suddenly got stronger, more independent."

Shari grabbed a black lace bodysuit from a rack and put it over her arm. "Well, she seems fine now. And she must not care about Julian anymore; she never told me about him. Carla, how'd you know about him?"

Carla laughed. "I was at her apartment once when *Entertainment Exclusive* came on. Taylor threw a shoe at the TV and cussed like a sailor. Then she kind of felt obliged to explain."

Danielle nodded. "Yeah, I've learned not to mention Julian's name. But I wonder what'll happen now."

Carla shook her head. "It could get ugly. Real ugly."

"Well, I'm rooting for her and Philip," Shari said. "Maybe after the wedding reception, I'll get Julian drunk and have my way with him."

"Oooh, Shari the sugar mama," Carla said.

Shari dangled the lingerie. "Maybe."

As Carla drove her blue Toyota Supra south on the Fisher Freeway toward Detroit, she phoned her police contact, Shawn Rutherford. Seeing those police officers with Taylor, and hearing about Gus Lemer at the neo-Nazi rally, intensified her desire to avenge her father's death by locking up Lemer for life.

"Shawn, it's Carla. Got any news?"

"Yeah, I was going to call you this afternoon," he said. "One of my sources saw Lemer yesterday at the white supremacists' rally."

"I heard," Carla said, gripping the steering wheel as contempt rolled through her. "It might not mean anything, since that's his beat."

"Either way," Shawn said, "I'll feel out my sources on Monday."

Carla wondered why Lemer's former partner who witnessed her father's death refused to talk to her or Shawn about the case.

"Has Duane Montgomery opened up yet?" Carla asked.

"Hell no," Shawn said. "That brother is strange. Before he retired, I never saw him talk to anybody. I call him at home, he hangs up on me."

"Maybe someday he'll talk. Thanks a lot, Shawn."

"So when can I take you out?" he asked.

"Pa-leese, Shawn, you're cute, but you're just like my brother

Jimmy—a player. I don't want to join your harem of hoochie mamas."

Shawn laughed. "I'm not that bad."

"But you are bad," Carla said, smiling. "I'll talk to you Monday."

Carla could not shake Gus Lemer's ratlike face from her mind. Even now, his image hovered over memories of her mother's screams when police had come to the door of their house on Oakman Boulevard. It was Monday, July 24, 1967, the second day of the riot, just hours after Papa had left to check on his grocery store on Livernois. He had been worried because he had not remembered to place a SOUL BROTHER sign in the window, which had deterred looters from black-owned businesses.

But, there having been no sign, looters had been helping themselves to the canned goods, money, and food inside the business that had made Papa so proud. When he entered, two police officers—already in a standoff with two other black men—mistook Gregory Jackson for a criminal. When he tried to approach them to explain that he owned the store, the white officer blasted two bullets into his chest, killing him instantly.

After the black smoke had cleared, the snipers' fire had quieted, and the National Guard's tanks had rolled out of the ravaged city, it was revealed that part of what sparked the riot was a police raid at an illegal nightclub and another incident at the Algiers Motel. There three white police officers had shot and killed three young black men who had been partying with two white girls. The three cops were tried and acquitted by white juries, as was Lemer. And there was a feeling in the black community, Carla's mother had often explained, that the white cops and trigger-happy National Guardsmen who had taken black lives over six days of fiery anarchy would never face justice.

But we always believed that Lemer would. He has to be punished for taking Papa from us.

Suddenly the freeway became a blur; Carla blinked to squeeze the tears from her eyes. She had been only three when he died, but the painful void where he should have been in her life ached as intensely as if he had died yesterday. Her memories of him were a collage of images lifted from Mama's treasured photo albums. Her favorite was the snapshot of Papa, a husky man of six feet, with a hazelnut complexion and wavy black hair, holding little Carla's hand outside the glass and brick storefront of Gregory's Grocery. She, in a frilly dress as red as the licorice rope in her hand, was grinning, her two pigtails sprouting high from her head. Next to her, Papa wore a white smock and a delighted smile.

Over the years, Carla had established a gentle, warmhearted relationship with her father in her dreams. While she was asleep at night, he would visit her, offering advice about growing up and the pressures of college and law school, even though he had had only a twelfth-grade education. Every day she sensed his presence with her, like an angel guiding her through trials, helping her administer the justice that his own death had yet to elicit.

Without Papa, when bad things happened in the Jackson family, it was not his image that appeared in Carla's mind. It was Gus Lemer's close-set brown eyes, his narrow face, his whiskerlike brown mustache. She had envisioned Lemer when her mother wailed that night after ten-year-old Debra died of an asthma attack in the yellow bedroom she shared with Carla. Lemer's face had appeared every time her mother spoke of losing the spacious house on Oakman and moving into the projects. Carla had seen Lemer when her mother served plain, boiled macaroni for dinner three nights in a row because the welfare money had run out. And she had thought of Lemer every time her brother Jimmy, who grew up fatherless, was arrested for skipping school.

Someday Lemer will see my face when he's rotting in prison, paying for Papa's death with his every breath.

Carla parked behind the Girls Center, a renovated Victorian house with blue gingerbread trim near Detroit's theater district. She had founded the nonprofit guidance center three years ago with grants and a vision of helping female teens navigate turbulent waters infested with boys, school pressures, and family problems.

On the porch swing sat fifteen-year-old Tamika Jamison, pouting in a denim miniskirt and halter top. Tiny braids hung in her eyes.

As Carla approached, she said, "Hey, Tamika, why you look so sad, girl?"

The girl shrugged and stared at the tree-lined sidewalk.

"You can tell me," Carla said, sitting next to her. "Your mother's boyfriend again?"

Tamika examined a blue and green acrylic fingernail.

"Your final exam in biology?"

"No, I got a B plus."

Carla hugged her. "So let's celebrate! You pushed your GPA up from an F. That's excellent."

Tamika fingered the laces on her Filas. "I'm mad about Davante," she said. "He say he won't go wit' me no more unless I have sex."

Carla sighed. "Well, you already know what I say about that."

Tamika nodded. "But he plays football, he can sing, and he likes me."

"If he really cares about you, he won't demand sex," Carla said. "Remember Melinda Davis? You think she'll be working at a law firm this summer like you?"

"No," Tamika said. "She's tryin' to get her GED 'cause she quit tenth grade for the baby. And she don't even go wit' the baby daddy. He go wit' LaKeisha now. She a cheerleader."

"There. You just found the answer to your own problem," Carla said.

"How?"

"Davante wants to use you for sex. You could end up like Melinda. You want that?"

"Oh no," Tamika said. "That's how my mother was. I want to be a lawyer like you."

"Do you think I let boys have sex with me when I was your age?"

Tamika turned her smooth brown face—large, curious dark eyes, a cute, flat nose—toward Carla. "Did you?"

"Not until I was eighteen," Carla said, "when I was in love in college. And then I used protection. If I had gotten pregnant by some ne'er-do-well boy, I wouldn't be an assistant prosecutor, and I wouldn't have opened the Girls Center."

"But what about when the boys be pressurin' you, sayin' you pretty an' they ain't gon' talk to you unless you give 'em some?"

"What's more important? Pleasing boys, who may not give you the time of day after you give up the you-know-what? Or doing things good for you?"

Tamika sighed. "But, Carla, it ain't like when you was my age."

"With boys, it's exactly the same," Carla said, "except for the metal detectors and drugs at school."

"I don't play that." Tamika twisted her hand in the air. "If a boy say he packin' a gat, I say 'See ya!' Drugs too."

"Good. Now, what are you gonna do about Davante?"

"I'm 'a tell 'im no," Tamika said.

Carla hugged Tamika. "That's my girl!"

Tamika grinned. "You so cool, Carla. I can't talk to nobody grown like I can talk to you."

"That's why I'm here," Carla said.

The front door squeaked open. A girl in baggy blue jeans, a beeper, and a plaid tank top sat down next to Tamika. She had a round, caramel face with red lips and a long, black ponytail.

"Carla, this my friend Rose Rodriguez."

"Nice to meet you," Carla said.

"Rose got a problem wit' her gang-bangin' boyfriend," Tamika said.

Rose shot Tamika a hard look. "Shut up, girl. I got my own mouth. He my *ex*-boyfriend, anyway."

Rose turned to Carla. "My boyfriend, he in the Latin Dukes, right, an' he say if I quit him, I might as well just shoot myself before he pop me hisself."

"How long have you dated him?" Carla asked.

Rose tilted her head toward the sky. "Six weeks."

"Naw," Tamika said. "You met him at the skatin' rink when it was snow on the ground. I was wit' you, knucklehead."

"Okay, so say three months we been tight," Rose said. "But I ain't down wit' all his gang stuff, and he act like he own me. Forget that."

"Did you break up?" Carla asked.

"Yeah, last night," Rose said. "But I'm scared of Rico comin' after me."

Carla drew her eyebrows together. "You think he'd hurt you?"

"He slapped me once," Rose said, "when I told him off 'cause he was rappin' to some hoe downtown. I shoulda dropped his gangsta butt then."

"I told you," Tamika said. "But you said, 'Naw, he so cute and he got fat cash.' You askin' for trouble if you go wit' roughnecks."

"I know," Rose said.

"How old are you, Rose?" Carla asked.

"Fifteen."

"How are your grades?"

"I had a two-point, right, but now it's two-point-nine."

"That's progress," Carla said. "You should tell your parents about Rico and tell him to leave you alone. On Monday come downtown and I'll help you get a Personal Protection Order in court. So if Rico harasses you, he'll be arrested."

Rose raised her eyebrows. "Arrested?"

"Yes, arrested. A PPO is like a restraining order. It's supposed to prevent people like Rico from acting out threats."

Rose buried her hands in her face. Tamika caressed her back.

"Don't worry, girl," Tamika said. "My mama had a restrainin' order against my baby brother Leon daddy. Once he got arrested, we ain't seent him since."

"For real?" Rose asked.

"Would I lie?" Tamika said.

"And I want you to enroll in our summer tutoring program," Carla said. "What do you want to do after graduation?"

"I like decoratin' houses," Rose said.

Carla led the girls into the house, where a Whitney Houston CD played on the stereo in the activity room, with its bay windows, wood floor, and fireplace. Hundreds of pictures of girls covered a bulletin board under a yellow heading, I AM SOMEBODY! Maya Angelou's poem *"Phenomenal Woman"* hung over two blue couches. In another room, girls and tutors studied textbooks, while others worked on computers.

"Come up to my office," Carla said as she started up the wooden staircase.

At the same time, Haifa Haddad and Marni Draper bounded into the foyer.

"Carla! We need to talk to you."

"Come on up," Carla said.

The two girls waited on the couch while Rose and Tamika looked around at the posters, books, and plants that filled the tangerine-walled office.

Tamika pointed to a black-and-white poster of Rosa Parks, the African-American seamstress whose refusal to forfeit her bus seat to a white man in 1955 in Alabama prompted the Montgomery Bus Boycott and galvanized the civil rights movement.

"Rosa Parks lives in Detroit," Tamika said. "I met her here last year."

"For real?" Rose said.

They turned to Carla, who was on the phone behind her desk in a circular window alcove.

"You do?" Carla smiled. "Great. I'll bring her over in about an hour. Thanks, Mary."

Rose's face lit up. "What is it?"

"One of our mentors needs a summer clerk at her interior design studio. She wants to meet you, Rose."

Rose appeared stunned. "For real?"

"Yes. But, Rose, if she gives you a job, you have to be on time and act professionally." Carla handed Rose a folder full of papers. "Here are the rules."

"Dang, all this?"

"It's not that bad," Tamika said. "I memorized it."

"Meet me downstairs," Carla said.

"Thank you," Rose said.

Haifa and Marni entered with swastika-covered pamphlets.

"Some skinheads visited our high school yesterday," Marni said, shaking her ponytail. "They were scary."

"They called me a sand nigger," Haifa said with an Arabic accent.

Disgusted, Carla scanned the pamphlets.

"Our principal called the cops," Marni said, "who made them leave. But my boyfriend, he met one of the guys later and thinks skinheads are cool."

Carla shook her head. "Marni, remember the reporter, Taylor James?"

"Yeah," Haifa said. "She took us on that cool tour of the TV station."

"Right," Carla said. "The skinhead leader threatened to kill her yesterday. These people are nothing to play with."

"Oh my gosh," Haifa said.

"I'm calling my boyfriend's mom," Marni said. "She'll be furious."

"Thanks for telling me about this," Carla said as the girls left the office. As she looked at the pamphlets again, her stomach tightened.

Lord, why is there so much hatred in the world? If anything good comes out of these hate mongers coming to town, it will be exposing Gus Lemer for what he really is. A racist murderer.

CHAPTER 20

Taylor perched on the cold lip of the fountain, stunned by Julian's confession. When his words sunk in, they struck with the stinging, paralyzing force of jumping off a cliff and smacking facedown on the water's surface. It knocked the wind out of her, set her skin ablaze, drowned her in pain.

After a few moments, Taylor found the strength to whisper, "What did you say?"

Julian's eyes projected anguish and guilt.

"I resented you because you look white," he said.

Nausea burned in Taylor's gut. *God no . . . There's nothing worse he could say. Race, what made us so special together, was the fatal wedge between us?*

Her limp hand slipped from his back, into the cold water. Taylor vacantly withdrew it, dropping it in her lap.

She held Julian's haunted gaze as the past decade of wondering and praying and crying over him flashed through her mind on fast-forward.

What a senseless, terrible waste. A curse of fate. God, why?

"But, it doesn't make sense," she said. "I was your ally, your comfort zone. At least I thought I was. And look what I've been through. Those cops over there are proof, and I'm scared to death."

Julian shook his head. "No, you and I, we're different. That's what I realized. You could pass for white, keep it a secret if you wanted. But me, look at me." He held out bronze arms.

In Taylor's mind his skin was beautiful, with its deep, rich color and baby-soft smoothness, taut over firm muscle. Why was the rest of the world blind to such beauty?

"You can walk into a store or a restaurant or a job interview," he said, "and no one would know you're black. With me, that's the first thing they see. It's like a signal to cops to pull me over. Clerks follow me in stores. And, until I became famous, rude treatment in restaurants. But you, you can just blend in with the majority."

"Physically, maybe," Taylor said, feeling bruised from head to toe. "But I've never tried to hide the fact that I'm half black. And I still don't understand, why did it take you so long to tell me this?"

"Tunnel vision," Julian said. "After the incident, I was so focused on proving those racists wrong, and proving myself, I lost sight of everything. I wanted to focus all my energy on my career, so I broke up with you. And I used women and partying to fill the void."

Numb with grief, Taylor stood up, staring into his sad eyes. "Julian, I would've rather gone my whole life confused about our breakup than to hear you say that," Taylor said, trembling. She felt as if she had scuba dived too deep, too fast, and the great weight and pressure of the water were crushing her mercilessly. It wrung perspiration and hot tears and oxygen from the grotesque gel that was now her body.

This is the worst day of my life.

Julian stood, putting an arm around her. "Taylor, baby, I am so, so sorry. Losing you was the biggest mistake I ever made, and the only way to rectify it was to find you, explain myself, and hope you'd love me again. I hope it's not too late."

He was a blur through her tears. She fingered her ring.

"It is too late," she whispered. "And even if I didn't have Philip, I could never risk loving you. Especially over some nonsense like this. Another breakup would kill me."

Julian pulled her into his chest and the warm wafts of his cologne. He placed a feather-soft kiss on her burning cheek.

"I'll never hurt you again," he said. "I want to hold you in my arms forever and make you smile and laugh and feel safe. I love you, White Chocolate."

A white-hot bolt of rage cleaved Taylor from his arms. *How dare he call me that now!*

Then, on the side of the fountain hidden from the police, she saw two skinheads in White Power Alliance T-shirts and combat boots. They were walking toward her.

No, not now . . . enough trauma for one day. For a lifetime.

Taylor gasped. "Julian! Hey," she shouted to the police officers.

"Rocky's gonna get both you mongrel freaks," said one boy, who wore a silver-studded dog collar.

Julian seized their tattooed arms.

"Let us go!" one shouted.

The cops arrived seconds after Julian pushed the punks into the fountain.

Taylor's heart galloped with fear, walloping already frazzled nerves.

"You okay, Ms. James?" Officer Edwards asked.

"I'm fine," Taylor said.

Julian glowered at Edwards. "You should've seen them coming."

"We reacted as quickly as we could," Edwards said.

"That's not good enough," Julian said.

Edwards glared at Julian. "Ms. James, let's go back to your apartment."

"Okay," she said.

Officer Young held the boys. "Show me some ID."

"We don't got none," the one in the dog collar said.

"How old are you?" Young asked.

"None a yer business."

Taylor and Julian sat in her car while a second police car detained the skinheads.

"This pisses me off," Julian said. "Those damn rent-a-cops have worse reflexes than a quarterback with broken legs."

"Julian, the guys snuck up on us," Taylor said.

"Exactly. Bodyguards don't let anybody sneak up."

As Taylor drove over the bridge, her stomach gurgled with hunger and stress. Julian's confession had left her feeling physically battered while this Pulaski ordeal had caused her nerves to go haywire.

Philip is out of town, I'm scared to death, and I don't want to be alone.

"What do you say we go back to my apartment, maybe order a pizza?" Taylor asked Julian. She kept her eyes on the utility vehicles and sports cars clogging Jefferson, one of Detroit's major avenues that paralleled the river with dozens of apartment buildings, marinas, and grocery stores.

Julian beamed. "Sounds great."

With the cops outside the apartment door, Taylor sat on the living room couch and ordered a pizza. Her eyes followed Julian's round, denim-clad butt as he looked around the apartment.

"What a view," Julian said from the balcony.

"Beautiful, isn't it?" Taylor answered.

"Yeah," Julian said as Puff purred and brushed her orange fur against his legs. Julian stroked Puff, then placed several CDs in the stereo. What used to be their favorite love song began playing as Taylor poured two glasses of white zinfandel.

Julian sang into a candlestick from the dining room table.

Taylor stared into Julian's eyes as she stroked Puff's silky fur. That song evoked memories of the first time they made love. They were sixteen, on the annual James-DuPont vacation at the DuPonts' summer cottage near the small, peaceful town that inspired Picasso— Mougins, on France's Côte d'Azur. First she and Julian had picnicked on luscious, local-grown grapes and olives. Then, as they lay on that hill amidst silvery olive trees, fragrant roses, and mimosas, a new hunger had overwhelmed their sun-bronzed bodies. After a beautiful sunset, they kissed and caressed each other with feverish need until Julian, whispering, *"Je te désire"* and *"Je t'aime,"* became one with her. It was horribly painful at first, like a knife plunging inside her. But after she relaxed, his gentle lovemaking carried her to a height of passion she had never known. After feeling him spasm with pleasure more intensely than he ever had, Taylor slept in his arms under the stars.

Julian crooned about everlasting love.

An odd sense of detachment possessed Taylor while she watched him. *How can he sing those words to me, words that I once believed were true between us, when he just shattered my heart all over again?*

When he finished, he sat next to her, his arm extended toward her at the back of the couch. "That song is perfect for us," he said.

"It was," Taylor said.

"It still is," Julian said.

"We don't even know each other any—"

The ringing phone interrupted her.

"Hello?"

"How's my darling?"

"Philip," she said, guilt stinging her cheeks. She walked to the balcony, feeling Julian's eyes behind her. "I wish you were here."

"I miss you, too," he said. "I sealed the K.C. deal and I'm on the plane back to L.A. How do you feel?"

Taylor explained Pulaski's threat.

"Rest easy tonight," Philip said. "You're safe with the police. And remember that I love you."

Taylor watched a sailboat glide down the river, now dark blue. Behind the downtown silhouette, the evening sun was a fuchsia disk in the orange sky.

For a second she wondered about Caroline, the woman Julian had alleged was Philip's mistress, but she suspected that was merely a ploy by Julian to divide her and Philip.

"I love you, too," Taylor said softly. She hung up.

"Do you really?"

Julian's voice startled her.

"Eavesdropping is rude."

"So what'd he say?" Julian asked. "Cheer up, darling, this crisis is good for ratings'?" Julian chuckled. "Philip Carter has absolutely no idea how you feel."

"He understands enough," Taylor said. In her mind she saw Philip during their argument last night.

"I doubt it," Julian said.

"Shut up," Taylor said. "We'll eat, you'll leave, and that's the last of talking about you and me. You have no right to—"

Julian stepped closer, staring intensely at her.

Taylor scowled. "Don't stand so close—"

Julian gently placed his mouth on her parted lips, cupping the back of her head in his palm.

Taylor pushed her hands into his chest, but he pulled her closer. The tension, the anger, the pain, melted under his kiss. Suddenly dizzy and hot, she closed her eyes. Electric sparks crackled along her spine, reigniting long-suppressed passion for her first love. *He feels so good. So good . . .*

Julian placed warm hands on her bare waist, under her cropped sweater, causing her nipples to strain against her lace bra. She crushed her breasts into his chest, kissing him with curious hunger.

His lips are so soft and hot. I can kiss him for a minute or two, that's all. One last kiss.

Taylor moaned as passion aroused every inch of her flesh. She slid her palms up from his hard stomach, over his chest, lacing her fingers through his silky curls.

Then Philip's cornflower blue eyes appeared in her mind. She heard him call her "superstar."

No, I can't cheat on Philip. And I can't give Julian the satisfaction of hurting me again. Especially after that twisted confession.

Taylor pried her lips away. She pushed Julian's chest. He drew her closer, kissing her again. Then he released her. She reeled into the glass door.

Julian's smoky eyes sparkled with lust and triumph.

"Now tell me, Taylor, that you have no feelings for me," he said with a sexy rasp. "No, don't tell me. Your eyes tell me how much you care."

Taylor glared at him. *How can I care for him after what he said today?* She hurried into the kitchen, gathering plates and silverware. In her haste, she spilled red pepper flakes on the floor. As she swept them up, the phone rang.

"Hello," Julian said.

Damn him! It could be Philip again. Furious, she darted into the living room and snatched the phone from his hand.

"Hello? Yes, please bring the pizza up to 25E. Thank you."

Her heart racing, Taylor glared at Julian. "That could have been Philip! What's your problem?"

"I'm going to tell Philip about us," Julian said.

"There's nothing to tell!" Taylor yelled.

"That kiss just convinced me that there's a lot to tell. Deny it all you want, White Chocolate, but I know you still love me."

"You arrogant bastard!" Taylor shouted. "You're gonna eat your pizza and leave. You cross Philip Carter and he'll ruin you. And I don't want you bringing me down with you. I've worked too hard—"

"I don't care," Julian said. "You're all that matters."

"I *do* care," Taylor said. "I won't let you trash my career or my engagement."

"Watch me," Julian said.

CHAPTER 21

On the balcony, with Julian sitting next to her on the rattan love seat, Taylor noticed her CD by a new age music group had begun to play. As she listened to the lustful lyrics, she wondered if she had left it in the CD player or if Julian had inserted it.

"This pizza is great," he said.

Taylor seethed as she chewed the pizza. She was annoyed beyond words that he was ambushing all corners of her life: work, her parents, her apartment. She watched the giant neon letters of the Canadian Club sign across the river flash red, white, and blue lights. It blinked off, then illuminated, reflecting on the black river. The sign, across from Taylor's balcony, rested atop huge white silos holding grain for producing alcoholic beverages. Now the pungent scent of yeast wafted across the river, which meant that intoxicating spirits were brewing.

"Taylor?"

"What," she snapped.

"You have to believe I'm a different person now," Julian said, sipping wine.

"I don't," she said. "It was easier to watch a cross-burning at Pulaski's compound than to hear what you said today. It makes me sick." Taylor dropped a pizza slice on the plate and stared at the water.

"I am so, so sorry, Taylor. I don't know what to say."

"There's nothing to say. Just finish your food and leave."

"I don't want to leave," he said. "I want you in my life."

Taylor faced Julian, her eyes blazing with anger. "If you're still so in love with me, why'd you get engaged to that stupid actress?"

"She helped me forget about you," Julian said with woeful eyes. "I figured you hated me by then, so I kind of fell into it with Brooke."

"That's the wrong answer," Taylor said, remembering the plastic-looking bimbo she'd seen on Julian's arm in *People*.

"It's the truth," he said. "She was part of the wild party scene with Philip that I wanted to get away from."

"What wild scene?" Taylor asked.

"Women, parties, drugs, you know," he said.

"No, I don't know. Philip doesn't use drugs."

"Maybe not in front of you."

"You're just saying this to turn me against Philip," Taylor said.

"Believe what you want, but I know things about Philip Carter that would—"

"I don't want to hear your lies," Taylor said. "It doesn't matter anyway, Julian, because you know what? I don't love you anymore."

"Look into my eyes and say that."

Taylor met his eyes. "I don't love you anymore."

"Could you love me again?"

"No," Taylor said. *That's a lie. When I don't think about the past or the future, and just savor the now, I could let myself feel safe and serene with Julian.*

Julian's piercing stare declared that he sensed her dishonesty.

After a few moments, Taylor realized that the passionate music was placating her distressed emotions. She took another pizza slice, the steaming cheese stretching upward. Julian ran his finger through the cheese, then pressed it to her mouth. She turned away, causing the greasy glob to strike her cheek.

"What—"

Julian licked her cheek, then poked his finger through her lips to plant the cheese on her tongue. His mouth sealed her lips. At first Taylor thought she would choke, but the delicious garlic-tomato taste and the hotness of his lips made her head swirl. Julian pulled away for a moment as she swallowed, then grasped her jaw in his hands. He kissed her, his lips satin-smooth and fiery-hot against hers.

Oh my goodness . . .

The torrent of emotions that had thrashed inside her like a whirlpool since she had first seen Julian now simmered and steamed under his searing kiss. She was melting, slipping into the dark realm where her heart and soul wrested all self-control and power from her rational mind. After a few moments of scarlet desire flaming through her, the molten mass that had become her feelings yielded a bittersweet syrup. After one taste, Taylor ached with a fiendish craving for more.

As if his lips were a lollipop, she traced their edges with her tongue, lapping at their smooth curves, then sucking them into her mouth, extracting and savoring their sweetness. When their tongues touched, it was like licking a giant, heated sugar cube, the rough surface empowered to enrich all that it touched. Next she tasted his cheek, as smooth and sweet as caramel, and so delicious that she needed more, a larger expanse of the delectable skin. So she nibbled her way down to his neck. A wide, strong neck, hot with the blood surging through ropelike veins, tender and spiced with an enticing scent unique to Julian LaMarre DuPont. She devoured his neck, savoring its scent even as she tasted his earlobe, biting it gently, then dipping the tip of her tongue inside.

All these flavors and textures tasted hauntingly familiar, because they had delighted her long ago. But the long famine between then and now made them spicier, aged to perfection and even more luscious. And Taylor wanted to taste everything, to gorge herself to the bursting point, then feast on more as soon as her body would allow. She relished this newfound gluttony without conscience or fear of what consequences it might bring tomorrow.

"Je te désire," Julian whispered, his warm breath tickling her neck.

The two plates on their laps crashed to the floor as he balanced his muscular bulk over her, melting her into a pool of butterscotch. His hot palms on her bare stomach set her flesh afire all over again, causing her to moan and writhe under his touch.

She stared into his smoky eyes, peering into the soul of the man she had always loved. She savored every feathery-soft stroke of his fingertips, every waft of his scent, every searing kiss, because he touched her more gently than any man knew how, and now aroused in her a passion that she had never known.

He removed his shirt, exposing a dark expanse of velvet skin that she ached to touch and taste. He pulled off her sweater and ran his cheeks over her bare flesh. Across her stomach, between and over her aching, lace-covered breasts. He cupped them in his hands, coaxing them to firm peaks, teasing them with hot breath. He removed her bra. Taylor moaned when he took the hot tips into his mouth, sucking gently, cupping the round flesh as he trailed his tongue between them. Golden sparks sprayed through her abdomen, lighting fire to the swelling flesh between her legs. She clung to the back of his neck, laced fingers through his hair, and thanked God for delivering such mind-numbing passion.

When another song began to play, with its Gregorian chants and sultry beat, Julian gazed at her with the most tender eyes she had ever seen. A wonderful languor overcame her, pulling her into a mellow state of limpness and heaviness and dampness. It was not inspired entirely by Julian's eyes, with their smoky brown color lined by thick black lashes, or his cheeks, rouged with passion, lips parted with hunger. It was the love she saw in his face, the gentle promise of a lifetime of care and compassion, happiness and heartfelt adoration. It provoked a shiver, a shoulder-twitching shiver that raised the fine hairs across her body.

At that moment Taylor became hypersensitive to the sensual stimuli around her—the seductive music, with its French pleas of passion. Above them was the full, silver moon, reflecting off the black river below.

And before her was the most beautiful man on earth, her soul mate, Julian DuPont. She loved that his eyes carried her to a place where nothing else existed, to a realm that promised an eternity of the enchantment she was sampling now. Taylor stared into his eyes over her heaving chest, inviting him without words, as she once had so often, to siphon her further into this intimate dimension known only to them.

He understood, because he scooped her into his arms. He pressed his lips to hers as he carried her to the bedroom and gently placed her on the bed. There he removed her sandals, her jeans, and lit candles on the dresser. Then, with eyes flashing sadness and regret and hope in the candlelight, he pulled off his loafers and jeans, towering over her at the side of the bed in white briefs. Taylor, her hair fanned around her near-nude body, ran a curious forefinger over his flat stomach, his iron-hard thigh.

Julian knelt on the floor next to her. He kissed her lips, then nibbled her shoulders, trailed kisses down her arms, and pressed his lips to all ten of her fingertips. He held up her feet, tracing their arches with his fingers, sucking her toes. He stroked her calves and knees and thighs with his hands and mouth, dropping feathery kisses on the insides of her thighs that made her squirm with desire.

Yes, I need you, I want you . . . Me and you. Us. Now.

Taylor marveled at his every move, burning the sight and feel and scent of him into her mind over the tattered, faded images of the past that once were so bright. His every breath enchanted her now, as he traced the lace arches of her white thong over her hips and across her quivering-to-the-touch abdomen.

She shuddered and cried out when he ran fingers over the moist fabric between her legs, again and again. The flesh there was like a wild, pink animal, wriggling and screaming for massage. Julian's eyes were glazed with lust as he grasped the lace, pulling it downward over her hips, thighs, legs, and toes. He dropped it to the floor, then dove between her legs with an open mouth.

Taylor cried out when his tongue penetrated her. The pleasure became nearly unbearable when he moved upward, lapping at the bursting berry, hot and swollen and juicy, devouring her as if she were his last meal. He nibbled as if she gave him sustenance. Like shooting stars, hot tingles radiated through her, engulfing her mind in a psychedelic swirl of sparkles and heat. She shivered when he slid a finger inside her, teasing her with pleasures yet to come. That, with his expert tongue, intensified these glorious sensations to the point that wild tremors wracked Taylor into a near-death seizure of ecstasy. Her body squeezed around Julian's finger as blue-white webs of electricity crackled across her trembling flesh. She cried out as she never had before, a cry for mercy and salvation and hope. With her eyes closed, the delirious pleasure seemed eternal as she floated to heaven on a silver lined cloud. After long moments, she opened her eyes to see Julian over her, naked, a huge erection hovering over her trembling body, pointing at her like Cupid's arrow.

Yes, ravish me. I'm all yours.

His eyes were haunted and ravenous. Taylor lifted limp arms to cup his face in her palms. He was so beautiful. And he belonged to her. He was home. Eyes connecting with hers, Julian descended and impaled her.

She whimpered, the shock of his size momentarily stunning her. Then, gloriously, it was as if he were reaching deep inside her and tickling thousands of nerve endings that spewed gold electric sparks. And this communion of souls promised to wash away the pain and suffering of the past and sweep her into Elysium.

Julian moaned as he thrust slowly, as if to savor every sensation. The heavy-sweet incense of burning passion enshrouded them as Julian channeled Taylor into a garden blooming with vibrant color and velvet textures and sheer bliss. Somehow this experience was far more powerful than their teenaged rapture. Now their bodies and minds were more mature, more seasoned by disappointment, more appreciative of the purity of love and commitment. The emotions gushing through Taylor, spinning like a funnel and pulling every morsel of her being into it, were as intense as the waves of pleasure that had consumed her moments earlier. She gazed up into the brown velvet of Julian's eyes.

Yes, my soul mate is home. We're one now, our spirits are swirling in the air above us as we float into Nirvana.

But something mysterious smoldered in Julian's expression as he thrust more urgently. More savagely.

"What's my name?" he demanded with a raspy voice.

Startled, Taylor stared up at him.

"What's my name?"

"Julian," she whispered.

"Say it loud."

"Julian." An otherworldly shadow suddenly appeared in his eyes, on his damp face.

He grasped the backs of her knees and pressed them forward, plunging deeper inside her, virtually nailing her to the bed. She gasped and closed her eyes to savor this erotic cataclysm.

"Say it!" he bellowed.

"Julian."

"Who do you love?"

Taylor probed his eyes. *Who do I love? Do I love Philip at this moment that Julian is making love to me? Do I love Julian, an apparition with a scheme to steal my heart?*

Taylor revered this passion-swept fantasy that Julian was hers again, that they were in another dimension where Philip and Rocky Pulaski and the police outside the apartment door did not exist.

That's what she loved, the escapist sensuality and soul-quivering beauty of the moment. And she did not want to venture past that.

"Who do you love?" Julian thundered. "What's my name?" Taylor panted, delirious with ecstasy.

"Who?"

"Julian," she gasped as orgasmic waves consumed her. "Julian, yes, Julian."

He began to tremble. Panting, he closed his eyes, moaned and spasmed for long moments. When his body stilled, he gently collapsed beside her, drawing damp fingertips across her forehead and chin and cheeks.

"My Taylor, my baby, my White Chocolate. I love you."

Hot, fiery tears clouded her focus, spilling from the corners of her eyes. She blinked, noticing that that tender expression remained on his face, pleading for repentance and salvation. Taylor lowered heavy lids to exorcise this vision of heartache.

CHAPTER 22

Jess Stevens cringed when Karl Kramer snaked his arm over the back of her chair in the fluorescent-lit basement meeting room in the Pulaski farmhouse.

"I told you we'd bail 'em outta jail and bring 'em home," said Kramer, his bushy, graying mustache and beard dominating a small face. He smelled like that same cheesy groin musk as her grandfather.

"Ssshh," she said, inching to the distant edge of the metal folding chair. "Don't talk while Rocky's preachin'."

Jess sighed, relieved when he removed his arm. She had been thankful that Kramer, Rocky's lawyer, had appeared in 36th District Court that morning with a briefcase stuffed with bail money, but he had been sitting much too near on that hard courtroom bench. And now he was doing the same.

Jess nibbled the jagged skin around her stinging fingernails. She had chewed them so low the previous night after seeing Rocky in jail that each tip was now a raw, red strip. Nail biting was a nasty habit that had grown worse in prison, after the rape. Jess shook her head to erase the images of those two lifers who had not seen a man in twenty years, ramming their callused fingers inside her, groping her breasts in the janitor's closet when the guards were not looking. She squirmed on the hard chair, unconsciously tightening her sphincter muscles to combat the bloody memory of the fingers sodomizing her, sharp teeth gnawing her breasts, that filthy sponge in her mouth to quiet her screams. Jess shuddered.

Kramer stroked her back. "It's okay, Jess," he said. "Rocky's home now."

Get your hands off me, pervert. You're just like Grandpa.

Jess battled memories of Grandpa—the way he always demanded that she bathe with him, and the way he forced her to bounce on his thing, hurting her and making her cry. She could still hear the bathwater sloshing around him, see the expression on his bushy-bearded face when his white goo squirted into the dingy water.

I hate him and the bitch daughter he raised. He deserves to lie in his own shit in that nasty nursing home, with his bedsores and drool.

Jess concentrated on Rocky, standing proudly before fifty or so comrades, quoting *Mein Kampf.*

"The mightiest counterpart to the Aryan is represented by the Jew," he said as his followers nodded silently.

Pride glowed within Jess. She dreamed of helping Rocky achieve his Utopia, and her work with the revolution instilled in her a sense of purpose and importance. She was forty years old, and Rocky Pulaski was her savior. Before she met him, shortly after his wife, Loretta, died, her life had been a series of wretched experiences strung together by booze and cold-blooded boyfriends.

My life was crap before Rocky, and Ma made it that way.

Too wicked to keep her husband, Betty Stevens had seldom been around for Jess. She preferred working at the truck stop, calling herself a waitress instead of a hooker, rather than taking her daughter to the circus or helping her with homework. She rarely came home to the tiny, cluttered bungalow in Dearborn where Grandpa's babysitting left Jess withdrawn, scared, and sore. At least Jess had discovered Ma's stash of marijuana and booze. She remembered sitting on the tattered living room couch, giggling in a haze of pot and vodka, as *The Brady Bunch* enjoyed a two-parent, middle-class life that was as foreign to Jess as the Latin American countries where her weed was grown.

She dropped out of school in ninth grade, spending days and weeks in drugged fogs at boyfriends' houses, heavy-metal music blasting, endless sex passing the hours. That lifestyle did not cease until she attended a white separatist meeting with a friend, where she met Rocky Pulaski. Now she gazed at him as his increasingly fervent preaching and hand gestures roused the crowd into an emotional, blood-hungry frenzy.

You changed my life, and I love you like I've never loved a man.

First he had explained to her the tenets of Aryan superiority. Her experience with blacks and Jews and Mexicans had been limited to the criminals on the television news, the prominent-nosed rich folks in Oakland County, and the short, greasy people she had seen at a Mexican Village restaurant on one of the few dates she ever had. As a result, she found it easy to embrace Rocky's authoritative, scientific explanations about genetic intelligence and social Darwinism, with white people always superior.

After that, Rocky had shared with her his vision of a better America. She regularly attended meetings at his house in Detroit, and when he fled the urban chaos that was engulfing the city—especially his frustration with having a Negro foreman at the auto plant and Billy Joe's repeated fights with black schoolmates—she relocated with him and Billy Joe to the farmhouse about two hours north of Detroit. The years that followed had been the pinnacle of her life. She had loved cooking sausage and eggs for him in the morning, making love in the afternoon, and working long hours to build the White Power Alliance into the newspaper, cable television, and computer empire that it had become by the early nineties.

Then Taylor James came along and dropped an A-bomb.

That bitch deserves a slow, painful death.

After the raid, Jess's life became a filmstrip of horrors. Suffering eighteen miserable months in prison. Witnessing her black cellmate's convulsive, screaming nightmares. Biting a cockroach in the beef stew. Staring at cement walls, seeing Taylor James's face in the compound, secretly videotaping everything. Pounding and screaming on her thin mattress to vent her hatred for that mongrel.

And for her to appear at the rally in Detroit yesterday with that proud smirk was like spitting in the face of the White Power Alliance.

"Comrades," Rocky shouted, "this is war! The mongrel has pushed us closer to the revolution."

Jess joined raucous applause. "Burn the bitch!"

Next to Rocky was a television playing a videotape of Channel 3's five-part series about the WPA. Angry shouts and jeers erupted from the assemblage.

Rocky, with Billy Joe at his side, calmed the crowd with outstretched hands.

"Tomorrow night, right here," Rocky said, "we'll have Taylor James in the custody of the White Power Alliance. In our own common-law court, we'll try her on criminal charges of betraying our mission, betraying the entire white race linked to her through her mother's blood. She stands accused of being a puppet of the Jew-controlled media and its conspiracy to portray productive white citizens like you and me as America's villains. And she's guilty of being

WHITE CHOCOLATE / 177

born into a degenerate union of Negro and Caucasian, then using her appearance to deceive Aryans to advance her career."

The crowd cheered wildly.

"Destroy her!" Jess screamed. Next to her, Lula and Nick Wallace, and their little girl, applauded.

"For these charges, comrades," Rocky said, "we'll hold a trial right here, before all of you, tomorrow night. She'll be found guilty. We all know that these are offenses punishable only by death. So you'll join me in inflicting merciless vengeance."

Jess beamed. The mongrel's death would signal the debut of a new era of Jess's life as an eager soldier in the white revolution.

CHAPTER 23

White-hot pain throbbed in Taylor's cheek.

Andy, we gotta leave . . .

She felt cold, damp grass under her.

Julian can't save me now.

"Wake up, honey," Lula shouted, slapping her cheek. "Wake up. It's okay." *Lula and Nick and the black sky swam above.*

Andy, let's go now . . . God, please don't let them kill us. No, Rocky. Don't hurt me—

"Sweetheart, are you all right?" Rocky asked. "Your boyfriend here is gonna take you home now. I'm sorry my son is such a hothead. He thought you were some girl who hustled him out of a hundred bucks at the pool hall."

Andy, there you are. He raised her up and walked her to the Ford Explorer in the garage.

"It's time to leave," Andy said. "It's okay now. It was a misunderstanding."

Heart racing, drenched with sweat, Taylor awoke; her eyes flew open.

Julian is here now to hold me when I'm scared.

A dull ache between her legs and the exhaustion that weighted her nude body were evidence of their delicious tryst, and Taylor longed to feel him again, holding her as he had all night, kissing her forehead, stroking her bare skin, radiating heat and love. She needed to hear him say her name and her nickname again, over and over, in that low, raspy tone.

Lying on her side, she inched backward, anticipating the hot, arousing touch of her back against his chest and torso, the bottoms of her thighs on his, her buttocks on something long and hard that promised more soul-felt, psychedelic quivering.

But the sheets were cold. She was alone.

CHAPTER 24

Taylor knew better than to wonder if she had imagined the night with Julian, but for a second she did. There was no note, no forgotten sock, not even a black hair on the pillowcase. Verification of his presence finally came in a very faint waft of his scent, drifting up from the sheets, assuring her that the night had been real.

"That bastard," she said, striking the side of the bed where he had slept. Just like before, like a ghost, he had slipped out of her life, leaving her wondering and hurting. She imagined him on a plane to California, smirking that his seduction skills were so smooth that he could enrapture his engaged ex-girlfriend, after a decade, within one day. Was all that talk about wanting her back sincere? What about that ache-to-the-bone confession about his resentment of her color? And the soul-searing passion they had shared? Taylor pulled the blankets over her bare chest.

I cheated on Philip.

She fell back on the pillows. The same fiery shame that had consumed her after that first night with Philip in New York suddenly engulfed her.

Did I commit adultery? Three weeks from her wedding night, she had celebrated by making love with another man.

Taylor ran to the shower. Under water as hot as she could bear, she asked God not to loathe her. It was Sunday morning and in a few hours she would be at her bridal shower, receiving gifts in celebration of her upcoming marriage. But she had just experienced the most delirious passion ever, with another man. Guilt rolled through her like a black storm cloud. Sudden, ominous, thundering. Though her skin was scarlet under the steaming water, she shivered.

How could I have been so gullible? Julian had ripped open the long-healed wounds that he had inflicted on her heart, leaving them now to throb and gush again. And, like before, she was now alone for the grueling recovery. Taylor held her face under the scalding stream of water until she gasped for breath.

Then she rationalized her dalliance with Julian as a momentary lapse in judgment. Pulaski's threats, the police escort, and the emotional trauma of seeing and hearing Julian had twisted her sensibleness into a tangle of confusion and pain that enabled her to commit a grave indiscretion.

It's over and done with. Nobody will ever have to know. As for Julian, I'll show complete indifference when we become colleagues.

Taylor dressed in an ankle-length, cream granny dress with peach flowers and tiny satin rosebuds around a scoop collar. She wore little makeup with the pearl earrings and pearl choker that were a high-school graduation gift from her parents.

Two police officers greeted her outside the apartment door.

"Good morning, Ms. James," said an officer with a thick black mustache. "We'll be with you until this evening."

"Nice to meet you," Taylor said.

"Your fiancé is so good-looking," the female officer said. "When he left here this morning, he seemed familiar for some reason."

A red flare of panic exploded inside Taylor.

"Listen, being on TV, I really cherish my privacy," Taylor said as they walked to the garage. Then another alarming thought sent her pulse racing: If Sergeant Scarlin was a Pulaski sympathizer, perhaps these two officers were as well. And with one phone call, they could inform Pulaski where she was, and he could simply come and kill her. Taylor shook her head to rid her mind of such paranoia. Pulaski couldn't possibly have that kind of power in the police department.

"We're here to make you feel safe, not uncomfortable," the male officer said.

Still, Taylor eyed them suspiciously as they walked to her car.

Taylor and the police pulled into the circular driveway of her parents' English Tudor home on Fairway Drive in northwest Detroit.

"My baby girl," her father said, hugging her tight against his warm, thick chest. His close-cropped, salt-and-pepper beard brushed her cheek.

"Hi, Daddy," Taylor said, relishing the security of her father's arms in the walnut-paneled, two-story foyer. As he stepped outside, she noticed he wore plaid shorts and a polo shirt.

"I'm going to play golf. Too many women in that house for me," he said, laughing, his brown eyes sparkling in the sunshine. "Enjoy yourself, honey."

"I will," Taylor said as her mother embraced her.

"My goodness, Taylor, you're glowing like the sun," Monica James said, her turquoise eyes twinkling.

Taylor smiled self-consciously as forks of guilt stabbed her. "Thanks, Mom, I'm just excited about the party."

Her mother, with a cloud of white-blond hair bouncing at her shoulders and a blue headband that matched her blue silk dress, examined Taylor. Maternal knowing drew her pale eyebrows together, parted her pink-painted lips, and raised the fine white hair on her cheeks like tiny sensors.

"You saw Julian," Monica said, smiling. "I've never seen you so radiant."

Hot gales of shame whipped Taylor. Perspiration seeped from her pores and she cast her eyes down.

"The wedding invitations are already out," Monica said, "but I'll gladly make a hundred phone calls to tell the guests that the name of the groom has changed."

"It hasn't," Taylor said. She glanced at the bunches of peach and cream helium balloons filling the paneled hallway. With their curly ribbons hanging to the floor, they were like a jury of stick people whose blank faces exclaimed a verdict: guilty of premarital infidelity. The aromas of confections drifting from the kitchen were so sweet that Taylor felt a bit nauseated, while the chatter of scores of women echoing from the living room, along with the soft strums on a harp, made her feel as though she were about to be sacrificed in some ancient female ritual. And all the women in the room would read the guilt and torment on Taylor's face as clearly as her mother did, as if her face were a TelePrompTer that said, *I cheated on my fiancé last night with Julian DuPont and I loved every orgasmic second of it.*

Like a ghost of Julian, his mother appeared in the kitchen doorway.

Janice DuPont consumed Taylor in a bear hug and a cloud of perfume. With her black hair swooped high and her dark eyes bright, she looked elegant, as usual, in a teal pantsuit with gold-embroidered stripes and fancy buttons. Her taut brown skin was ageless, and her facial structure was a carbon copy of her son's.

"Hello, Aunt Janice," Taylor said, squeezing her.

"You look so young and innocent," she said. "Doesn't she, Monica?"

Her mother flashed a knowing smile.

Taylor dabbed her damp upper lip with the back of her hand. Her secret was obvious to the X-ray eyes of the two women who had known her since birth.

"Taylor," cried Aunt Bernadette, her father's sister, with her daughters, Yvonne and LaTonya.

Aunt Bernadette kissed Taylor's cheek, then scrutinized her with jet button eyes and a smile. She thrust a gift at her.

"Here, child, something pretty for you," she said before heading to the kitchen with Monica and Janice.

"Girlfriend," cousin Yvonne said, a gold rope glistening at her neck, "I can't believe you're 'bout to marry that rich old white man."

"Yeah, why you wanna sell us out like that?" LaTonya asked, crossing thin arms over an orange sheath dress.

"Sell you out?" Taylor asked.

"Yeah, you black, you should stick with the black race," Yvonne said. "Seem like you tryin' to pass for white now that you on TV."

Anger hummed through Taylor. Her childhood tormentors— who had called her "whitey," teased her for "talking white," and flirted ruthlessly with Julian—suddenly wanted to claim her as one of their own.

"I'm not selling out anything," Taylor said. "Philip is a wonderful man and we're in love."

"Well, I heard Julian is back in town, and I *know* you want a piece of that," Yvonne said. "I know I do. He's makin' big dough now. Shoot, if I got him . . . no more food stamps, no more hearin' my three kids complain about 'Why can't I have these two-hundred-dollar gym shoes?' I'd get me a house, a Benz, everything. I'd have the finest man in Detroit."

LaTonya playfully slapped Yvonne's arm. "Dream on, girl," LaTonya said. "Julian would run if he met your bad-ass kids. And after livin' large in L.A., I don't think he'd step foot in your ghetto crib."

Then LaTonya posed like a model, smiling. "I think I'm more Julian's type," she said.

"Maybe, when you're not in rehab," Yvonne said. "He'd know somethin' was up when his VCR and jewelry started to go up in smoke when you came around."

LaTonya glared at Yvonne. "Shut your mouth."

Taylor set the gift on the hallway table next to a vase of roses, then said, "LaTonya, Yvonne, why don't you go into the dining room and get some punch."

Minutes later, Taylor's entrance into the crowded living room prompted a chorus of cheers. Champagne flowed, scrumptious finger foods beckoned from the coffee table, and the harp music played by a woman in a flowing dress soothed her rattled emotions. As friends and relatives cooed over her, Taylor began to enjoy the party.

"That dress makes you look young enough to be Philip's daughter," Shari said, evoking smiles from Danielle and Carla. "Talk about robbing the cradle. All you need is a pacifier."

"Very funny," Taylor said.

"I like it," Danielle said. She pointed to a mountain of pastel boxes and bows. They glowed under beams of sunshine penetrating the beveled windows along the back of the living room that faced the bright green of the Detroit Golf Club. "I bet there's enough stuff in those boxes to corrupt every inch of you."

Danielle elbowed Taylor softly. "So yesterday Julian told Peter he's hired at Channel Three. And that he was visiting you."

"We talked," Taylor said coolly. "I congratulated him on the job; he congratulated me on the marriage. That was it."

Shari's hazel eyes enlarged with curiosity. "That was it?"

"Yes," Taylor said, holding up her ring. "Julian missed his chance a long time ago and I—"

A gray-haired woman pushed past Taylor's friends with long, fleshy arms. "My baby girl!"

"Grandma Willa," Taylor said, hugging her father's mother, whose arms and breasts felt like giant sacks of warm Jell-O. She always smelled like witch hazel and menthol and had worn the same silver cat-eye glasses since Taylor was a baby.

"All grown-up and gettin' married," Grandma Willa said, leaning on a cane in her purple flower-print dress and brown orthopedic shoes.

Taylor smiled and introduced her to her friends.

"Why, I remember when you were just a little yellow butterball squirming in my lap," she said, extending a waxy brown hand still strong after decades behind a sewing machine.

"I'll never forget that day I took you to the department store," Grandma Willa said, grasping Shari's arm, "when a security guard asked me for some identification because he wanted to know why I was carryin' around a little white infant. Thought I kidnapped my own grandbaby."

Shari shook her head.

"But I love all people," she said, looking at Danielle. "It doesn't matter the color, as long as they're good inside, you see. And God will forgive your other grandparents, child, for their hateful ways." Piercing dark eyes stared out from a wrinkled oval face, powdered pink-brown.

Taylor glanced around the room, noticing with sadness the absence of her mother's family, whom she had never met—grandparents and her mother's two sisters, Helga and Hellen.

The tinkle of a crystal bell drew everyone's attention to Taylor's mother.

"Ladies, it's time to enjoy a buffet prepared by Janice DuPont, my best friend and owner of the catering company La Cuisine Noire. Come on into the dining room and fill up your plates."

As Taylor piled her plate high with fried chicken, quiche, croissants, and collard greens, Janice whispered over a huge pan of her incredible macaroni and cheese. "Taylor, my son is lovesick."

And I've been heartbroken for a decade. Taylor stared stiffly into Janice's eyes. Her and her mother's comments, considering the occasion, were insulting. They completely disregarded her feelings for

Philip. And she especially did not want to talk about Julian with cousin LaTonya eavesdropping over the relish tray.

"How was your visit yesterday?" Janice asked as she led Taylor into the kitchen. "I didn't get to talk to him before his flight this morning."

"His flight?"

"Yes," Janice said. "He went back to Los Angeles to pack up his house. Taylor, I know for years you asked me and François to send messages to Julian. Now I hope you'll hear him out before it's too late."

"That's really unfair," Taylor said.

"Maybe," Janice said. "But sometimes we have to swallow our pride and make difficult choices."

Taylor stiffened. "Aunt Janice, excuse me, but you've made all this food, I don't want it to get cold."

Taylor regretted her harsh tone, but it welled from her gut as forcefully as a heave. Her cheeks burned as she joined her grand-mother at an umbrella table on the patio.

"Your daddy just passed by on a golf cart," Grandma Willa said.

"Yeah, I think his right arm is going to turn into a golf club one of these days," Taylor said, attempting to smile.

The women gathered in the living room, where Taylor sat on the couch and Danielle handed her gifts. Every negligee, fancy bra, and nightgown evoked cheers from the women.

"This is from Shari," Danielle said.

Taylor pulled a purple satin bustier, garter, and stockings from a Victoria's Secret box.

"Oh my," her mother said.

"In my day that would've been illegal," Grandma Willa said.

Taylor examined the gift. Guilt tugged at her insides when she envisioned herself wearing it for Julian instead of Philip. "Thank you, Shari, I love it."

Leaning against the mantel, Shari smiled and twirled her tennis bracelet.

"She got herself the same thing," whispered Carla, sitting next to Taylor with a notepad to record the gifts for thank-you notes. "I think you need to watch out for Shari. She's trippin'."

"What?" Taylor whispered. "She's just upset about her marriage. All this probably makes it worse for her." Taylor placed the box on the coffee table, which resembled a small lingerie boutique, overflowing with pastel silks and frilly baskets of bubble bath and perfume.

Next Taylor opened Carla's gift, a sheer white nightgown and robe.

"Oh, they're beautiful. Thank you, Carla."

"There's one more," Carla said.

Taylor retrieved white lace panties from the tissue paper. "Oh my goodness!" Taylor exclaimed. "They're crotchless."

The women exploded with laughter.

"Grandma Willa, don't look," Taylor said, blushing. "Mom, you either."

"Looks like dental floss," Grandma Willa said. "I couldn't get that little thing around my wrist if I tried."

When the wild laughter subsided, Danielle gave Taylor a box. "This is from Janice DuPont."

I bet it's a chastity belt or a voodoo doll of Philip impaled on a TV antenna.

The pink paper held a beautifully carved wooden jewelry box. Inside, on blue velvet, was a gold, heart-shaped locket on a chain. Taylor was afraid to open it, fearing Julian's picture inside, but it was empty.

"This is so pretty," she said, hugging Janice.

Next, her mother handed her a box. "Taylor, you are the most precious gift God has ever given me, and I want you to know that nothing is more important to me than your health and happiness," she said tenderly. "So I want you to have this."

In a small box Taylor found a gold bracelet with a half dozen crystal charms. Emotion stung Taylor's eyes and clogged her throat.

"Mom, this is so beautiful," Taylor said as her mother fastened the bracelet on her right wrist.

"My grandmother gave it to me when I was a girl," Monica said, fingering each charm. "This crystal star symbolizes you reaching for the stars in all your life's endeavors. The figurine of a woman stands for good health, and the tiny sword represents safety. This heart symbolizes that you'll always choose the love truest to your heart."

Taylor hugged her mother, wishing she were still a little girl sheltered from the emotions and decisions of adulthood.

"Thank you, Mom. I'll never take it off."

"I also have this for you." Monica handed Taylor a box containing a silver eight-by-ten picture frame with a spot for engraving at the bottom.

As if she doesn't know Philip's name and our wedding date.

The blank spot reminded Taylor of the newsroom storyboard early in the morning, before the assignment editor had written any names of stories or reporters on it. It changed daily.

CHAPTER 25

"Man alert!" Yvonne shouted from the entrance hall.

Taylor's father stepped into the room and waved. "Hello, everyone. Don't mind us. I'm just helping some of Detroit's finest get a plate since they're protecting the guest of honor." The two police officers who had accompanied Taylor that morning waved.

At the same time, Danielle handed Taylor another box. "Last but not least, from me."

Taylor pulled frilly bra and panty sets from a Victoria's Secret box.

"Thank you, Danielle," Taylor said. "I love them."

"Good, they're equally sexy and innocent," Danielle said.

Taylor smiled, displaying the ensembles for her guests until hard footsteps in the entrance hall drew her attention. Two tall police officers—unfamiliar ones—in navy blue uniforms appeared at the hallway. They stepped down into the living room, staring at Taylor with foreboding expressions.

Her pulse quickened.

Oh no, something happened. Maybe Pulaski broke into my apartment or tried to break into the house here. How infuriating that he's violating my shower, too, just when I was relaxing. Is he gonna disrupt my wedding as well? Follow us to Hawaii and stalk me on the beach?

"Ms. James," said the officer with the bronze skin and strong facial features of a Native American. All eyes in the silent room were on him.

"Is everything all right?"

"No," he said, walking toward her. His partner had a wide chest and an intimidating stance.

"Please stand up," the first officer said.

Shari brought a dining room chair and set it near the windows.

Taylor knitted her brows as her heart raced. "What's going on?"

"Please, ma'am, for your own good, step over to the chair," he said.

Taylor sat facing the guests as the officers cuffed her hands in her lap. "What'd I do?" she demanded of the scores of smiling women. Loud disco music started playing.

Taylor smiled. *Strippers. Very funny.*

The men knelt before her. "We're here to serve and protect . . . and please you," they said in unison.

"I'm Jeronimo."

"I'm Black Thunder."

Taylor smiled at Carla, Danielle, and Shari.

But as the men leaped to their feet and tossed off hats, Taylor's cheeks burned with embarrassment that her mother and grand-mother were watching.

The men spun, shaking bodies whose muscles bulged through uniforms. They gyrated hips and shimmied chests.

The women clapped to the beat as the men danced. Jeronimo, with lustful dark eyes locked on Taylor, pulled his long black hair out of a ponytail and shook it wildly.

Shari shrieked.

He grasped his shirt collar and pulled, causing buttons to pop at Taylor, then tossed the shirt toward the wide-eyed harp player. The men strutted around the living room, past the enthusiastic women.

Suddenly self-conscious, Taylor glanced up at the dark-beamed and white stucco ceiling. A few moments later, she noticed her mother and Janice clapping as their amused eyes followed the men's washboard abs and buff physiques. Danielle's cheeks were a little pink, but she exchanged excited whispers with Shari and Carla.

Taylor smiled nervously as the men continued teasing her. She was relieved when the music finally stopped and they bowed.

"Can you uncuff me before you leave, please?" she asked, pro-voking wild laughter among the women.

"Yes, ma'am," Black Thunder said as he produced a key and let her loose.

"Thank you very much," Taylor said as the men retrieved their clothes and departed with a standing ovation.

"I think we could all use a cold drink now," Taylor's mother said. "So, ladies, let's go into the dining room for punch and cake."

Taylor snagged Danielle and Carla with an accusing, teasing look.

"It was Shari's idea," Carla said, pointing to Shari on the patio, talking on her cellular phone. "Listen, I have to tell you something," said Carla, who wore a pink suit.

"What?" Danielle asked, smoothing down her white dress and clear crystal pendant. She wore her long hair in a French braid.

"This morning at church I met a man," Carla said, beaming.

"We want juicy details," Taylor said, smiling.

"His name is Ben Robard and he's a doctor at Henry Ford Hospital. He moved here from Atlanta last year."

"Date? Phone number?" Danielle asked.

"Yeah, we're having dinner Friday night at the Summit," Carla said with a twinkle in her eyes. "Me and him, steak, shrimp, and candlelight."

Taylor caressed her back. "I hope it works out, Carla. You deserve a nice man."

"Is he cute?" Danielle asked.

"Very," Carla said. "He's kinda square, and he talks really proper, but I like that."

"My fingers are crossed," Taylor said, smiling. She rummaged through the sexy goodies on the coffee table, then tossed a red lace bra and panties to Carla.

"Here, wear these for good luck," Taylor said playfully.

Shari approached with a stressed expression. "That was the assignment desk," she said. "You know the activist who was beaten unconscious at the rally Friday, the white guy with dreadlocks?"

Taylor nodded. "Yeah, Lloyd Pryor."

"He died this afternoon," Shari said. "The cops are going out to the Pulaski farm to arrest Rocky and Billy Joe. We're talkin' second-degree murder charges here."

Sourness bubbled in Taylor's gut. *The man I interviewed is dead. Rocky and Billy Joe are murderers.*

"Now you see the monster you're dealing with here, Taylor?" Carla said.

Taylor nodded.

"I'm going into the station," Shari said, "to see how this arrest goes. Something tells me it'll be ugly. Tomorrow I want you to cover the arraignment."

Taylor nodded. "Right."

CHAPTER 26

Taylor teetered under a tower of boxes as she led Carla and Danielle into her bedroom, where they created a mountain of shower gifts in the corner.

"You could open your own store," Danielle said. "Taylor's Temptress Trap."

"You got that right," Carla said.

"Very funny," Taylor said.

The police officers announced that their shift was over and that replacements had arrived. In the living room were two officers, both white men in their early thirties. They smiled and shook Taylor's hand.

"We'll be outside the door all night," one said. "So don't you worry about anything."

After they went into the hallway, Taylor played a Mariah Carey CD, then poured three glasses of white zinfandel. Carla wandered onto the balcony.

"I saw Julian yesterday," Danielle said, sinking into the corner of the ivory leather couch. "He's desperate."

"What do you—" Taylor started.

"What in the world happened out there?" Carla asked as she walked inside. "Looks like a tornado struck. Plates on the floor, pizza crust all over, *two* wine glasses, and this!" Carla held up Taylor's bra.

Taylor smiled. "Okay, I'm busted."

"Julian?" Danielle asked, grinning.

"Scandal in the house tonight!" Carla said loudly, smiling.

"You two can't tell anybody," Taylor said. "Especially Shari."

"So you've got your wedding dress," Danielle said. "All Julian needs now is a tux."

Taylor sighed. She sipped her wine, letting the cold liquid warm her. Danielle slid closer and put her arm around Taylor. "I've been thinking a lot about you and Julian. Peter and I were talking and—"

"Don't tell me you told Peter what I said," Taylor said angrily.

"Julian told him. But, Taylor, maybe this is how your life plan is supposed to be."

"My life plan?"

"Right," Danielle said. "As a teenager, it was like you were almost codependent on Julian for emotional support. You needed him, kind of like Prozac, to help you cope."

Anger shot through Taylor. "Codependent? Prozac? What kind of psychobabble is this, Danielle?" She sunk deeper into the couch, crossing her legs Indian style under her dress.

"I see what she means," Carla said, sitting in the cream leather chair facing them.

"Maybe the past ten years of your life happened the way they did," Danielle said, "because God wanted you to be alone. That way you could become independent and strong, by yourself."

Carla nodded. "Think about what you've accomplished without Julian, how you've grown."

Through tears, Carla was a pink and brown blob. Taylor squeezed her eyes shut, letting teardrops fall onto her lap, as Carla came into focus.

"You earned two degrees," Carla said. "You worked in Miami, you busted the white supremacists, and you became the Wolf Network's angel." Carla looked pensive for a moment. "Sometimes I think I became a good lawyer and I work so hard because I haven't had a man to distract me. And who knows? If I had a husband and kids, maybe I wouldn't be so consumed with my job."

Danielle nodded. "Yeah, and maybe if you and Julian had stayed together, your relationship might have been your first priority, and you might have become just another run-of-the-mill TV reporter." Sadness flashed in Danielle's eyes. "I regret that I didn't have any time alone. I wouldn't know Danielle Mancini if Peter Anderson was suddenly taken away from me. But you know exactly who Taylor James is, without Julian DuPont. See my point?"

"Yeah," Taylor said.

This realization struck like a torrent of floodwater, crashing into Taylor's face, sucking out her breath. Tears stung her eyes. She sighed, staring down at her ring, then the crystal heart on the bracelet her mother had given her that afternoon. Marriage and true love. She had to choose between two things that were supposedly synonymous.

After Carla and Danielle left, Taylor bolted the door and activated the alarm, which would let out a deafening noise if the door opened. A few minutes later, Philip called.

"How's my darling?" he asked.

"I'm okay," Taylor said, as she carried the cordless phone onto the balcony.

"How was the shower?"

"It was nice, but I don't know about all the gifts," Taylor said. "Some of them come with a warning label that says: Caution, wearing this lingerie for an older man carries the risk of heart attack due to extreme sexual arousal."

Philip chuckled. "Hey, that's a risk I don't mind taking. If it's my time to go, let me be tangled up between your legs."

Taylor smiled. "So how's L.A.?"

"Good," he said. "Me and the kids went sailing today. I fried."

"Aw, poor baby," Taylor said softly, watching a lighted freighter cut through the black river. "Miss me?"

"Immensely. Are the police still with you?"

"Yes," Taylor said. She explained that Lloyd Pryor died and that Pulaski would be arrested.

"That barbarian's about to get a lifelong lease on a prison cell,"

Philip said. "The important thing is that you don't have to worry anymore."

"I hope you're right," Taylor said. As she leaned against the rail, her wineglass toppled and shattered.

"What was that?"

"Nothing, I just knocked something over," Taylor said. "I wish you were here to hold me."

"Mmmm, so do I," Philip said. "I'm throbbing just thinking about it."

There he goes again. Thinking sex when I need emotional support. She glanced at the half-eaten slices of pizza.

"Taylor?"

"Yes, I'm here."

"Promise me you won't worry tonight," Philip said.

"That's easier said than done," Taylor said.

"Just try," Philip said. "Hey, we hired Julian DuPont yesterday. That's my man."

Guilt slithered through her.

"He takes his work seriously, gives everything his all," Philip said.

Taylor felt devilish. *Oh yes, he does.*

"Ambitious, determined," Philip added. "When I first met him six years ago he had this fire in his eyes like nothing could stand in the way of what he wanted."

Yes, I saw that look last night in bed.

"Sounds like you know him pretty well," Taylor said.

"Yeah, I do," Philip said. "I take care of my people. Work hard, do me right, and the universe is yours. Cross me, then you might as well take the next train to Timbuktu 'cause you're finished in this business."

A sudden wave of weakness threatened to buckle Taylor's knees. She fell back on the rattan love seat.

Philip chuckled. "Like this guy Rick Hilton in Chicago. That arrogant son-of-a—"

Philip's malicious tone drew sweaty goose bumps across Taylor's body. *That could be me.*

"I'm sorry, darling," Philip said. "Don't get me started. This doesn't apply to you. Not my superstar. You'll take the network by storm. Soon as we get back from the honeymoon, we'll start preparing your résumé tape for New York. The interview process will only be a formality."

Taylor fought for her voice. "Wonderful. You know that's my dream."

"You'll be there," Philip said. "I'll just sit back, watch your meteoric rise, and say, 'That's my darling.' "

Taylor imagined him smiling with that proud gleam in his eye that he had had at the Journalist of the Year banquet.

"You're so quiet," he said. "You must be tired. Tuck yourself in bed, curl up with Puff, and pretend that's me who's purring in your arms. And remember that I love you."

"I love you," Taylor said, a heavy wave of guilt consuming her. *Philip can never find out about me and Julian. Never.*

As Taylor headed into the kitchen, she heard angry voices in the hallway. She peeked through the peephole.

Scarlin was outside the door. Anger contorted his thin face. His eyes were narrow slits as he snapped at the officers, against the wall and out of view. *What is he doing here?*

More angry than scared, Taylor deactivated the alarm, unbolted the door, and opened it.

"Is there a problem?" she asked.

Scarlin looked at her coldly. "I was informing my men that Mr. Pulaski was arrested this evening."

"Why couldn't you have just called or radioed them?" Taylor asked.

The officers appeared agitated.

"Everything is all right, Ms. James," an officer said. "This is routine. Sergeant Scarlin wanted to make sure we're keeping you safe."

With hard eyes and pursed lips, Taylor probed the three men for signs of deceit. If Scarlin was a Pulaski sympathizer, it was a frightening possibility that the other two cops outside the door were the same. If so, they could direct Pulaski right to her and thrust her into the arms of terror. Taylor quickly closed the door, bolted it, and reactivated the alarm.

Tense with fear and distrust, Taylor changed into a knee-length Detroit Pistons T-shirt, then flipped on the eleven-o'clock news. Seeing Kendra Vaughn doing the lead story did little to lift her mood.

"This is Kendra Vaughn, live at Rocky Pulaski's farmhouse about two hours north of Detroit. Big, breaking developments tonight."

Yeah, and aren't you glad you're the one reporting it. Taylor scowled. Kendra's face glowed in the camera light in front of a three-story white house. Her eyes seemed to look right at Taylor and say, "Watch me now, bitch. I got your story."

Video of Lloyd Pryor, then Rocky and Billy Joe Pulaski at the rally, flashed on the screen.

"The action started tonight," Kendra said, "after community activist Lloyd Pryor died in the hospital and the Wayne County prosecutor issued arrest warrants for Rocky and Billy Joe Pulaski, who are shown here beating Pryor at a neo-Nazi rally in Detroit on Friday. When police came here to arrest the men, the Pulaskis fired from that attic window."

Video showed SWAT officers in black ducking behind police vehicles as they fired rifles. The camera focused on a Cape Cod–style awning where a thin curtain fluttered over broken glass and the black tip of a gun.

"Two officers were shot, including, as you see here, one SWAT officer who fell two stories from the roof when Pulaski reportedly shot him at close range," Kendra said.

Taylor cringed as the man slid off the roof.

"He is hospitalized in stable condition with a gunshot wound to the chest, while the other officer is in serious condition with a graze wound to the arm," Kendra said. Video showed Rocky, Billy Joe, and Jess being led from the house in handcuffs.

"Fifty-year-old Rocky Pulaski, his twenty-eight-year-old son, Billy Joe, and his forty-year-old girlfriend, Jess Stevens, were taken to the Wayne County Jail. Police told me the Pulaskis will be charged with second-degree murder. In addition, the Pulaskis and Jess Stevens will probably be charged with assault to commit murder, police said, because all three of them fired on police officers here tonight."

The screen showed about twelve skinheads being led from the house.

"These men were arrested and taken into custody as well," Kendra said. "Now there's another disturbing twist to this story. Police told me they found evidence of a plot to kidnap and murder Channel Three News reporter Taylor James. Police say—"

Those words struck Taylor's chest like a cannon.

"—some of the men arrested confessed that tonight's raid interrupted their plans to kidnap and murder Taylor James—"

Taylor froze, her heart pounding against her rib cage.

God, please help me. How could they kidnap me with police protection? Is that why Scarlin was outside the door? If Pulaski hadn't been arrested, would I be dead?

CHAPTER 27

Julian leaned on his elbows on the wooden rail of his deck overlooking Malibu Beach. He stared at wave after wave, first rolling in quietly, gaining momentum, curling under, crashing into water and sand, then slipping quietly back to the ocean, leaving a thin foam fizzling on the beach.

Warmth stirred in his groin, as it had all day when he thought of his night with Taylor. He saw her face, her quivering body, the tender curves that had enlivened foreign yet familiar feelings in him. It was as if the Taylor he had known as a child and teenager had been an imprecise watercolor portrait, but the woman he had spent the night with was an exquisite impressionistic painting, each tiny dot of intellect, emotion, and will uniting to form the perfect woman for him. He had sketched himself into the picture, but his permanence would depend on many more flawless strokes to seal their fate as one.

On a cordless phone, Julian dialed Philip.

"Hey, DuPont, thought you'd be packing."

"I have been," Julian said, "but I want to stop by for a minute. I need to talk to you."

"Sure, you know where to find me."

Julian hopped into his black Porsche and zipped down Pacific Coast Highway to a gated community of mansions on a cliff overlooking the ocean. After the guard phoned Philip and allowed Julian to enter, he followed the familiar curving drive up to the Spanish Mediterranean–style house. How many times had he driven this route to join Philip for wild nights of women, parties, and intoxication?

Like bullets from the past, a barrage of images shot out of his memory. Just months ago, they were in Philip's limousine, club-hopping, when they picked up five girls no older than twenty. The blonde in black spike heels and a micromini perched on Philip's lap, his face in her swelling chest, his hands kneading her bare thighs. Her friends, one with spiky black hair and a sheer pink cat suit, the other in a leopard-print dress, writhed seductively on both sides of Philip. Two girls flanked Julian, licking his ear, tugging at his clothes, but his breakup with Brooke and desire to return to Detroit, and Taylor, had made him feel repulsed by the scene. In his earlier days he would have enthusiastically participated.

"DuPont, video time," Philip said, pouring champagne and sharing a vial of coke with the girls. Julian reached into a compartment under the bar and television to retrieve a camcorder. Philip, smiling, continued drinking, sniffing, and groping as Julian depressed the record button, even when one of the girls buried her face in Philip's unzipped trousers. Videotaping his own lasciviousness, Philip had explained early in their friendship, was a way for him to preserve the fleeting moments when he could forget about his tremendous responsibilities at Wolf and his father's puritanical preaching. He enjoyed playing the videotapes back later to relive every moment of carnal indulgence.

Now Julian pulled into the circular driveway. He walked through an iron gate, onto the columned porch, and rang the doorbell.

"DuPont," Philip said. He wore baggy white drawstring pants, no shirt, and windblown hair. White cream streaked his face, chest, and shoulders, which were the color of raw steak, and he smelled antiseptic.

"Forget your sunblock?" Julian joked as he stepped inside a cavernous expanse of beige Italian marble, columns flanking sunken living and dining rooms with sharp-angled beige furniture.

"Yeah, sailing," Philip said. "Can you believe it? My mind's been on Taylor and that Pulaski joker. I don't know, all weekend something's been eating away at me. Can't put my finger on it."

Julian followed Philip to the bar between the living room and dining room.

"I wish that Neanderthal would just find a cave and crawl in," Philip said as he dropped ice cubes into tumblers.

Julian perched on a barstool. "I hear you, man."

"Grand Marnier?" Philip asked.

"Yeah," Julian said. A knife twisted in his gut every time he glimpsed Philip's lips, his bare chest, his hands. Those were the instruments Philip had used to kiss Taylor, to press his body over her during sex, and to grope her breasts and crotch as he'd done to countless whores. It was difficult for Julian even to look Philip in the eyes, not out of guilt for spending the previous night in Taylor's bed and not out of regret for betraying his relationship with Philip. Julian detested the eyes that had so many times devoured Taylor's body and face, watching her cry and laugh, look serious and somber, but not possibly appreciating her, inside and out, the way Julian did. That blade in his gut sliced the other way now, because Julian had been too selfish and cruel to realize he had been destroying a perfect love, pushing Taylor into the arms of Philip Carter.

Julian sipped the fiery-sweet orange liqueur to drown his remorse. He raised his glass to Philip.

"To you, the great Philip Carter, for making me rise from street slave to big-time anchor, now hometown hero," Julian said, smiling and meeting Philip's stare. "Let me officially thank you for all you've done for me. I appreciate it, man."

Philip nodded as they tapped glasses. "I'm gonna miss you, pal."

"Hey, it's a new start for both of us," Julian said.

"You're right," Philip said. "I just hope when I tie the knot this time, it's not the nightmare I had with Andrea."

"Taylor seems sweet enough," Julian said.

Philip smiled. "She is."

"Man, I never thought you'd take the plunge again," Julian said, remembering when Philip had been forced to buy a new wardrobe because his wife had taken a pair of scissors to his suits and ties after seeing him leave a hotel with the star vixen of a prime-time soap opera.

"Me either," Philip said. "But with Taylor, I don't know, I just had to have her. She makes me feel like a school kid with a crush and a dick that won't quit."

Julian steeled himself against the red cloud of anger threatening to consume his coolness.

"To the power of a woman," Julian said, clinking his glass with Philip's.

"It's wild, DuPont, that I can go into any board room, and I got the biggest balls in the universe. Nobody can fuck with me. But man, sometimes when I'm with Taylor, I'm a weak little puppy and she's holdin' the leash. Call me pussy-whipped, what the hell."

Julian joined Philip in deep laughter. It was all he could do to keep from punching him. But Julian felt whipped, too. Whipped by his own regret and hope, and the awesome pleasure of being alone with her yesterday, feeling that unspoken bond, smelling her hair, forfeiting his soul to her.

"Never thought I'd hear this, man," Julian said. "I guess Brooke did that to me for a while, until I saw the beast within."

"Hey, sweet as it was, there was poison in that apple that Eve gave to Adam," Philip said.

"Yeah," Julian said.

"Speaking of Brooke, she was at the marina today on her dad's boat," Philip said. "That guy is one sleazy motherfucker. Calls himself an investor. He's nothing but a nickel-butt hustler. Wouldn't surprise me if somebody makes shark meat outta him one day."

"That racist lowlife," Julian said. "What the hell was I thinkin' about with her, man?"

"Pussy," Philip said. "Brooke's a card-carrying temptress. That's her job. Blind men with T and A, then take 'em for all they've got. Cash, clothes, and fake tits."

"You could've warned me, man," Julian said.

"Hey, I didn't know you'd fall so hard, pal," Philip said. "Thought you could see she was just one stiletto heel above a call girl."

Julian shook his head. "I know one thing. She was a bad omen, telling me it's time to head back to the more wholesome Midwest."

"But this was good for you," Philip said. "You had to stake your claim on the world. That's more than I can say. I've been under my dad's reins all my life. Be glad you got the chance to come out here."

"Couldn't've done it without you, man," Julian said.

"I saw the fire in your eyes," Philip said, pointing to his own face. "I said, here's a guy who's going somewhere. And we'd been talking about diversity and that whole spiel, especially in the anchor chairs. There you were."

"So I was your affirmative-action baby?" Julian asked.

Philip turned down his mouth and walked around the bar. "No,

DuPont," he said, patting him on the back and sitting on a stool next to him. "I never said anything, but I heard what happened to you at GNN, back when you were an intern."

Julian's cheeks burned with embarrassment and shame. He thought GNN had squelched that before it hit the media grapevine. Then again, Philip always seemed to know things before anybody else. A pang of paranoia shot through him. Could Philip know about his past with Taylor? Did he notice, for example, that both their résumés listed Detroit Country Day School? Could there have been any pictures of himself and Taylor in her parents' house when Philip visited?

"You knew?" Julian knitted his eyebrows.

"Don't worry about it," Philip said. "I heard long before you came to *EE*. So I kept an eye on you, you know. Maybe you were a troublemaker. But they were wrong. When I looked at you, I saw a diamond in the rough. And man, were you trying to polish yourself to brilliance."

Julian sipped his drink, somehow feeling that he did not want to hear what Philip was about to say.

Philip grimaced. "Wilbur Franklin is the sleaziest cocksucker on the planet. Been my mortal enemy since he hired snitches to spy for him in Wolf newsrooms. Can you believe that?"

Julian shook his head.

"So I try to piss him off whenever I can," Philip said, chuckling. "I outbid him on the Bel Air house where Andrea and the kids live. I've paid maître d's at the best restaurants to give him the worst tables and bad service. I even fucked his daughter and FedExed her come-stained panties to his office. He knew it was me 'cause I put my business card inside."

Julian chuckled. "You're ruthless, man. But what's that got to do with me?"

"Franklin said you'd fail in television, right?"

"Yeah," Julian said, feeling a jolt of anger at the memory.

"So I made you a star, just to piss him off," Philip said.

Julian stared in disbelief as sardonic laughter shook Philip's red-and-white-striped chest.

I was just a stooge in Philip's egotistical puppet show.

It was one thing to think Philip was using him to make himself appear supportive of minorities, but to be motivated by spite against a terrible man, as some kind of roller-coaster ride on Philip's lifelong ego trip, was devastating. That meant that Philip initially did not give a damn about Julian DuPont. He was just a tool, like the come-stained panties and the Bel Air mansion. And what demented scheme was Taylor caught up in?

Still laughing, Philip shrugged. "Course, your hard work and talent made it easy. Never thought we'd be road dogs, too. C'mon, DuPont, you look like I just cut your balls off."

No, you just cast them in stone. And your words just invigorated me with superhuman determination to seduce your bride. Again. Forever.

CHAPTER 28

In the lobby of 36th District Court, beyond the metal detectors and security guards, Taylor penetrated a swarm of hundreds of people. The air was hot and stale. Fluorescent lights cast a greenish pall over the aggravated faces of those waiting to pay traffic tickets and bonds for people who had been arraigned for various offenses.

With cameraman Patrick McIntyre and the same police escort as Friday, Taylor entered courtroom 1067, whose double doors opened about twenty yards from the courthouse entrance.

"I hate that mongrel bitch," a skinhead hissed from the pewlike rows of wooden benches.

"Eat this, freak." A guy with swastika tattoos on his forearms grabbed his crotch and thrust at Taylor.

Officer Edwards stepped between her and the cluster of White Power groupies.

"Sit down, be quiet, or you'll be ejected from the courtroom," he told them.

The tattooed man made a mocking face. "Ooh, I'm scared."

Another man glared at Edwards. "No self-respecting white man would work for a Negro police chief."

Taylor kept walking with a cool, stiff expression that, with the help of extra makeup, masked her sleepless night.

The one positive thought she had was that from now on, the only place she would have to see Pulaski was in a guarded courtroom during proceedings that would hopefully send him to prison forever. Enough television cameras had caught his assault on Lloyd Pryor that convicting him would be simple.

With her microphone, notebook, and leather shoulder bag, Taylor took the first seat off the center aisle in the first row. Officer Edwards and Officer Young stood in the aisle next to her.

"You're creating quite a drama, Taylor," said Sheila Dane of Channel 5, who was sitting next to Taylor.

"Just doing my job," Taylor said, noticing Rocky Pulaski's lawyer at the defense table in front of her. Surprisingly, Carla sat at the prosecutor's table. Nearby, between the sectioned-off public seating and the judge's bench, Patrick set up his tripod and camera amid a cluster of videographers and print photographers.

"I'd say you're going above and beyond," Sheila said, "facing the guy who wants to see you wearing nothing but a toe tag at the morgue."

"I guess," Taylor said. "Three weeks from now I'll be on a beach in Maui on my honeymoon, and all this will be a long-forgotten blur."

Sheila smiled. "If we could all be so lucky to marry network execs. But I think we're both better off than Lloyd Pryor's wife and kids over there."

Across the aisle in the first row sat a puffy-faced woman and two children whose pink and black tennis shoes dangled over the edge of the bench. Mrs. Pryor blew her nose and stared blankly toward the front of the courtroom.

Taylor stepped across the aisle and crouched next to her.

"Excuse me, Mrs. Pryor, I'm Taylor James from Channel Three. I interviewed your husband Friday afternoon. I'm sorry about what happened."

Mrs. Pryor's face twisted into a sob. "He was doing something positive. It's not fair. I wish Michigan had the death penalty."

"Can I interview you about that after the arraignment?"

Mrs. Pryor looked up with bloodshot eyes.

"I think you have a message that people want to hear," Taylor said.

Mrs. Pryor nodded.

"Thank you. I'll talk to you right after the arraignment." Taylor stood up and slipped through the thigh-high swinging door to the front section of the courtroom. "Carla," Taylor said.

"Hey, girl," Carla said softly.

"Hi, Taylor," said the male assistant prosecutor, who was flipping through files and papers on the table with probation officers.

"Hi, Gary," Taylor said. "Carla, how in the world did you pull this off?"

"The woman who should have been here called in sick, so I volunteered to take the case," Carla said. "Tell me, why do you think Gus Lemer is here, in the back of the courtroom? It really rubs me the wrong way. This isn't his beat."

Taylor glanced back and saw Lemer's ratlike face. "That is strange. I knew something wasn't right when I saw him talking to this cop named Scarlin. He's got neo-Nazi written all over him."

Carla shook her head. "I think something's up. It's beyond coincidence. I really think we—"

"All rise!" the bailiff bellowed.

"I'll talk to you later," Taylor whispered, then hurried back to her seat.

"Court will now come to order," the bailiff said. "Magistrate Yolanda Jeffries presiding. You may be seated."

The skinheads in the back row snickered loud enough for the magistrate to hear their racial slurs.

"Officers, eject those men from the courtroom, please," said Magistrate Jeffries, annoyance creasing her broad, caramel face framed by a close-cut Afro.

Taylor turned around to watch them be escorted out.

Oh my God . . .

All she saw were Scarlin's malicious eyes.

He was standing in front of the double doors at the back of the courtroom, glaring at her. His gaunt face and thin body were as still as a mannequin. And next to him was Gus Lemer.

What a scary pair. Are they here to show support for Pulaski—while on duty? Or something worse?

Taylor scribbled a note: "Please film the officers by the back door." She passed it to Patrick, who nodded.

"Thank you," Magistrate Jeffries said, scanning the packed courtroom through round spectacles. "Any more disturbances will be dealt with in a similar manner."

Jess, Rocky, and Billy Joe appeared with skinheads and several black men in the large window of the twelve-by-twelve lockup cell. It was situated to the right of the judge's bench and commonly called "the box."

"Case number 97-325533, *the People versus Jessica Ann Stevens,*" the court clerk said.

Two police officers escorted Jess out of the box. Her dark hair was a wild mane. Standing in front of the judge with her lawyer, Jess glared over her shoulder at Taylor.

"If looks could kill," Sheila Dane whispered.

Taylor showed no reaction.

"Face forward," the magistrate said.

The lawyer cleared his throat. "Magistrate Jeffries, I am attorney Karl Kramer, here on behalf of Ms. Stevens. My client stands mute to the charge, Your Honor."

Taylor knew that meant that Jess was pleading neither guilty nor innocent to the charge, and that she would still be able to speak during the proceeding.

"Please state your name," Magistrate Jeffries said.

"Jessica Ann Stevens," Jess said.

"Do you understand the charge against you?" the magistrate asked.

"No, I didn't do nothin'," Jess shot back in an angry tone loud enough to evoke startled whispers throughout the hushed courtroom.

"We are not here today, Ms. Stevens, to determine your guilt or innocence," the magistrate said. "It is my duty to simply inform you of the charge against you and to inform you of your constitutional rights."

"I still didn't do nothin'," Jess said.

Magistrate Jeffries knitted her brows. "Please listen carefully, Ms. Stevens. You have been charged with assault with intent to commit murder, which, if you are convicted, carries a maximum sentence of life in prison. You have the right to remain silent. Anything you say orally or in writing can be used against you in a court of law. You have the right to an attorney. If you cannot afford one, one will be provided for you. You have the right to have the attorney with you now and any time when you are questioned about the charges."

Magistrate Jeffries flipped through a file. "Ms. Stevens, I am setting bond at fifty thousand dollars cash. I note that you have a parole hold. The file indicates that you are presently on parole for weapons and conspiracy convictions. You must attend a preliminary exam on Monday, June twenty-fifth."

A court security officer in a black jumpsuit guided Jess back to the lockup box. Jess glared at Taylor, then spit at her, as she walked away. "Mongrel bitch," she hissed. Cameras recorded her every move.

"Case number 97-325534 and 97-325535, *the People versus James 'Rocky' Pulaski and Billy Joe Pulaski,*" the court clerk said.

Rocky and Billy Joe, wrists handcuffed to belly chains, shuffled out of the box, chains jingling in the courtroom silence.

Taylor relished a newfound sense of relief over the Pulaskis being in police custody, at least for now. *They're both right where they belong. I can finally relax.*

Lloyd Pryor's widow sniffled, then raised trembling hands to blow her nose.

All eyes and cameras focused on the two men in blue jeans and T-shirts.

Rocky glanced at Taylor. His eyes were calm. They were not the usual roiling black pits. And his face was serene, not taut or sneering as it had been during his trial three years ago. Billy Joe also appeared relaxed.

Something is wrong. Suspicion swept through Taylor. She set her pen on her notepad and pressed clammy palms to her beige skirt.

As the Pulaskis turned to face the judge, their lawyer between them, Rocky locked eyes on Taylor. A wicked grin lifted his cheeks. Kramer nudged him to face forward.

An icy boa of fear circled Taylor's throat and chest. *Something is very wrong. Pulaski isn't acting like a man who stands a good chance of spending the rest of his life in prison.*

Attorney Kramer addressed the court. "My clients stand mute to the charges, Your Honor."

Magistrate Jeffries advised the Pulaskis of their constitutional rights.

"James 'Rocky' Pulaski and Billy Joe Pulaski, you are both charged with one count each of second-degree murder and assault with intent to commit murder," she said. "If you are convicted, each offense carries a maximum penalty of life in prison. Bond is set at one hundred thousand dollars cash for each of you."

Taylor glanced around the courtroom. At the lockup box were two Detroit police officers. Two guards, in black jumpsuits marking them as the courthouse's private security force, stood behind Billy Joe, Rocky, and Kramer. In the back corners of the courtroom stood two pairs of Detroit police officers.

At the back door were Scarlin and Lemer. Taylor was sure that Scarlin was a Pulaski sympathizer, and the more she thought about it, the more she believed that Lemer's presence in the courtroom today was suspicious.

An ominous feeling seeped through Taylor, raising the hairs on the back of her neck. She nudged the female police escort, Officer Young, who stood in the aisle next to her.

"Does anything seem strange to you in here?" Taylor whispered.

Officer Young glanced around and shook her head.

In her peripheral vision Taylor saw Scarlin glaring at her.

Magistrate Jeffries continued with Rocky and Billy Joe. "You also each have a parole hold. Your files indicate that you are both on parole for conspiracy to overthrow the government and weapons convictions. Your preliminary exams will be held on Monday, June twenty-fifth."

A police officer opened the door to the box, signaling that Rocky and Billy Joe would soon file back through that door to jail.

As Taylor watched, moments seemed eternal. *Yes, I hope you go back to jail forever.*

Then the metal-on-metal clink of guns being cocked echoed around the courtroom. In the front, in the back, at the door.

Taylor froze.

God, no. This can't be happening.

Magistrate Jeffries looked up with knitted brows. "What was—"

Spectators shrieked.

"Everybody freeze!" deep voices bellowed in unison.

CHAPTER 29

Stunned, Taylor watched the security officers flanking the Pulaskis and their lawyer as they pulled shotguns from their jumpsuits. Black metal flashed.

One of the phony guards aimed his gun at the judge. The other pointed at Taylor.

"Anybody move and the bitches' heads fly," the man said.

Taylor stared into the black hole of the shotgun.

No, this can't happen.

Every heartbeat felt like a firecracker exploding inside her chest. She felt she should do something. But what? She was helpless with a gun in her face.

Officers Edwards and Young were blue columns in the aisle. *A lot of good they are now.*

She raised her eyes to look at the face of the man pointing the gun at her. Nick. The platinum blond man she and Andy had befriended at the compound. The man who caught her when Billy Joe punched her. All that charm he'd shown back then, calling them brother and sister, was now venom in his eyes.

Rocky and Billy Joe Pulaski quickly turned around. Rocky's handcuffs jingled to the floor, as did his belly and ankle chains. Had they not been locked in the first place? Their lawyer stepped toward the gate to the public seating area, then opened it with the grace of a well-trained butler. The packed benches of people were still and silent as the convicts turned to leave.

"Somebody do something!" Carla shouted from her seat at the prosecutor's table. She looked at Taylor with eyes like black saucers.

No, Carla, be quiet. Do as they say.

The man with the gun on the judge looked back.

"Call the police!" Carla yelled. "They can't get away!"

Billy Joe stopped in his tracks. He approached Carla, glared—

No!

He slammed his fists down on Carla's head.

She went limp. Thudded on the table. Facedown. Still.

Taylor went numb.

Gasps and shrieks erupted from the crowd.

Lloyd Pryor's children wailed in the front row. Nick waved his gun at them. "Shut up!" he shouted.

With zombielike calm, Rocky passed through the gate. He stopped inches from Taylor.

"I should kill you right now," he said with wicked delight in his black marble eyes.

God help me . . .

Taylor was frozen with fear. She felt as if her fluttering heart pumped slush through numb limbs.

Rocky shot a thick hand at her. His swastika tattoo flashed before her eyes.

Her scalp stung. There was a ripping sound.

Rocky was clawing her hair, lifting her like a rag doll.

He threw her into the aisle.

She grunted. A red rod of pain shot through her right temple.

Taylor hugged the floor.

Rocky's deep, devilish laughter echoed through the courtroom. He leaned inches above her, sending a waft of jailhouse funk toward her.

"Watch your back," he hissed.

Billy Joe's face appeared next to his father.

"You're mine, bitch. All mine."

Both men roared as they stepped over her.

Something stabbed her left buttock.

"You're gonna burn, bitch!"

It was Jess, kicking. She bolted out of the courtroom behind Rocky and Billy Joe.

The lawyer, Nick, and the other gunman passed. Then the phony and crooked cops, including Gus Lemer, filed through the double doors behind Scarlin.

CHAPTER 30

Chaos erupted in the courtroom. Shrieking people scattered like ants.

"Call the police!"

"Call 911!"

"Get them!" Lloyd Pryor's widow screamed. Her children wailed.

Officers Young and Edwards dove toward Taylor. They lifted her onto a bench, laid her down, and examined her.

Pain hammered her right temple. A knot like a baseball was growing and throbbing and stinging.

"It's bleeding," Officer Young said.

Officer Edwards radioed for ambulances and police backup. A half dozen police officers from the courthouse lobby poured into the courtroom.

Taylor sat up, but Officer Young became a dark blue blur, swimming above her. She lay back down.

"Carla," she said. "Help Carla."

"The other officers are taking care of her," Officer Young said.

Patrick appeared above her. "Taylor, are you all right?"

"Yeah. Did you get all that on-camera?"

Patrick nodded.

"Don't stop," Taylor said. "Get all this action. How's Carla?"

"I don't know," he said.

"Patrick, get me my purse, please?"

"Sure."

Taylor dug her cellular phone out of her purse and dialed Shari. "Shari, they escaped," Taylor said. Her face muscles quivered with fear, making it difficult to talk. "Pulaski. He escaped."

"Escaped? How?"

"His army of Nazis drew guns. They just left the courtroom," Taylor said. "His son hit Carla and knocked her out. And I—"

"Our friend Carla? The prosecutor?"

"Yes." Taylor plugged her left ear so she could hear Shari over the frantic din.

"Christ! Are you okay?"

"Rocky threw me to the floor and I hit my head, but I can still do my noon report."

"You sure? I can send another reporter over. You should get an X ray."

Taylor imagined smirking Kendra Vaughn strutting into the courtroom, microphone in hand. "No, no, I'll get an X ray after my report."

"What about your police escort?"

"They're here, but they couldn't do anything when that rifle was pointed at my face," Taylor said.

"Unbelievable," Shari said. "Is Carla conscious?"

"I don't know. I tried to sit up, but I was too dizzy."

"Taylor." Shari's voice was shrill with alarm. "You can't work if you can't even sit up."

"I'll be fine. Listen, I had this hunch that the White Power Alliance had contacts in the Detroit police department. I must have been right. How else could they have pulled this off?"

"You're right," Shari said.

"I think Sergeant John Scarlin is the ringleader," Taylor said.

"I'll get Tony Martin over to police headquarters to check out Scarlin," Shari said. "And I'll have him find out how the hell the police are going to catch these guys."

"Ms. James, the paramedics are here," Officer Edwards said. "We need them to take a look at you."

"Shari, I gotta go," Taylor said. "What time is it?"

"Ten-thirty."

"Good, I have plenty of time for interviews."

A female paramedic stood over Taylor. "Ma'am, can you please get off the phone?"

Taylor nodded.

"This is lead at noon," Shari said. "But let me know if you don't feel up to it."

"I'm fine." Taylor set down the phone as the paramedic wiped blood off her temple. "Ow!" Taylor sat up. An ice pack soothed her throbbing bump. "How's Carla Jackson, the prosecutor?"

"Here she comes," the paramedic said.

Taylor slid to the edge of the bench as paramedics pushed a gurney down the aisle.

Oh God, please help her. Raw emotion overwhelmed Taylor when she saw her friend. Blood caked her forehead and nose. A gray pallor dulled her normally radiant complexion.

"Carla."

She half opened unfocused eyes.

"What hospital are you taking her to?" Taylor asked.

"Henry Ford," a paramedic answered.

"Carla, I'll call your mother," Taylor said, holding back tears.

Carla closed her eyes.

Taylor shrank into the bench. The horror of what happened came crashing down on her like a lightning bolt, burning, shocking, illuminating the grave danger that she was now in.

Taylor interviewed witnesses inside and outside the courtroom. Then she and Patrick went out to the Channel 3 News van to feed video back to the station. She called Henry Ford Hospital, where a

spokesman said Carla was in serious condition and was being monitored for a head injury.

Then she dialed Shari.

"Tony Martin talked to a police source in internal affairs," Shari
said. "This Scarlin guy is a known Nazi. Been on the force thirty
years, cited five times for violations, the first of which was handing
out hate literature to other officers."

"The others?" Taylor asked.

"There's a slew of complaints against him from people of color
who says he uses racial slurs and roguish behavior during routine
traffic stops," Shari said. "And he's got some complaints about how
he's dealt with domestic violence, not taking the women's reports seriously."

"I knew he was bad news," Taylor said.

"Yeah, in one case a couple years ago, Scarlin refused to arrest a
known abuser who turned around and killed his wife that same night
Scarlin answered a call to their house," Shari said. "Martin is trying
to ask the chief why this guy was allowed to stay on the force."

"What about the others in the courtroom?"

"Two had clean records," Shari said. "Let's see, Gus Lemer and
Matt Zakowski. Lemer was charged with manslaughter in 'sixty-
seven but was acquitted."

"That was Carla's father," Taylor said weakly.

"Christ," Shari said. After a pause, she added, "We'll have Tony
work that into his report. The others were impostors. Fake security
guys in the jumpsuits, fake police officers. Seems strange to me that
the legitimate officers wouldn't notice the impostors. You sure you're
up to this report?"

"Yes, Shari. I'll be fine."

A few minutes later, as Taylor and Patrick set up for the live
shot inside the truck, she ignored the pain throbbing on her right
temple and her left buttock.

"You're gonna have a black eye," Patrick said. "I can see it."

Taylor pulled out a mirror. A pillowy arc of pale purple hung
below her right eye. She quickly dotted cover-up on it.

Patrick adjusted a knob on the video transmitter. "I have to admit I'm a little shaken up. It's hard enough to get justice when a courtroom works the way it's supposed to. But for those thugs to just bust out like that . . ." Patrick shook his head.

"I agree," Taylor said.

Patrick angled the camera and tripod in front of the 36th District Court, a modern, six-story beige building.

"Taylor James, how ya doin' out there?" asked Mike Covey, the show director in the studio control room, in her earpiece.

"I'm okay," she said. "Ready to roll."

"We're changing your name to the Bionic Reporter," Mike said. "I heard Sheila Dane say in a promo that you had a concussion."

Taylor glanced at Sheila, about ten yards away, preparing for a live report.

Mike chuckled. "We have the pictures edited and we're ready to go. Taylor James, you have two minutes at the top of the show, then we'll go to your wrap, then answer Noelle Keats's questions. Give me a roll cue."

"Courthouse security," Taylor said.

"Got it. Stand by."

CHAPTER 31

Taylor's usual live-report adrenaline rush stirred her raw emotions. She glanced down at the sidewalk, praying for strength. *Yes, I can do this.*

Officers Edwards and Young stood nearby.

"Taylor James, ten-oh-eight," Mike said.

"Good afternoon, everybody, welcome to Channel Three News at Noon. I'm Noelle Keats. A hate group leader escapes from a Detroit court this morning, sending the prosecutor to the hospital and stunning the police chief and court authorities. Channel Three News reporter Taylor James is standing by live to give us the very latest. Taylor, what happened?"

Taylor took a deep breath and stared into the black camera lens, letting her on-air autopilot take over.

"Noelle, what happened here at Thirty-sixth District Court this morning can only be described as dramatic and shocking. It started when White Power Alliance leader Rocky Pulaski faced a judge on charges of second-degree murder. An almost surreal chain of events followed. Bogus police officers aimed shotguns at me, at the judge, at children, paving the way for Pulaski, his son, and girlfriend to escape from the courtroom.

"Police and the FBI are launching a massive manhunt to find the three convicts and the dozen or so phony and/or corrupt policemen who participated in the escape. Police say this is the first time that chained, handcuffed defendants have actually bolted from a courtroom, and they say this raises serious questions about citizens' trust in police as well as courthouse security."

"Go to wrap," Mike Covey said in her ear.

Taylor watched the monitor as her prerecorded voice corresponded with a video package that had been prepared back at the station.

Taylor cringed when she saw, for the first time, video of Rocky Pulaski yanking her like a doll and throwing her to the floor. Then the video cut to the magistrate, interviewed later in her chambers.

"In my twenty years in the judicial system, I have never seen nor heard of such unconscionable behavior," Jeffries said, shaking her head. "Today is a sorry day for American justice."

Taylor's recorded voice played over video of the puffy-faced widow: "Justice is something that Lloyd Pryor's widow is afraid she might never see."

"Please," Mrs. Pryor said, staring into the camera, "wherever you are, turn yourselves in now. You have to pay the price for what you did to my husband. He never would have hurt you. He was a good man. But now I'm alone to raise two babies." She sobbed.

Next the report showed two legitimate police officers who were in the lobby near the exit when the Pulaskis escaped.

"At first I thought it was all right because the police officers were leading them outside," said Officer Tina Tate. "But then I realized we don't transport prisoners through the front door. So I tried to block them, but they knocked me down. That's when I radioed for help."

Next, the report showed Jared Jones, the man who ran the fruit stand in front of the courthouse. "They just walked outside like they were going for a Sunday stroll," he said, "and hopped into a van that was waiting by the curb."

"Taylor James, fifteen-oh-six," Mike said.

"I knew it wasn't right because they had chains around their waists but no handcuffs," Jones said. "And I seen that guy on the news Friday and I recognized him as the one who beat that poor man to death. If you can't feel safe in a courthouse, it's a damn shame."

"Taylor James," Mike said.

Taylor ignored her throbbing temple. "Shame is exactly what courthouse and police officials are feeling this afternoon as they scramble to figure out just how something like this could happen," Taylor said into the microphone. "It's obvious that someone from inside the Detroit Police Department orchestrated this breakout today, and we'll be pressing them for answers as they develop."

She stood by for the anchor to ask a question.

"Taylor, yesterday we reported that police discovered a White Power Alliance plot to kidnap and murder you because you broadcast that daring exposé three years ago that sent Pulaski and his son and girlfriend to prison. How are you taking this?"

"I was just as shocked as everyone else in the courtroom. Fortunately I escaped with only a few bruises. This is Taylor James, reporting live from Detroit's Thirty-sixth District Court."

"Shocking is right," Noelle said. "Thank you, Taylor. Now we have Channel Three News reporter Tony Martin at Detroit police headquarters for a report about the manhunt and an investigation into how this—"

Taylor pulled the IFB from her ear.

"Good job, Taylor," Patrick said. "Now I'm taking you to the hospital."

CHAPTER 32

In the crowded hospital waiting room, Taylor and Patrick sat between a little boy with a bloody leg and a man rocking with apparent drug withdrawal. A baby's wails drowned out the dialogue of a soap opera blaring from a television.

Taylor's cellular phone rang inside her purse.

"Hello?"

"Darling, are you all right? I heard what happened."

Relief eased her tense muscles when she heard Philip's voice. "I'm okay, but I'm at the emergency room now." Taylor explained what happened, plugging one ear to block out the noise.

"I'd fly to Detroit this afternoon, but I have two important meetings. How do you feel?"

"I have a headache and I feel nauseous."

Philip sighed loudly. "We should have taken you off this story. You're too involved with it now. You can't report objectively about a man who wants to kill you."

"You weren't concerned about that Friday," Taylor said.

"I was thinking of the drawing power of the story. But now I see just how dangerous this situation is."

Taylor grimaced.

Patrick drew his eyebrows together and mouthed, "What?"

She rolled her eyes. "This is *my* story. I broke it three years ago and I'm going to continue covering it until Rocky Pulaski and Billy Joe Pulaski and his witch girlfriend are all rotting in prison."

"Don't get upset, darling. All this racial animosity is taking its toll on you. I could hear it in your voice when I called over the weekend, and it worries me. We have a wedding coming up, and I want you rested and at peace when you walk down that aisle to become Mrs. Philip Carter."

Taylor's stomach cramped.

"I think you should take the afternoon off. Maybe the doctors can give you a tranquilizer."

"I don't need drugs," Taylor snapped.

"Well, at least take a painkiller," Philip said. "And stay with those police officers."

"Yeah, a lot of good they did in court this morning," Taylor said.

"Darling, relax, would you?" Philip said. "I'll call you as soon as my meeting is over. I love you."

Taylor watched a man cradle a crying woman on his shoulder across the waiting room. Maybe the woman was upset because a loved one was dying, or perhaps she was ill or injured. The man holding her truly loved her, Taylor could tell, because his face mirrored her pain as he rocked her gently, kissing the top of her head. That couple was united in spirit as one. When one hurt, the other ached.

Philip was incapable of such compassion.

Julian understood it like no other.

"Taylor?"

"Yes."

"I said I love you," Philip said, annoyed.

Tears burned Taylor's eyes. The pain throbbing at her temple became unbearable. "I . . . I love you, too."

"Just think of Maui," Philip said. "You and me, making love on

the sand, snorkeling, and anything else your pretty little heart de-
sires."

"Yeah," Taylor said, feeling heavy and hot, as if she were sinking
into wet volcanic ash.

A speaker above crackled with static. "Taylor James."

"Philip, I have to go."

"Okay, darling. I'll check on you later."

Patrick patted Taylor's back as she wiped her tears on her beige
suit jacket sleeve. "You all right?"

Taylor nodded.

A nurse led her to an examination bay where a doctor examined
her for neurological damage, then told her not to sleep for twenty-
four hours, or if she did, to have someone wake her every forty-five
minutes to make sure she was not comatose. The X ray revealed no
fracture, so the doctor put a bandage on the cut and gave her a pre-
scription for a painkiller and antibacterial ointment for the cut.

After that, Taylor led Patrick and the police escort up to Carla's
room. Carla's mother stood over her, holding her hands, while a
handsome man in a white coat stood on the other side of the bed.

"Taylor," Mrs. Jackson whispered. "How are you, baby?"

Taylor hugged Mrs. Jackson. "I'm worried about Carla."

"They're watching her, making sure she doesn't have a seizure.
Her X rays came up negative, thank the Lord, and they gave her
some medicine. I already lost a husband and a daughter. Lord knows
I couldn't stand to lose my Carla."

"She's tough," Taylor said.

Mrs. Jackson's usually bright eyes were dim and hooded. "On the
news they showed that monster who killed my Gregory. It ain't right
for all this to be goin' on in a civilized society. It just ain't right."

Taylor hugged Carla's mother as Mrs. Jackson sobbed. After a
while Taylor said, "Carla has worked too hard for Lemer to get away.
He'll get what's coming to him." Then Taylor glanced at the man in
the white coat. "Are you her doctor?"

The man wore wire-rim glasses and had an open, clean-shaven
face. He smiled. There was something very gentle about him.

"No, I'm her friend," he said. "Dr. Benjamin Robard. Ms. Jackson and I met in church on Sunday."

Taylor smiled. *All right, Carla.*

"I just happen to work here at the hospital, in pediatrics, and when I saw the news, I came down to check on her. I don't think she recognized me when she opened her eyes."

"I'm sure she did," Taylor said.

CHAPTER 33

Taylor's entrance set the Channel 3 newsroom abuzz. Everybody flocked around her desk, staring at her forehead and her purple eye. Even Andy Doss had concern in his eyes when he asked how she felt. But not Kendra Vaughn. She circled like a vulture, barely veiling her regret that Taylor was not laid up in the hospital alongside Carla.

Otherwise, there was a strange stillness in the newsroom. Why wasn't Shari at producer's row, barking orders at reporters and producers? Taylor shrugged it off as an afternoon lull as she listened to her phone mail.

"Message one."

"This is Mom. Call me as soon as you can."

"Message two."

"White Chocolate, it's Julian."

Taylor's heart galloped. *Yes, Julian, I need to hear you, feel you.*

"I saw you on GNN this morning," he said, sounding alarmed. "You're probably still mad at me. I don't blame you, but it would mean a lot if you could just call my parents and let them know you're all right. Or if you want to call me—"

As Taylor replayed the message and scribbled Julian's phone numbers in her day planner, a strange glazed feeling overcame her. The numbers and his name blurred. She touched the bandage on her forehead. Maybe the painkillers were making her dizzy. Or maybe she was reeling with the realization that she had wished for that phone call countless times. In New York, in Miami, in Detroit. And it never came until the eve of her wedding to another man, a man she wasn't even sure she loved anymore.

As Taylor stared blankly at the phone, Shari called, asking her to come up to the conference room. Her empty stomach burned with stress as she ascended the steps and entered.

"Hello," Taylor said as she took the seat. To her right were Shari, William, then a man in a Detroit police uniform. To her left was an unfamiliar man in a gray suit.

Why is everyone looking at me with such pity in their eyes?

"How are you feeling?" William asked, eyeing her bandaged forehead.

"Fine. It's just a bruise."

"Taylor," Shari said, twisting her tennis bracelet. "This is Detroit Police Detective Green and Brian Schuler from the FBI."

"Hi," Taylor said.

"Ms. James, our bomb squad checked out a package delivered to you here today," Green said. From a box on the table he retrieved a headless black doll, then a white head with matted blond hair. Across the body was written, "You're next, half-breed."

"We believe the White Power Alliance is responsible for this," he said.

Shari, with concern radiating from her hazel eyes, said, "Taylor, we need you to go into hiding until Pulaski is caught."

CHAPTER 34

The horrendous pain atop Carla Jackson's head caused her to imagine an ax lodged in her skull.

"Do you need more pain medication?" A blurry expanse of white hovered above.

"Ye . . . aaaahh."

Was that me? I sound like a rusty muffler. What happened? The courtroom, the guns, Lemer, shouting. Nothing.

"Baby? Carla baby, did you say something?" She heard ruffling newspaper and her mother's voice.

A brown circle appeared. "Carla, you woke up."

"Wha . . . aaaaa . . . haaapppin?"

"There was an accident, baby, but you're all right," her mother said. "You got a bump on the head and some stitches, but the doctors said you'll be all right."

Through her sore, swollen nose, she noticed an institutional smell, like disinfectant and overcooked peas, and her mouth and throat were dry as sawdust.

"Waaaa—"

"You want some water? Here." A straw poked through her lips and she sucked. Her mother's face began coming into focus.

Carla's arms felt heavy at her sides. A tape-covered tube extended from her left hand up to an IV bag of clear liquid.

"Did they shoot me?"

"No, baby, you got hit on the head. They just showed it again on the news," her mother said, pointing to a muted television hanging from the ceiling above the foot of the bed. On the screen, Buck Norton was giving the Channel 3 sportscast.

"This hurts my heart," Mrs. Jackson said, "to see that Gus Lemer. He escaped with those white supremacists today."

Carla tried to concentrate. *They escaped?*

The heavy force of grief and outrage suddenly dropped on Carla like a cement slab. Despite her drug-fogged mind and the extreme pain, an anger unlike any she had ever experienced stunned her. And her mother's emotion-cracked voice only made it worse.

Gus Lemer killed my father, enlisted in Pulaski's racist army, and laughed in the face of justice today. Again. Jesus, how can you let this happen?

Her mother wiped Carla's hot, tear-streaked cheeks.

"I'm gonna get him, Mama," Carla said softly. "Lemer can't get away with this. He can't. I swear on Daddy's grave that I'm gonna get Lemer if it's the last thing I do."

"Hush, child," her mother said, holding Carla as she sobbed into her chest. "Shhh. You just hush and rest for now."

After a few minutes, Mrs. Jackson said, "Your brother and the girls from the center have been calling and stopping by all afternoon, and that young gentleman from church came, too. Says he works here."

Ben.

"We're at Henry Ford?"

"Yes, he even sent up these flowers," her mother said. "See?"

Carla saw a red and green blur nearby. "Roses?"

"Yes, a dozen red ones."

Carla closed her eyes, desperate to divert her thoughts from her father and Lemer to romance. Roses from a man, a gentleman. Dr. Benjamin Robard. *God, please let him be the one.*

Her mother said, "The card says, 'My thoughts and prayers are with you.' And it's signed, 'Ben.' Isn't that sweet?"

As Carla attempted to smile, there was a knock on the open door.

"Maybe that's your dinner," her mother said.

Two white faces above navy blue uniforms appeared at the foot of the bed.

Her heart raced. A panicked cry rose from her scratchy throat.

Cops. Pulaski's phony cops. Lemer. They killed Papa, now they've come after me.

She pulled the stiff white sheet up to her chin. Images of Lemer and the bogus officers in court, with guns drawn and pointed at the judge and Taylor, flashed in her mind.

"Get away!" she shouted.

"Carla, baby, it's the police," her mother said. "They came earlier to take a report while you were asleep. They want to help find the men who hurt you."

An officer approached the bed.

Carla cringed.

"Ma'am, we understand that you're afraid," he said, "but we are legitimate."

Both men stepped closer with notebooks.

"Do you remember any distinguishing characteristics of the policemen in court this morning?" an officer asked.

Yes, one of them is the man I see every night when I close my eyes. The man who murdered my father.

Carla imagined these men drawing guns with silencers, shooting her and her mother, and never having to pay for it. Just as Lemer did to Papa in his store.

"How do I know you're for real?" Carla asked.

Another man in navy blue entered the room. *The lookout man.*

Carla shook her head.

No, he's different. Black and familiar.

"Ms. Jackson, I'm Chief Bernard Goodson. I came to personally apologize on behalf of the Detroit Police Department for the tragedy that occurred today at Thirty-sixth District Court."

He removed his hat and shook her mother's hand, then hers.

"I've followed your work with the prosecutor's office," Goodson said. "You have an impressive track record. And I want to assure you that we are doing everything we can to catch the man who did this to you."

Pain shot like lightning across the top of Carla's head. She remembered Billy Joe Pulaski, stepping toward her with a demonic expression on his razor-stubbled face . . . raising his fists . . .

"Where are the Pulaskis?" she asked.

"We're trying to determine that ourselves," Goodson said.

"What?"

"They escaped from court this morning," he said softly.

"But, how could—"

"Ms. Jackson, I must admit that I am, quite frankly, just as astounded as you are," Goodson said. "We believe a sergeant arranged the escape of the three convicts today, and Internal Affairs is investigating as we speak."

"You haven't caught them yet?" she asked. "But we had all the evidence we needed to convict them of second-degree murder and lock them up for life."

Goodson nodded. "I know."

Carla saw Goodson through a red-hot cloud of anger, which intensified the dizzying effects of the medication.

Suddenly two blinding lights shot toward her, hurting her eyes. She squinted and raised her right hand over her face. TV cameras. And the mayor!

Detroit Mayor Norman Johnson, a tall, almond-skinned man in a stiff brown suit, stood next to a surprised Mrs. Jackson. He shook Chief Goodson's hand over the bed. Both of them angled compassionate expressions toward the cameras, then looked down on Carla.

I feel like a prop in a campaign advertisement. Resentment rumbled through her; here she was laid up in the hospital, two murderers on the loose, and the police chief and mayor were making a PR stunt of it.

"How do you feel, Ms. Jackson?" the mayor asked.

Carla scowled. "Pretty bad."

The mayor placed a manicured hand on her arm. "I am confi-

dent that the Detroit police," he said with tender eyes, "working with
the FBI and law enforcement agencies nationwide, will apprehend
your assailants and have them back in jail before daybreak."

"Do you have any leads?" Carla asked.

"We do, but we cannot divulge them at this time," the mayor
said.

"We're working around the clock until the suspects are caught,"
Goodson said. "And we're weeding the force of any officers with
hate-group connections. We've come too far from the turbulent sixties and early seventies when racism was rampant on the police force
to let today's tragedy further tarnish the four thousand shining badges
in the Detroit Police Department."

Carla tensed. She'd prosecuted police officers, too, for domestic
abuse and excessive force and drug possession. And the recent Malice Green trial, in which two white officers were convicted and imprisoned for beating to death a black motorist, proved in the eyes of
many that racism still festered on the force. The chief's rhetorical
sound bites made her stomach churn.

She glanced toward the camera lights, squinting, trying to see the
reporters. Taylor would never bum-rush someone in a hospital bed
without calling first. *Huh, no wonder, it's Sheila Dane and Kendra
Vaughn.*

"Ms. Jackson, if there is anything we can do," the mayor said,
handing her a business card, "please call my office. I want to extend
my most sincere regrets that this happened, and I wish you a speedy
recovery."

"Thank you," Carla said as the cameras came closer.

"And feel free to call my office anytime for updates on the investigation," Goodson said.

Carla nodded at them.

"Do you remember anything?" one of the police officers asked.

"Yes," Carla said loudly. "One of the police officers was Gus
Lemer. He killed my father, Gregory Jackson, during the 'sixty-seven
riot and was acquitted of murder. The jury bought his self-defense
claim."

Goodson appeared perplexed. "Gus Lemer? I know about the unfortunate occurrence with your father, but since then Lemer has been an exemplary officer. Why, we recently honored him at a banquet for saving a child from drowning."

He's trying to earn points with God so he won't go to hell.

"I know Gus Lemer when I see him," Carla said. "Believe me. He was in court this morning."

"We'll definitely look into that," Goodson said. "Thank you very much, Ms. Jackson."

"Please catch them," she said.

The bright camera lights and the reporters, now joined by more newspaper and radio reporters, closed in on the mayor and police chief. The journalists' loud, rapid-fire questions, all at the same time, made Carla's head throb.

She raised her arm. "Please, take it to the hallway."

The mob moved into the hallway like an amoeba engulfing the mayor and police chief.

Carla rested her pounding head on the pillows. "Isn't that nurse bringing me medicine? I really need it now."

Her mother stroked her cheek. "That was so thoughtful of the police chief and mayor to visit you."

"Ma, it was a publicity stunt. They feel like idiots because of what happened. And Taylor said the hospital never lets camera crews just wander around like that without a patient's consent. How rude."

The nurse entered with a tray of baked chicken, mashed potatoes, and peas. Carla had no appetite.

"This should help the pain," the nurse said as she injected a syringe into the IV tube.

"Thank you," Carla said. "Ma, can you dial Taylor at her office, please?"

"Sure, baby." Taylor's answering machines came on at her desk and apartment. Then her mother called Channel 3 and got Shari on the line.

"Shari, it's Carla."

"You poor thing, how do you feel?"

"I got stitches and my head hurts," Carla said.

"You and Taylor both," Shari said. "She got a bump on the head when Pulaski threw her on the floor. It was awful to watch. As tough as I think I am about the news, it's a whole new ball game when your friends are crime victims."

Carla sighed. "Who are you tellin'? Where's Taylor?"

"We sent her away."

"Where?"

"To Philip's in L.A., until they find Pulaski. Police protection does no good at this point if White Power freaks are on the police force."

"I know she was pissed," Carla said.

"Spitting fire."

Carla smiled and glanced up at the television as *Entertainment Exclusive* began. "Ma, turn up the volume."

"What?" Shari asked.

"*EE* is coming on," Carla said. "Shari, look, it's Julian DuPont."

"—a special tribute tonight for Julian DuPont, who will be leaving us after tonight to return to his hometown of Detroit—"

"Got it on in my office," Shari said. "Funny, he's coming here to be with Taylor, but we sent her to L.A. with Philip. Now she's out there with both of them. You really think Philip's clueless about her past with Julian?"

"As far as I know." Carla watched a succession of images of Julian reporting at the Academy Awards, interviewing famous actors, and anchoring on the *EE* set. "That man is gorgeous."

"Imagine how I felt interviewing him last week," Shari said. "I wanted to jump him right here in my office. I mean, I thought Philip was sexy, but Julian set my thirty-five-year-old love-starved libido on fire."

"Shari, please."

"What? You think I'd have a chance with Julian?" Shari asked.

"I don't think Taylor would like it."

"Why not? She's doesn't want him."

Don't be so sure. "Shari, I think you should get divorced before you go having an affair."

"Prude," Shari said.

"I'm a church girl. Adultery is a sin."

A warm, cloudy feeling, as if her limbs and head were being massaged by tiny waves, began to engulf Carla. She sunk into the pillows, welcoming the numb, tingly sensations of the medication.

"Carla?"

"Uh-huh."

"You okay?"

The phone slipped down her shoulder.

"This is Mrs. Jackson. I think Carla's medicine just—"

Carla closed her eyes as her breathing slowed and a wonderful euphoria tickled her brain. After a few moments, she heard a deep voice call her name. She lifted heavy lids.

A white jacket and stethoscope. Tender brown eyes behind gold glasses . . . a warm smile . . . Ben . . . a man she could love.

CHAPTER 35

Taylor's empty stomach gurgled for food as she rummaged through the ornate but barren wooden cabinets in Philip's gourmet kitchen. She found only a box of macaroni and cheese, but realized she could not prepare it because she could not find a can opener.

Furious, Taylor flung the macaroni and cheese box into the breakfast nook. It thudded against the wall. Macaroni rained noisily on the granite floor. The cheese can rolled under the table and chairs.

Taylor leaned on the island, chest heaving, eyes misting. She was enraged that she was being held captive in Philip's outlandishly expensive clifftop mansion. Though it was eleven o'clock at night, he was still at work, or at some meeting.

Taylor stared blankly through the kitchen windows, where the ocean shimmered under the moon like an ominous black eternity.

This whole ordeal was Pulaski's fault. She wondered if he had Internet contacts in Los Angeles who might somehow track her down. He and his thugs had already posted her name and picture on neo-Nazi sites on the World Wide Web. And after today's courtroom escape, anything seemed possible.

Everything in her life suddenly seemed wrong: cheating on her fiancé with her ex-lover; thinking about Julian during her bridal shower; getting assaulted by a man she thought she had defeated; watching Pulaski walk out of court with crooked cops; being sent to stay with Philip; doubting she loved him; wondering how far away Julian lived.

I hate this. My life was perfect just three days ago. Now it's a mess.

Taylor trudged to the breakfast nook and slumped in a chair, a black fan of elegant, hand-wrought iron. But the hard chair bruised her back, so she leaned forward on the cold granite tabletop. This dinette set, which she had once through so pretty, now seemed too painful to enjoy.

She walked through the cavernous living and dining room area, where her purse and travel bag sat on a round stone table in the middle of the foyer. She was glad that she had changed into blue jeans, a denim shirt, and white Nikes, but when she caught her reflection in a mirror, it startled her: the bandage on her forehead, the purple ring under her eye, the tiny white scar on her cheek, the haunted look in her eyes.

I feel as horrible as I look.

CHAPTER 36

When Philip finally came home, he stopped short of kissing her.

"Jesus, Taylor. You win the Rocky Balboa look-alike contest. I hope that's healed before the wedding."

Taylor stiffened. "You're not concerned about how I feel?"

"Shari told me you were fine," he said. "And before you pass out from hunger, here. I went to a going-away party for Julian DuPont. It's still hot."

Taylor took the bag, stunned at the irony of eating leftovers from Julian's send-off to Detroit.

"I hate this whole thing, Philip," Taylor said in the kitchen as she slid the lasagna onto a plate. "I'm on the run and Pulaski has the upper hand. And all that in court this morning, I mean, those guys escaping with phony cops, it just made me realize that I'm really in danger."

Philip removed his suit jacket, then leaned back on the wrought-iron chair and put his hands behind his head. A polished loafer rested on his knee.

"No, you're not," he said. "Pulaski and his goons are just a bunch of military wanna-bes with too much time on their hands. They're probably coming all over themselves thinking about their little commando drill this afternoon. They're through with you, darling. They're fugitives now. If they have one shred of intelligence, they'll be in the hull of a freighter headed for Australia."

"Then if I'm not in danger, why am I here?" Taylor asked.

"Because I wanted you with me," he said. "I've had a bad feeling all weekend, like you were in danger. I just want to play it safe."

Yeah, I was in danger—of falling back in love with another man. Your protégé.

"I should've known," she said as her plate and silverware clattered on the table. "This is more about you than me."

"Of course it's not, darling."

Taylor stabbed the salad with a fork. "What am I supposed to do out here, paint my fingernails and take bubble baths?"

Philip chuckled. "I wouldn't mind that."

"Well, I would," Taylor said. "I haven't worked and gone to school all these years just to pick up and run at the first sign of trouble." Taylor took a bite of lasagna, ignoring a twinge of guilt when the tomato and garlic scent reminded her of the erotic prelude to making love with Julian Saturday night.

"That's good stuff," Philip said, patting his stomach. "I ate too much. Soon as you finish, I want to take you to bed and hold you."

Oh, for once he's not thinking about sex.

"I'm supposed to wake up every forty-five minutes," Taylor said. "To make sure I'm not dead, I guess. Doctor's orders."

"Set the alarm," Philip said. "You call your folks?"

"Soon as I got here," Taylor said. "I still can't believe it. You don't know how it felt today, watching Pulaski and his thugs escape like that. It was unreal. Those guns . . . the handcuffs just fell off Pulaski's wrists . . . him coming at me."

Philip watched her with tender eyes and stroked her back. "I'd like to rip that caveman's throat out."

"I wish somebody would," Taylor said. "I've never been so scared."

"That's what you get for picking a fight with lowlife scum," Philip said, "even if you were doing society a favor."

"But it kind of makes me feel like race relations are doomed," she said. "It really bothers me."

"Dammit, Taylor, how many times do I have to tell you not to carry the weight of the world on your shoulders? It's not up to you to solve America's race problem. It's been around for a long time, and it'll still be here when you're six feet under."

"But I don't know," Taylor said. "I feel like it *is* my responsibility to do something. I always have."

"Well, you need to stop," Philip said sternly. "You really need to get off this race thing and be glad you look white, not black. Jesus, if you knew some of the crap blacks go through in this business, it'd send you to the freakin' nuthouse."

Taylor stopped eating, her stomach aching.

"Like DuPont," Philip said. "He had some racial shit happen that could have cost him his career. Lucky for him, I swooped in and saved the day."

"What do you mean?"

"Huh, I just told him this last night when he was here. There's this guy, Wilbur Franklin at GNN. I can't stand the greaseball. Well, he told DuPont years ago that he'd never make it. So I made DuPont a star just to piss this guy off." Philip chuckled. "Now every night when Franklin turns on the TV, there's Julian DuPont smiling back at him."

Taylor reeled. *What a sick bastard.* All that time Julian thought Philip really cared. But Philip was just playing with Julian's life with the same I-always-win cockiness that he had at the baccarat tables in Monte Carlo and Vegas.

"So am I just a pawn in a game of yours, too?" Taylor asked. "Say, maybe some divorcés bet who could find the youngest trophy bride?"

Philip's face became taut. "That bump on the head today really knocked you into the bitch zone."

Taylor glared at him, anger prickling through her.

"Let me tell you something," Philip said with a harsh tone. "I'm trying to do what's right for you. So don't use me as a punching bag just because you're mad about Pulaski. You ought to be glad he didn't kidnap or kill you today. He sure had the chance."

Taylor bolted to her feet. "You are so insensitive."

Philip grabbed her arm, anger flashing in his eyes. "Look, you need to step back and see the big picture, Taylor. Today was a PR dream for you. Your name, your face, you were all over the news on five different networks. People in newsrooms from New York to L.A. are talking about Pulaski's escape—and you. Some reporters would kill for exposure like this."

Taylor stepped back, causing the chair to screech across the tiles. She snatched her arm from Philip's grasp.

"I want to be known as a good reporter, not a crime victim," she said.

"You should worry about being known, period," Philip said.

With a knife Taylor noisily scraped her plate in the sink. "I can't believe how callous you're being."

"You call it callous, I call it concerned," Philip said, snatching up his jacket and leaving the kitchen.

"Wait, Philip." Taylor followed him through the foyer and up the stairs. He walked quickly through the upstairs hallway to his bedroom, where he began unbuttoning his shirt. His face was stiff.

"No, you wait," he said. "Let's get one thing straight. I'm not the villain here. I do what I think is best for you, and you blow up at me. And how the hell could you question why I'm marrying you? That was a low blow, Taylor. It really was."

Guilt rumbled through her. *I already cheated on Philip, now I'm lashing out at him with anger at myself, at Pulaski, at Julian.*

"I'm sorry," Taylor said. "I just don't feel like myself tonight. My head is killing me, I'm exhausted and . . . Just hold me."

Philip pulled her close.

She leaned on his chest, inside his open shirt, and closed her eyes. She wanted to savor his warm hug, but anger still stiffened her limbs.

"I want my darling calm and happy," Philip said, stroking her head.

Taylor tried to absorb comfort from him. She pressed closer and inhaled his scent, Lagerfeld and herbal shampoo and—

Perfume.

Taylor's eyes flew open. Her heart raced.

A long pink smudge lined his collar. *Lipstick!*

She pulled away. "What the hell is on your shirt?"

"Where?"

"Inside your collar," she said.

"I don't know."

"It's lipstick," Taylor said, crossing her arms.

Philip was calm. "DuPont's going-away party, it was emotional. His anchor partner, Shanna George, cried on my shoulder. Maybe her lipstick brushed my shirt. So what."

"I suppose that's her perfume I smell, too."

"No, it's probably yours, darling."

"I'm not wearing any."

CHAPTER 37

Doubt and anger rampaged Taylor's senses. Another woman's perfume stung her nostrils. Philip's insincere voice collided with her pounding heartbeat in her ears. She heard his ex-wife saying "stable of whores." Then Julian, warning "womanizer."

Taylor scanned Philip for more telltale signs of sex.

Through a new filter of distrust and annoyance, Philip appeared not as the usual charming, sophisticated man whom Taylor had agreed to marry, but as a slippery, sneaky man.

At that moment in his silk boxer shorts, surrounded by a fortune's worth of handmade suits and China silk shirts and Italian shoes, he reminded her of the Francisco drug lord during his double murder trial in Miami. Despite the mountain of evidence against him, he sat each day amidst witnesses and lawyers, smirking as if it were all a grand charade, fixed in his favor, and at the end he would ride away in his limo drinking Dom Perignon.

That same slick aura now framed Philip. His eyes seemed to taunt, "You have no evidence, so don't bother pressing charges." But Francisco was wrong; he went to prison for life, no parole. Likewise, Taylor was not about to let Philip get away with duping her.

"Some late-night meeting," Taylor said. "Looks more like a casting-couch rendezvous."

"Darling, a colleague gave me a hug," Philip said calmly.

"I might be twenty years younger than you, but I'm not that naïve," Taylor said. "A hug does not smudge lipstick inside your shirt like that, or cover you with perfume."

Philip stepped close and began unbuttoning her denim shirt.

She stepped back. "Don't touch me. I don't know where your hands have been."

Annoyance flashed across his face.

"You cheated on Andrea with me," Taylor said. "Now you're cheating on me and we're not even married yet."

"Darling, I have no reason to stray from you," he said.

"Then who's Caroline?"

Philip held her stare, but something strange stirred behind his eyes. "Who?"

"Caroline in Kansas City," Taylor said.

"Who told you about her?"

"That's not the point. The point is that I heard you have girl-friends at Wolf stations all over the country. Is that true?"

"Stop with the inquisition," Philip said. He sat on the bed and pulled off his socks. "You're tired and upset. Now, let's forget we ever veered into this insulting exchange and go to bed."

Taylor wanted to say she had never cheated on him, but that would be a lie. "Why should I marry you if you aren't faithful? I mean, we just made love Friday night. Is your libido so insatiable that you couldn't wait until the weekend when you saw me again?"

"But Friday night you were so tired, and I have needs," he said.

"So you did sleep with someone else tonight."

"Not necessarily," Philip said. "I'm just saying you weren't very enthusiastic about sex Friday night."

"I doubt you'd be so obsessed with sex if your life was threatened by a neo-Nazi convict," Taylor said.

Philip let out an exasperated sigh. "All I'm saying, darling, is that Andrea stopped sleeping with me, so I satisfied my needs elsewhere. Men need sex, and their wives are supposed to give it up whenever they need it."

Taylor glared at him. *This is so wrong. The most traumatic day of my life and Philip is lecturing me about the male libido.*

"I have needs, too," she said, "and you don't have a clue how to meet them."

"What's that supposed to mean?" he asked, the vein on his forehead bulging.

"My feelings, you don't care about them," she said. "You called me one lousy time today to see how I felt. And you had your peons tell me to come out here, like I'm some package of yours that they're FedExing somewhere."

"How dare you accuse me of not caring about you," Philip said. "Doesn't that rock on your finger mean anything?"

"A stupid ring can't hold me when I'm scared," Taylor shouted.

"Stupid ring? That ring cost more than you make in a year," Philip yelled. "Enough of the bitch act. I don't like it."

Taylor glared at Philip as he entered the dressing room and put his socks in the hamper. When he turned his back to her, she noticed two thin red lines arcing over his left shoulder blade.

Fingernail scratches! And they were in a spot that he, with his always smooth manicures, could not reach with his own hands.

Taylor's heart surged to her throat. He really had been with another woman tonight. Hot bolts of disappointment and anger zigzagged through her.

"You bastard!"

Philip spun around. "What now?"

"You cheated on me," she shouted. "You lied to me. You couldn't even cancel your tryst with your whore of the day to come home early for me."

Philip stepped close with stormy eyes and pursed lips. "I left my first wife because she was neurotic and paranoid," he said angrily. "And you, Taylor, are starting to sound a lot like her."

"Maybe you made her that way," Taylor said. "I've never questioned you before, but tonight I have reason to."

"No, you don't," Philip said. "As a matter of fact, it was your confidence and security with yourself that attracted me to you."

" 'Naïveté' is a better word," Taylor said. "I was too blinded by your charm to question your fidelity."

"Then why on earth are you doing it now?" Philip yelled.

"Because I'm starting to see the real Philip Carter, and I don't like him at all," Taylor shouted. "He's selfish and controlling and cold-hearted and—"

A hard, open palm whacked her cheek.

CHAPTER 38

Taylor was so stunned that she froze, staring at Philip.

Oh my God. He hit me.

Stinging, swelling pain drew tears.

Philip gripped her arms, pinching her flesh between his fingers. He shook her violently.

"Stoo . . . oooo . . . ooooop!" she shouted, her head rolling.

Philip's teeth glistened. "Don't you ever talk to me like that."

An icy fist of terror squeezed Taylor's chest. Her legs wobbled. "Let . . . me go!" she shouted. "You can't—"

"Shut up! I can do whatever I want. Stupid mulatto bitch!"

A devilish gleam in Philip's eyes chilled Taylor to the bone.

She sucked in air, remembering to breathe like she learned in self-defense classes. She twisted downward, escaping his grasp.

Philip stooped over, surprised.

Taylor balled her right fist . . . bashed it into his stomach.

"Uuuugggghhhh." His face reddened. He clung to his gut.

She shoved his shoulders and face into the carpet.

Wild with fear, Taylor scrambled out of the room. She flew down the staircase, grabbed her travel bag and purse from the foyer table.

Taylor bolted outside, ignoring the house alarm.

God, please help me . . .

It was dark except for the landscape lights close to the house. She hoped the alarm would draw no attention.

At the end of the walk, her trembling fingers fumbled with the gate hook. Finally it opened. She pushed through.

On legs like pistons, pumping, flying, she sprinted across the yard to the winding asphalt drive.

Her lungs ached as she gasped for breath. Sweat oozed under her shirt and jeans. Thank goodness for her Nikes.

Philip's house alarm became fainter as she ran down the drive. Headlights flashed. A car screeched. A man shouted.

"Watch it! Damn joggers!"

Taylor ran past mansions. She had to escape, but all around the development was a high fence of black iron spears. And she knew of only one exit, the guarded gate at the road.

She realized that Philip might call and tell the guard to catch her. She ran faster.

"Taylor!"

It was Philip, far behind.

She heard a car, so she crouched in a row of bushes as it passed.

Then she darted to the gate and hid behind a stone column opposite the guard booth.

Inside was a young man, scowling. He was on the phone, looking up at a map of the complex. A red light flashed on Philip's mansion.

I'll slip out while he's not looking.

As she inched from behind the column, watching the guard, bright headlights flashed. She withdrew into the darkness.

A woman in a Mercedes stopped at the guard window and said something. The guard bent down, flipping through a directory.

Taylor bolted through the gate.

Running, panting, praying.

Silver moonlight guided her down the winding road lined by walls of blasted rock. At certain angles the black ocean stretched eerily before her, as if she could leap from the hillside and plunge into its mysterious depths. She could hear waves crashing and cars roaring at the bottom of the road, on Pacific Coast Highway.

Something hard, buzzing loudly, struck her face. She frantically swiped a giant bug.

Dizzying fear and the damp, cool air gave Taylor goose bumps. She heard a car behind her.

If it's Philip, he'll see me and catch me and take me back and—

Taylor scanned the dark road for a hiding place. There were only rocky walls too steep to scale.

The car was getting closer. It sounded like Philip's Jaguar.

Taylor sprinted around a curve.

Ah! A pile of boulders. She jumped behind them, hoping she was not invading a wild animal's home.

A red Jaguar XJS convertible crept along the road. It was Philip, scanning the darkness.

"Taylor! Taylor, darling, where are you?"

Taylor crouched lower between the rocks. Her muscles burned, her head throbbed . . . cheek stung . . . lungs couldn't get enough air.

He hit me on the same cheek as Billy Joe. And he called me a stupid mulatto bitch. Assaulted and insulted by Philip on the same day as Rocky Pulaski. It's over. I have to get away. Can't marry him . . .

Taylor battened down a cement hatch over her raw emotions as Philip's car rolled past. When it sounded like he had reached the main road, she crept out of her hiding space. She ran.

She reached the bottom. Across the road was the dark beach. To the north a young couple strolled near the road and teenage boys clustered around a sporty Blazer with surfboards.

Several cars whizzed past.

Taylor gasped.

A convertible with double circles for headlights was coming toward her.

Philip.

She slid into a ditch. Philip turned back onto the road to his house, driving slowly.

Taylor darted across the street and ran south. Two men on motorcycles blew past, whistling. She wondered how crazy she looked running down Pacific Coast Highway with a large bag and a bandaged forehead.

Up ahead was a party store. She could call a cab and go to a hotel.

Frantic honking made her turn around.

It was Philip, pulling onto the shoulder.

Taylor shot toward the beach. Her shoes dug into the sand, making it difficult to run, but she plodded on. *I can hide in those rocks and bushes—*

"Taylor! I'm sorry, darling! Come back!"

Taylor kept running, praying that he wouldn't catch her.

She dashed toward a rock formation near the water's edge. There she scrambled over the rocks like a frightened crab.

Anything to get away from Philip. The man who was supposed to protect her had become yet another brute out to get her.

CHAPTER 39

Taylor crouched behind wet, jagged rocks. The waves roared before her, spraying her with salt water. Save for the moonlight, she felt as if she were standing at the edge of a huge black hole—the ocean and sky formed an intimidating void that made her pulse race.

She struggled to catch her breath, but Philip's cries were becoming louder.

Then she remembered Julian.

With trembling hands she rifled through her purse, pulling out her cellular phone and day planner. She used the dim green light from the phone's keypad to read the phone numbers Julian had left on her voice mail.

It rang five times. "Please answer. Please."

"Hello."

"Julian! Help me! Please, I'm—"

"Taylor?"

"You gotta help me," she squeaked.

"Where are you?"

"On the beach. On the rocks by—"

"What!" he shouted.

"I'm near Philip's house, on the beach, on the rocks."

"Why are you on the rocks? Why are you here?"

"Hiding from Pulaski. I mean, Philip. Can you come get me?"

"Good God. Of course. Where exactly are you?"

"By that party store at the foot of the drive up to Philip's. He's on the road, looking for me in his car. Hurry, please."

"How are you calling me?"

"On my cellular."

"Give me the number," Julian said.

"It's 555-2898."

"I live about fifteen minutes from there," Julian said. "Can you hold out that long?"

Taylor looked around. The dark ocean crashed at her feet. The salty wind stung her face. And gulls shrieked above, circling angrily. Philip was still calling her name.

"Hurry," Taylor said.

"I'll call you right back on my car phone," he said.

"Okay." She crouched low.

"Taylor! Where are you?" Philip called.

She gripped her phone, willing it to ring with Julian at the other end.

Something yellow appeared over the rocks. *Philip!*

"Taylor! I'm sorry, come back. What are you doing out here?"

She scrambled on the rocks, but her foot caught in a hole. She lost her balance, then crashed, shoulder first, into the wet sand. A wave, shocking cold, splashed her face and body. Water stung her nose. She tasted bitter salt.

At the same time, her phone plunked into the salty froth.

Her twisted ankle stung. Bullets of pain shot up from her shoulder. Dazed, she lay sprawled at the edge of the black water.

CHAPTER 40

Taylor willed her body to rise from the wet sand. She yanked her foot out of the hole, scraping her ankle. It stung horribly. Her shoulder ached.

"Taylor! Come back!"

Philip's voice sent another gush of adrenaline into her limbs. She dove for the phone, plucking a handful of water and sand with it. She shook it.

"Ring!"

Throbbing all over, she sprinted off the rocks, stumbling over dry sand. Wet clothes stuck to her skin; water dripped from her leather bag and purse.

"Goddammit!" Philip shouted.

She glanced back. He was sitting on the rock holding his knee.

Good, he's injured.

Taylor ran back toward the party store where Julian could find her. Peeking from around the dark side of the fluorescent-lit building, she saw two teenaged girls in a Jeep drinking sodas in the parking lot. Aching everywhere, she tried to catch her breath.

Sand caked the keypad on her phone. It was dead. Now Julian could not call, and she did not know what kind of car he drove.

God, please let him find me.

A car pulled in front of the store, but Taylor was too scared to peek. So she listened.

It was Philip's voice. "Hey, girls, have you seen a blonde wearing denim and a face bandage running around here?"

They giggled. "No, sorry."

Philip peeled away.

"What a weirdo," one girl said.

"Should we call the cops?" the other asked.

"No way. He might come after us, too."

Taylor closed her eyes as another car screeched into the parking lot.

"That's the guy from *Entertainment Exclusive*," one girl said. "I see him jogging on the beach all the time."

"He's cute," the other girl said. "He must recognize you, 'cause here he comes."

The girls laughed.

"Excuse me, but have you seen a blond woman anywhere around here?" It was Julian.

"Um . . ." the girl said.

Taylor ran into the parking lot. *Yes, it's Julian, thank God!*

"Julian! Let's go!"

His mouth fell open. "Taylor, what happened?"

The girls in the Jeep snickered. "Eewww, swamp thing!"

Taylor swallowed a hot gush of emotion. "Hurry! Philip was just here!"

Julian opened the door of a black Porsche convertible and took her bags off her shoulder as she slid into the car. Then he hopped in the driver's seat and they sped away.

"Sorry I'm all wet. I just—" Taylor bit her lip.

No, I will not start bawling in front of Julian like a helpless, pathetic crybaby. I will not. I'll be strong.

"Can you take me to a hotel, please?"

"No, I'm taking you home with me," Julian said. "What the hell did he do to you?"

She shivered as Julian sped up Pacific Coast Highway. Suddenly he spun onto the road to Philip's mansion.

"No!" she shouted. "Where are you going? Don't take me back there."

Julian floored it. "He can't get away with this. He just earned himself an ass-kicking, Detroit style."

"No, Julian, don't. Don't get yourself in trouble."

Julian did a U-turn. "What's going on?"

Taylor explained what happened as they drove. Fifteen minutes later, they pulled up to a contemporary white house.

Inside, her sneakers sloshed muddy tracks on the pine floor. "Sorry," she said, looking down.

Julian's eyes were soft as brown velvet as he held out his arms. "Let me hold you, White Chocolate."

Oh yes, I need this now. Thank you, God, for Julian.

Hot waves of fear and anger and shock surged through Taylor's still-trembling body. Julian clutched her to his chest. He squeezed his arms around her as raw emotions burst forth in fierce sobs and tears.

"I'm here for you," he said softly. "You're safe. Nobody can hurt you now."

Taylor closed her eyes.

Yes, it feels so good. This is where I should be, in heaven, in Julian's arms. My sanctuary from the world. This is where I should have been all along.

CHAPTER 41

Taylor pulled out of Julian's arms and looked at the huge living room. A zebra-skin rug and oversized black leather furniture sat in front of a white marble fireplace. Glass and pewter tables matched sconces on the walls. Enormous windows stretched to a cathedral ceiling, offering a view of the shimmering black ocean.

"I shouldn't be here," she said.

"You should," Julian countered.

"I don't know."

"I do know," Julian said. "In a hot shower, then in bed. You've had one hellacious day, and you look like . . ."

A faint smile broke through Taylor's gloom. She glanced at her muddy clothes and touched her sand-matted ponytail. "I guess I could use a shower."

Julian led her upstairs to a guest bedroom and bathroom, where she took a long, steaming shower.

"I feel horrible," she said to herself, staring in the steamy mirror at the purple bruise on her forehead and her black eye. Philip's slap had not left a physical mark, but it had obliterated the last bits of love she had for him.

As she donned a warm cashmere robe, in came Julian with a tray. On it was a steaming cup of tea and a small green jar.

"Where are you going with that Porter's Salve?" Taylor asked. "I hate that stuff."

"But it works," Julian said. "You know this was the first thing our parents reached for when we got cuts and scrapes as kids."

"But it smells. Speaking of parents, I need to call mine."

"The phone's on the nightstand," Julian said.

Taylor sat down and dialed her parents.

"Hello?" her mother said groggily.

"Mom, I'm with Julian now."

"That's strange," she said. "Philip just called and asked if we'd heard from you. He sounded pretty upset. What happened?"

"I left him," Taylor said.

Julian grabbed her foot and, with a Q-tip, smeared Porter's Salve on her scraped ankle.

"That tickles," she whispered with knitted brows.

"What?" her mother asked. "He said you two had a small misunderstanding. He thought you'd be on the next flight back to Detroit. And he said he's coming here to be with you. What's going on?"

"Don't worry, Mom," Taylor said. "Philip and I argued. So I called Julian. Please don't tell Philip where I am."

"So the wedding is off?" her mother asked.

Taylor imagined her mother in a frilly nightgown, sitting up in bed, grinning.

"Mom, I dont' want to talk about it," Taylor said. "It must be four A.M. there. I just wanted to tell you that I'm safe."

"Call us in the morning," Monica said. "And let me talk to Julian."

Taylor rolled her eyes. "Why?"

"Just let me."

Taylor handed the phone to Julian.

"Hello, Aunt Monica. Yes, I'll take care of her . . . I know . . . all right." Julian hung up and scooted toward Taylor with his Q-tip.

"Where are you going with that?"

"To your forehead."

Taylor shook her head. "No, it's too close to my nose."

"C'mon. You won't have a scar if you use this. I'll put a Band-Aid over it so you won't smell it."

Taylor let Julian play doctor as she called Shari.

"Sorry to wake you. It's Taylor."

"Wha . . . Are you all right?"

"Yeah and no. I just wanted to tell you I'm not at Philip's tonight."

"Why not?" Shari asked.

"We argued and I left."

"Then where the hell are you? A hotel?"

"No, Julian DuPont's house. Here's the num—"

"What did you say?" Shari asked.

"I'm with Julian. It was either that or I'd just fly back to Detroit tonight."

"No, don't do that," Shari said, sounding more awake. "Pulaski is still at large. Does Philip know where you are?"

"No, and don't tell him."

"Christ, this is career suicide for both of you," Shari said.

"Tell him and William that I'm at a hotel."

"I'm not lying to them," Shari said. "Management has to know where you are, since we sent you away. You're playing with fire here, Taylor."

Taylor's stomach cramped as she remembered Carla's warning about being suspicious of Shari when it came to Julian and Philip.

"Shari, please, as my friend," Taylor said. "I don't want Philip to find me. He hit me and called me a mulatto bitch tonight. If he comes here, I'm calling the police."

Julian's eyebrows drew together angrily.

"Why'd he slap you?" Shari asked.

"We were arguing," Taylor said. "Please, Shari."

"All right, all right."

"Thank you," Taylor said. "I'll call you tomorrow."

"Be careful," Shari said.

Taylor hung up, then sipped the warm tea, which soothed her nerves.

"Sorry you're going through this," Julian said.

"It's your fault," Taylor said. "If you hadn't done me wrong in the first place, I would never have given Philip Carter the time of day."

Julian embraced her and kissed her forehead. "Please forgive me," he said softly. "It'll never happen again."

Taylor wanted to believe him, but in her mind there was still a dangerous electric fence around her feelings for him, and now it was zapping and buzzing like never before.

CHAPTER 42

Shari cursed at Charles as she climbed out of bed and wrapped a satin robe around her nude body.

"Be quiet," he grumbled before turning his back and snoring loudly.

You're such a shit-head. Disdain for Charles and anxiety about Taylor's call intensified Shari's cigarette craving, which possessed her like an evil spirit. After three days, she needed a nicotine fix more urgently than air.

Shari hurried to her closet, pulled a shoe box from the shelf, and retrieved the pack of Benson & Hedges Menthol Lights that she had hidden from herself. With a frantic hand she grabbed her gold lighter from the vanity and headed for the door.

The phone rang. Charles moaned loudly.

"I'll get it downstairs," Shari said.

She ran to the kitchen.

"Hello?"

"Mrs. Gordon, this is the Channel Three operator. I have Philip Carter on the line."

Shari sighed loudly.

"Shari, have you talked to Taylor?" His speech was hard and fast.

"Hi, Philip," Shari said. She nervously peeled the plastic off the box, retrieved a cigarette, and placed it between her lips. "Where are you?"

"I'm in my fuckin' car, looking for Taylor. She disappeared, running like a goddamn lunatic on the beach. You heard from her?"

Panic whirled in Shari's head as an orange flame danced before her eyes. As the tip of the cigarette glowed red, she sucked smoke, deep down. She closed her eyes in anticipation of the nicotine tickling her brain, calming her nerves.

Should I protect my friend and lie to my boss? Or should I tell Philip the truth and betray Taylor? But if Taylor sleeps with Julian tonight, her engagement is history, and Philip will be a free man—

"Shari?"

Her nipples stiffened. Philip sounded like he had a lot of ferocious energy that he needed to unleash.

"Yeah, sorry, I just woke up," she purred.

"Well, has Taylor called you tonight?"

"Yes, she did," Shari said. "Brace yourself."

"What, goddammit? Tell me."

"Taylor is at Julian DuPont's house in Malibu," Shari said. She took a long drag on her cigarette to suffocate tendrils of guilt and wickedness creeping up from her conscience.

Through the phone, Shari heard screeching tires.

"Say that again," Philip said.

"She's at DuPont's house."

"But she just met him Friday," Philip said. "Well, I'll be damned. I thought I was smooth, but— Shit, what does he have, radar? Me and Taylor have one little argument and that Mandingo pussy hound is right on the case. He's probably fuckin' her right now."

Shari sighed. *This is ugly. And it's only gonna get worse.*

"Philip, relax," Shari said coolly, blowing out smoke. "Taylor and Julian are childhood sweethearts. She's the reason he's coming back to Detroit."

"No fuckin' way," Philip said, his voice deep and raspy. "I got him that job. And Taylor, after all I've done for both of them, this is the thanks I get?"

"Taylor has gotten to where she is on her own," Shari said. "She works her butt off. But she was depending on you to help her get to the network."

"She better put her head between her knees and kiss her ass good-bye, because that ain't gonna happen," Philip said. "Both of them are through in this business."

"Relax," Shari said.

"That slut," Philip said. "Nobody makes a cuckold of Philip Carter. Even DuPont. He's a whore, she's a whore. They belong together."

"Taylor is not a whore," Shari said.

"Now she is," Philip said.

"She said she left your place because you hit her."

Philip sighed. "She punched me in the stomach, knocked the wind out of me. I couldn't believe it. She needed a good slap with all the shit she was giving me tonight."

Shari's raging libido was like cotton in her ears; she did not let his violence register on her mind. She sensed that fate was thrusting a much-longed-for lover into her arms, and she was going to seize the moment at all costs.

"Philip, I was going to call you in the morning," Shari said. "We're having some problems with the morning program."

"What problems?"

"There's a major budget glitch," Shari said. "It looks like someone neglected to allot money for salaries for the technical staff as well as a morning producer."

"Shit," he said.

"And construction of the new studio is on hold because the engineers ordered the wrong lights, and the cameras that arrived are defective," Shari said. "We really need you here to help iron this out."

Philip cursed loudly. "Yeah, you need me to fire whoever the fuck made all those mistakes."

Lustful tremors rippled through Shari's body, lingering in a moist ache between her legs. *The raspy violence in his voice is so sexy.*

"I don't know, but I think this constitutes an emergency, Philip,"

Shari said softly. "And I think this is a fire that only you can extinguish."

"Fine," Philip said. "I'll call my pilot now. I'll be there in the morning."

Shari smiled in the orange glow of her lighter as she lit another cigarette.

CHAPTER 43

Philip zoomed toward the airport, unconcerned about his attire of gray sweats and flip-flops. Those clothes were the first things he had grabbed after Taylor fled the house.

Sweat poured from him, despite the cool wind, and his chest muscles spasmed. He thought about Taylor and DuPont looking at each other like strangers in his office Friday. It was a trick. All along they were former lovers, fooling him, laughing at his ignorance, probably scheming for a secret rendezvous when he left town.

Just like Dad. The woman I love betrayed me with a lover. DuPont is probably fucking Taylor silly right now.

Philip hit the steering wheel with his palm.

I'm a cuckold. And if I don't marry Taylor, I'll never be legitimized in Dad's eyes. Dad will think I'm unstable. He'll divide the company between Horace and Jonathan. I can forget any chance of being CEO of Wolf Media Corp.

He envisioned his father's disapproving eyes. Dad would think he was a failure at work because of the morning program fiasco. A loser by birth because he was another man's son. And a failure at marriage, with one ex-wife and an ex-fiancée. Chances of finding another woman like Taylor were as minuscule as finding a diamond in the sand on the beach.

What was left in his life? Should he strive for forty-eight more years of trying to please the man who was not his father? Working endless hours, fucking countless women, always feeling empty in the end?

No. Philip's likeness to his father ended there. He did not have the diplomacy of Gerald Carter. No way would Philip sacrifice his hankering for vengeance in the name of reputation. Taylor and Julian's betrayal had punched a gargantuan hole in his ego, and Philip was determined to deliver even more destructive blows to both of them.

Neither of those mulatto whores will work another day in broadcast news.

CHAPTER 44

A mellow smile lifted Jess Stevens's cheeks as the engine's loud roar lulled her further into a cottony euphoria. Her only irritation now was her allergy to mold; she had sneezed scores of times over the hours as the old Chris-Craft sped north across Lake Huron.

"That's good, Jess," Rocky said, reaching back to stroke her hand as she kneaded his thick shoulders.

"This here's the beginning of the end," Rocky said, looking across the faux wood table at Scarlin, Billy Joe, Kramer, and the nine comrades who had posed as cops during the escape. At the safe house they had all changed into army green fatigues and combat boots.

"It's a triumph," Rocky said, "and it'll galvanize the movement. It'll show the world that we have the power to conquer enemies and rise to greatness. Now we need to start back training, buying weapons—"

Jess sneezed. "Excuse me."

The men ignored her.

"Führer Pulaski," Scarlin said, "if it was up to me, I'd say we make a move for Canada, lay low awhile, then come back to the States in a couple months. After the heat dies down."

Lemer and Billy Joe nodded.

But Rocky shifted on the chartreuse plaid booth. "No, we need to act now, keep the momentum going."

Jess sneezed again and blew her nose loudly on a napkin.

"Jesus, woman," Rocky said. "Get ahold of yourself."

"Allergies," she said, embarrassed.

A short time later, the boat stopped. As they climbed on deck, she heard Gus Lemer laughing with Billy Joe.

"Thanks for whackin' that black bitch, man," Lemer said. "I blew her daddy away, and I'd love to pop her, too."

Billy Joe laughed. "Jess, you got the mongrel good."

Jess smiled. "I hate that bitch."

On a small wooden dock stood Fred Lutz, the private developer who was one of the White Power Alliance's most generous benefactors. Jess hugged him and kissed his clean-shaven cheek. He was very tall, with gray-brown hair and a large Adam's apple.

"How're you, Jess? Brunette again. The natural you."

"Thanks for helpin' us out here," she said.

"I'm just doing my duty for white brothers and sisters in need," he said. "Stay as long as you want."

After hugging the men, Fred led them down a wooded path under bright moonlight. Jess walked close to Rocky. The boat engine still roared in her ears despite the quiet stillness around her, broken only by the cries of whippoorwills and feet crunching leaves and twigs.

They followed Fred into the kitchen of an enormous cedar log home, with a stone chimney and expansive deck. Inside, Fred's wife, Daisy, urged them to indulge in a spread of cold cuts and cheese that she had prepared.

"We seen you on the news," said Daisy, who wore a jet black beehive hairdo and an apron over yellow polyester cigarette pants and a sleeveless blouse. "That musta been one God-awful boat ride."

"Was better 'n jail," Billy Joe said as he joined Nick, Scarlin, Lemer, and Kramer in loading their plates.

"You outdid yourself, Daisy," Rocky said. "I'm so hungry I could eat everything on that table."

"There's more where that come from," she said. "You boys, Jess, dig in."

A woman almost as tall as Fred, bearing his features and endless legs, strode into the kitchen in pink shorts and a bikini top. She flashed a wide smile at the men and twirled a lock of long brown hair around her fingers.

"Rocky!" she shrieked, hugging him.

Who's that slut? Jess watched, anger surging through her, as Rocky squeezed her and kissed her mouth.

"Sweet young thing," Rocky said. "You get prettier every time I see you." Rocky turned to Fred. "With a daughter like this, man, I know you keep the shotguns loaded."

Fred chuckled.

Jess glared at Rocky through a red veil of anger. She wanted to slap him and that girl, especially when she noticed the other men had frozen to gawk.

"This must be your girlfriend," the woman said, giving Jess a once-over.

"Yeah," Rocky said in a tone that made Jess feel unwelcome.

The young woman held out her hand. "I'm Sally, Fred and Daisy's daughter."

"I'm Jess."

Sally spun, her hair hitting Jess's shoulder. Then Sally lifted herself on the counter, smiling when Rocky stared at her bare thighs.

Rocky must think Sally's dinner, the way he's lookin' at her. Jess stabbed a kielbasa with a fork. She piled her plate high, then sat at the table to eat.

"Rocky, I thought you were starving," Jess said.

"Don't worry 'bout me," he said without looking at her.

Jess glared at him. *Asshole. I devote my life to your cause, and you treat me like a dog. You cheat on me and act like I'm bothering you when I ask for affection. And you never paid me one dime when I ran your communications network.*

But Rocky did not notice Jess's anger; he was too busy ogling Sally's legs.

After dinner, while Jess helped Daisy clean the kitchen, she could hear the men outside on the deck, talking about the White Power Alliance. And she could see, through the window over the sink, Sally giggling on Rocky's lap.

That son of a bitch.

A short while later, Fred showed them to the cabin. It had four bedrooms, a kitchen and a living room on the first floor, a sleeping loft on the second floor, and a full basement, set up like an office with three computers linked to the Internet, phones, and a stocked gun closet.

After Jess and Rocky went to the upstairs loft to sleep in a double bed, Rocky said, "I'm goin' for a walk."

"You're goin' to meet Sally," Jess said. "I'm your woman, and I don't want you sneakin' into the woods with that girl half your age."

"You're my woman, not my wife, so lay off," Rocky snapped.

"No, I'm tired a bein' treated like dirt," Jess said.

Rocky pointed at her, his eye twitching. "I got your washed-up ass out of jail."

"It was your fault I got arrested," Jess said.

Rocky pinched her arm. "Shut up before I shut you up myself." He shoved her onto the bed, then stormed out of the cottage.

Motherfucker. I went to prison for you, but you just give me grief.

She massaged her throbbing arm as she listened at the open window.

There were giggles, Sally's giggles, and two sets of footsteps crunching on the wooded path.

Jess slumped to the floor, wondering why her life was so miserable. She could not simply leave Rocky because she was a fugitive of the law. And she had nowhere to go.

CHAPTER 45

In the enormous mirror in Julian's gray marble bathroom, Taylor marveled at the ivory-bronze contrast of their skin and the striking difference between their black and blond curls.

How could he scorn something as exotic and beautiful as the two of us together?

Julian met her questioning eyes in the mirror. He turned off the blow dryer.

"What?" he asked, feeling her hair. "It's all dry."

"Thank you," she said.

"I still can't believe you're here," he said.

"Only because I'm on the run from two other men," Taylor said.

"No, it's fate," Julian said. "This is meant to be."

Julian cupped his hands over her jaw, pulling her close. He pressed his fiery-sweet mouth to her lips, arousing a hunger in her, physical and emotional, for him and only him.

He feels so wonderful, I never want to leave his arms. Yes, Julian, kiss me like this until I breathe my last breath.

He scooped her into his arms and carried her into his bedroom—an immense room with a glass rotunda overlooking the ocean, sleek gray furniture, and a pedestal bed at the foot of which lay a zebra skin. He laid her down, letting the cashmere robe fall open around her nude body.

"Taylor, I love you," he whispered. "I will never, ever hurt you again."

"I missed you so much," Taylor said. "Now I finally—"

Loud chimes interrupted her.

Alarmed, she sat up and covered herself. "Could it be Philip? Who else would ring your doorbell at two in the morning?"

Julian stood up. "I'll kick his ass if it's him."

When he left the room, Taylor went to a window. A silver Nissan sat in the driveway. She could not see the doorway, but she heard a woman's voice.

Her heart raced. *Julian had a tryst tonight, just like Philip. That bastard.* Taylor quietly opened the window.

"Julian, baby, what's wrong?" the woman asked. "Why don't you want me anymore? You got somebody else up there?" The woman sounded as if she had been crying.

"Leave, Brooke, now," Julian said loudly.

"What's wrong? Are you gay? You're crazy to let me go."

"Go now," Julian said.

Taylor watched the woman, a tanned blonde in a minidress and high heels, drive away. Taylor's limbs trembled with anger as she stood at the top of the stairs with crossed arms, glaring at Julian as he ascended. She felt sick and hurt, aching from one more blow after a traumatic day.

"That was your fiancée, wasn't it?"

"Used to be," Julian said. "Now she won't leave me alone."

"Why is she coming over at this hour?"

"She comes over at all hours, begging me to take her back," Julian said. "She was just part of the grand fuckup that my life became when I lost you."

Taylor rolled her eyes, wondering how many times that woman, and probably many more, had slept with Julian in his bedroom.

"I wish you had never come to Detroit," Taylor said. "Now my whole life is screwed up. My job, my wedding, my future. If Philip finds out I'm here, it'll be the end of both of us. Take me to the airport right now. I'm going home."

"No, you can't," Julian said, blocking the staircase. "Pulaski's still out there. It's too dangerous."

"I'll take my chances," Taylor said. "I was happy until you and that racist maniac invaded my life."

She glared at Julian, then ran into the guest bedroom and slammed the door. She called the airline to reserve a seat on the first flight to Detroit in the morning.

CHAPTER 46

Her body aching with lust, Shari Gordon joined her colleagues at the assignment desk for morning story conference.

"I want a segment about courthouse security," Shari said. "How people are feeling at courts in the city and suburbs in the wake of Pulaski's escape."

And I want Philip Carter to fuck me senseless. She squeezed the muscles between her legs, tantalizing the hypererogenous throb that had burned for attention since she spoke to him.

"We'll have Tony Martin continue with the cops and FBI, see if they've got any leads," Shari said. "And have Kendra Vaughn follow up with the condition of the prosecutor, Carla Jackson, in the hospital. Anybody calls asking for Taylor's whereabouts, the answer is no comment. Got it?"

Everyone around her nodded.

"We need someone to check on a shooting on Belle Isle last night," said Jerry Spinx, the assignment editor. "Sounds like two kids were fighting over a girl. Add Uzis, and the kids made Swiss cheese of each other."

"I'll have Mary Lawrence check that out," Shari said.

Jerry checked a notebook. "We already have Roland doing a Grand Prix promo story, and Art is in Lansing for the governor's press conference."

"Fabulous," Shari said as the group dispersed. She stopped William by the Newsflash desk.

"Morning, Shari."

"I have to tell you something confidential," she said.

"What?"

"Taylor James left Philip's place last night. She's with a friend nearby."

William flashed a facetious expression. "Now, why on earth would she leave warm, caring Philip at a time like this?"

"I guess they had a disagreement," Shari said. "But just so you know, Philip is coming back today to deal with the morning show snags."

William sighed angrily and pushed up his pewter glasses. "I don't need his help. I can handle all those problems on my own."

"Don't worry," Shari said. "I'll keep him out of your hair."

When Shari entered her office, Philip was pacing with crossed arms. He wore a tapered beige suit; his tense face was pale despite his tan, and his eyes seemed smaller and sharper.

Yes, come to me. I have a luscious outlet for all that fury surging inside you.

"Well, good morning," she said.

"Shari, I want the names of every imbecile working on the morning program," Philip said. He slapped a newspaper on the desk, causing papers to float to the floor.

Shari closed the door. "Philip, calm down. I know you're upset because of last night, but—"

"But my ass. I've never been more furious. So tell me, Shari, how long has Taylor been planning to jump Julian's bones?"

She stepped closer to him. "Philip, stop. On Saturday she was pretty pissed off that he was here."

"You should have told me about their connection," Philip said.

"I thought it was innocuous," Shari said. "Taylor said she wanted you, not him. But I guess something happened last night to change her mind, I don't know. Just don't be too hard on her."

"Oh," Philip chuckled maliciously. "Hard doesn't begin to describe it. She and DuPont will wish they'd never seen a television set when I get through with them."

"But we need them," Shari said. "Taylor helped make Channel Three number one. Viewers love her."

Philip shook his head. "I don't give a flying fuck."

"Besides, she's got enough problems with Pulaski on the run," Shari said.

"She should've thought about that before she went running to DuPont," Philip said. He sighed loudly and turned his back to her, shaking his head.

Now's the time to make my move. Shari unbuttoned her electric blue suit jacket, under which she wore only a black lace bodysuit. Her stiff nipples poked through its floral pattern as its snug design lifted and rounded her full breasts. With her back to the office door and windows, she stepped close to Philip, putting her hands on her hips to hold open her jacket.

"Philip," she purred.

He turned around. Shock, then lust, flashed across his face.

Shari gave him her best seductive pout. *He'll either fire me for indecent conduct and sue me for sexual harassment, or he'll fuck me delirious.*

A hungry expression washed away Philip's scowl.

Electric sparks shot through Shari's abdomen when she looked into his eyes. She wanted to bite his parted, pink lips and crush her cheek against his rugged face, bury her mouth in his neck and ride him until it killed her.

Shari was so aroused that she felt dizzy. She smiled slightly as the soaking wet crotch of her bodysuit pressed delightfully against her swollen flesh. And her nipples were pointing at Philip like the tips of a magnet drawn to a rod of steel.

"Shari," he said softly. "You know just the remedy for my troubles."

She devoured him with lustful eyes.

"Come up to my office so we can discuss this," he said.

Shari's heart thundered as she buttoned her jacket and followed Philip out of her office, across the balcony, and to the elevator.

When the elevator doors closed, Philip turned to Shari with a cocky smile. "So how long have you been scheming to fuck me?"

Shari looked at her watch. "About six hours."

Philip ran his fingertips over her lips, sending a tremor of lust through her.

"I see you're at your best under deadline pressure," Philip said. "I like that."

Shari's senses went wild. His cologne . . . his warm breath . . . his hungry eyes . . . the throbbing between her legs.

She slid her hand into his three-button beige suit jacket, then wrapped her fingers around a rock-hard erection, hot even through his trousers.

One side of Philip's mouth rose in a sly smile. "You want it bad, don't you?"

Shari nodded.

Philip spun her around and pushed her against the elevator wall. He pressed his erection into her backside, humping her hard.

"I oughta take it right here," Philip said through clenched teeth.

Shari shivered. *Good God. I need it so bad. And he's so deliciously rough.*

He released her as the elevator door opened.

Breathless, Shari smoothed down her hair and skirt.

"Good morning, Ms. Gordon," the receptionist said.

"Hello, Ms. Small," she said softly as she trailed Philip through the sun-drenched atrium.

In his office, Philip locked the door and drew the blinds. He hung his jacket on a brass hanger near the television, then sat in a wing-back leather chair.

"Come here," he said with hungry eyes.

Shari felt savage with sexual hunger, but suddenly guilty and self-conscious. She was about to blow her marriage vows to hell, screw her close friend's fiancé, and have sex with her superior. But her marriage was over, Taylor did not want Philip, and Shari would just have to roll with whatever consequences unfolded in the office. It was more than worth it.

Shari stepped in front of Philip and pulled off her jacket. Her perfume wafted from her chest as Philip gripped her thighs. She shivered as his fingers grasped her buttocks under her skirt, pushing it up to her waist.

The sexual charge pulsating through Shari was so strong that she felt she could illuminate a light bulb with her fingertip.

She cried out when Philip ran his hand between her legs.

"You need it bad, sweetheart," he said.

The wonderful tingles radiating under his touch squelched all emotions except for unbridled lust.

Philip stood up, kissing her wildly, groping her breasts and back and butt.

Shari stroked his erection through his pants, then unfastened them and let them fall to the floor. She pushed Philip back on the chair, his legs outstretched, and knelt in front of him.

Then she pulled a glorious erection from the golden nest inside his beige boxers.

Shari moaned as she stared at it, remembering how wonderful that strange shaft of flesh looked and felt. It had been so long.

Yes, I've struck gold. And I want all of it.

She ran the tip of her tongue from its base to its tip, inhaling that sweet male scent as Philip sucked in air.

"Yeah," he said softly. "Do that."

She slid him inside her mouth, her lips touching every satin-smooth surface, every vein, every angle of its head. Shari closed her eyes, sucking and licking and moaning. And every lick made her hotter and wetter.

"Come here," Philip said, tapping his tanned, muscular thighs.

Shari straddled his lap, locking the backs of her knees over the arms of the chair. Philip reached down and unsnapped the crotch of her bodysuit, then shoved his fingers inside her.

Shari threw back her head and cried out. "Fuck me, please," she moaned.

Philip roughly grasped her thighs, his fingertips kneading her flesh. Then he yanked her down onto his rock-hard erection.

Shari groaned.

The friction of him inside her swollen, slippery flesh sent hot waves of numbing, electric bliss through her. He gripped her thighs more tightly, pulling her down and pushing her up. A snarl twisted his sweaty face.

Shari cupped his cheeks in her hands, ran her fingers through his blond hair.

I found a lover, and oh, what an expert lover he is. Shari bit her bottom lip to keep from screaming. She imagined for a split second the receptionist dialing 911.

But Shari cried out again when Philip slid his thumb across her clit as he pumped her.

"You do that so good," she purred. "So good."

Within seconds, a seizure of raw passion consumed Shari. She never wanted that amazing, electrified feeling to end. Hot, glistening skin quivering, her breasts tender and tipped by hard pink peaks, a pulsating firestorm between her legs.

Philip poked his fingers into Shari's mouth as she climaxed, letting oral stimulation intensify the overwhelming sensations that pushed her over the edge.

When she stilled, Philip guided her on trembling legs to his desk. He bent her over the front side, then rammed inside her.

This is incredible, better than I ever dreamed.

Shari closed her eyes, delirious with pleasure. Her damp cheek and palms stuck to papers on the desk while Philip pounded her ferociously. She imagined that he was thinking about Taylor and Julian, and each thrust unleashed fury over losing his fiancée to his protégé. Shari almost felt sorry for him, but her absolute glee over the fuck of her life made her numb to everything but the wild hammering between her legs.

Philip pulled her by the hips back closer to the edge of the desk, causing her arm to hit something. She turned just in time to see a brass frame around Philip and Taylor's tanned, smiling faces on a boat. The frame crashed to the floor, shattering glass.

"That whore," Philip said under his breath as he thrust even more violently.

"Yes," Shari said. "Give it all to me like that."

CHAPTER 47

Taylor bolted out of bed. She was disoriented, her head was throbbing, and she was furious that she had missed her flight.

She started to charge out of the bedroom, searching for Julian, until she caught her reflection in the dresser mirror. Purple ringed her right eye below the bandage, and she wore only a lace-trimmed white nightgown.

Damn him, I'm trapped. And he stole my clothes.

"And where do you think you're going?" Julian said as he entered with a breakfast tray. "Blueberry pancakes just for you."

"Where are my clothes?"

"In the laundry room with your bag, drying out," Julian said. "They were stained with salt water and sand." Julian placed the tray on the bed. "Come on, Taylor. Eat."

"Fine, but I'm flying back to Detroit today," she said. She climbed into bed and pulled the blankets around her waist. "When did you learn to cook?"

"My mother owns a catering business, remember?"

"Yeah, but you're never around enough to pick up any culinary skills."

"I know," Julian said with a shamed expression. "But that'll change. I take it by the way you're wolfing down those pancakes that they're good."

Taylor rolled her eyes. "I'm just hungry. And mad. My whole life is turned upside down."

"Do you remember me waking you up every forty-five minutes last night?" he asked.

Taylor locked on his compassionate gaze. Despite the desperation in his eyes, she questioned his sincerity. At the same time, however, it felt so wonderful with him, like climbing into a soft, warm bed after a grueling day. Taylor had the feeling that she had endured a solo trip across a frozen tundra, lacking food and water, battling hungry packs of wolves and polar bears. Now she had finally reached the tropical island, which could either mean a lifetime of lush pleasures or a deadly case of hemorrhagic fever.

"You did that?" she asked.

"Yeah, I slept right there," he said, pointing to a leather settee in the corner. "You look confused. Maybe a jog on the beach would help you sort your thoughts."

Taylor glanced at her nightgown. "I'm not dressed for it. And I need to call the airline."

Julian frowned. "It would be insane to go back to Detroit. Pulaski could be anywhere, and if he's got police contacts, you're easy prey. Channel Three ordered you out here, so stay awhile."

"Fine," Taylor said. "But it's only because of Pulaski and my bosses, not because I want to stay with you."

"As long as you stay," Julian said. "I'll get your clothes. I think I saw a pair of bike shorts in there."

"You did, along with all my underwear," Taylor said, tossing a pillow at him.

Taylor marveled at the sight of the blue ocean through huge living room windows. Sunlight poured in at every angle, splashing onto plants, white walls, and polished wood floors.

She followed Julian to a lower level, which held a gigantic room with a large television, a pool table, a dance floor, video games, and a long bar. The entire back wall was sliding glass doors leading to the beach.

Outside, Taylor shielded her eyes against the hazy sunshine as she gazed at the ocean. Sadness tugged at her like an undertow as she remembered early visits with Julian: strolling on Venice Beach, watching street performers and the eye-popping cornucopia of humanity, like the one-armed midget on the skateboard begging for cigarettes, and the woman in the leather bikini with a python around her shoulders, and the motorcycle guys whose tattooed skin resembled wallpaper.

Back then, she and Julian had been ebullient in each other's presence—splashing through the waves, kissing, body surfing. And there was the time when they were swimming far out at Zuma Beach when they saw a large sea animal leaping into the air and diving back into the water. Terrified they had seen a shark, they swam as quickly as they could back to the beach.

Taylor chuckled. But the ocean was also where she had sought solace in Miami. She loathed all those lovey-dovey couples along Ocean Drive on the South Beach strip, holding hands and gazing at each other the way she and Julian had once done. And the one time she did have a boyfriend there, an artist named Andrew Johnson, she remembered sitting at the News Café under an umbrella table, eating couscous, hummus, and stuffed grape leaves, when he told her that she spoke "too white" and that she should try to get a tan to darken her skin so his black friends would not ask so many questions about her race. Taylor stopped dating him, choosing solitude instead. So she had often jogged by the water or sat on the sand, wishing and praying in vain for Julian to return her phone calls and letters.

"Ready?" Julian said.

Taylor's stomach felt acidy and her head was still pounding.

"What if one of Pulaski's fanatics sees me?"

"Nobody knows you're here," Julian said. "Come on, running will work off your stress."

Taylor followed Julian, scrumptious in red shorts and a tank top. For a moment she let him jog ahead so she could watch his muscles. She wanted to marvel at his gorgeous physique, but raw memories of their breakup kept causing her to avert her eyes to the sand. Looking at him was like staring at the sun; he radiated warmth and brightness and incredible power, but he also hurt her eyes, and she feared that staring at his beautiful exterior too long might blind her to the danger of loving him again.

Taylor caught up, keeping his pace, as they ran past houses and people and surfers.

"I jog every day," Julian said. "Clears my mind."

Taylor did not speak until they returned, a half hour later, to Julian's house.

"How's your headache?" he asked, stretching on the wooden staircase that led from the beach up to his deck.

"It's gone," Taylor said, watching the waves.

It sunk to my heart.

CHAPTER 48

Julian pulled the car into a parking spot marked DUPONT behind a huge, box-shaped building in Burbank. As Taylor got out of the car, a white Rolls-Royce pulled up next to them. A leathery, silver-haired man in olive trousers, a mock turtleneck shirt, and loafers stepped out and removed sunglasses.

"DuPont, there's my man," he said, smiling.

"Hey, Roger, how was your trip?"

"Cabo San Lucas has never been better," he said. "I took this babe who made me feel half my age. I feel like a million bucks."

"Glad to hear it," Julian said. "Taylor, this is the executive producer of *EE*. Roger Gold, this is Taylor James."

"Where have I heard that name before?" Roger asked, scanning Taylor from head to toe. She was glad she wore white jeans and a white blouse that covered most of her body, and makeup on her black eye. She realized that this was Philip's friend, the one he had invited to their wedding. *God, please don't let him figure out who I am.*

Uneasiness gripped Taylor's gut as she shook his hand and followed them inside, past a security guard and receptionist.

"DuPont, you got the house packed up yet?"

"Not yet, but it won't take long," Julian said.

"Spectacular," Roger said. "Your timing couldn't be better. The Malibu place is perfect for my reentry into bachelorhood."

Julian joined Roger's deep laughter until the elevator opened.

"Nice meeting you, dear," he said to Taylor. "And good luck, you'll need it hangin' around this guy."

As Roger left, relief surged through Taylor. "What was he talking about?"

"I rent my house from him," Julian said. "He's moving back in after his divorce."

"Philip invited him to our wedding," Taylor said.

"Birds of a feather flock together," Julian said. "They're both rich, powerful, and they love young girls."

"And they act like you're their best buddy," Taylor said with an accusing tone.

Julian led her through a bustling newsroom, where colorful, autographed posters of stars lined the walls. As he unlocked his office door, Taylor recognized *EE*'s female anchor, Shanna George, who wore a curve-hugging coral suit and a bouncy blond bob.

She kissed Julian's cheek. "I thought I'd seen the last of you."

Julian smiled. "Shanna, meet Taylor James."

"Is this Philip's girl?" Shanna asked.

"Yeah," Julian said, entering his office.

"Philip never told me you were so young," Shanna said. "But he's got you in good hands."

Taylor smiled. *Did Philip fuck you, too?*

"Good luck with your marriage," Shanna said, smiling. "And you better keep in touch, Julian."

"Will do, see you later," Julian said.

Taylor scanned the office, which was more like a dressing room, with its mirrored vanity and trays of makeup and a rack of clothes on one side, a paper-strewn desk and couch on the other side.

Julian began packing things in large boxes.

"Dude, DuPont!" A tall, brunette man bounded into the office, smiling.

"Kris Carson, this is Taylor James, an old friend."

The man squeezed Taylor's hand. "The question is, how old, and how close a friend?" Kris guffawed and patted Julian's back.

274 / Elizabeth Atkins Bowman

"We grew up together," Julian said.

"Oh, a healthy midwestern girl! Just get her some sunshine and she'll be centerfold material."

"Kris, man, cut it out," Julian said. "I told you about eating sugary cereal for breakfast."

"Hey, dude, I'm just a little emotionally disturbed about you leavin' and everything," he said. "Who am I gonna hang out with? You're the coolest guy to come through here in ten years."

"Thanks," Julian said, "but—"

"Hey, we're all goin' out tonight, dancin', partyin'," Kris said. "C'mon, you better get your fill of L.A. night life before you leave."

"I got my fill long ago, Kris. Taylor, want to go out tonight?"

"I'm not in the mood," she said.

"C'mon, guys, it'll be fun," Kris said. "I'll catch you later."

"What's he on?" Taylor asked after he had bounded from the office.

"He's always like that," Julian said. "He's a studio sound technician. Going out would help you forget everything."

"I didn't bring going-out clothes," Taylor said. "And I said I'm not in the mood."

"What if I buy you a dress?" Julian asked.

"I have my own money," Taylor said.

"Okay, what if I take you to a store and you buy a dress?"

Taylor huffed. "Listen, I don't want to be here. I don't want to be with you. And I definitely don't want to go out with that obnoxious guy. So just drop it, will you?"

Taylor plopped on the couch and brooded while Julian packed. After a while, she glanced around at the photographs of him and stars on the walls, including Quincy Jones, Oprah Winfrey, Sylvester Stallone, and Hugh Hefner.

"Ugh," she said aloud, staring at Julian surrounded by four chesty women in bikinis. Everything was confirming her suspicion that Julian was a certified playboy.

Julian taped up the last box. "Ready?"

"Yes," Taylor said.

Suddenly Roger appeared in the doorway, his face taut with anger. "I just talked to Philip," he said, squinting at Julian. "What the hell kind of friend are you, DuPont, stealing Philip's woman? This is low-down and dirty."

Roger banged the open door with his palm. "DuPont, you'd better get the hell out of my sight before I do something I might regret. And take this tramp with you. You ungrateful ni—"

Julian raised his eyebrows. "Say it, Roger. Say what you really think of me."

Roger turned a shade redder. "No, that's the point. Until now I didn't see color. I saw you as a friend. But now you've acted like—"

"Like what?" Julian asked. "As soon as I do something you perceive as wrong, then race comes into play. Now you have a long repertoire of insults to draw from."

Roger huffed. "I want you out of my goddamn house by Friday. How dare you double-cross the man who gave you everything." Roger stormed away, cursing under his breath.

Taylor realized that she was trembling. *My career is over. Philip will ruin me.*

CHAPTER 49

Julian took Taylor to have lunch at Roscoe's House of Chicken 'n' Waffles in West Hollywood. Shortly after they ordered, a black woman in a blue business suit approached the table.

"Can I help you?" Julian asked.

"The only way you can help me, brotha, is if you stop sellin' out the black race by going with Barbie doll–lookin' white women like her," the woman said through curled lips.

"And it's white bitches like you," she said, pointing a rhinestone-studded fingernail at Taylor, "who are stealin' our good black men, successful men like Julian DuPont. But naw, he think he livin' large on *Entertainment Exclusive,* so now he can sell out his brothas and sistas and go with a white woman."

A hot gush of anger consumed Taylor. "First of all, you don't even know what race we are, and second—"

"Taylor, stop," Julian said. "Her ignorance isn't worth a reaction."

"I *am* worth a reaction," the woman said loudly, drawing stares. "It's a damn shame for a brotha to bring his snowball into a soul-food restaurant. You need to stick to your own kind."

Julian looked up at her calmly. "Just how do you define your own kind?"

"Black," she said. "There are a lot of beautiful black women for you to pick from in L.A. She need to take her white ass and find a white man."

Julian cast a contemptuous glare at the woman. "For your information, she and I are both mixed—half black, half white. *Et je suis français.*"

The woman drew her eyebrows together and looked back and forth between Julian and Taylor.

"See?" he said. "We are the same kind, biracial, mixed, métis, whatever you want to call us."

The woman's neck jerked as she pointed a long fingernail. "Mixed is right. Your parents was mixed-up. And if you mixed, you black."

Julian held up a palm to her. "Go away."

The woman glared at both of them. "You still a sellout, brotha, hangin' with this girl tryin' to pass for white. Make me sick."

"Hey," Julian said as he doused his fried chicken with hot sauce. "Don't let it get to you."

"I can't help it," Taylor said. "We get flack from both sides. Sometimes I think I need to wear a sign that says, 'I'm not black, I'm not white, I'm both.' Then maybe people would understand."

Julian was devouring his waffle. "Probably not."

"This is the exact kind of thing they talked about at this interracial group I did a story on last year," Taylor said. "I couldn't believe it when I walked into this room full of families just like ours, with kids who look just like you and me. It was the best feeling, like I finally fit in somewhere. They're even trying to get a 'multiracial' category on the next census so—"

Julian shook his head. "Bad idea. Sounds like the 'coloured' category when South Africa had apartheid. Or a throwback to slave times when they had 'mulatto,' 'quadroon,' and 'octoroon' for the babies when Massa took a black mistress. There's enough divisiveness, as Miss Thing over there just showed."

"That's the point," Taylor said. "Mixed people are just looking for a space of their own."

"Good for them," Julian said. "I don't care what kind of categories or groups they have. What it comes down to, if you have one drop of black blood, you're black."

"I hate that," Taylor said. "Why can't we all just be human?"

"Save the idealistic, we-are-the-world drama, please," Julian said. "The bottom line is that mixed kids need to know about racism. When that kid feels racism for the first time, he can't say, 'Oh, wait, my mama's white and I check 'multiracial' on the census.' That's not gonna mean a damn thing when Billy Joe Pulaski is beating the shit out of him."

Taylor suddenly felt sad. Ten lifetimes of her hard work, it seemed, would not be enough to make a dent in the hatred so tightly woven into the fabric of America.

CHAPTER 50

After lunch, Taylor and Julian returned to his house, where she sunk into a chaise longue on the deck. Finally she felt mellow as she took in the sounds of chirping birds and crashing waves. The heavy, humid air and her full stomach brought a wonderful languor.

Until she looked up and saw a red-brown crew cut. It was rising on the staircase from the beach.

Taylor froze.

A plain white face . . . sunglasses . . . an auburn mustache. Thick upper body . . . tattooed arms.

Oh God, no. It's Rocky Pulaski!

Taylor's heart crashed against her rib cage. Cold sweat prickled across her body.

The sun was so bright behind him, she could not focus on his face. But he was charging at her with those oarlike hands.

He found me. And now he's gonna kill me.

"Julian!" Taylor screamed.

Rocky was getting closer, smiling wickedly.

No, I won't let him kill me.

A sudden surge of adrenaline made Taylor leap from the chair.

She jumped toward him, fists balled tight.

She socked him in the groin.

"Aaahhh-uuhhgg," he grunted, doubling over.

Taylor, surprised at her strength, dove for the door into the house.

Julian appeared. "Taylor, what's— Don? Are you all right?"

"Don?" Taylor gasped, her chest heaving. "I thought . . . I thought he was Rocky Pulaski."

"What?" The man lifted a hand from his groin and removed his sunglasses. "Shit! What's goin' on here?"

Taylor's cheeks burned with embarrassment. "I'm sorry," she said. "Really, I am. I thought you were someone else."

Don turned to Julian. "Who is this, man?"

"Don, man, I'm sorry," Julian said. "She's hiding from someone who looks a little like you."

Don grimaced, then glared at Taylor. "Remind me to call next time. I was just coming to tell you my jewelry shop has what you're looking for. I hope it's not for her."

Julian chuckled. "You all right, man?"

"Yeah. She packs a mean punch."

"I've gotten a lot of practice lately," Taylor said.

CHAPTER 51

Taylor sat in the passenger seat of Julian's Porsche as he sped down the dark, fog-shrouded Pacific Coast Highway. She glanced at the red minidress and heels she was wearing, an outfit Julian had bought her that afternoon after lunch.

"I don't want to go out," Taylor said. "Let's go back to your house. This dress, everything, is reminding me of that night ten years ago."

Julian, drop-dead sexy in a black Edwardian suit, glared at her.

"Well, this is now. I'm not taking you back to the house so you can brood. It'll be good for you to get out." He faced the road.

Taylor grabbed the steering wheel. "Turn around. I don't want to go."

Suddenly Julian spun the car onto a roadside perch over the ocean.

Taylor glanced around at the fog and black cliff, waves crashing violently below. "Drive!" she shouted. "We could get carjacked out here."

Julian turned off the engine and buried his face in his hands. "I need a minute to cool off."

"Then I'll drive," she said, removing her high heels.

"No, you drive like a maniac," he said.

She glared at him. "Why are you being such a jerk?"

He stared back blankly.

"Move and get out!" she said. "I'm driving."

Taylor climbed out of the bucket seat, reaching over him for the door latch.

"No," he said, pushing her.

She knelt on her seat, pushing his knees toward the door. "Move! I ran from Philip onto the beach, and I don't want to sit here in the fog with you. This is insane!"

Julian did not budge.

Stupid bastard, trying to get us killed out here—

Taylor pushed harder. Her knee slipped; she tumbled into his lap. She grasped his thigh, holding herself up, trying to balance. The seat belt dug sharply into her leg.

Their faces inches apart, their angry eyes locked.

Hot, blinding wrath charged every cell in Taylor's body. She wanted to lash out, strike something, scream. The expression on Julian's face mirrored her rage.

"I hate you!" she shouted, hitting his chest. "You think you can just take over my life—"

Julian cupped her jaw and kissed her, hot lips plying gently.

Taylor desperately needed to release the knots of emotion shackling her heart and mind and body. She felt wound up, tense and taut like a ball of wire and string wrapped around a snarled nerve center.

Julian's kiss warmed the cords that were her muscles and teased the fibers of her heart. Her iron core began to melt.

His fiery mouth, his full lips against hers, thawed rage into lust. Her temperature rose, degree by degree, as molten drops of desire trickled through her, flooding and engorging her erogenous zones.

Yes, Julian, I want all of you. Now.

Taylor sucked his lips, then tangled her tongue with his. She straddled his lap, ripping open his jacket, unbuttoning his shirt.

Panting, she cried out when he planted searing lips on her neck. She tossed her head back, staring into the misty black sky as the wind howled against the cliff. Waves roared below. Her breasts ached for his mouth; the steaming swell between her legs craved savage pounding.

Julian, his eyes frenzied, moans escaping his mouth, nuzzled her chest. He unhooked the halter top of her dress, letting it fall. Her nipples, tight in the cool air, tickled his face. When he drew them into his mouth, Taylor gasped, then buried her face in his hair. She grasped his muscular shoulders, rocking on his lap.

Julian reached under her dress, squeezing her.

A wild sexual hunger overwhelmed her. She had forgotten about everything that had plagued her mind and emotions in recent days. Her singular thought and goal was to quench the erotic chaos that had seized her body.

"*Je te désire,*" she whispered.

"*Je suis à toi,*" he answered.

She clawed his trousers, unfastening them. Then she pried his throbbing erection from black cotton briefs and stroked its length, as smooth and hard as granite.

Julian lifted her up, pulling her panties to the side.

Poised over him, she stared into his cinnamon brown eyes, deep wells of love and lust and mystery.

She closed her eyes as his rock-hard rod slid inside her, impaling her on his lap. His erection was like a magic wand from which tiny stars floated, tickling and tingling through her body, numbing her mind like the purest opiate. Then, when he touched her there, intensifying the pleasure of his strokes, she moaned and shivered and succumbed to carnal delirium.

This sexual fantasia spread down her trembling thighs and calves, through her hypersensitive abdomen and aching breasts—which she pressed against Julian's lapping tongue—and into her head. It created a mental kaleidoscope of brilliant reds and purples and golds, which spun faster and brighter with every thrust, dazzling her with cataclysmic shudders.

Julian sucked in air, his eyes enraptured and ablaze with need.

Their lips seared together, uniting them in body and soul, making Taylor wish she could spend her life in such erotic oblivion. But deep beneath her lust-swept emotions laid an abyss of distrust and fear that she knew would forever keep her from loving Julian again.

CHAPTER 52

Monica James concentrated on Grandma Willa's antique pearl headpiece in a stoic effort to obliterate a constant chorus of worries resonating in her mind.

But as she affixed the bridal veil to the pink head of the mannequin on which stood Taylor's wedding gown, she fretted about her daughter's well-being. At the same time, the horrifying news report of Pulaski hurling her child to the courtroom floor flashed vividly in her mind.

The dress became a white cloud through a veil of tears. Monica sunk to the living room couch.

When will it end?

It seemed that little had improved since July 23, 1967, when she and Ramsey had cowered in the house on Boston Boulevard as sirens wailed and acrid black smoke spiraled into a thick gloom over the city. And how tragic it had been for them, an interracial couple fearfully clinging to one another as their respective races waged a bloody battle that would claim forty-three lives. For those nightmarish six days, as the National Guard seized the city, they remained confined to a domestic prison of terror and dread, wondering if the mayhem would spread to their middle-class neighborhood.

Monica still remembered the *Detroit News* headlines: TANKS, TROOPS BATTLE SNIPERS ON WEST SIDE and GUERRILLA WAR ERUPTS ON RIOT-SCARRED 12TH. And the nightly news reports were a frightening collage of fires, marching troops, and mobs as gunfire crackled constantly.

But the riot had most distressed baby Taylor. She had been only ten days old, and sheltered from the violence, yet her uncharacteristically relentless screams had made Monica and Ramsey wonder if perhaps she had sensed the racial devastation exploding in gunfire and flame across the city, and the disharmony that awaited her as a child and adult in such a fractious world.

And now, almost twenty-nine years later, my poor baby is hiding from a racist madman.

Monica sobbed loudly, spewing forth the limb-trembling anxiety and outrage that had welled within her since the White Power rally on Friday. She begged God to grant her daughter safety and peace of mind, and demanded of Him, as she had so many times, why such a gentle symbol of unity must be subjected to such antagonism.

"Monica, honey, what's the matter?" Ramsey bolted into the living room and gathered her languid frame into his arms. He kissed the top of her head, rocking her gently. "I know you're worried about Taylor, but she couldn't be any safer than with Julian."

Emotion weakened Ramsey's deep voice, so he began humming, very softly, "Lift Ev'ry Voice and Sing," by James Weldon Johnson. The melody soothed her, and the inspirational words of the black national anthem—about continuing to rejoice in freedom and hope for a brighter future despite the bloody past of slavery—rejuvenated her faith that God would prevail. Taylor would be safe, and someday that vicious political and biological construct of race would no longer divide people or nations or families.

It had been thirty-two years since the Larsson family expelled its youngest daughter. Yet that final Sunday evening in the Huntington Woods colonial was still clear as crystal in her mind. Her father, Hans Larsson, whose parents had settled in Detroit when his engineer father was hired at General Motors, had postured imperiously at the head of the table, opposite her mother, Tessa, her white-blond braid draping her shoulder. In between, Monica and her two older sisters, home for the weekend from college, had been chattering about clothes and classes as they enjoyed the Swedish staples of cheese, strömming (Baltic herring), hard bread, sausage, and buttered potatoes. Dessert promised sweet cloudberry sauce atop ice cream.

"I'm going to marry Ramsey James," Monica had announced.

Her father blanched and pinched the bridge of his sharp nose. The bald spot on his head shined red as a ripe tomato as he glared at her, his blue eyes as icy as a fjord in winter.

"You will not marry a colored man," he said, his full bottom lip trembling. "If you do, you lose your family." He stormed away from the table.

Helga pushed her plate away, as if disgusted. "You're so foul, always going to those concerts and civil rights marches, acting like a Negro."

Monica watched in disbelief as her two flaxen-haired sisters abandoned her at the table. Her mother, until then silent, whispered something about disgracing the family as she fled the room in tears.

That night Monica had returned to her Ann Arbor apartment, her education classes at the University of Michigan, and her fiancé, Ramsey James. And she had not seen or talked to her family since.

Many times, however, she had passed her father's Saab dealership. She stopped once, but he had refused to see her.

Even after thirty-two years, it astounded Monica that the woman who had birthed and reared her, and her father, who had been affectionate until that night, could extinguish their love for their child over a reason as shallow as skin color. They had never met Ramsey, even though, when she had initially told her parents that she was being courted by an architecture student, they were pleased. Until she mentioned his race.

Now Monica gazed up at her husband's tender eyes, pink-ringed and glassy with emotion as they shared anxiety for their daughter.

"Do you remember," Ramsey said softly, "when we were sitting next to the reflecting pool on the Washington mall, listening to Dr. King's speech in 1963, when both of us had tears streaming down our faces, and we pressed our cheeks together, and you said something about uniting the tears of black and white in the struggle against bigotry?"

Monica nodded.

"I have to believe Dr. King's work was not in vain, and that good will defeat evil men like Rocky Pulaski," he said.

"I need to hear that," Monica said.

"Good. Monica, can I ask you something?"

"Sure."

"Why are you bothering with Taylor's wedding dress?" he asked.

"I'm hoping there will be a wedding, for Taylor and Julian," she said, smiling. "I trust my maternal intuition."

CHAPTER 53

As Monica continued working on the dress, the doorbell rang.

"I'll get it," Ramsey called from his study.

"Be sure and look first," Monica said. "And turn on the lights. It's almost dark."

She heard the door open.

"Well, I'll be," Ramsey said.

Monica, alarmed that one of Pulaski's men or Taylor was at the door, darted down the hallway. *Oh my goodness. My sisters.*

"Hellen? Helga? Is that you?"

Two women in their fifties smiled and extended their arms.

Stunned, Monica stared at them, holding Ramsey's hand as she contemplated slamming the door or inviting them in.

"What . . . what are you doing here?" she asked.

"We saw Taylor on the news," Hellen said. "And we heard about her wedding. We just realized that our separation was a terrible waste. We want to make amends."

Grief and hope collided inside Monica, squeezing her heart. *Can I ever forgive them?* After long, tense moments, she embraced her sisters and cried for the bygone years and lost love.

"Please accept our apologies," Helga said.

"Come in," Monica said.

Ramsey, warmth radiating from his chest, gazed down at her and stroked her back. "You okay?"

Monica nodded as her sisters looked around.

"You have a beautiful home, Monica," Helga said. "We never expected you to do so well."

Monica's face drooped. "Why not? Because I married a black man?"

Silent tension charged the air between them.

Helga laughed nervously. "No, of course not. It's just that your work with civil rights, we just thought you'd be a hippie all your life, living in a peace van, making posters and marching on Washington."

"There was a time and a place for that," Monica said. "But I'm a teacher now, and Ramsey is an architect."

Her sisters smiled awkwardly. They both wore their hair in short, stiff swirls around their heads, like lemon meringue. Hellen sported a green jogging suit with faux-leather flats; Helga wore a yellow striped dress.

"When I saw Taylor's wedding announcement in the paper," Hellen said, settling with Helga on the living room couch, "I got this terrible feeling that her whole life has passed us by. Of course, you sent those baby pictures, but that's not the same as holding the baby."

Monica perched on a tufted rose chair by the fireplace. "So you, they . . . you received the pictures? I didn't know, since I heard no response."

"We got them," Helga said. "But at the time, we just weren't ready to . . . well, I wanted to see your baby. She was so white, but—"

"But you didn't call because she's half black?" Monica asked, her hands trembling in her lap with the shock and anger of their sudden presence.

"Well, I don't think that . . . well, we watch her on television every day," Hellen said. "We're very proud."

Monica smoothed her blue cotton dress over her legs. "Then tell me, why in the world did you abandon me?"

"We were just following Mama and Papa's bad example," Helga said. "We're both nearly sixty. We realized it was an awful mistake to lose our little sister."

Hellen nodded.

"Can you forgive us?" Helga asked with pleading eyes.

"I don't know," Monica said softly. "I've been a virtual orphan, but Ramsey's family has loved me like a daughter. You don't know how I've suffered over this."

"It really hurt Mama and Papa," Helga said. "Not that Papa remembers anymore. He has Alzheimer's. Mama spends all her time taking care of him, even with her arthritis."

Monica felt nothing. She chose to remember her parents as the loving man and woman who taught her to ride her bike under the shady oaks on their street and helped her do math problems at the kitchen table and tucked her in bed with kisses and fairy tales.

Mama and Papa stopped loving me. They abandoned me. And I can never forgive them. The old couple her sister described were strangers, and Monica wanted to leave it that way.

For the next half hour, the three sisters chatted about the past thirty-two years of their lives, laughing and crying. When Monica went to the kitchen to make tea, the doorbell rang.

"I'll get it," she told Ramsey as she looked through the peephole in the door. "Oh, it's those Jehovah's Witnesses again." Two dark-haired white women, wearing large crucifixes around their necks and carrying Bibles, stood on the porch.

Monica opened the door. "Sorry, ladies, we're already active in our church."

Suddenly an ominous feeling wrapped around her like a cold mist.

Oh my God, it's Jess Stevens. The woman who kicked Taylor in court. Monica's heart pounded as frigid fear surged through her.

"You're a traitor to the white race," Jess said, squinting.

"No!" Monica shouted. *I have to slam the door and call the police.* She stepped back and grabbed the edge of the door.

Jess and the other woman clawed her arms and dress, yanking her through the door.

"Ramsey!" she screamed. "Call the police!"

Monica tumbled onto the grass. *God help me . . .*

The women clawed and growled over her like hungry lions.

"You dirty, Negro-loving slut!" Jess shouted. "Your freak of a daughter is gonna die a painful death. Just like you."

"Stop!" Monica shouted. Lying on the ground, she kicked and swung and scratched at the women in the darkness.

She heard her sisters shrieking near the door. A windowless van with a loud muffler rattled at the curb.

"Drag her," Jess said to the other woman. "Take her feet."

"No! Ramsey! Help!"

Monica thrashed wildly to escape their grasp. She freed a hand and tugged Jess's crucifix.

Jess's head snapped forward violently. She fell to the ground.

"Bitch!" Jess shouted.

Monica kicked the other woman in the stomach, causing her to double over. She scrambled on trembling limbs toward the door.

The two women pounced on her. Monica fell to the sidewalk.

A hard metallic kerchunk echoed in the darkness.

"Freeze or I'll shoot!" Ramsey shouted.

Out of the corner of her eye, Monica saw the black steel tip of his shotgun.

The women froze.

"Monica, get up, honey," he said.

Thank God. She crawled from beneath the women. She reached the porch, where her sisters embraced her.

"Lie on the grass," Ramsey shouted.

Jess spit at him.

Boom! Ramsey fired into the ground next to her and pumped his gun.

"I said lie on the grass. Facedown."

Jess glanced at the other woman. "Run, Lula!"

The two women bolted.

Ramsey fired, just missing Jess's back. The bullet pierced the van at the curb.

He fired again as Jess and Lula climbed into the van, but it sped away.

CHAPTER 54

"What do you mean I'm suspended?"

William, in a starched blue shirt, silk tie, and navy trousers, paced near the television, stroking his pocket watch.

"Taylor, we specifically told you," he said sternly, "for your own safety, to stay out of town. You disobeyed; you're suspended. Plain and simple." His eyes had a hard, judicial glint.

A spear of indignation shot through Taylor, raising her to her feet. "I know Philip is behind this. You do everything he says."

William glared at her. "Think what you want."

"Where's Shari?" Taylor demanded. "I suppose Philip's harassing her, too. Where's Philip? I'll straighten this out myself."

"Try his apartment," William said.

Taylor shook her head. "This is so unfair. When can I return to work?"

"When we decide," William said.

"Whoever heard of punishing someone for wanting to work!" Taylor said.

"You're too close to the Pulaski story now," William said. "We don't want you in harm's way. You'll still have police protection. Rest easy, the police chief says he's fired all white supremacist sympathizers on the force."

Taylor darted toward the door. "I'm calling my agent. This suspension violates a labor law."

"Which labor law, Taylor?" William asked mockingly.

"I don't know, but Thad Wilson will know," she said. Taylor left the office and hurried down the stairs with Officers Edwards and Young.

"So they got rid of the white supremacists on the force?" Taylor asked as they headed into the garage.

"That's what Chief Goodson said today, but he can't be a hundred percent sure," Officer Young said. "Scarlin was always polite to me, never said anything inappropriate. Same thing with Lemer and the other guys."

"Yeah, I thought they were all nice guys," Officer Edwards said. "Guess you never know."

Ten minutes later, Taylor knocked on the door of Philip's apartment. She could hear a Joe Sample CD playing, but he did not answer. She used her key to enter.

Laughter drifted from the bedroom, so she hurried down the hallway and pushed open the door.

"Philip, you can't—"

Taylor froze.

Oh my goodness . . .

Her mouth fell open.

Clothes, blankets, and pillows covered the floor.

The sticky-sweet scent of sex hung in the warm air.

On the bed was a writhing tangle of bare flesh.

She saw a purple bustier, stockings, and garter.

And a mop of brown hair.

Taylor's heart raced. *Are those Shari's legs flopping over her head as Philip bangs her?*

"Shari?"

Philip stopped and scowled. "What are *you* doing here?"

Shari looked up, scrambling to cover herself. Her eyes, smudged with mascara, were large as prunes. Perspiration glistened on her bare skin.

"Taylor, I'm so—"

"Don't even bother," Taylor said, her stomach cramping. "You're both sick."

The vein on Philip's forehead bulged. "What do you want?"

Trembling with rage, Taylor twisted the diamond ring from her left hand.

"The wedding is off," she said, squinting. "And if you try to sabotage my career, I'll sue your sleazy ass all the way back to California."

Taylor threw the ring, striking his chest.

She spun and left the apartment.

I can't believe I almost married him. He's taken me for a fool, all these months of our engagement, all these years of courtship. I actually loved him.

Taylor, police in tow, stormed to her car and peeled away. She had expected an ugly confrontation with Philip, but what she had just seen was abominable. Now she was losing a fiancé and a friend. Those two adulterous nymphomaniacs deserved each other.

How could Shari backstab me? And how long has this been going on?

All that mattered now was getting her job straight. She drove to the downtown office of Thaddeus Wilson.

Philip's not going to get away with destroying my career.

CHAPTER 55

Early evening heat radiated from the sunbaked asphalt like thick, greedy fingers, squeezing Shari's breath and searing her panty hose to her legs.

She and Philip hurried from his private jet to his limousine on the tarmac at La Guardia Airport in New York. Shari slipped into the crisp air conditioning before she became a sweaty, wilted mess.

"It's a sauna out there," Philip said.

Shari smiled. *It's felt like a sauna between my legs for two days now, thanks to you.*

"Shari, remember, when you get to the interview in the morning, you have to sell yourself. It's all about promotion. Talk fast, be confident, and answer every question like you're the boss."

Shari nodded and stared at Philip's heart-shaped lips as he spoke. She wanted to remember everything, yet her constant state of sexual arousal diverted her concentration.

"I brought several tapes of my best shows, including the White Power Alliance exposé," Shari said.

"Good," Philip said. He rested a hand on her knee. "Everybody remembers that. Now, my brother Jonathan will probably drill you hard about your experience and why you think you're worthy of Wolf's program-development team."

"I think my work speaks for itself," Shari said.

"I agree."

"Thanks for arranging this, Philip. This is a good thing for me, moving away from Detroit. A divorce, a new job, new town. This is very good."

"Your ballsy style will be good for national programming," Philip said.

"Thanks, but I feel so bad about Taylor," Shari said, staring blankly at the buttery soft beige leather upholstery. "She was a close friend. I go from being a bridesmaid in her wedding to having sex with the groom. Doesn't that bother you?"

"No," Philip said. "There's no wedding now. It doesn't matter. And William says she got pretty pissed off when he told her she's suspended, so we have a meeting Friday with Thad Wilson. She thinks we're violating her contract."

"Go easy on her," Shari said.

"No way," Philip said. "I respect Thad, but this time he's up the creek. I want to fire Taylor. Frame her, if necessary."

The ominous tone of his voice prompted Shari to reach for her cigarettes. "I'll forget you said that," Shari said. "Taylor James has been an exemplary employee since day one. She's got more integrity and commitment to the craft than ten reporters put together. So I say just leave her alone, let her work, and move on with your life."

Shari sucked in smoke, eager for that nicotine rush to numb her guilt over betraying her friend and the disquiet she felt from the sinister glint in Philip's eyes.

"Nope," Philip said. "She and DuPont are through. Taylor knows what's coming to her. And I told William that if DuPont calls, tell him he's out of a job."

Smoke plumed from Shari's nose. "You can't do that, Philip. He has a contract, too, a watertight one, and I think he'll be good for our newscast. Dwyer has big shoes to fill, and DuPont can do it. Besides, we need to find another female anchor. Did you hear?"

"What now?"

"Alison Smith had twins yesterday and decided to take a year off to be a mom," Shari said.

"Shit," Philip said.

"So now that we have two empty anchor chairs, DuPont should start ASAP," Shari said. "We don't want viewers to think we're playing musical chairs here, a different anchor every night."

Philip poured himself a tumbler of Grand Marnier. "I fired all those fuckin' idiots who screwed up the morning show."

Shari tensed. "You fired them?"

"Yes, after you left my office. That'll keep people on their toes. You fuck up, you're through."

Damn, he's ruthless. Shari closed her eyes and shook her head. "The problems could have been resolved without firing those poor people," she said. "So we rework the budget, get the cameras replaced, and find staff for the program. Big deal."

Shari smoked frantically to ease gut-gnawing guilt; she had used the morning-show problems as a seduction ruse to draw Philip to

Detroit. But it had backfired and now a half dozen people were un-employed.

This is so bad. I betray my friend, get people fired. Now what?

Philip slid his hand under her short skirt and leaned close. "Ever fucked in a limo?" he whispered, his eyes ablaze with lust.

"No," Shari whispered, "but I've always wanted to."

CHAPTER 56

Rocky Pulaski seemed to revel in his dominance over Jess as her fingers fluttered over the keyboard in the cool, damp basement of Fred Lutz's cabin.

"No, erase that," he said coarsely. "This bulletin has to be clear to our comrades, yet confusing to our enemies."

Jess slouched and dropped limp hands to her lap. "Dammit, Rocky, you're changed it six times," she snapped, glaring up at him. "Maybe you're not thinkin' straight because you spent the night in the woods with that slut."

Rocky yanked Jess's ponytail, causing her glasses to slip down her nose.

"That hurts," she said.

"This is nothing compared to what I'll do if you don't act right," he said, his eye twitching. "Now, type every goddamn word I say or it'll be my steel-toed boot in your ass."

Jess rested her fingers on the keys. *I hate him. I've given him everything and gotten nothing but misery in return.*

"That's better," Rocky said. "Now—"

Over the monitor, Jess watched Sally—in denim cutoffs showing two white crescents of her behind—descend the steps with a tray of food.

"Lunchtime, boys," she said. The dozen men working on computers, reading weapons magazines, and talking around the paneled basement swarmed the food like flies.

I hate that slut. And I hate the way Rocky drools over her.

"Ham and cheese for you," Sally said, handing Rocky a plate with a huge sandwich. "Made it myself, just for you."

Rocky smiled and patted Sally's butt.

Well, I'll be damned. He's feelin' her up right in front of me.

Jess sucked her teeth. "Don't I get lunch? I've been working all morning, too."

Sally glanced down as if Jess were a flea. "Maybe, if there's anything left after the boys get through."

Trembling with anger, Jess wanted to slap the dewiness off Sally's perfect complexion.

"Rocky, I'll be by the pool," Sally purred. "You can come inspect my tan lines if you want."

Chewing loudly, he watched her saunter away, bouncing her dark mane.

"Now, let's try this again," Rocky said. "We have to let our comrades know that we're having a cross-burning here, and we'll be killing Taylor James. Type this: 'The day of revolution is dawning.' "

Jess stabbed the keyboard with her fingers, imagining that every letter was a knife into the faces of Rocky and Sally.

"Our führer has set the example," Rocky said, "to free himself of the chains that confine us to a dark world where our Nordic superiority is abhorred. We will christen this new day with a celebration of fire and the death of our pariah at the tip of the Thumb."

Rocky let out a lusty sigh. "Good. You think people will know that means cross-burning Friday night on Lutz's property, and Taylor James dies?"

"Yeah," Jess said. "But how are you gonna get her this time? We don't even know where she is."

"Don't worry about it," Rocky said. "Nick hacked into the airlines' computers. The idiots who sent her away were too dim-witted to give her an alias. She went to Los Angeles Monday, came back Wednesday. And Scarlin heard she's got police protection again. Piece a cake."

"But why risk it?" Jess asked. "Somethin' might happen and let the cops know where we are, and we'll all be back in jail."

"No revolution started with that defeatist attitude," Rocky snapped. "You think Hitler ever said, 'No, I can't conquer Europe'? Hell no."

Jess shrugged. "I just think it would be less risky to keep working here on the computers, building up our weapons, instead of all the hoopla of a cross-lighting. What if a helicopter sees it and calls the police?"

Rocky's dark eyes flashed angrily. "Why are you so fuckin' paranoid all of a sudden?"

"I'm just hungry."

"You don't get up from this chair until you E-mail all comrades in Michigan and surrounding states," Rocky said. "Then send the bulletin to contacts worldwide. Let them know I'm free. You hear me?"

"Yeah," Jess said.

"Sour bitch," he hissed as he headed for the stairs.

CHAPTER 57

That evening in Taylor's apartment, she described every detail of her ordeal to Danielle and Carla.

"And if that wasn't bad enough, Shari had on the same purple lingerie she gave me at the shower," Taylor said as the six-o'clock news droned on the television in her living room.

"I knew it," Carla said. She wore a MADE IN DETROIT baseball cap to hide five stitches at her hairline directly above her nose, and her black hair hung straight around her shoulders. "I could smell it. Didn't I tell you to watch your back, girlfriend?"

"You did," Taylor said, "but I didn't expect it to be that graphic."

Danielle pointed to the television. "Look, Pulaski's on the news."

"—and authorities are questioning all people whose names were on the White Power Alliance membership lists seized during a federal raid," said Kendra Vaughn. "Local, state, and federal law enforcement agencies are working together to find clues—"

Taylor sighed. "I know Kendra's loving every minute of this."

"I'm sure it's temporary," Danielle said, sitting on the chair between the couch and balcony in a plum business suit. Her long black hair was gathered in an art deco barrette with wisps around her face. "Carla, tell us about your new doctor friend."

In yellow sweats at the end of the cream leather couch, Carla beamed as she stroked Puff. "He came to see me twice a day and sent me flowers. We're supposed to go to dinner Friday night, if I feel up to it."

"And?" Danielle asked.

"I get this warm feeling when I'm with Ben," Carla said. "Not nervousness, but more like comfort. It's hard to explain."

"That's how I felt when I met Peter, and I still do," Danielle said.

"I used to feel that way with Julian and Philip," Taylor said.

"But even though Ben is handsome, that's not what attracts me to him. He's polite, works hard, and goes to church. He brought my mother coffee and candy while she sat with me. And the way he looks at me—" Carla fanned herself "—makes me burn up inside."

Taylor and Danielle exchanged knowing smiles.

"I'm happy for you," Danielle said. "There's nothing more special than being in love. Except having kids, but that comes later."

"So, Taylor, besides wild sex in California, what's the scoop on you and Julian?" Carla asked.

Taylor's stomach cramped as she sunk deeper into the couch. "Uh, I don't know."

"Liar," Carla said playfully. "You know you want him."

"What's your excuse now?" Danielle asked. "Philip is history, Julian's here, and—" Danielle pointed at the TV.

"Hello, I'm Julian DuPont. I'll be joining the Channel Three News staff next week, and we're planning very special programs for you."

The shock of seeing Julian on Channel 3 dumbfounded Taylor for a moment. She turned up the volume.

"He's so handsome," Danielle said.

"Whew," Carla said. "Tell me about it. Taylor, you're crazy to let him go."

Taylor rolled her eyes. "Shh."

Somber music played while the camera shot widened to show a video screen behind Julian on which flashed video that she had taken at the White Power Alliance compound.

"That's *my* story!"

More video showed the federal raid, the rally and riot, the crying widow, and the courtroom escape.

Arrows of anger shot through Taylor. She stood up, stunned. *How can Julian sell me out like that?*

"The wake of a fatal neo-Nazi rally has cast a shadow of gloom over race relations in metropolitan Detroit," Julian said over the music and video. "That's why we're inviting Channel Three viewers to join us next Wednesday evening for a special town hall meeting to discuss how this tragic event has affected our community. Please join us, with the mayor, the police chief, and a panel of race-relations experts, for this special program. To join our studio audience, just dial the telephone number on—"

Taylor grabbed *TV Guide* from the coffee table and hurled it at Julian's image. "He bogarts into my station, uses my work to promote his first appearance in Detroit, while I'm suspended, and expects me to be with him?" Taylor shook her head. "No way. This is the most sneaky, low-down—"

"Taylor, I'm su⌐ there's an explanation," Danielle said.

"Yeah, cool out " Carla said. "Don't assume the worst."

"Wonder what other tricks he's got up his sleeve," Taylor said. "I'm so mad I could take a baseball bat to the TV."

"Please don't," Danielle said. "You'd only have to buy a new one, and with your job up in the air—"

Taylor glared at Danielle.

"Sorry, I mean, it just wouldn't be smart to destroy your TV," Danielle said. "I'm sure Julian has a good explanation."

Carla shook her head. "Maybe Philip made him do it to make you mad. And Shari, maybe she wants you to hate the other man who's after you."

"Philip, yes, but Shari isn't that devious," Taylor said.

Danielle stood up with her car keys. "I say give Julian the benefit of the doubt. Now, let me get to the day-care center before seven."

As she and Carla were leaving, the phone rang.

It was Julian. Anger hissed through Taylor like steam. "Taylor, I've been out of my mind worried about you. Why the hell did you leave in the middle of the night while I was asleep? That was the dumbest—"

"Well, here I am, you found me," Taylor snapped. "More importantly, I just saw you on TV."

"What'd you think?" he asked.

"I'm mad as hell."

"Why?"

"Because I'm suspended and you're using my work to bust onto Detroit TV with a bang."

Julian sighed. "Wait a minute. William called me this morning and asked me to come in and tape that promo today. It wasn't intended to slight you."

"You're in Detroit? How did William know that? You weren't even supposed to start working yet."

"He called my parents' house," Julian said. "Philip called me yesterday in L.A. saying don't bother coming to Detroit because I didn't have a job here. You know Philip and William don't get along, so I think William wanted a rush job on my promo while Philip is in New York with Shari."

"Why is Philip in New York with Shari?" Taylor asked.

"William said she's interviewing for a network job."

"A network job, good," Taylor said. "I hope she gets it because I can't work with her now. Or you. This is such a slap in the face."

"Calm down," Julian said. "Don't be mad at me."

"Me, me, me. That's all you care about. What about me? I lost a fiancé, a friend, and a job, all in two days."

"You can't blame me for all that, Taylor," he said. "It's not fair. Just cool down."

"I'll cool down when I get my job back," Taylor said angrily.

CHAPTER 58

Philip looked coolly across the conference room table at Thad Wilson, who appeared calm and invincible with Taylor's contract laid out before him. Next to Thad was Taylor, but for the past half hour, since he had entered with Shari, William, and Wolf lawyer Fran Burton, Philip had been too disgusted to even glance at Taylor.

"Look," Thad said, "you either reinstate her now, or I'll take you to court so fast it'll make your satellite dishes spin. And toss in a twenty percent salary bonus to take the sting out of this mess. That way I won't have to take out my big gun."

Philip laughed loudly. "Get real, Thad. You don't have a case."

Thad set his fountain pen on the contract. "Laugh till your balls turn blue, Philip," Thad said. " 'Cause I got you red-handed. Let's start with the unlawful suspension. Then there's the sexual harass-ment, coercion, and extremely dangerous working conditions. Not to mention the criminal assault charges I'll file in California."

Thad leaned back, chuckling. "The tabloids would eat this up. I can see it now: MEDIA MOGUL ATTACKS FIANCÉE, STALKS HER ON DARK BEACH. How do you like that? Better yet, how would your fa-ther like it?"

Philip's head felt like a pressure cooker ready to blow its top. He could feel the vein in his forehead protruding and throbbing, and sweat soaked his armpits. He glowered at Taylor. Her eyes were like green marbles.

You whore. You annihilated my plan to appear honorable and stable in Dad's eyes, so I'm gonna shit on your network dream. You're gonna re-gret this for the rest of your racially tormented life.

Philip leaned forward on the table, staring at Thad's haughty face. "Guess what, buddy," Philip said. "You've stepped way beyond the boundaries of agenting and lawyering. This is what we call black-mail. Sue me, call the cops, do whatever gets you off. But I don't ever want that slut's face on a Wolf broadcast again."

Thad shook his head. "You're going to regret this big time."

"Shoot your best wad," Philip said, bolting from his seat. He nodded at William, Shari, and Fran Burton. "Let's get out of here."

Fran Burton removed her tortoiseshell glasses, a somber expres-sion on her plain, cosmetic-free face. "Mr. Carter, I think we should talk in private for a moment."

"Fine, in William's office," Philip said. "Excuse us."

Philip sneered down at Taylor in her navy blue suit, trying to look innocent with the white blouse, pearls, and hair pulled back. "You really fucked up," he said. "You could've been a star. I was going to make it happen for you. For us."

Taylor stood up. "Rot in hell," she said. "I don't need you or your sleazy smooth talk to make it big in this business."

"Now, that's where you're dead wrong, sweetheart." Philip but-toned his sand-colored suit jacket and exited to the balcony. There his rage surged up another notch when he saw Julian DuPont, waiting outside the conference room.

"Well," Philip said, "if it isn't the second career catastrophe of the week. You sure look cocky for a guy who's out of a job."

Grinning, William stopped in the doorway. "Julian, your promos look fantastic on the air. Good job."

DuPont smiled. "Thanks, William. Glad I could help out."

Philip glared at William and Julian. The two of them together made his blood boil even more. "What promos? You haven't been on-air yet."

An arrogant smile spread across William's face. "I specifically remember you saying that Wolf wants more special programming, i.e., town hall meetings."

"And?" Philip said.

"I got the ball rolling," William said. "Julian here is going to host our first program about race relations next week."

Arrows of anger stabbed Philip's insides as he stared, stunned, at DuPont's smug face and William, in his off-the-rack gray suit. "I *told you* DuPont was fired," Philip said. "You don't make decisions like that. I do. So you'd better cancel the show or you'll be on the fast track to the unemployment line with DuPont here."

William pushed up his silver-framed glasses, which magnified the defiant gleam in his eyes. "You can't just negate a signed contract, Philip. I'll see you in my office." He walked away.

So that cocksucking shit-head finally got some balls, and now he's using them against me. He'll pay for this.

"Philip, I need to talk to you," DuPont said.

Philip squinted at DuPont. "No, you son of a bitch. Let me talk to you. I gave you everything. You were nothing without me, and I gave you the world. Your manhood. Money, fame. Women. And this is how you thank me? You turn around and shove it all up my ass?"

Trembling with rage, Philip used every ounce of self-control to keep from punching the self-assured smirk on DuPont's face.

But Julian did not flinch. "We should talk."

"Get the fuck out or I'll call the cops," Philip said. Suddenly he imagined DuPont and Taylor in bed, her moaning, him humping furiously. *I bet that whore screamed like the devil when DuPont rammed his dick inside her. The motherfucker.*

"Leave now!" Philip shouted.

DuPont shook his head, then pulled three videotapes from his pocket.

CHAPTER 59

Philip knew immediately what they were. Sweat oozed from his pores, soaking his once crisp white shirt. His heart raced.

"You devious motherfucker," Philip said. The burning rage of betrayal consumed him. He thought of his father, of his brothers getting everything.

"Now that I've got your attention," DuPont said, "you'll listen to me or I'll send these tapes to Mr. Gerald Carter, chairman and CEO of Wolf Media Corp., so he can see just how sleazy his illegitimate son really is."

Static crackled in Philip's ears. "You do that and you'll not only never work in this business again, but you might not see your next birthday."

Julian chuckled. "Oh, so now we're adding a murder plot to your long list of dirty secrets."

"Don't push your luck, pal," Philip said. "Besides, I don't think you have the guts to ruin me. You're already on a kamikaze flight as far as your career goes. The only thing left for you to do is crash and burn. You're not walkin' out of this battle alive, pal."

Julian met his glare. "Don't be so sure. Why don't you come into my office." As he stepped backward toward his office, Julian removed a tape from its case and read its label. "Let's see, this would be Melinda, the stripper with the wandering tongue."

Philip's entire body hummed with fury. He stepped toward Julian and snatched the tape out of his hands.

Julian laughed. "I have plenty more. Like this one."

Now inside the office, Julian popped a tape into the VCR. Philip slammed the office door as women's moans began playing loudly.

"What do you want?" Philip asked.

"A few things," Julian said with an unflinching stare. "First, I want you to promote Taylor James to fill Alison Smith's anchor position and triple her salary," DuPont said.

Philip stood still as a statue, listening in utter disgust as the man he had created bullied him into submission under the lethal whip of blackmail.

"That's an outrageous proposal," Philip said.

"It's not a proposal," Julian said, pointing to the television screen.

Philip watched himself snorting cocaine with a bare-chested girl on his left, a girl licking his ear on his right, and another with her bare behind toward the camera, her head bobbing in his lap.

DuPont crossed his arms. "You might remember the girl engaged in fellatio was fifteen. That's statutory rape. And this was taken the night you announced your engagement to Taylor."

Philip was dumbfounded. "You backstabbing motherfucker. You've been scheming to do this since day one."

"That's not true, but it doesn't matter now," DuPont said. "My career was just a hundred-dollar chip on your high-stakes poker table. I won you high ratings for *EE*, positive press, and I was your road dog. Now it's my turn to cash in."

Stunned, Philip glanced at the television again. A heavy cloak of shame fell upon him when he saw his own sweaty face, twisted with ecstasy, his glassy eyes ogling the girls, his tongue rimming his lips. How many times had he repeated that scene in front of DuPont and a camera? Before, when he had watched the videos at home, he had been too aroused to feel shame. But now, in the bright light of day, Philip felt humiliated and mortified that his father, or anyone else, might view this self-produced smut.

"What else do you want?" Philip asked.

"I want you to keep your malicious hands off my job and my three-year contract, and I want Taylor to be my anchor partner on the six- and eleven-o'clock shows. And I want her to comoderate next week's forum on race relations with me. Oh, and get Andy Doss a videographer position at *EE*. That's it."

"This is preposterous," Philip said.

"That's exactly what dear old dad will say when he sees this," DuPont said.

CHAPTER 60

Taylor paced the conference room, where Thad Wilson explained that her best option might be a lawsuit. Her muscles were tense as wires and a sour acid taste rose from her cramped stomach.

"Forget a lawsuit," Taylor said. "I just want my job back."

Thad shook his head, but smiled seconds later when Julian walked in.

A geyser of resentment surged through Taylor. *He's in here so confident and happy while I might be out on my butt on Woodward Avenue.*

"Thad," Taylor said, "is there any recourse for me if another journalist is stealing my work to promote himself?"

Julian's smile withered. "Taylor, I didn't—"

"I told you I don't want to talk to you until after I've resolved this," she said. She could see the hurt in his eyes, but she hoped that he saw the same in hers.

"You'll see," Julian said. "Everything will work out for you."

"You are so arrogant," she snapped. "How do you know?"

"I just do," he said, eyes sparkling with confidence as he headed for the door.

At the same time, Philip was entering the conference room. He snatched his shoulder back quickly to avoid bumping Julian in the doorway.

Philip's face was grayish. Locks of hair hung at his temples. Tiny beads of sweat glistened at his close-cropped sideburns. And fury seethed in his eyes.

Behind him, the rest of management streamed in like a funeral procession.

Taylor's heart began pounding. *They're about to tell me I'm fired. Or I'm suspended indefinitely. Or I'm demoted to the graveyard shift, or a PA, running around, delivering scripts to Julian in the studio. I'd rather die!*

Next to Philip, Shari and William sat down, looking sullen. Triumph glinted in William's gray eyes, but his face was stiff. And a limp pallor had zapped Fran Burton's previous self-assurance.

Next to her, Shari appeared neutral. But every time Taylor glanced at her, she saw her rocking under Philip's thunderous thrusts, the purple lingerie, her shocked face, trying to cover up.

"Thad," Philip said, "if you and your client could give us an hour, we can wrap this up this afternoon."

"No problem," Thad said, glancing at his watch. "It's eleven forty-five. We'll be back in exactly one hour."

Thad and Taylor exited the room to find Julian on the balcony talking with the two police officers still trailing Taylor.

"Taylor, can I talk to you?" Julian asked.

She sneered. "What?"

"How 'bout the three of us get some lunch? Thad?"

"You two go ahead," Thad said. "I need to call my office. Mind if I use your phone?"

"Be my guest," Julian said.

Taylor glanced down at the newsroom, where Kendra Vaughn was standing by the assignment desk, talking with Jerry Spinx. Kendra, noticing the cluster of people up on the balcony, flashed a triumphant smile at Taylor.

Taylor shuddered with rage at the situation.

"Taylor," Thad said. "You really should get some fresh air."

Brooding, she followed Julian and the police officers, two she had not seen before—a white man with a boyish face and a white woman with very long legs and a dark braid down her back. They took the elevator to the main-floor lobby. Taylor eyed them suspiciously, wondering why they had replaced Officers Young and Edwards.

"How does pizza sound?" Julian asked.

"Great," the female officer said. "America's Pizza Café is just up the street."

The male officer nodded. "That's quite a walk. I'll drive."

"The quicker the better," Taylor said to the female officer. "I'm counting the minutes until we get back here and straighten out this mess. I still can't believe a crazy man comes after me and *I* end up suspended. This whole thing has been one big, ugly nightmare."

Julian turned to her as they entered the garage, "It'll all work out for the best," he said. "You'll see."

Taylor cut her eyes at him, then turned toward the female officer. "Is this job boring enough? I'm sure Pulaski has more on his mind now than coming after me."

"Wouldn't be so sure," the woman said. "Sounds to me like he'd love to get his hands on you."

As the female officer opened the back door of an unmarked police car, she locked her eyes on Taylor. There was something strange about the woman's stare. It made Taylor uneasy. She glanced at Julian, who was entering the other side of the car, and the male officer, who was in the driver's seat, starting the engine.

Her gut instinct was warning her of something. But she brushed off the paranoia as an emotional short circuit in her overtired brain.

Inside the car, the female officer announced on a two-way radio where they were going as the male officer drove the brown car out of the Wolf garage into the rain. People in business suits and raincoats scurried on the sidewalks under umbrellas. Thunder crashed above.

"Where is this place?" Julian asked.

Taylor glared at him, then turned away, looking out the car window.

"It's just up Woodward, by the Fox Theater," the male police officer said.

Julian grasped Taylor's arm. "Listen, Taylor, it's unfair to blame me for your problems. If anything, I'm trying to help."

"Yeah, right," Taylor said, snatching her arm back. "If it wasn't for you, Philip wouldn't be out to ruin me."

"Listen to Miss Innocence here," Julian said, a hard edge to his voice. "It takes two to tango, baby."

Taylor squinted at him. "Shut up. Just shut up and leave me alone."

She crossed her arms and turned toward the window. Through the red veil of anger clouding her thoughts, she noticed that the car was speeding past the restaurant.

"Hey," she said to the driver, pointing. "There's the restaurant."

But he only accelerated.

CHAPTER 61

Taylor's heart raced. She thrust her head and shoulders over the seat, jabbed her forefinger into the male officer's shoulder.

"Hey," she said loudly. "Turn around. We passed the restaurant."

Neither officer turned around as the car sped up Woodward.

In a heart-stopping second, Taylor realized that this was a trick. *These are phony cops, just like in court. Pulaski's foot soldiers. And we walked right into their trap.*

"Where are we going?" Taylor asked frantically. The cold shock of danger clutched her chest.

The woman ignored her as the car raced across the freeway overpass into an eerie urban wasteland. There was the pink neon BURLESK sign glowing on a lone building on a littered, vacant lot. Dark figures, homeless people, wandering sidewalks like ghosts. A pile of rubble where a building once stood. Dark windows and doorways of vacant houses, ghoulishly distorted through rain-pelted windows.

"Stop! Take us back."

Thunder crackled above them. Rain thudded on the rooftop. Taylor spun toward Julian. He fumbled for door latches. There were none.

We're trapped. We'll disappear without a trace.

"Stop the car!" Taylor shouted. "You can't do this."

Julian flung his shoulder against the car door. It did not budge.

Taylor pushed the power window button. Stuck.

Then Julian lunged over the front seat, diving for the steering wheel.

"Pull over!" he shouted.

Taylor heard clinking metal.

A gun. Pointed at Julian's head.

"Get your black ass back on the seat with the mongrel," the woman said.

Julian raised his hands and sat down. His eyes were wide; sweat glistened on his forehead. Taylor had never seen him appear so frightened.

The woman's dark eyes were slits and her full lips were stiff. She turned the gun on Taylor.

"Sit still, shut up, and nobody gets hurt," the woman said. "We got a long drive. Try any shit, an' you're both goin' in the trunk."

CHAPTER 62

Jess hurried up the staircase, shielding her eyes from sunlight pouring into the cabin's living room. She approached the television, around which sat Billy Joe, Nick, and Gus Lemer.

"—interrupt regular programming to bring you this report—"

On the screen was a reporter in front of Detroit's 36th District Court.

"Police say the disappearance this morning of two Detroit television journalists may be linked to Rocky Pulaski, a fugitive white supremacist who has evaded a law enforcement dragnet across the state for five days."

Jess, her eyes aching from hours at the computer, squinted as she watched the news clip of Rocky, then Taylor James, Julian DuPont, and the courtroom breakout. For the first time, Jess saw herself on television, kicking Taylor.

Is that wild-haired woman me? I look like a witch. Rocky has turned me into a freakin' witch.

Jess sunk into the old green tweed sofa, reeling with self-loathing. Rocky had bewitched and degraded her for so many years that she had become oblivious to the evil that had possessed her. She had never intended to become that crazy woman on the news. That awful image of herself on television provoked a sudden flash of insight: Booze, men, and hatred had consumed forty years of her life, leaving only a gray haze of heartache and emptiness.

"Ha!" Billy Joe shouted, pointing at Taylor's image on the television. "Look at that bitch, lookin' so scared. She'd shit her pants if she knew what she was in for tonight. And that punk Julian, I used to beat the shit outta him in school. This oughtta be some reunion with his face and my fist."

The men laughed as Billy Joe described violent sexual perversions that he intended to inflict on Taylor. Profanity and racial slurs peppered their speech; malice blazed in their eyes.

Sudden queasiness wracked Jess's entire being. She was repulsed by the animosity Rocky and everyone constantly spouted against anyone who was not white. She abhorred the sight of herself on television—wild-eyed and brainwashed by Rocky's evil doctrine. And disgust surged through her as she contemplated Rocky's viciousness toward her and his vindictive obsession with killing Taylor James. Why couldn't he just get over it and move on to more important things?

"I get to squeeze the last breath outta that whore," Billy Joe said. "Soon as Sally and Ken get here, the mongrels fry."

Jess shuddered. In prison she had hated Taylor James so much that crying fits and nightmares plagued her daily. Now, however, it seemed that Taylor was a victim. Through Jess's newfound clarity, she could see that Taylor had simply been bettering society when she sought to destroy Rocky's stinking cesspool of malevolence.

I can't let Rocky rebuild what he had. It's wrong. It's cost me my life and it may cost two more lives tonight. I gotta stop him.

Billy Joe's voice drew her attention.

"All women are whores," he said, his swastika tattoo rippling on his pudgy chest. "My mom was no different. She got what she deserved."

Nick shook his head. "Man, that must've been rough seein' your old lady die like that."

"My dad didn't think so, since he's the one who pushed her," Billy Joe said, scratching his brown razor stubble. "The cops didn't even question him. That's when I knew my dad was a warrior."

Jess's blood froze; her limbs numbed.

Rocky killed Loretta? He'd always said she fell, tripped on a rug, with the baby during a feeding. If he could murder his wife and child, then surely he could kill me.

Jess felt as if she were slipping into an oily, bottomless pit. She was a fugitive of the law, and if she fled Rocky now, with all his secrets, he would certainly hunt her down and kill her.

Maybe she could turn herself in, work a deal with the cops, prioritize her life in jail, then embark on a new life in a faraway place. And perhaps she could mend her relationship with her mother. Maybe then she would be free of fearing Rocky because he would be in prison for life.

Suddenly she noticed a bra, her bra, flying like a white bat from the staircase leading to the loft where she and Rocky slept. She darted up the staircase, only to get smacked in the face with an avalanche of bedsheets.

"You'll need these on the couch," Rocky said. "Sally's sleepin' up here with me."

His words struck with the brutality of a fist in her gut. "You're kickin' me out of your bed?"

"You're swift, Jess."

Motherfucker. Jess dropped the sheets and ran toward Rocky, who wore only tattered briefs and his Iron Cross, his thick middle and chest bare.

"How can you do this?" Jess spat. "After all I've done for you—"

"You haven't done shit but give me a headache," he said.

"But all the computer work at the compound," Jess said. She felt as if her life, like the last grains of sand in an hourglass, was being sucked into a black hole. "All these years," she said softly, more to herself than to Rocky.

"Your meter's expired, Jess. A man like me needs a cute little thing like Sally, not a washed-up rag like you, always giving me flack."

Jess shook her head as the hopelessness of her situation consumed her like a steamy vapor cloud.

"You been nothing but trouble," Rocky said. "Back when Taylor James and Andy Doss were filming us at the compound, you were having a fit about me lookin' at her. Should've been using some female intuition to figure out she was a phony. Then I send you to get her mother. You can't even do that right."

Rocky pressed fingertips to his spastic eyelid, then threw a pillow at Jess. "I should've done this a long time ago. Now, get your sour ass back downstairs. Back to work. After tonight, I need you to rebuild the Web site and do recruiting on the Internet."

Jess shook her head. "No way, man. I'm outta here." She turned toward the staircase.

Rocky snatched her arm, pinching her flesh. "You stay," Rocky said, his eyes violent and piercing. "You got no money. No job. Nothing. Besides, you know too much. I'd have to kill you, just like Loretta and Taylor James. That's what I do to bitches who get in my way."

Jess met his glare without flinching. *I'm gonna get in your way, all right, and you're not gonna like it.*

CHAPTER 63

Philip sat at his desk, chewing a handful of Tums and watching news reports about Taylor and DuPont's disappearance.

Those whores are getting what they deserve.

His secretary buzzed the intercom. "Mr. Carter, your father is on the line; he'd like to talk to you alone before the weekly family conference call."

"Shit," Philip said. "Put him through."

"Philip?" His father's furious tone squeezed the already tight bands of stress around his chest.

"Yes, Dad."

"Are you on a mission to self-destruct yourself and the company?"

"Of course not," Philip said, feeling as if he were shrinking.

"From my vantage point, it appears that you are. Your engagement goes up in smoke, you cavort in New York with a married woman, your ex-fiancée and star reporter disappear with *EE*'s anchor, and I hear the morning program is a disaster."

Philip closed his eyes. After this morning's bout with DuPont, this was the last thing he needed.

"I just watched it on GNN," Gerald Carter said. "You'd better do your damnedest to make sure the rest of your problems don't leak out. I loathe gossip, especially when it's my name being whispered about."

Go ahead and say it, Dad: "This is what I get for raising a bastard."

It's only your name I have, not your blood, so I can never live up to your impossible expectations.

Philip could hear his father breathing. He imagined him at his desk, his fleshy face flushed with anger, a hard glint in his dark, watery eyes, his thick gray-black hair in angry tufts.

He thinks I'm a failure. In marriage, at work, in life. Now I really have to bust my ass to be CEO.

"There's nothing more for me to do," Philip said. "We're working with the police and Feds to find Taylor and DuPont."

His father huffed. "This is an outrage. How could you let something like this happen?"

"I didn't—"

"And you show up in New York with a married woman?" Gerald said. "What's gotten into you?"

"It's not what you think, Dad. It was strictly business. I arranged an interview for her."

"Jonathan said she's very bright. But he tells me he went to your hotel room and heard the two of you engaged in the lowest type of debauchery."

A choking cloud of shame engulfed Philip, just as it had when he was fifteen and his father discovered him masturbating with an adult magazine in his bedroom. Horace had given him the magazine and showed him how to release the sexual pressure that constantly distracted him. And, Philip later learned, Horace had snitched to Dad that Philip stole the magazine and masturbated nightly.

"What kind of sexual beast have I raised?" his father asked, then and now. "You bring me shame in the eyes of God."

"Dad, c'mon," Philip said. "You're overreacting. I've done nothing wrong."

"You run our family name through the mud, muddling promiscuity with professional responsibilities, and you say you've done nothing wrong?"

Philip closed his eyes.

"Well?" his father asked.

"What can I say?" Philip said. "I'm doing everything in my power to remedy all these problems. I've already fired the people responsible for the morning-show problems."

"I'm not sure that's good enough," his father said. "Today you will be excluded from our weekly conference call so that we can discuss your status in the company. I'll call you tomorrow with our verdict."

His words hit Philip's sweaty chest like a wrecking ball against a brick building. His chest ached as his pride and aspirations thundered to the ground, rubble under a cloud of dust.

The loud dial tone blaring in his ear was like an alarm saying, "Sorry pal, your time is up."

CHAPTER 64

"Get in."

The gaping back door of the dark blue eighteen-wheeler resembled the mouth of an enormous whale, waiting to suck Taylor and Julian into oblivion.

"I said get in," the woman said. She stomped her foot on the truck's metal ramp, which echoed like a death knell.

Taylor frantically scanned the highway rest area.

"Run and I'll blow your legs off," the woman said, pointing the gun at Taylor.

The truck driver, a skinny man with bushy hair under a cap with a Confederate flag patch, lit a cigarette. "Dammit, let's get a move on," he said. "Sally, I'm doin' this as a favor to Rocky, and I'm already behind schedule. Now, let's go."

The hair on the back of Taylor's neck bristled. She had no choice but to get into the dark trailer. She glanced up at Julian, who subtly nodded, as if to say, "Get in." Taylor climbed the metal ramp into the hot, unlighted metal box. Julian followed.

"We're ridin' with you," Sally told the trucker. He slid the metal ramp under the truck and bolted the doors.

Taylor was engulfed in blackness; seizures of terror wracked her body. Her eyes were wide-open, but she saw nothing.

"Julian?"

She felt his hands grasp her arms and pull her against his chest, where she closed her eyes and tried to forget the absolute horror of their situation. The truck reminded her of the tales she had read about the Holocaust in which European Jews were crammed at gunpoint by the hundreds into train boxcars and trucks, then transported to Nazi death camps. Many never survived the grim journeys.

"We're gonna get out of this alive and in one piece," Julian said.

"How do you know?" Taylor asked.

"Because I have faith," he said.

Still, Taylor's heart raced as the truck's engine roared.

CHAPTER 65

Taylor and Julian sat on the floor of the truck against the wall, so that the sides of their thighs and elbows touched. Taylor was sweating and uncomfortable in her suit, panty hose, and pumps.

"Do you have your phone?" Julian asked.

"No, it broke. Do you?"

"It's on my desk back at the station," Julian said.

The truck started picking up speed. Taylor and Julian jiggled on the hard floor.

"Taylor?"

"Yeah?"

"If anything happens to me," Julian said, "I want you to know that I love you."

A hot lump grew in Taylor's throat. Just as she had had an epiphany under the brights lights on the Wolf auditorium stage three years ago, the blackness around her inspired a flash of insight.

Julian is mine now. Fate moved Philip out of the way, just in time, so I could join my soul mate. Forever. Even if we die today.

"And," he said softly, "I have to know if you've forgiven me, if you still love me. I don't want to die without hearing you say you love me."

Julian put his arm around her. She rested her head on his shoulder, relishing the comfort of his body and his deep voice in the darkness.

"The past ten years," Julian said, "were an absolute waste. Now it looks like we might not have much of a future."

"Don't say that," Taylor said. "The police will find us, or maybe we can escape, or hit Sally and steal her gun. I don't know how. But we'll make it."

He stroked her head. "All I care about is now. You and me, right now. Please say you forgive me. And that you love me."

A river of raw emotion coursed through Taylor. "I'm working on the forgiving part. That'll take time. But . . . yes, I still love you." Mouthing those words released so much passion and anxiety that had been trapped inside her that she literally felt her tense muscles loosen as she spoke.

Julian pulled her closer and kissed her forehead.

"I always have," Taylor said, "even when I told myself that I hated you. Even when I was telling Philip that I loved him."

"Did you love him?" Julian asked.

"Yes," she said. "In the beginning I thought we were both outsiders; me because of race, him because of his strange family. But we weren't really alike. I was so caught up in his charm. And, I don't know, I think the marriage was an act of defiance against my parents' overprotectiveness. In the back of my mind, I probably did it to help get over you, too."

Julian sighed. "You don't know how happy you just made me."

"Maybe I do," Taylor said. "But you've caused me more grief than—"

"Shhh." Julian pulled her closer. "I want to spend the rest of my life making that up to you."

"Talk fast." Taylor laughed nervously. "You may have only a few hours."

CHAPTER 66

It was no longer raining when the truck stopped and the trucker opened the doors.

"Get out," Sally said, pointing the gun at them.

Taylor, squinting in the late afternoon haze, exited on wobbly legs with Julian. They were on a two-lane paved road in a wooded area at the mouth of a dirt road.

The male police impostor nervously scanned the forest, leaves rippling above in the breeze, as the truck pulled away. They marched Julian and Taylor down the wooded trail. As their feet crunched leaves and twigs, blackflies and dragonflies buzzing around them, Taylor searched the woods for an escape route. But she saw none.

They were in the middle of nowhere, and this time—unlike the exposé at the White Power Alliance compound—there was no heli-copter waiting in a nearby barn, no cellular phone, no tracking device. No escape plan.

After a while they reached a clearing and a beautiful cedar log home with a stone chimney and wide wooden deck. A woman with a black beehive hairdo appeared on the deck.

"You do us proud, Sally," the woman said. "You too, Ken. Take 'em to the cottage."

They led Taylor and Julian at gunpoint past an in-ground swim-ming pool and down another wooded path, which led to an A-frame cottage. Dense woods surrounded it. Taylor noticed a path whose distant end was a blue expanse. A lake. A large one, Taylor figured, because she could not see the other side.

As they stood in a small clearing before the cabin, its front door flew open, crashing loudly against the wall.

In the doorway stood Rocky Pulaski, in camouflage and black jackboots, a holster and gun on his hip. His face was stiff as he ex-amined Taylor and Julian.

"Special delivery," Sally chirped.

Suddenly Rocky belted out deep, sardonic laughter, echoing off the trees and overcast sky.

"Looks like we hit the double jackpot," Rocky said. "Two mon-grels for the price of one."

Taylor struggled to stand still and tall on trembling legs. She glanced at Julian, whose face was taut. He was glowering at Rocky with the same defiance in his eyes as when he was a child in meet-ings with their parents, Pulaski, and school officials. Julian was not going to surrender without a fight.

"I know who you are," Rocky said. He jogged down the small ce-ment porch and shoved a thick, accusing finger in Julian's face. "You're that half-breed son of a bitch who knocked my son out cold in the fifth grade."

Julian stared, nostrils flaring, but did not speak.

"Aren't you?" Rocky bellowed.

Julian pursed his lips.

Rocky punched him in the stomach.

Julian grunted and bent over, but quickly stood back up.

Taylor flinched. She tried to project an unfeeling mask, a tough facade, but her insides were mush. And seeing Rocky assault Julian caused her own stomach, and heart, to ache.

"Julian DuPont," Rocky hissed, his thick fingers encircling Julian's neck. "I'm using every ounce of self-control to not rip you to shreds. Nope. I'll wait until tonight, when I show my comrades how to cleanse the world of vermin and black degenerate mongrels like yourself."

Julian's eyes glowed with malice as he glared at Rocky, who locked eyes on Taylor. Dizzying fear swept through her.

"And you. You! The pariah of the White Power Alliance. You, Taylor James, will be the first human sacrifice marking the revolution. We'll slaughter two mongrels as we usher in our long-awaited dominance."

Taylor squinted at Rocky. "You can't get away with this," she said. "You can't! The police know where you are."

Fury flashed in Rocky's eyes, one of which twitched as he glared at her. Then he laughed.

Taylor scowled at him.

Rocky stepped closer. "There's nothing I hate more than you, Taylor James. I've waited a long time for this. My dick gets hard at the thought of killing you."

He leaned close, his face inches from hers. Taylor could feel his hot breath on her cheek. He still had that beef jerky smell, and his black eyes were like liquid venom.

"I oughtta take you right now, in front of your boyfriend here," Rocky said. "Show you what it's like to be with a real man."

Though more frightened than she had ever been, Taylor felt a surge of defiance surge up from deep in her gut. "I'd rather die," Taylor whispered, staring deep into his dark eyes.

He pushed closer, his mouth open. Then on her cheek she felt something sharp, something wet. Rocky was biting her face!

"Get off her, man!" Julian shouted. He lunged at Rocky, whose teeth unclamped from Taylor's cheek. Julian wrenched Rocky away from her.

Disgust and fear rippled through Taylor. Then she noticed that Julian seemed oblivious to the fact that Sally and the fake cop were aiming guns at him. Julian punched Rocky's jaw.

"Stop it!" Taylor shouted.

The front door of the cottage flew open. Out ran Billy Joe, Gus Lemer, John Scarlin, and several other men whom Taylor recognized from the court breakout.

"What the hell is goin' on?" Billy Joe shouted. "Dad!"

The cluster of men charged toward Julian and Rocky.

"Stop it!" Taylor screamed, every inch of her quivering with fear. This mob of hate mongers could kill Julian in minutes, with their hands.

Julian and Rocky scuffled on the ground, punching each other, shouting obscenities. Billy Joe and his gang dove into the fray.

Then a single, earsplitting gunshot caused everyone to freeze.

CHAPTER 67

The handcuffs were pinching Taylor's wrists. The cold cement of the basement floor was hard and damp; the metal pole to which she and Julian were roped back to back bruised her spine. Her sole consolation was the fact that they were still alive, and that their disappearance must have triggered a massive search by now.

Taylor's mind spun incessantly in an effort to hatch an escape plan. The relief of just a few minutes ago, when Sally had fired her gun into the sky to stop the men from brawling, had dissolved under Billy Joe's taunting.

"I've been hopin' we'd meet again," Billy Joe said, looking down at Julian. "The nigger bastard who thought he was so tough when we were kids. How tough are ya now, big boy?"

Taylor could not see Julian's face, but she imagined him glaring at Billy Joe. On her side of the pole was Gus Lemer, his ratlike face and silver-brown crew cut glowing eerily in the dim light of the computers, where Jess typed noisily without looking up. A cup of coffee and a handgun sat next to her keyboard.

"After we do you," Lemer hissed at Taylor, "we're goin' after your friend the prosecutor." He caressed the barrel of the Glock on his hip. "I killed her daddy and I'll pump her fulla bullets, too, then piss on what's left. The both of yous."

Taylor projected ice-cold eyes at him. Here was a man in his fifties enacting some childish G I Joe fantasy in Michigan woodland. What a loser. Sworn to serve and protect, and now he had disgraced the department—again—and chosen instead to serve as henchman to a racist barbarian.

Someday, somehow, justice will come crashing down on you. For Carla and her family, for me and Julian. For society.

Taylor ignored him and glanced down at the handcuffs holding her wrists together in her lap. The metal rings seemed inescapable. She found some comfort, or perhaps a mental diversion from this horrifying experience, in the fact that she was still wearing the charm bracelet that her mother had given her. If there was any power in that crystal sword that Mom had said symbolized safety, Taylor prayed that it would work some magic now.

"You're stuck right here where we want ya," Lemer said. "Ever felt fire on your skin?"

Taylor looked up at him, his eyes aglow with malice.

"Sounds like steak sizzlin' in a fry pan," he said. "SSSsssstttttt!"

Taylor tried to ignore him and Billy Joe's loud insults to Julian.

"That'll be you and him, tonight," Lemer said. "Sizzlin' like fajitas at a freakin' Mexican restaurant."

Billy Joe came into view, laughing. "Yeah!" he said. "You're gonna burn. And we're gonna party down when you beg for mercy."

Taylor cut her eyes at Billy Joe. *I hate you. You and your father are psychotic monsters. And I'm gonna put up the bravest fight I can, because I don't want to give you bastards the satisfaction of watching me and Julian die.*

"You're pathetic," Taylor said, glaring at Billy Joe.

Violent intrigue sparkled in his eyes. "Hey, I'll show you pathetic," he said, tugging at the top of his cutoff shorts. "When I shove my meat down your throat, you'll see pathetic, all right. When you gag on my—"

"Get away from her," Julian shouted. Taylor could feel him writhing, trying to break free of the rope binding their chests and arms.

"Shut up," Lemer yelled at Julian.

At the same time, Taylor grimaced when Billy Joe unzipped his pants. She clenched her teeth, pursed her lips. No way would she let him violate her like that. No way.

Billy Joe made a gleeful grunting sound as he stepped toward her, his hand on the white fabric of his exposed briefs.

"Whooo-weee!" he shouted.

CHAPTER 68

Jess stood up. She kicked her chair away from the computer, causing it to crash loudly on the floor.

"Goddammit!" she shouted, charging at Billy Joe and Lemer. "I'm tryin' to get this work done before tonight."

Billy Joe and Lemer glanced at Jess with annoyed expressions. "Crazy bitch," Billy Joe said. "Who are you talkin' to like that?"

"You," Jess said. "And him. Now, get outta here so I can get some work done. If I don't finish, Rocky'll have both your tails. Now, go!"

As he and Lemer headed toward the stairs, Billy Joe glared at Taylor. "I ain't done with you."

Taylor ignored him. She glanced up at Jess, grateful that she had saved her from Billy Joe's perversion. But the angry gleam in Jess's eyes provoked yet another pang of fear. After the vicious way Jess had kicked her in court, Taylor did not dare imagine what Jess might do to her and Julian in this awful basement in the middle of nowhere.

"Shit," Jess hissed, glaring down at Taylor. "Got so much damn work."

Jess returned to the computer and typed noisily as several heavy pairs of footsteps descended the creaky staircase.

First came Rocky, then Nick and Sally. Then came Fred Lutz, who patted Sally's back. They gathered around Taylor and Julian, ogling like visitors at a zoo.

"Good job, girl," Lutz said. "Who woulda thought my pretty daughter would be so good at cops and robbers?" He let out a wheezy laugh, opening his mouth wide to show gold molars. Then he spit, projecting a wet glob on Taylor's skirt. She did not look at it; she kept her eyes on her bracelet and prayed for a rescue.

"Can't wait to see that hussy burn," Lutz said. "Who's the nigger?"

"An old friend," Rocky said sarcastically, glaring at Julian. "He's the half-breed who knocked Billy Joe out cold in the fifth grade."

"Yeah, I remember that story," Lutz said.

"It's payback time," Rocky said, then glanced over at Jess. "Hey, Jess, you got all those bulletins sent out yet?"

She ignored him.

Rocky took two long steps toward her, his combat boots slapping the cement floor ominously. He grabbed her ponytail, flipping back her head so that she looked at him. "I'm talkin' to you."

"I'm almost done," she said softly.

"What's takin' you so long?"

"It's a lotta work," Jess said.

Rocky pushed her head toward the monitor. "Hurry up, stupid cunt. You only have a few hours left, so get with it."

Unfazed, Jess resumed typing.

After the men went upstairs and, judging by the sounds of their footsteps, outside the cottage, Taylor heard Julian whisper.

"You okay?" he asked.

"Yeah," she said softly.

"I think I got a plan," Julian whispered.

Taylor glanced at Jess, who was typing furiously. She turned her head toward Julian. "What?"

"When they—"

"Shut up over there," Jess said loudly. Taylor locked eyes on Jess, who was staring at her in a peculiar way. Jess tilted her head, causing the computer screen's green glow to reflect eerily in the lenses of her glasses. There was enough light for Taylor to see Jess rest a hand on the gun on the table. Then Jess picked it up, shoved it into her waistband, and stood up. Taylor, her empty stomach a crampy, burning pit, cast her eyes down to her wrists.

But she could still feel Jess's piercing stare. Her heart raced when she heard Jess's chair scraping across the floor, then Jess stepping toward them. Taylor looked up at her. Strangely, she did not see the same hatred in Jess's eyes that she had seen in the courtroom just days ago. Something odd—perhaps even tenderness—glimmered in Jess's gaze. But any such hope Taylor felt was dashed when light reflected off the shiny steel handle of the gun at Jess's waist.

"Shh," Jess said, holding a forefinger to her mouth. She glanced at the dark staircase. "Don't make a sound, either of you."

Taylor eyed her suspiciously. *This is probably some sick mind game. She'll be nice, then pistol-whip me.*

Jess knelt in a spot where both Taylor and Julian could turn their heads to see her. "It's okay," Jess said. "I want to help."

"Yeah, right," Julian said.

"I do," Jess said. She glanced nervously at the stairwell. "Listen. I just E-mailed the FBI and the state police. I let 'em know where you guys are, and what's gonna happen tonight."

Taylor knitted her brows and studied Jess. "Why should we believe you?"

Jess cracked a tiny smile. "Your choices are kinda limited right now, I'd say."

"Did the cops answer your E-mail?" Julian whispered. "Are they coming?"

"Yeah," Jess said. "Only thing is, by the time they get here, it might be too late. They got a long ways to come. We're kinda far out, at the tip of the Michigan thumb."

"What do you mean, too late?" Taylor asked.

Jess stuck her hand deep in the pocket of her blue jeans. "There's gonna be a cross-burning tonight. Rocky and Billy Joe want to kill you in front of the crowd. Here it is." Jess pulled a tiny silver key from her pocket.

Taylor's doubt about Jess's intentions eased when Jess—with trembling hands—unlocked the handcuffs. Taylor was speechless. Relief and terror surged through her as Jess freed Julian's hands, then untied the rope binding them to the pole.

Taylor massaged her wrists and stood on cramped legs. Her stomach fluttered with intense hope tempered by the horrifying thought of Rocky returning, catching Jess's apparent act of kindness, then killing all three of them. "I thought . . . I mean, why are you doing this?" Taylor asked.

Jess pressed the key into Taylor's palm. Her brown hair formed a messy frame around her gaunt, weary face; her eyes, full of fear and grief, darted around quickly. "This is all bad," Jess said. "It's wicked, and I don't want a part of it anymore."

Julian glanced up the staircase, then turned to Jess. "Got any more guns?"

Jess hurried to a closet in the corner. "Yeah," she said, opening the door. "Damn him. He moved the guns."

Taylor joined Julian at the foot of the steps. They stared up the dark tunnel together, listening for footsteps in the silence.

"My gun should be enough," Jess said, stepping toward them. "Listen, everybody's at the main house for dinner. We got maybe an hour before they'll be back. So I say we make a run for it now. We get to a main road and hitch a ride, or find a boat and take off—"

Upstairs, the front door creaked loudly. Then a heavy footstep thudded on the floor. More footsteps, heading toward the staircase.

Taylor's heart pounded in her ears; her palms became clammy. She stepped into a dark shadow by the staircase.

Julian pushed Jess to one side of the stairway, then picked up a metal folding chair.

The top step creaked. "Jess!"

It was Billy Joe.

CHAPTER 69

Taylor could see Jess's chest heaving in the dim light.

"Jess!" Billy Joe shouted down the staircase. "Dad wants you in the house now."

Taylor glanced at Julian, who held the chair over his head. He nodded at Jess.

"Jess?" Billy Joe called.

"Sure thing," Jess said with a steady voice. "Come on down and help me carry this stuff for your dad."

"Shit," Billy Joe said, stomping down the steps. "Can't even finish supper, always runnin' around for somebody."

When Billy Joe reached the bottom step, worry flashed across his face. "Hey, where the hell are—"

Julian smashed the chair down on Billy Joe's head. Billy Joe crumpled to the floor, moaning.

"Get the rope," Julian said as he dragged Billy Joe across the floor. Taylor and Jess quickly bound him to the pole.

Julian grabbed Taylor's hand. They flew up the stairs, two at a time. Taylor's legs felt as they always did when she was running in dreams, as if her legs did not touch the ground, and that she was so full of energy that she was gliding, flying through the air.

Julian led the trio up the stairs, through the dark, musty living room, where the television cast eerie shadows on the dusty furniture. He peeked through the front door, then bolted.

They ran into the woods, the opposite direction of the grand log cabin. Taylor could hear loud voices and the clatter of plates and silverware coming through the house's open windows.

Adrenaline fueling her legs, she ran behind Julian, Jess behind her, faster than she ever imagined. Feet crunching leaves and twigs, they whizzed past trees and fallen branches, knee-high ferns and pine thickets. She ignored the brush slicing into her panty hose and skin.

It was overcast and near dusk, the dark blue-gray sky looking as if it would rain any moment.

Ahead, Taylor fixed on Julian's dark suit jacket in the dim woods. An oddly thrilling terror consumed her; they seemed so close to freedom, yet so near danger. They had to come to a road soon.

Over the sound of her gasps for breath, she heard shouting. Deep voices, echoing in the woods behind them. Still running, Julian turned around. He motioned with his hand to surge ahead.

Taylor pumped her legs faster.

A gunshot cracked like thunder, rebounding off the clouds, crashing down on them. Then came the foreboding chorus of barking dogs.

Taylor felt ice-cold yet sweaty, terrified yet hopeful. *God, please . . . please let us get away.*

"No!" Jess screamed.

Taylor ran faster without turning around. She heard a gunshot, then heard Jess thud to the ground, dry leaves crumpling under her.

Julian and Taylor froze. Glancing back, she saw Jess's pink shirt now splattered red. Jess's mouth and eyes were open, as if staring at the sky, astonished at what had happened. She was dead.

Taylor froze, horrified. *We're next.* Julian, perfectly still except for his heaving chest, searched the woods.

It was darker now. They could not see anybody. They could hear the dogs and voices—getting closer.

Panting, Taylor scanned every direction with wide eyes, but all she saw was the white bark of birch trees, the gray of poplars, the brown of oak. They all blurred into a murky shroud for Jess's assassin. Their assassin.

"Should we run?" she whispered.

Julian nodded. They bolted.

Another gunshot. Closer this time.

They kept running.

Then they heard another sound. Cars. On a paved road.

Taylor and Julian surged forward at what seemed like bionic speed.

She could see the road now, a red sedan whizzing past.

Finally they reached the edge.

Taylor stumbled down a sandy bank, landing on her chest, knocking the wind out of her. She lay stunned until Julian pulled her up.

"C'mon, Taylor, we're almost there."

Julian gripped her hand as they ran on the double yellow lines in the middle of the road.

Cars. We need cars. Rescuers. Police.

They ran and ran, but saw only woods.

Taylor ignored the pain in her feet and her aching lungs.

We've got to escape.

Suddenly a green pickup truck appeared about five yards ahead. It barreled out of the woods and screeched onto the pavement, shining headlights on Taylor and Julian. *Maybe they can rescue us, drive us to safety. No—*

A man with a shotgun balanced atop the cab. It was Rocky, aiming at Taylor. Her hope wilted under the terrified trembles wracking her body. Julian grabbed her hand, trying to yank her into the dark woods.

The truck skidded to a stop in front of them.

"Stop or you're roadkill," Rocky shouted.

CHAPTER 70

Julian licked the caked blood on his swollen, split lip. He was bruised and aching from the beating by Billy Joe and Lemer. Taylor's screams still rung in his ears. Thank God they had not raped her.

That horrifying episode over, Julian was now numb with terror. He and Taylor sat handcuffed to a post on a wooden platform, which was nothing more than a flat trailer on wheels pulled by a tractor, to which it was still hitched. Behind them was a towering wooden cross. And before them, hundreds of menacing faces thundered, "White Power!" and "Kill the mongrels!"

It was a carnival of malevolence, hidden deep in the dark woods, under a black sky, and he and Taylor were the freak show. But through his eyes, it was the contrary. The tattooed, bearded man at the front, howling and gulping a forty-ounce bottle of beer, appeared maniacal. As did the two women in short shorts and tank tops, hanging on a muscular man in a black leather vest and sunglasses. And the scores of skinheads, their faces contorted and red as they shouted, were horrors unto themselves. The rest of the throng was a sea of perverse frivolity.

It would soon become more so, Julian suspected, when the cross blazed behind them. The scent of gasoline hung in the air, presumably from the gas-soaked cloth wrapped around the cross. A red and yellow gasoline can sat on the grass near the platform.

Julian's powerlessness to protect Taylor inspired in him a rage he had never fathomed. Her left arm, against his right, trembled. Her teeth were chattering, and her legs, dirty and covered with red lines where sticks has sliced through her panty hose and skin, quaked violently.

My baby is scared out of her mind and I can't do a damn thing about it.

His rage was for God, for entangling them in the clutches of evil and imminent death, and for permitting such pestilence to fester in the world. In that eighteen-wheeler, he had imagined that he was Jonah in the belly of the whale, begging God for forgiveness for all the anguish he had caused Taylor. But now it seemed that he would be punished rather than forgiven.

And his anger was for himself, for losing Taylor and somehow allowing her, in her quest to better society and carve her own journalistic niche, to defy a monster like Pulaski. Now, as he stared down death, a profound sadness and shame joined the maelstrom of emotion squeezing his chest. He might not live to enjoy Taylor's love.

If Jess had been telling the truth about the police and FBI, where the hell are they?

Suddenly the crowd exploded with Hitler-style salutes and cheers.

Rocky, Billy Joe, Scarlin, and Lutz—all armed—stepped onto the platform. They saluted the crowd, where Sally and the rat-faced man named Lemer stood near the front with Nick.

"White brothers and sisters, this is a historical day," Rocky shouted into a microphone. "The revolution has begun!"

An earsplitting roar rose from the throng.

"I am the Aryan messiah," he bellowed. "And I will lead my

brethren to a safe, white society, free of the vermin we see here tonight."

Julian's heart raced as the crowd focused—with eyes hungry for violence—on him and Taylor.

"These are the despicable offspring of Negro and Caucasian, the muddling of pristine whiteness with filth," he yelled. "Tonight we begin a cleansing, a cleansing by fire, of the mongrels polluting America."

Pulaski's flock cheered wildly as Scarlin held a torch to the cross. A noisy gust of acrid heat blasted Julian and Taylor as the cross ignited.

Dammit, why do we have to die this way? Haven't we endured enough hatred? This wasn't supposed to happen in the 1990s. It was more like Alabama or Mississippi in the 1860s or 1930s. A modern-day lynching. What had changed? He and Taylor had both attended college and attained wonderful careers that would have been impossible to people of color back then. Yet the power of racists, at this point, seemed just as strong as during Reconstruction and before the civil rights movement. He thought about his parents, how devastated they would be to learn that their only son was dead. Taylor's parents, too. They would be crushed.

No. This can't happen. We can't let this happen. Somehow, someway, we have to escape.

Julian glanced at Taylor, whose ashen face pained his heart. The crowd began chanting, "Blood! Blood!"

Taylor's mind spun frantically. Even though she had the handcuff key in her pocket, she knew it would be suicide to run from the armed mob.

"They call it the browning of America," Rocky shouted. "I call it a call to arms!"

Just as she cast terrified eyes at Julian, hoping he would have some magical escape plan, a thunderous noise and violent wind silenced the crowd.

All faces turned skyward.

Helicopters.

CHAPTER 71

Three black choppers hovered above the crowd. Then, like an attack of giant black ants, helmeted men in black filed out of the woods from all directions, guns drawn.

"Do not surrender!" Rocky shouted. "This is Armageddon. We must fight to the end!"

Rocky, Billy Joe, and their followers drew guns, firing on the helicopters. Lemer, Lutz, Scarlin, and Nick surrounded the platform, as if to protect their führer.

Gunfire crackled from all sides. The clearing became a battleground; White Power Alliance members, many armed, wrestling with and shooting at law enforcement agents.

The chaotic scene filled Taylor with uneasy relief. At last their rescuers had arrived. If she and Julian did not get killed by stray gunfire, perhaps they would escape alive. She quickly pressed closer to Julian and said, "The handcuff key is in my left jacket pocket."

She maneuvered so that he was able to reach in her pocket, then unlock her handcuffs. Her hands free, Taylor took the key from Julian and, with trembling fingers, freed his hands.

At the same time, a cluster of SWAT officers was rushing toward Taylor and Julian. *Yes, get us out of this nightmare.*

Taylor glanced around, noticing that the White Power Alliance members were so busy fighting the law enforcement officers that nobody was watching them. But as she and Julian stood up, Billy Joe lunged at Taylor. She fell down, her elbow and knee crashing painfully into the wooden platform.

Billy Joe fell on her, his weight squeezing the air from her lungs. Staring up at the black sky and the flaming orange cross, Taylor writhed beneath his heavy bulk, despising his smell and the hot, suffocating feeling of him. She tried to push him away, but he was too heavy.

"Get off me!" she shouted.

Julian lunged at Billy Joe, slamming him into the wooden platform. Taylor quickly scooted back onto the grass. At the same time, Billy Joe rose up and shot a brutal punch at Julian's jaw.

Then Billy Joe snarled at Taylor. On his hands and knees, he surged at her like a wild animal. "I'm gonna get you if it's the last thing I do," Billy Joe shouted over the deafening chaos.

"Do not surrender!" Rocky shouted into the microphone. He was still standing on the platform, waving a gun under the searing glow of the burning cross.

The crowd before him was fighting, screaming, blasting guns. As a helicopter landed in the center of the clearing, a SWAT officer shouted over a loudspeaker for the crowd to surrender peacefully.

Taylor met Billy Joe's glare, then glanced at Julian, who cast a reassuring gaze at her. The SWAT officers were closer. Soon they would be safe, away from this hellish mayhem. Hope soaring, Taylor scrambled away from Billy Joe. She scampered to the grass behind the podium, where she crouched as the SWAT officers approached.

At the same time, Julian lunged at Billy Joe. They scuffled on the platform. Julian bloodied Billy Joe's nose; Billy Joe punched Julian's gut. The men rolled onto the grass before Taylor, who watched in horror. In an instant, Billy Joe knocked Julian with brutal force, propelling him onto his back at the edge of the dark woods.

The SWAT officers were just feet away, their rifles aimed at Billy Joe.

"Help us!" Taylor screamed. But she became silent and still when she felt the cold steel tip of a gun at her temple.

CHAPTER 72

Taylor had never known such terror. Her muscles spasmed uncontrollably. A cold, clammy sweat clung to her skin.

The gun at her head, Billy Joe forced her to stand.

Compounding her fear was the fact that she could not see Julian. He could be anywhere in the dense mayhem. And with so many guns blasting and people screaming, Taylor's graphic imagination provided horrifying possibilities for what had happened to Julian. But she did not dare turn her head to increase her range of vision.

No, she was profoundly helpless, despite the four SWAT officers' rifles aimed at Billy Joe.

"Put the gun down," a SWAT officer shouted.

Billy Joe did not budge.

Out of the corner of her eye, Taylor could see his thick fingers wrapped around a silver gun. Her back to his chest, she could feel his sweat and heavy breathing. Seconds seemed eternal.

"You shoot me," Taylor said, "and they'll blow your head off."

"Shut the fuck up," Billy Joe grunted into her ear, pressing the gun into her skin.

"Take it easy, man," a SWAT officer said. "We can settle this without bloodshed."

"Shut up!" Billy Joe screamed above the chaotic din.

Taylor could feel the heat of the burning cross at her back. She could hear Rocky screaming wildly into the microphone on the platform. Gunfire rang out in every direction.

But where was Julian? Her heart thundered with fear.

Suddenly, before them, the platform began to move. It jerked toward the cross, toward the woods. On it, Rocky continued to scream about Armageddon, thrusting his gun into the air. Nearby, on the grass, Scarlin, Lutz, Lemer, and Nick scuffled with SWAT officers.

Taylor, perplexed, watched. Then Billy Joe, the gun still pressed to her head, spun Taylor around, enabling her to see what was moving the platform.

It was Julian! He was sitting atop the tractor that pulled the trailer-platform. He was steering the tractor sharply toward the woods, pulling the platform toward the burning cross. The image of Julian—on a tractor, surging through the violent chaos—was surreal. Taylor squinted in an effort to comprehend what he was doing. Hope surged within her that whatever it was that Julian was trying to do, it would wrench her from Billy Joe's death grip.

The platform continued moving. Now it caught Rocky Pulaski's attention.

He stopped screaming. His rage-distorted face paled. He had a bewildered expression as he looked around, as if trying to figure out why the platform beneath him was suddenly shifting.

Rocky spun around, looking toward the burning cross, trying to see what was pulling the platform.

At the same time, Julian's trick drew Billy Joe's curiosity.

"What the fuck—" Billy Joe began.

Now Julian drove the tractor faster, causing the platform to jerk quickly. It was getting closer to the burning cross.

Then, with a loud thud, the platform rammed into the base of the cross.

There was a great whooshing sound. A searing gale of heat.

A blinding flash of light.

The flaming cross toppled toward the platform.

Rocky looked up. His mouth opened with shock. He raised an arm to shield his face.

The cross crashed atop Rocky Pulaski.

It pinned his body to the wooden platform, blanketing him with flames.

An eerie hush stilled the crowd.

Horrified faces gawked at the fiery outline of Rocky's lifeless body.

Stunned, Taylor watched with relief. *That's right, burn in hell.* The evil, racist Rocky Pulaski was dead. And this death by fire was oh-so-appropriate for him. Now Taylor would no longer have to fear him, or his violent race war.

But her relief suffocated under sheer terror.

At her back, Billy Joe shook with rage. And the barrel of his gun was still at her temple.

CHAPTER 73

Billy Joe suddenly loosened his grip on Taylor. The gun slipped to her cheek as he absorbed the gruesome reality before him.

"Dad!" he screamed.

He shoved Taylor to the ground. The four SWAT officers who had aimed guns at Billy Joe helped her to her feet. *Thank God! Now Julian and I can get out of here safely. But where is he?*

"Let's get you out of here," a SWAT officer said, taking her elbow. "To the chopper." He pulled her toward the woods.

Taylor pulled her arm back. "Julian, I have to find Julian."

"Ma'am, we need to evacuate now," the officer said.

"No, wait, please." Trembling with panic, Taylor scanned the chaos.

She saw Billy Joe, running toward the yellow-red inferno. Flames now engulfed the entire platform, shooting ten feet in the air.

"Dad! Somebody save him!" Billy Joe bellowed.

Scarlin, Lutz, and Lemer tried to lift the burning cross. Nearby, Sally shrieked horribly.

"Get him outta there!" Billy Joe shouted.

But the men, working frantically, could not touch the red-hot cross.

Flames shot up Scarlin's arms; he patted them out. Lutz shouted for someone to find a tree branch with which to pry the cross off Rocky's body.

Then there was a thunderous roar. An explosion.

A scorching flash of blinding flame lit up the night.

Taylor jumped back. She raised her hands to shield her face from the heat. It was so hot that she scanned herself for flames. There were none, but fire was everywhere. Heart-stopping terror consumed her.

My God, where's Julian? He might be behind that cloud of fire.

Julian had caused the cross to topple Pulaski, thus saving Taylor from Billy Joe's wrath. But she cringed at the thought of Julian being hurt in the process.

Taylor heard spine-chilling screams, which only intensified her fear.

"Ma'am, let's go," the SWAT officer said.

"No, I can't," she said. "We have to find Julian DuPont. The man who was kidnapped with me. Julian Dupont. Have you seen him?"

The SWAT officer's expression was blank.

He doesn't know where Julian is either.

"Ma'am—"

Taylor darted away from the SWAT officer, toward the fire.

She saw flame-covered figures running in all directions. There was a tall shape raising his flaming arms like a bird. Then he fell to the ground. *God, don't let that be Julian.*

Nearby she saw a thin figure engulfed in fire. And another, resembling Billy Joe's stocky build. A fourth one, trying to roll on the ground, snuff out the flames.

Nearby stood Sally, tears streaming down her contorted face. She let out earsplitting screams. "Daddy! Rocky!"

The scene was as close to hell as Taylor ever wanted to be. And not knowing Julian's whereabouts was nothing short of torture. As she studied the chaos, she realized that perhaps the gas can that had been near the platform had exploded.

Could those burning figures be Billy Joe, Scarlin, Nick, Lutz, and Lemer? All wiped out in a cloud of fire? But not Julian. No. It would kill me.

A spasm of horror rolled through Taylor's shock-numbed body. She desperately scanned the mayhem. She could not see the tractor anymore; there were too many people clustered around the burning men, trying to extinguish the fire.

Another SWAT officer took Taylor's arm. "Let's go!" he shouted.

But she snatched her arm back. She was not going anywhere without her long-lost love.

CHAPTER 74

A horrible sense of doom consumed Taylor. She ran in the direction of where she had seen the tractor. And Julian. But she froze in her tracks when she saw the tractor, on its side, consumed in flames near the edge of the woods.

"Julian!" she shouted. "Where are you?"

Taylor's chest heaved. She realized that she was so frightened that she was panting. As she raised a hand to her chest, she saw two men scuffling nearby on the grass.

"Julian!" she yelled.

There he was, fighting off the punches of a burly man in a leather jacket.

As if floating, Taylor rushed to the edge of the forest. She grabbed a large stick from the ground, then surged toward the burly man, who was now pinning Julian to the ground.

Taylor, with strength and violence that she did not know she had, drew the stick back with the concentration of a major league baseball player in the World Series. Then she whacked it with all her might, striking the man in the face. He fell backward. Thudded to the ground.

Julian stood up.

"That's one mean swing you got there," he said, eyes smiling despite a bloody lip and tattered clothes.

Trembling with relief, Taylor grabbed his hand. "Let's go!"

SWAT officers surrounded them.

"We've got to leave now," one said.

The men ushered Taylor and Julian into the woods. As they ran, bullets whizzed past, splitting the bark of trees just feet from their heads.

Finally Taylor saw something black and shimmery through the trees. The lake. And she heard the deep rhythm of helicopter blades.

The SWAT officers led them to a helicopter at the lake's edge. The door flew open. Men lifted her trembling body inside the chopper's metal belly.

Julian followed. Taylor could hear bullets ping against its outer shell, and an officer fired a gun mounted to its side.

Sitting on the floor, Taylor fell back on Julian's chest. She felt bruised and exhausted and shaky, but finally safe in his arms.

"I'm never letting go of you," he whispered in her ear. "I got my White Chocolate back for life."

Taylor closed her eyes, savoring the warm blanket of security and relief that was his embrace.

CHAPTER 75

Monica James wiped her wet, puffy eyes with a clump of tissues as Janice DuPont paced the floor. Ramsey and François sat around the kitchen table, eyes glued to the television. Carla and Danielle, who had been there since dinnertime when they brought over a bucket of fried chicken, were preparing tea and coffee. Outside, a horde of reporters, TV cameras, and news trucks crowded the street.

When they heard the Channel 3 News theme song, they clustered around the television.

"Good evening, I'm Noelle Keats and this is Channel Three News at Eleven."

Monica held her breath.

"Breaking news from Michigan's Thumb region. Moments ago Channel Three learned from law enforcement authorities that two Detroit journalists are alive and safe at this hour in a police helicopter—"

Hot sobs of relief wracked Monica. Ramsey embraced her.

"Thank God!" Monica shouted, looking up at the ceiling.

"Everything is all right," Ramsey said.

Janice and François cried and hugged.

"—say Rocky Pulaski and his son, Billy Joe, died in the siege. The body of Jess Stevens, the forty-year-old girlfriend of Pulaski, was found in the woods, while businessman Fred Lutz, and two men believed to be Detroit police officers, all perished in a fire—"

Carla shrieked. "Lemer. He's dead. I know it. The man who

killed my father is dead!" She covered her mouth with trembling hands, then sobbed into Monica's shoulder.

She stroked Carla's head. "Go ahead and cry. This has been a long time coming for you."

CHAPTER 76

Carla placed wildflowers on her father's grave.

"We finally got justice, Papa. Now you can rest in peace."

An airy serenity, like a soft breeze, brushed across Carla's cheeks. Then tears of joy streamed down her face, dripping into the soil.

Several hours later, Carla and Ben Robard, their ears popping and stomachs flipping as the elevator ascended seventy-three floors over the black river, reached the Summit, a rotating circular restaurant at the top of the Renaissance Center.

Carla shivered with joy as she gazed into Ben's enamored face. All around them through glass walls were endless sparkling city lights. And Carla felt like she was on top of the world, in the candlelight with her new man. Carla wanted to melt under his twinkling eyes.

I think I've found the one.

CHAPTER 77

Philip delighted in watching Shari pry her sweat-soaked body from his and pad into the bathroom. He grudgingly answered the phone.

It was his father. "Philip, your siblings and I have reached a decision about you. First, I want an apology for your rude tone yesterday. Philip?"

"No," Philip said. "I've spent forty-eight years apologizing to you. Never again."

"You disrespectful little bastard," his father said.

"That's right," Philip said confidently. "I'm the pool man's bastard baby. And you're a hypocritical cuckold. There. The truth is out. Take me or leave me, Dad. I know enough people in this business that I could get another job with one phone call."

Philip's nipples stiffened with an overwhelming gush of emotion and relief. It was as if a boulder had been lifted from his shoulders.

"Son," his father said for the first time. But it was too late. "Of course I want you to stay with the family business. My goodness. Whatever happened with Taylor must have sent you off your rocker. Take a vacation. Relax."

Philip was stunned.

"I was simply calling to congratulate you on the Kansas City deal," his father said.

"Twenty-one down, seven more to go," Philip said, walking nude to his bedroom window, where he watched boats sailing the blue-green river. Elation surged through him.

CHAPTER 78

As she drove home, Shari's body felt raw and achy from a day and night of savage sex with Philip.

Excitement hummed inside her at the prospect of a new, challenging job in the media capital of the world. And she was thrilled at the thought of getting blue-ribbon stud service from Philip whenever she needed it. She never would have guessed that just a week ago, her life could be transformed so dramatically, so wonderfully. It was as if a new person had been born out of the despair she had wallowed in just days ago.

I'm happy and I love my life again! And nothing is gonna stop me now.

Pulling into the driveway, she saw Charles standing in the front doorway.

"Oh, so I finally got his attention," Shari said aloud as she extinguished her cigarette. She pulled into the garage and entered through the kitchen.

"Where the hell have you been?" Charles demanded. "I've been worried sick about you. I called everyone. Nobody has seen you since last night. What's going on, Shari?"

She brushed past him on the staircase. "I've been wondering that for months now."

He appeared panicked and pale. "What do you mean?"

Shari stopped and looked down on him. "Face it, Charles. You need to find a fertile young nymph who'll have your babies."

Charles blocked her path. "Shari, I don't want anybody else."

In the bedroom, Shari began packing a suitcase.

"What are you doing?" he asked.

"I'm leaving you," Shari said, loving the way that felt. "I'm moving to New York to take a job at Wolf headquarters. I'll be developing new programs for stations across the country, and I'm so excited about it I could scream."

"But you can't just leave!" he cried.

"Oh yes I can."

CHAPTER 79

Saturday morning, Taylor signed her new contract, euphoric that she and Julian were now Channel 3's new anchor team. As they taped promos announcing their debut and the upcoming race-relations forum, William bolted out of the second-story control room above the anchor studio.

"This is hot!" he said, scrambling down the staircase.

Taylor beamed. What she had envisioned so many times was happening—she and Julian, a team, behind the Channel 3 anchor desk, working together, doing news, bringing viewers a fresh perspective on race through special projects. Her goal of getting to the network by age thirty would have to wait, but she surprisingly did not feel she was forfeiting any career goals in the name of love.

"There's a chemistry between the two of you that the camera loves," William said. "You're going to send our ratings through the roof. You two were made for this."

Yes, and each other.

She glanced at Julian, who was smiling proudly.

"I'm so happy," Julian said, "I'm speechless."

William chuckled. "Whoever heard of a speechless anchor?"

Later, in the Jameses' backyard, family and friends gathered for a celebration around a cake that said CONGRATULATIONS! TAYLOR AND JULIAN.

Under an umbrella table, Taylor talked with Grandma Willa and Grandpa Duke, a smooth-skinned man with silver waves.

"Back in my day," Grandpa Duke said, "colored folks couldn't get jobs like you young folks got. We didn't even have the TV news."

"We're so proud of you," Grandma Willa said.

A short while later, Taylor's stomach flipped when she met her mother's sisters.

"We're sorry about missing this much of your life," Helga said, "but we hope we can get to know you now."

Taylor smiled. She felt anger at these two women for hurting her mother, but, as she did with Julian, she felt warm hope for a new beginning.

"Excuse me, everybody," Julian said. He was holding a microphone and standing near Taylor's father, who held a camcorder. "Taylor, can you come here please?"

She stepped to his side.

"This backyard is where it all began," Julian said. "As kids, Taylor and I used to play newscast right here, using that stone planter as our anchor desk. As you all know, our childhood game is an adult dream come true. So I'd like to ask you, Ms. James, how does it feel to be an anchor on Detroit's top-ranked news program?"

Taylor smiled. "Wonderful."

"And," Julian said, holding the microphone to her mouth, "how do you feel after your long ordeal with Rocky Pulaski?"

"It was like a roller coaster ride that dipped to hell and soared to heaven," Taylor said. "I'm still dizzy."

"Most importantly," Julian said, "will you marry me?"

Shock and exhilaration bubbled inside Taylor. She beamed.

Julian dropped to his knee, then slid a ring on Taylor's trembling finger.

"The two emeralds remind me of your eyes, and the diamond symbolizes forever," Julian said. His eyes were glassy; his voice cracked on the last word. In his eyes was the most tender expression Taylor had ever seen.

She swallowed the lump in her throat and dabbed happy tears.

"To answer your question," she said softly, "there's nothing I'd like better than to be your wife."

Julian swung her around as friends and family cheered. It was the happiest day of Taylor's life.

EPILOGUE

The scene appeared surreal through the white veil. The perfect blue sky, bright green grass, the rainbow of tulips and lilacs and apple blossoms blooming around the yard—it could not have been more perfect.

And in the center, a hundred guests sat beneath a scalloped white tent. There was the rose-covered trellis, the petal-strewn white aisle.

Taylor tried to absorb every wonderful detail as she emerged from her parents' house onto the patio, hooking arms with her tuxedoed father.

"Stunning," he said softly. "I'm so proud."

Taylor smiled; her stomach fluttered as an organist began playing the wedding march.

Her father chuckled. "I'm just glad your mother and Janice had enough time to uninvite Philip's people and invite Julian's guests."

Taylor beamed. What a wild tangle of fate that the wedding she had planned for Philip would mark her marriage to the man she had tried to forget.

Taylor had never imagined the sheer happiness that electrified her now. After so long, she finally had him back.

And there he was. Julian DuPont, her soul mate. Radiant in a white tuxedo, waiting to unite his heart with hers forever.